THE
LOVE OF MY
OTHER LIFE

The perfect uplifting story to read this summer
full of love, loss and romance

C.J. CONNOLLY

JOFFE
BOOKS

Joffe Books, London
www.joffebooks.com

First published in Great Britain in 2022

Cover art by The Brewster Project

ISBN: 978-1-80405-310-2

For Oscar and Felix,
May you choose the right paths for your lives,
or know there are always others

PART ONE: ME

CHAPTER 1

November 30

"I'm Josie Cavendish and you've been listening to Open House on Talk New York. That's all for today. If you have any real estate questions, email the studio—"

Ting-ta-ding.

Dammit. A text. Loud. Right next to the on-air mike.

"—Email the studio, openhouse@talknewyork.com, or text 555387, and we'll tackle it tomorrow. Until then, happy house hunting!"

I remove my headset and enter the production booth, wincing slightly as Abby, my producer, makes a "doh" face.

"Josie, seriously? Two years doing this show and you don't turn your cell off?"

"Sorry, Abs. I'm a mess today."

She wags a finger. "You're forgiven — this time. Hopefully listeners think it's someone texting for your real estate wisdom."

"Ha. I doubt it, but thanks. It's my brother; he's leaving for Australia. I'd better call him."

I hit David's UK number as I step out onto Second Avenue. It's a bright November day in Manhattan. A plastic bag blows around my feet, and to the west, above a row

2

of shabby concrete buildings, the tip of the Empire State is glinting in the sun.

"Happy birthday, sis! Get my text?"

"Yes. Right as I was signing off the show. I forgot to turn off my phone, so half of New York heard it."

"Oops. How'd you manage that?"

"I'm a bit delicate today. Heavy night. Drinks after rehearsal. I stayed behind for another with Peter."

David groans. "The bloke you've been pining after? From your choir. Isn't he attached?"

I huff down the phone. "Okay, for one thing, I'm not pining. And he's probably breaking up with her. But I'm not holding my breath. What about you, loser? Any unlucky women fall for your questionable charms recently?"

He laughs. "Hundreds, but, you know. Nobody special. Not that I need anyone special."

"Absolutely. Me neither."

"Right. So, birthday girl, how are you celebrating?"

"Dinner with Suzie and some choir peeps. We're going to a posh restaurant in SoHo."

"Please. Hardly the real Soho. Anyway, hope they let you in. Be a shame to be turned away on your birthday."

"You're hil-a-rious. Gotta run. Take it easy."

"'Take it easy'? They're turning you into a Yank. Resist!"

"I'm hanging up now."

"Okay, kiddo. Happy birthday. I'll call you when I get back. Have a good one. Love you."

"Have a brilliant time. Love you too."

I hang up, suddenly uneasy. My brother's words have hit a nerve.

Having feelings for someone who's unavailable doesn't mean I'm pining. Does it?

Peter's been living with Michelle since long before we met, slightly over two years ago, when he joined our choir. That didn't stop me developing a huge crush on him. How could it? He's just so . . . lovely.

And, last night, in the bar after rehearsal, when he looked at me, there was something different about it. I first felt it a few weeks ago, when we were rehearsing our duet, gazing into each other's eyes, singing words of love. It's acting, I told myself, a performance. But yesterday, from the other end of the long bar table, he looked at me the same way. . .

I had been chatting with the altos when I got the text.

Stay behind tonight? I need to talk to you. :P

What could he want?

I hardly dared think it was what I've been hoping for — that he and Michelle had finally split and he'd realized what was in front of him.

Me.

I smiled at Peter, giving him a tiny nod. He responded with a double thumbs-up.

Once the choir had dispersed, I moved to the bar to finish my wine. A male hand with freckles and a smattering of fair hair appeared on the counter beside me. Peter squeezed right up against me, maneuvering his lanky frame onto a stool.

He pushed his black-framed, geek-chic glasses up his nose and wiped away a lock of sandy hair. "Finally, I get you alone." He signaled at the bartender, ordering a beer.

"What's up? You're coming to my birthday dinner tomorrow, right? What couldn't wait?"

Peter took a slow sip out of the cold bottle and looked at me. A thrill ran from the back of my neck down my spine. In two years of friendship, we'd never been on our own in a bar. So intimate. Like a date.

"I needed to talk, alone. We're always with other people."

"Not when we're rehearsing our duet," I replied.

"No. I think it's been spending that time together that has changed things for me." He paused. "Michelle and I had another of our fights. She said I'd rather be with my band or choir friends than her. And I admitted that's true. Then she

4

said, 'You'd rather be rehearsing with Josie, too, wouldn't you?'"

Peter took another swig of beer. "And I admitted that was also true. I don't know when it happened, Josie, but things have changed for me. With you and me, I mean. I realized the thing I most look forward to is rehearsing with you, and going out with the choir, but only if you're there. You're the bright spot of my week."

He put his hand on mine, cool and gentle. "I don't really see you as just a friend anymore. And I think you feel the same. I hope there's a chance for something more."

He was right, of course — there was every chance of more with me. But I'd never have started anything. Not while he was in a relationship.

"You know I've always liked you, Peter. I've never been any good at hiding it. The entire choir knows." I laughed. "I think you've only just gotten it, though, in the past weeks."

He squeezed my hand. "I've been an idiot, Jose. Michelle and I haven't been happy. Not for a while."

"But you didn't actually break up with her?"

Peter watched a bead of condensation make its way down the bottle. "It's hard. We live together, our lives are meshed together. But . . . we're in the process of separating."

Despite my relief at his words, I didn't want to make it too easy for him.

"Well, I'm happy to hear that. But nothing can happen between us until you're moved out. And I won't make you any promises. I think you're here to see if I'm available if and when you do break up with Michelle. I won't be your fallback, Peter."

I looked him in the eyes a little defiantly and drained the last of my wine. A big, dark-haired guy stepped back into me, nearly knocking the glass out of my hand, and muttered an apology.

Peter leaned in. "Let's get out of here."

He paid for our drinks, helped me into my raincoat, and pulled me outside into the cold November night.

"What now?" I asked, my breath fogging in the freezing air.

"Josie, I get it. I need to make a clean break. But you're not my fallback, I swear. Wait for me to prove it, okay?"

My teeth started to chatter. "Well, don't take too long. I'm not going to be strung along.".

"I won't. Man, it's freezing. You want to share a cab to Brooklyn? Just to talk."

I glanced across the street at where Electra was chained to a railing. "I'm on my bike, and I don't want to leave her. Besides, I'm not sure what more there is to say."

"Fair enough. I'll talk to Michelle again tonight. Hopefully I'll have more news tomorrow."

We crossed the street to Electra. Before putting my helmet on, I rose on my tiptoes to kiss Peter's cheek. Tenderly, with just a hint of a promise. "Sounds good. I'll see you at the restaurant. Six-thirty, under my name."

"Ride safe."

* * *

Peter texts me before lunch.

Happy birthday, beautiful. Can't wait for tonight. :P

My heart soars.

Yeah me too :) See you at the restaurant. Jx

Aside from that sweet exchange and a cupcake my co-workers present, along with a tuneless rendition of "Happy Birthday," it's a day like any other. I make another attempt to book Hans Halstein, luxury realty brokerage owner and star of *Luxury Listing NYC,* as a guest on my radio show. But his communications manager, one Angela DeMarco, is having none of it.

By the time I post my interview with a city planner on the station's news website, my lower back is killing me. Oh, for an ergonomic office chair.

It's 5.37 p.m. — too late to make the hour-long round bike trip to my Williamsburg walk-up and be back in Manhattan in time for dinner. Fortunately, the station has a shower room.

As the warm water soothes my aches, I poke disapprovingly at my rounded belly and dimpled thighs, and let my mind wander to the possibility of things getting heated with Peter tonight. I really should pay more attention to my ladyscaping. To shave and suffer the itchy regrowth, to get another excruciating Brazilian wax, or to let it run wild? I cringe at the thought of Peter discovering my unruly undergrowth.

Stop it. He's still living with another woman.

I blow-dry my hair sleek and smooth and add a silver-and-black scarf to my gray sweater and black pants. Not very dressy for a birthday dinner, but it'll do. It's not like thirty-six is a special birthday.

Out in the bitter night, I ride down Second, negotiating my way through the gridlock of rush-hour New York traffic and thick clouds of steam from subway grates. I take a right onto 25th, intending to cut through by Baruch College into Madison Square Park. It's an intersection I'm always nervous at. A few years ago, I came off my bike here while swerving to avoid some students and sprained my ankle.

In my peripheral vision, I register a garbage truck exit an alleyway too quickly. A black sedan swings to the wrong side, another cyclist approaches, a screech of brakes—

And this is where it happens.

CHAPTER 2

November 30–December 1

The alarm intrudes on my peace.

I turn to hit the clock but can barely move. Wow, my back is bad today . . . And why so bright?

I open my eyes cautiously, squinting.

"I think she's awake."

The man's voice is low. Peter? No. That's not his voice.

There are other voices, quieter ones. And the alarm persists — an unfamiliar, intermittent beeping. No, the sounds are all wrong for home.

The room comes into focus. Suzie looms over, beaming at me, her trademark red lips close to my face. "There you are! You're in the hospital, sweetie — Bellevue." Her voice is uncharacteristically gentle. "You crashed your bike. Electra's toast, but you're okay. How are you feeling?"

"Ah," I croak. "A bit early to say." I attempt a smile that probably translates as a grimace.

"Of course, Josie."

She squeezes my left hand. Except . . . she's on my right. I turn my head to see who else is there.

Sitting by the bed, holding my hand in both of his, is a large man with light brown skin, thick, black hair and a dark, dense, neatly trimmed beard.

I have never seen him before.

I pull my hand away, and the man's brow furrows.

"You okay?" He leans in as if to show me his face better.

"Do I know you?" I whisper. I'm drawing a total blank but feel bad about it, as he seems kind. Nice brown eyes.

"Josie, it's me. Rob." He says it as if that should mean something.

"I'm sorry. I can't . . ." I twist away, but the movement sparks shooting pains across my torso.

I look at Suzie for help.

"Josie, honey, that's Rob. Rob. You don't remember him? Shit, Rob, she could be worse than they think. Amnesia . . ."

None of this makes sense. "Should I know him?" I'm starting to panic. "Do you know him?" My head now hurts, along with my body.

"Of course, sweetie. It's Rob. Your husband. Wait . . ." She holds up a hand. "You know who I am, but not who Rob is?"

I am still trying, but failing, to catch up. "Husband?"

"Baby, you've got to remember." The man's voice breaks. "We love each other. We're married. For over two years. You have to . . ." He grabs my hand again, tightly.

"I'm sorry." And I mean it. He sounds so heartbroken. "I don't know you — and you're hurting my hand." I tug it free. "Please go. I need to rest and I don't understand what's going on. *Suzie*?"

"Rob, give us a few minutes. Find a doctor? They need to do, like, a brain scan. You hear about it all the time, right? People have amnesia and then it comes back. It'll be fine."

She doesn't sound like it'll be fine.

The man gets up and leaves, closing the sliding door gently behind him. Through the glass, he raises his palms to his forehead, unaware of nurses and gurneys pushing past. Then he turns and disappears from view.

"What's going on, Suzie? Who is that guy, and why are you saying he's my husband? What the hell?" My voice is coming back, panic raising its pitch.

"Josie, that's Rob. The love of your life. The man you stood up with in front of us all in Hawaii and promised to love forever. The man you live with in domestic bliss, just a few blocks from here. Your husband."

"What? I've never even seen that guy! I'm not married, you know that, Suzie. And I don't live near here. I live in Brooklyn — you've only been to my place a million times."

"No, honey. You've never lived in Brooklyn, you've lived in Manhattan ever since—"

The door opens. It's the man again, this time with a doctor in scrubs.

"Hello, Josie. I'm Dr. Lin." The doctor's toothy smile doesn't reach her tired eyes. "I hear there is some confusion. You're having a hard time remembering your husband?" She flips through a chart.

"No, I don't recognize this man. He isn't my husband. I'm not married."

She looks up at me, then pointedly down at my left hand. "Well, you're wearing a ring."

On the fourth finger of my hand are two exquisite rings — one a plain wedding band, the other displaying a rectangular, pale-blue gem flanked by two diamonds in an art deco design.

It's the ring I've dreamed of.

The doctor folds her hands. "So, Josie, you've been in an accident. You were unconscious but didn't sustain a major head injury. Normally when we see memory loss, it's because of brain trauma. You have bruising on your ribs, hip and leg, and your right wrist is sprained. We'll do a scan to ensure there's no brain damage. Most likely, the trauma of the crash is causing your confusion."

"Thank you, doctor," the man called Rob says. "Will she be okay?"

"Memories usually come back, but we'll have to monitor her." The doctor turns to leave.

"Wait." My voice sounds weak. "I'm not suffering memory loss. I haven't lost any time. I remember waking up this morning, going to work . . . Hold on, what's the date?"

"November 30, 2017. Your thirty-sixth birthday." Suzie examines my face, gauging whether the information will shock me.

"Exactly! That's what it is. Trump is President, right? And, Suzie, I was meeting you and the choir gang tonight, at that new restaurant in SoHo. I haven't forgotten my life, but I don't know this man. I've never seen him before. I'm not married. And these are not my rings. Beautiful as they are." I tug them off, the setting catching on my knuckle, and let them fall from the bed. The man — Rob — bends to pick them up, his expression bleak.

Suzie shakes her head. "We weren't going to dinner tonight — you and Rob had a gallery thing. But I did tell you about that restaurant—"

"Let's not fuss over details," Dr. Lin interrupts. "We don't want Josie getting distressed. We'll run tests. For now, you need to let her rest." She makes a rapid exit.

"Suzie, does my family know I'm in hospital?" Mum, David, and my sister, Laura, wouldn't lie to me. "I do have a family in your crazy version of my life?"

"Of course," Suzie replies in a small voice. "I called Laura, and she told your mom. They're flying out from Heathrow now."

A relieved sob catches in my throat. I tilt my head away from the stranger who says he is my husband, and a fat tear drips down the side of my face.

"Come on, Rob, we need to let Josie rest." Suzie's tone is kind, but I can hear the strain. She leans forward. "Honey, I understand you're confused, but we'll get you better. Try to sleep, sweetie. We love you." She strokes my hair, then rises, crossing to the door, where she waits.

The man is still sitting at my bedside, and I can almost feel him wondering what to do next. Finally, he scrapes his chair back and, in silence, walks out with Suzie.

This is messed up.

I lie in the hospital bed, unable to sleep as I replay my conversation with Suzie and that man. Nothing makes sense. What's more, there's no way my health insurance would cover this fancy private room, with its plush armchairs and hotel-style curtains over a massive window.

What seems like hours later, I'm taken in a wheelchair to have an MRI, which is loud and unpleasant. A nurse helps me back to bed and gives me "something to help you sleep, honey," as the lights in the corridor dim. Before the pills kick in, I struggle out of bed to the private bathroom. Switching on the light, I catch myself in the mirror and step back in shock.

The woman looking back at me is . . . not quite me. She's *me,* but different. Hair a paler, more golden blonde, much longer and thicker than my own. And my body . . .

I take my gown off, ignoring the stab of pain that causes, and examine my body under the fluorescent light. It's bizarre. This is my body, these are definitely my generous breasts, that's the mole on my stomach, but I'm now so much slimmer. About 30 pounds lighter. And my pubic hair! It's nothing more than a tiny landing strip, perfectly presented. This is my body as I always wished it would be — aside from the strapped wrist and reddish bruising down my side.

Yep, this whole thing is seriously messed up.

I pee for the first time in hours, my butt bony on the seat, and I'm overcome with fatigue. I climb back into bed and fall asleep instantly, disturbed by strange dreams that my sister can't find me in the old attic of our family home.

In fact, she's calling my name, "Bosie! Hey Bosie!" — her nickname for me since childhood, over and over. It feels so real.

"Bosie! Bosie—"

And there she is, Laura, looming over me. For a moment, everything seems okay. Then I remember.

"Laura, oh, I'm so glad you're here. I don't understand what's happening." My voice is thick with emotion. "Where's Mum? Is she here?"

"Talking to the doctor. How are you? Suzie told us all about your accident. She said there was some memory loss? How are you feeling? You poor thing . . ."

"That's the thing, there isn't," I protest. "I know the date, who I am, and where I live. But people keep saying I'm married to this man, Rob. But you know I've never been married! I was supposed to be seeing Peter and my choir friends last night. I have to text Peter. I've no clue what's going on."

"Bosie, I'm sorry. I don't know who Peter is, and it's a couple of years since you left the choir. It must be the trauma, right? Some amnesia has set you back? Mum and Rob are asking the doctor about what care you need, so you can go home. 'Cos you're fine physically, and I'm sure you don't want to stay here."

"That guy — he's here?"

My question goes unanswered as my mother walks in, her shoulder-length hair even grayer than the last time I saw her, its strawberry-blonde colour almost leeched out. Impeccably dressed, as always. The dark-bearded man, easily more than a foot taller than my petite mother, follows just behind, his hand on her shoulder. Rob says something and Mum smiles, then he visibly starts as he meets my eyes.

"You're awake, baby — how are you feeling?" He pulls an armchair up to my bed.

Now I'm getting mad. Everyone's in on it, even my family. I turn to the guy. "Look, I don't know you, so for the love of God, *stop calling me baby*." I twist back to my mother, whose perfectly plucked brows are raised by my outburst.

"Mum, I'm so glad you flew here, thank you — but why the hell is everyone saying I'm with this guy?"

Mum leans in to kiss my cheek, her powdery rose scent a small comfort in this strange reality. She sits down with a sigh, taking my hand. "Darling, I understand you're confused, it must feel like we're ganging up on you, but I promise we're not. The doctor said you can go home, the scan seemed healthy. You'll have outpatient sessions to help you with this memory loss, if it persists. Let's get you dressed and we'll all go home, okay? Laura and I will stay a few days, make sure you're sorted out."

Home. The word seems the only bright point in a sea of darkness. At least home will make sense. But then I have a horrible thought.

"*He's* not coming too, is he?" I can't even look at Rob.

Mum and Laura glance at each other, and my mother pats my hand, providing scant comfort. "Of course he is, darling — Rob lives there, too. And don't worry, he'll take care of you."

"So . . . where do you think I live?"

Please say Brooklyn, please say Brooklyn.

The man finally speaks. "We live close, baby — sorry, Josie. On Union Square. We moved in just before we got married."

I look away. The realization I am not actually going home to the apartment I love begins to sink in.

"I live in Williamsburg," I mutter.

There's a heavy silence broken by Dr. Lin's arrival. "How is the patient this morning?" She examines the clipboard in her hand. "Better? Physically, at least? . . . You're clear to go, Josie. We'll set up specialist appointments to monitor your amnesia."

Mum smiles. "Thank you, doctor. We're getting her ready now."

"Here are some painkillers for the wrist and bruising. It'll be sore for a while. No more than six a day. Feel better, Josie." The doctor departs with her customary abruptness, having barely glanced at me.

"Right, let's get you up, darling." Mum looks across me at the bearded man. "Rob, her clothes?"

Behind me, Rob reaches into the tall bedside cabinet. Curiosity makes me turn to watch. He retrieves a pair of slim gray pants, a plum blazer, a gauzy blouse, gray ankle boots, and a bra and panties. I don't recognize any of them, although I do have a similar blouse at home.

He hands me a watch, the face smashed, the hands stuck at 6.17. That must be when I had my accident.

"I'll get that fixed for you." Rob lays a silvery-gray trench, a burgundy purse, and my bike helmet, the one with the green flowers, on the armchair. The helmet is the only thing that's mine.

"You were riding through Manhattan in this outfit?" Laura frowns, fingering the blouse. As a young mother in suburban England, she is usually in jeans and drives everywhere.

"Josie always rides in her work and social clothes." Rob doesn't wait for me to respond. "She refuses to stop riding, even though I've told her it's dangerous. Says it's much quicker to ride than get a car, and having money doesn't mean we should throw it away."

I half-smile at that — I've never said those words to this man, but it sounds a lot like me. And I do love riding past all those drivers stuck in gridlock.

"Well." Mum's tone is brisk. "No more riding for a bit, I think. Your bike was a write-off. Now, Josie, up!"

She helps me sit upright. I'm aware the man behind me can see my bare back and the top of my butt in the gap of my gown.

"Not with him here."

"Oh. Sorry," Rob mutters. He moves away.

Laura smiles sympathetically. "Give us a few minutes, Rob."

His footsteps retreat, and the glass door closes.

"Now, sweetheart." She hasn't called me that since I was a child being punished for naughty behavior. It's a loving endearment but intended to soften something sterner. "Put your undies on, and try to remember this is hard for Rob, too, you not remembering him. He loves you and wants to take care of you. Here are your trousers."

I do as I'm told. What must this be like for him? He believes he is my husband. He certainly seems kind, and Mum, Laura and Suzie all clearly care about him.

15

"Sure, I can be nice." I bare my teeth at my sister, in the fake grin we used to share as children. Even if she's as deluded as the rest of them, having Laura in the room is reassuring.

The fact that I'm about to go to a home that isn't mine, with a man who isn't my husband, is too overwhelming a prospect to dwell on. Clearly, I have no choice. I'll stay there with Mum and Laura for a while, while everything gets, as Mum said, sorted out. And I'll call Peter and tell him about the accident. That's the only way I can deal with all of this craziness.

I'm glad to get out of the room. Ever since Dad died, I've hated the smell of hospitals.

The man I'm told is my husband is waiting in the corridor. "Ready?"

I shrug, following him out of the hospital, flanked closely by Mum and Laura.

In the parking lot, Rob beeps open a peacock-green Lincoln with cream leather interiors.

"Nice." I can't help but show my appreciation. It *is* nice.

He senses my hesitation at where to sit. "How about we let Iris ride shotgun and you go in the back?"

"Good idea," I reply, as Mum starts to protest. "Really, Mum. I'm happier in the back with Laura."

Rob drives expertly through the wide streets, quieter than usual after the morning rush. In less than ten minutes, he pulls into a well-kept alley behind a tall, glass-and-stone building overlooking Union Square Park. He gets out as a valet emerges from the back of the building.

"Welcome back, Mr. Billing. Happy to see the patient is with you." The young man opens my mother's door first, then mine. I step out onto the pavement, my body sore and stiff.

Rob hands him the keys. "Thanks, Will."

"Recognize your building, darling?" Mum examines my face carefully.

I look about me. There's visitor parking and a large double entrance door into the building. I don't really recognize the tower, except it might have been on a recent episode of *Luxury Listing NYC*. If it's the one I'm thinking of, the penthouse has an epic wraparound terrace.

"Sorry, no . . . Maybe I've seen it on TV?"

Laura puts her hand on my arm. "Don't worry, it'll come back."

I doubt that, but say nothing. I avoid looking at Rob. I can almost feel his disappointment.

Rob flashes a fob at the side of the entrance doors, which swing open into an elevator corridor. Beyond that, the opulent front lobby has a triple-height ceiling and a vast, modern, chainmail chandelier dripping luxuriously into the lofty space. Past a tall set of glass doors is a hotel-style porte-cochère, with a smartly dressed concierge standing in its shade. And beyond the entrance, the busy street of Union Square East and the park are gleaming in the late morning sunlight.

This place is intimidatingly glamorous.

Mum guides me into a wood-paneled elevator, and Rob presses the button for the eighteenth floor. There are only nineteen and twenty above that. I know from my job — and watching too many episodes of *Luxury Listing NYC* — that the better the view, the higher the price. Seriously, how much money does this guy have?

The elevator doors open smoothly, and we step out in silence. Leading us to the end of a long corridor, Rob unlocks a set of double doors marked 1802 and throws them open.

I pause, taking it in.

The space inside is nothing short of gorgeous. We're in a bright foyer with white flooring and a circular table with a huge vase of delphiniums and hydrangeas — my favorites. Despite my confusion, I feel a spark of joy at their beauty.

The high ceiling has elegant moldings, and the recessed lights cast a shimmer on a smaller version of the chandelier downstairs. The central wall opposite displays a semi-abstract, moody ocean painting, with a gap to either side offering glimpses of the open space beyond. I suspect this will be the most fabulous property I've ever seen — and, as a real estate journalist, I've been in some pretty spectacular places.

This is way too fancy to be my home.

"Anything ringing a bell?" asks my sister.

I shake my head. "It's lovely, though." My voice sounds floaty, like I'm not quite here.

"You chose it." It's first time Rob has spoken to me since the hospital. "Everything. I mean, I love it too, but I wanted you to have your dream home." He pauses, as if waiting for me to say something. When I don't, he dips his head. "You guys all want tea? Iris?"

Mum nods. "Please."

I am still processing what Rob said. *I* chose this? All of it? I scan the room again, my gaze landing on countless lovely objects. How can I not remember?

"Three teas, please, Rob," calls Laura, moving her case into a bedroom. I glimpse a painting I recognize before she closes the door and walks into the area beyond the wall.

"Come on, darling, let's get you comfy on the settee." Mum guides me forward, and the living space opens up before us.

Directly ahead, several steps lead down into a vast living-dining room with a wall of sliding doors beyond, through which I can see a wide terrace. The ceiling height soars above this sunken area, which is flooded with light. To my right, on the upper level, is a modern kitchen, complete with a marble island and leather bar stools. Past the kitchen is another set of steps down into the living room, and another corridor beyond.

This place is unbelievable.

Aside from being vast, every piece of furniture, every light fixture, every detail is perfection. In the lower area, to the right, two white couches with gray and teal pillows look like they'd be heaven to ease my aching body onto. There's a pair of dove-gray armchairs in front of a marble-surround fireplace on the right wall. To the left is a long dining table with at least a dozen chairs for the glamorous dinner parties

Rob must host. And above each area, a matching chainmail chandelier ripples in the cool light.

It is everything I would choose, if, of course, I had that kind of money. Which I don't. But clearly Rob does.

"Shoes, sweetheart, and your coat," Mum prompts gently. I tug my trench over my strapped wrist and wince with pain as I bend to remove my boots. My mother pushes open a hidden closet door in the wall. "Go sit down, darling. Rest. Turn the fire on, Laura."

As I sink into the soft couch, Laura makes a fuss of supporting my wrist, then grabs a small remote from the coffee table. She presses a button, sparking on the fireplace, which is glass-backed and shared with a room beyond. Above the fire hangs another ocean painting, this one in shades of teal. But it's the ornaments on the mantel that intrigue me most. Is that my stone hand sculpture? And the vase from David for my thirtieth? I want to examine them, but I'm too sore to get up. I lean back, trying to absorb the place, reeling from its opulence.

"How are you doing, my darling?" Mum places a mug of tea carefully in my good hand, making sure I've got it before settling into one of the gray armchairs.

"Not great," I tell her, struggling with the heavy mug. "I'm pretty confused. As far as I'm concerned, I've never been here, and you're saying it's my home. But I'm glad you and Laura are here." I look about me. "And this apartment is amazing, so I'm going to . . . process it for a while. Let it just wash over . . ." My voice is cracking, so I stop. I glance up at the kitchen, where my sister is stirring sugar into her tea and talking quietly to Rob, who's staring at me.

Mum follows my gaze. "He's a wonderful man. He loves you very much. He's made you happy. You thought you might never marry, but then he came along and it all made sense. I'm sure it'll make sense again. Soon."

"I hope so, Mum." I'm trying hard to sound cheerful. "So . . . how did we meet?"

"At a hotel bar — the W, on this square — after a real estate conference. He was playing piano in the lobby, and you assumed he was a jobbing musician. You asked him if he knew a particular song, and the two of you hit it off. He didn't tell you he was a hotel and condo developer who happened to be playing the piano. He liked you not knowing he had money." She smiles. "You were shocked when you found out."

"I bet. But . . . I've never been to a conference at the W. Well, I nearly did. I was registered for one when I was working at Crain's, three years ago, before the radio station. But I crashed my bike on the way — no big deal, just a sprained ankle — so I didn't make it."

"Radio station?" My mother wrinkles her brow. "What radio station? Did you do some freelance work before Halstein & Faust?"

"The brokerage? Luxury real estate?" I'm as confused as my mother looks. "What's that got to do with anything?"

"Well, that's where you work, darling. After they let you go at Crain's, you got the communications manager job there. Rob got you the interview with Mike and Hans."

Now I'm even more perplexed. "I'm familiar with the brokerage, but I don't work there, Mum. I work at Talk New York. I have a real estate talk radio show. Two-and-a-half years now. You *know* that."

"Well, I don't." Mum's worry line between her eyes deepens. "Clearly this is another memory your accident has affected. You don't work at a radio station, darling. You need to take things slowly, step by step, and it'll fall into place." But she doesn't sound convinced.

Feeling nauseated, I focus on not dropping my tea on the spotless white couch. I take a tentative sip. At least it's warm, comforting. "Good tea," I mutter — and then, "Oh. This is good tea because it's my favorite brand, right?"

My mother's lips curve thinly in answer.

"Everyone okay?" Rob asks as he and Laura join us, not sounding okay himself.

"We're fine," Mum replies. "Some confusion about Josie's job. I suppose it's to be expected that if she has memory loss about one thing, it might extend to other areas. We'll work it out." But she sounds as if she's reassuring herself.

A spark of irritation flares in me. "And how are we accounting for the fact that I have a totally different set of memories, and a different job, and a different home? How will we 'work' that out?"

"Josie." Laura's voice is quiet.

"I can't handle this." I put down my tea, fight my way up off the couch and turn to Rob, whose eyebrows are raised. "Where's my room? I need some alone time."

He glances at Laura questioningly.

"Right." I catch the reason for his hesitation. "I don't mean the primary bedroom — I mean the room I'll be sleeping in. Because until this mess is sorted out, I'm not sharing a bedroom with you, no matter how pleasant you are."

"Iris and Laura are staying in the two spare bedrooms." Rob's voice is quiet. "But you could have our bedroom and I can go in the den."

"No, Rob." Laura gets up. "This is your home. I'll go in the den. You stay in your room. Josie can go in the art room — she'll be comfortable there. Mum can go in the green room. I'll move our stuff. That suit you, Mum?"

"Yes, thank you, darling." Mum nods. "Excellent idea. Josie will have all her paintings . . ." She trails off, clearly unsure whether I'll remember the paintings.

"Thank you," I reply, glad of one tiny victory. "Which one is the 'art room'? It sounds very fancy."

"Here." Laura strides past the dining table and opens a tall door to the left of the wall of windows. I follow her into a corner bedroom, from which a glass door leads out to the end of the terrace. I catch my breath at the sweeping views of the park and across the city. A million windows glint in the midday sunlight and, at street level, late-autumn trees flutter scarlet and amber leaves.

Overwhelmed by the relentless beauty of this home, I sit on the edge of the large bed, which has four metal posts and a white gauzy canopy hanging from the lofty ceiling. Then

I gasp as I face a collection of artwork, hung gallery-style on the deep blue interior wall. *My* beloved artwork — all the paintings and prints I've collected over the years.

I shake my head. "My art—"

"She recognizes the pictures, Mum! Rob!" Laura yells back into the living room. "All is not lost!"

"Thank goodness." My mother sounds relieved.

"So," my sister continues, "what do you need? Stuff from the master closet? I'll move your toiletries to the main bathroom."

"Thanks." Suddenly I'm exhausted. My wrist is throbbing. My body aches. "And those painkillers, please."

"Sure, big sis."

Laura leaves me sitting on the side of the bed, staring at my favorite English landscape, by my grandfather. It makes sense I would hang it right there.

Even though the door is open, my mother knocks as she enters. "Thought you might like to finish your tea." She sets the mug on the mirrored nightstand.

"Thanks, Mum. It's good to see these paintings. I was thinking how perfectly hung they are."

"We did it together." She sits beside me on the bed. "After you and Rob moved in, I came to stay and we hung all your smaller pieces together. That lovely forest painting is in the green room, but most of them are in here. You and Rob started to buy bigger statement works together after that . . . It's lovely, isn't it? The flat, I mean."

"Really, Mum, I can't fault this place. It's a dream. Makes me wonder if I'm dreaming this whole thing."

"Well, you're not. I'm not sure if that's good news or bad. But there it is." Mum pats my hand, then stands to leave as Laura returns with an armful of clothing that she hangs inside a closet.

Laura hands me a set of gorgeous gray silk pajamas. "Your makeup and toiletries are in the main bathroom. Need me to show you where it is?"

"Please. While I'm still dressed." I don't want to wander around searching for the bathroom in those slinky PJs.

I avoid eye contact with Rob as we pass him talking to Mum in the living room. At the top of the steps, I slow at the open door of a bedroom — the 'green room,' from the pale painted colour of the walls — stopping as I glimpse the forest painting I bought after arriving in New York. "That picture," I say to Laura, peering in.

"Yes, you had it in that tiny Murray Hill studio, before you met Rob."

"That's right," I reply.

And then it came with me to the home I bought for myself in Williamsburg.

Laura beams. "At least some stuff is consistent, huh?" She pushes the next door open. "Bathroom."

"Thanks." I smile at her. "The painkillers?"

"On the counter. See you in a bit." She kisses me on the cheek.

In the bathroom, I stare at this more glamorous version of myself, wearing clothes that are my style, but clearly pricier. It's beyond weird to see this slimmer me. I realize I haven't eaten in a long time, not since I slipped into this crazy parallel universe.

The last thing was an indulgent birthday meatball sub with Abby yesterday lunchtime at the diner near the station, followed by that cupcake. That was less than twenty-four hours ago, according to the bathroom clock, but it seems worlds away. It is worlds away. Still, my stomach is in knots, and I doubt I'll eat for a while. It doesn't look like this body has seen a meatball sub in years.

I slug down two painkillers and quietly pad back down the steps to the living area, past the three people who are clearly talking about me. I slip into the bedroom and change into the silk PJs, wondering whether anyone can see me through huge terrace windows. I explore the walls and find controls for the blinds, which obediently glide down. It's a shame to hide such a stunning view, but I need to be cocooned. I slide between the softest of white sheets and close the gauzy canopy. If I'm going to live in a crazy parallel universe, I guess this is pretty much the best way to do it.

* * *

Knocking.

Where am I?

The room is dark, the bed unfamiliar. Every part of me aches. The door cracks open, and Laura is silhouetted against the chink of light. Then I remember. The accident. The man who thinks he's my husband. The incredible apartment. Not a dream, then.

"I made you another tea." Laura opens the door wider. "It's nearly 6 p.m. You've been asleep all afternoon. We wondered if you might eat dinner with us? Rob's promised to cook chili prawns." She puts the mug down on the table beside me, picking up the previous mug. She turns on the light.

It doesn't seem right to eat in a universe that isn't my own, to be cooked dinner by a husband who isn't mine. But it won't help to starve. My stomach growls in agreement. "Yeah, I could eat. I haven't had anything since yesterday."

"I'd better shower, though." Could be interesting, with this new body.

"I wasn't going to say anything, but . . ." Laura screws up her nose, then winks as she backs out of the room.

I ease out of bed and slip on a robe that matches the pajamas. I check the mirror on the closet door. My hair is messy but not too bad — not only longer but also thicker than usual.

I run my good hand through it and feel a line along my scalp with thicker hair underneath. Extensions. I've thought about getting them, but they're expensive, and my life doesn't require that much glamor. Perhaps this version of my life does. I pick up a clip from the bedside table and fix up the locks in a twist before venturing out into the living–dining area.

My mother and Laura are on the couch, Laura showing Mum the latest photos of Theo, her three-year-old son. Rob is nowhere to be seen.

"He's getting groceries," Laura says, watching me look around.

I'm relieved. "Right. I'm going for that shower."

Walking up the steps, I realize I have a free moment to explore. I open the door on the other side of the foyer and find the primary bedroom. It's so huge, I can't help but laugh as I take it in.

Ahead of me, against the right wall, is a vast, super king-sized bed dressed in rich plum silk bedlinens, a cityscape painting above it. Past the bed, a tall, thin window reveals a north-facing view that frames the Empire State Building, lit up triumphantly against the now black sky. To my left, the richly carpeted room sinks down to the lower level, which offers a generous sitting area and a huge wooden desk and chair.

This is the biggest bedroom I've ever seen — larger than the entire Murray Hill studio I used to live in — and so sexy I'm almost turned on.

Nervous of being caught trespassing by Rob, I quickly descend to the lower level and peer inside some cabinetry on the interior wall. A flatscreen TV and state-of-the-art smart-home system. At the end of the room is the wall of windows that stretches across the whole apartment, with doors to the terrace and more westerly city views beyond.

Back up on the bed level is another interior door, which must be the en suite. Instead I find a luxurious dressing room with fitted cabinets and a velvet ottoman. I resist the urge to examine the clothes in the cabinets to see if any are mine — that will have to wait. Another door beyond the dressing room opens to a stone-clad wet room, with a soaker tub under another Empire State-view window, and a huge walk-in shower. I laugh again, shaking my head at the idea of living in this level of luxury.

I'm startled by a distant thud, a door closing. What would Rob think, finding me poking around his bedroom suite? I scuttle out of the room, across the hallway and slip into the main bathroom, closing and locking the door with a click. *Phew.*

Under the hot shower, my new body feels strange and angular beneath my hands. It's also a major challenge not to soak the strapping on my right arm. But I realize I'm almost glad of the injury. It's a visual manifestation that something is wrong. People can see I'm not myself — although they have no idea how much that is true.

Washing my hair is even tougher with one hand, and I've no idea what to do with these extensions. I make a mental note to ask my hairstylist. The amnesia excuse will help with a lot of problems. That is, if I don't wake up and find myself back in Brooklyn, in bed with Peter — which is what I'm hoping.

Slipping my robe back on, I clutch the PJs to my body, in case Rob is back. I walk back through the living room, smiling at my sister and mother. "Tricky keeping my bandages dry."

"I'll redo them soon," Mum replies.

The front door opens, so I give them another, more rueful smile and scurry into the bedroom to get dressed. When I emerge minutes later, a delicious smell hits me, bringing home just how hungry I am.

Rob is in the kitchen, absorbed in stirring a sizzling pan. Laura is carrying bowls of salad and rice to the table. "Hungry?" she asks me.

"Starving," I admit.

My mother sets down four plates and reaches into a drawer in the long walnut sideboard. I glimpse a mix of old and new cutlery, including some inexpensive stuff I recognize. I bought it years ago. She pulls out some beautiful, contemporary silverware. When she sees me admiring it, she murmurs, with a half-smile, "Wedding present from David."

"Better than that cheap set of mine," I tell her, watching as she moves gracefully around the table, setting out the cutlery. I sink down into a chair.

Rob brings the chili prawns. "Dig in." He sits across the corner from me. "I'm glad you found your place."

"Do I usually sit here? Seemed like a good spot." I don't like fitting in with his idea of me, but he's being welcoming. "Thanks, this looks delicious." I help myself to a generous serving and eat with unabashed gusto. This Rob guy is going to have to take me as I am.

"Seems like the appetite is back," says Mum. "You're so slim, we thought you've hardly been eating."

I want to tell her about the meatball sub but figure it wouldn't be well received, so I smile and keep eating as my mother and sister discuss plans for tomorrow. But I'm distracted — the silverware from my brother reminded me of him. He'd be on his surfing trip in Australia by now, so the time difference is probably why he hasn't called.

"Speaking of David, did you tell him about my accident? I know he's away, but I'd love to talk to him."

Rob, Laura and my mother glance at each other. Mum puts down her fork. Rob coughs. Laura's avoiding eye contact. They say nothing.

"What? Didn't you tell him?"

My mother breaks the silence. "Sweetheart, I'm so sorry. We didn't even think about that. You not remembering. About David."

"What about David? Is everything all right?"

Laura rises abruptly, her chair scraping against the floor. She walks to the windows. My mother moves around the table to sit beside me, twisting her chair so it faces mine.

I'm gripped by fear. This is not going to be good.

She takes my hand in hers, her eyes reddening. "It happened in Hawaii, darling, the week we were all there for your wedding. A few days after the ceremony. David and cousin Charlie took a helicopter ride with two girls they'd met. The pilot had a heart attack mid-flight, and they crashed." Her voice breaks. "I'm so sorry to have to tell you, none of them made it. We've been grieving their loss for more than two years, and it's been getting better for us, for you — everybody."

Her words are distant, as if she's speaking through fog. The terror in my stomach has expanded to fill every cell in my body. "David? Dead? Charlie too?" I push back the food that now looks repulsive and try to rise, but the ground falls away.

Moments later, when I open my eyes, I'm not where I thought I was.

I'm lying on something soft, white muslin draped above me. Mum is sitting on the edge of the bed, Laura standing by the art wall. Rob is nowhere to be seen.

"What happened?"

Mum takes my hand. "You fainted, darling. After I told you about David."

So that's true, then. Another thing that isn't a dream. In this version of the world, there's no David. No big brother, whom I adore. I spoke to him only yesterday, on my birthday. But in this world he's been dead for more than two years, killed because of my not-real wedding.

Sobs rack my body, and I let them consume me. When the wails come, I let those happen too. My mother continues to hold my hand tightly between hers, and my sister kneels by my bedside.

After a long time, Mum reaches over to the bedside table and opens the pill bottle to give me more painkillers. My throat is so dry, so dehydrated from all the crying, I can barely swallow them down.

As she and Laura finally leave me, Mum switches off the light at the door. The room, along with my thoughts, is plunged into darkness.

CHAPTER 3

December 2

I open my eyes. It must be morning, as there's a sliver of light around the edges of the blinds. This time I know exactly where I am. And the nightmare comes crashing back.

David is dead.

I wallow in memories, recalling the love between us, how charismatic he was, how vibrant his life.

What a stupid waste.

Stupid. Stupid.

I have a sudden, desperate urge to call Peter. I need to hear his voice, to try to make some sense of all this. He must be wondering what in the world has happened to me.

Rising, I creep out of my room, through the empty living room and up into the kitchen, only to stop at the bank of cupboards facing me. If I were me, where would I store coffee? I open a door above the espresso machine and find a selection of teas and a jar of ground coffee. Right first time. The neighboring cupboard yields mugs. The large coffee I make has skim milk, hardly optimal, but at least it's hot and comforting.

What now? I glance at the wall clock. It's 7.14 a.m. too early for Mum and Laura to be up on a Saturday. I don't know about Rob. I scan the room and spot a sleek pale-gold smartphone charging on the sideboard. Turning it on, I find my usual passcode works. That's something, at least. Now I can get hold of Peter.

I step onto the terrace. The outdoor space is huge, stretching across the whole width of the building, and divided into three areas by low box hedges. The nineteenth-floor terrace acts as a roof for the area, supported by thick, square pillars. Set between the pillars, instead of a railing, there is a frameless, waist-height glass barrier between me and the street, eighteen floors down.

It's another crisp fall morning. The sky is a vivid blue, and the last of the leaves offer splashes of gold and red in the park below and across the city.

What a fabulous place to live.

Sinking down onto the patio sofa, I tap the phone's screen and open the text messages. Scrolling through, there's nothing from Peter. His text from after rehearsal in the bar and on my birthday — all our previous rehearsal texts are gone. I check the contacts: his number isn't even there.

This is the wrong phone. I need my real one. But that one, the one in the green case, doesn't exist in this world. I don't even have my black purse with all my stuff.

In this world, am I even friends with Peter? I'm still in the choir, right? But what had Laura said? That I'd stopped going to the choir two years ago.

Still, I check my emails for messages about rehearsals and concerts, and again there's nothing, aside from an invitation in May to buy a cut-price ticket to the summer show. Searching for the name of our group, Sound Eclectic, I have to go back to September 2015 to find emails about rehearsals. The most recent, titled "Re: Thanks for everything," is a response from the director to me, after I decided to leave the group ahead of my wedding to Rob that fall. And, in this world, I never went back.

I would never have met Peter, if I hadn't been in the choir these past two years. He joined that same fall. Peter doesn't know me. Even if I find his number, I can't call him to tell him what's happened. He'll think I'm some crazy woman.

I stare out over the rooftops, wondering where he is, whom he's with. Maybe he's happy, still with Michelle.

But then it hits me.

It's only in *this* world, this totally wrong, alternate timeline that Peter doesn't know me. And *David*. David is only dead in this world, not in real life, my world. In the real world, he's very much alive, on a surfing vacation in Australia, getting drunk with his mates and picking up tanned girls. And in that world, Peter is breaking up with Michelle, hoping to be with me. All I have to do is return to that real life and I'll get them both back.

Sure, I have no idea how to do that. But considering I managed to shift onto this parallel timeline, maybe there's a way to shift back.

Feeling immeasurably better, I finish my coffee and glimpse movement at the master bedroom end of the terrace. Rob walks to the railing, where he stands for a moment, looking out. I'm not sure whether to say anything and decide to make a noise so he'll notice I'm here. I set down my mug with a clatter on the glass-topped table and study the phone, keeping him in my peripheral vision.

"Good morning." His voice is low and gentle. I glance up as he steps through a gap in the hedge. He is dressed in sweatpants and a hoodie, his brown feet bare on the paving.

I force a smile. "Good morning."

"How are you doing, after last night?"

"As well as can be expected. Better today. Last night was rough."

He shakes his head. "I can't even imagine. What a shock for you." He looks down awkwardly and notices me holding the phone. "You found your cell, then. Your Mum recharged it, as people will be calling."

I hadn't even thought about calls from strangers, people who will no doubt have all kinds of expectations of me. Fantastic.

"I was going through it, seeing if anything helps."

"Any luck?"

"Well, I've only just started."

"Right." Rob nods. "I'd better get dressed. I'll make some breakfast if you're hungry? Still like your eggs scrambled?"

"Thanks."

"No problem." He pauses, as if he wants to say something else, but instead turns and walks inside.

He seems nice. While I'm figuring out how to get home, he'll be a decent roommate in this spectacular place. But there's no way in hell I'm staying here, in this reality, without David or Peter. No way.

What else can this phone tell me? I click on the text icon again. Rob's name is at the top of the list. I hesitate a moment. Maybe there are some intimate messages between Rob and . . . who? His real wife. The Other Me. Wouldn't I be infringing on the privacy of that married couple? I shake the thought off. This is legally my phone, after all, and any messages were intended for the person inhabiting my current body, so there's nothing wrong with reading them.

I scan the most recent text, from the day of the accident, two days ago.

> Hey handsome, going to be a bit late at work, will have to ride straight to the gallery tonight, starts at 6, want to meet me there 6.30?

> > Coolio, see you there, birthday babe. I'll be the beardie guy in the sharp suit X

> You're such a cheeseball :D xx

Huh. They seem like a fun couple, him and this Other Me. Although, perhaps there's something forced about the joviality?

Other threads are more varied. The texts with Suzie, who lives with her husband and kids in Brooklyn, are relatively normal. But there are none from Lisa, my closest choir friend. And, of course, nothing from David or Peter.

I go to my Instagram account, scroll through. There are lots of images of life in New York, often with people I don't recognize, and some stunning photos of a vacation with Rob in Mexico. Then further back, a trip to Seattle with him and two people who look like they must be Rob's parents — a tall, white, gray-haired guy in his 60s and a pretty, short, Indigenous woman. There's a single photo of me with them, in which I'm looking pale and thin.

Finally, a couple of years back, I find what I'm searching for: Hawaii. The last photos ever taken of David and of our brash, banker cousin, Charlie. Photos of me and Rob with them, drinking at a bar, tanned, happy, surrounded by love. My breath hitches as I take in these captured moments, a joy I never experienced — to have my brother by my side at my wedding.

I scroll back and reach images of the wedding itself, informal shots that must've been taken by a guest using my cell, as almost all have me in them. I'm in a sleeveless white dress, with lace over the top and a flippy skirt that ends at the knee, and white flowers twisted into my hair. Perfect for a Hawaii wedding.

David again, walking me down the aisle on a clifftop lawn, with an adorned pergola overlooking the deep blue Pacific. Rob in a casual, pale gray suit, taller than everyone else, handsome and goofily happy. My own face, sun-kissed and filled with joy. Several of my mother and sister, dabbing their eyes. None of us knew David and Charlie would be dead a few days later.

I can no longer bear it, and turn back to finding out more about this world. I tap on another email app, and the messages are work-related. Lots from Hans Halstein from Halstein & Faust, the brokerage Mum said I work for. The same Hans I can't manage to book as a guest on my radio show, no matter how many times I ask. In my real life, that is. In this one, I work for him.

There are also conversations with a Mike Jones about communications strategies, as well as some with an Angela DeMarco. Why have I heard her name? Then it hits me — I've been in touch with her in my real life. She's the communications manager at Halstein & Faust. I called her to invite Hans on my show.

But in this reality, the comms manager at Halstein & Faust is me. I examine Angela's email signature. *Executive Assistant to Hans Halstein*. Seems in this world I have the job that she got in my reality, when I went to work at the radio station.

The phone tinkles, startling me. "Angela DeMarco," the screen says. Think of the devil. I let it ring, and I'm turning the phone off when a text chimes. It's also from Angela.

Hey Josie.
Heard you'll be off work after a nasty cycle accident. Mike said something about amnesia . . . ? We all send our best wishes. If it's too hard to talk, pls get Rob to call me with an update. Hope you haven't forgotten all about us!!

Wow. I don't have amnesia, but that last line would be a bit insensitive if I had.

I turn off the phone, fearful others might call, and go inside. Mum and Laura are drinking tea in the living room and Rob is in the kitchen, now dressed in jeans and a blue sweater.

I collapse on the couch next to my sister. She hugs me. "How are you doing, Bosie?" she asks.

"Better than last night. I guess you're used to David being gone, but it's new to me. I'll have to go through the whole grieving process. Again, I suppose."

"It was very hard on you the first time, on us all. I'm so sorry."

"I'll be okay. It's weird, but because it's mixed up with everything else, being here, not remembering Rob, or anything . . . That kind of dulls the pain. Another thing that is wrong about all this." I wave my hand around.

Laura nods, her poker-straight blonde bob swinging. "Maybe when that straightens itself out, you'll remember the healing you've done too. Dr. Lin recommended a specialist for patients who've had memory loss."

"Yeah." I'm doubtful but don't want to dash her optimism. "Hopefully."

"Eggs." Rob sets a steaming bowl and a plate of stacked toast on the dining table.

"Yummy, weekend scramblies," Laura claps her hands gleefully. "Guess this is your influence, Bosie."

I look at Rob, unsure.

"Yeah," he confirms with a smile. "We have oatmeal — sorry, *porridge* — as our weekday breakfast. But Josie loves scrambled eggs on weekends." He settles his large frame into a chair.

"Speaking of weekdays," I interrupt, "I had a call from Angela DeMarco, which I didn't answer, and a text asking after me. I guess we are colleagues? Anyway, Rob, she wants you to call her."

Rob nods. "Sure. I told Mike about your accident, but I can call Ange too."

I pile some fluffy eggs on buttered toast and take a big bite. "My manager? Mike Jones?"

"Yes, he's a Berkeley buddy and close friend. Best man at our wedding. He was the one who told me about the comms job at H&F, where he works with his partner, Hans. You and I had been together a few months by then."

So, nepotism's alive and well in Manhattan. Get your college buddy to give your new girlfriend a swanky job. Lucky Other Me.

"It was perfect timing, after you were laid off at Crain's," Rob adds, reading my expression.

"Sure. I just don't remember."

"Well, you're great at it. I told Mike you have amnesia, dating from before working there, so you'll have to start from scratch. Whenever you're ready."

He's right. Assuming it's going to take a while to figure out a way home, I'll have to go to work at some point. I can't keep padding around this apartment in Other Me's lovely, skinny-person clothes. I'll have to do her job, hang out with her friends, live her life, too.

Until I figure out how to get back.

I watch Rob eating his eggs. What now? Will he be okay with me sleeping in the art room, being his wife but not his wife — not in the ways that matter? Does he love me enough to wait for my memories to return? Not that they will.

Poor Rob. He thinks I'm his wife, but I'm not.

And what about his real wife — the Other Me? Does she exist separately from me? If I'm here, in her body and in her life, where is she? Maybe she's at my place in Brooklyn, as confused as I am. Or maybe I've simply . . . replaced her.

After dressing, I gaze out of my bedroom window at Union Square Park. I can't go back into the living room and keep having the same confusing conversations. Even in this lofty apartment, I'm feeling increasingly claustrophobic.

Mum is in the kitchen, cleaning up.

"I need some air, Mum, I'm heading out to the park. I'll be back in a bit."

Mum, always approving of a brisk walk, hands me a Coach purse, the silver-gray trench, and a pair of flat boots from the closet. "Off you go. Here are your keys. Take your mobile, too, and don't go far. We don't know how deep your amnesia runs. We'll have lunch together later." She practically throws me out of the door.

Downstairs, I exit toward Union Square East, the concierge holding the lobby door. "Morning, ma'am. Hope you're recovering." He smiles widely.

"Better, thank you," I reply. "What's the best place for coffee?"

"Your usual is Carluccio's, around the corner. The coffee from the kiosk in the park is also good, although they don't have the milk you like . . . Mr. Billing told me about the memory loss, ma'am. I'm sorry."

"Thanks . . . I'm sorry, what's your name?"

"Edward, or Ed is fine. The valet you met yesterday is my son, Will. Have a nice day, ma'am."

I nod before walking off slowly. I study my surroundings with interest. I've been to Union Square many times, but I've never hung out in this neighborhood. Rob's building must be new, as it wasn't built when I was last here. Crossing the street into Union Square Park, I turn around for a better view. It's an attractive tower of gray stone and glass, narrowing at the upper floors and narrowest where there seems to be a single penthouse at the top. The eighteenth- and nineteenth-floor terraces are visible, and the square pillars between them are an elegant, modern take on art deco.

At the foot of the building, across the busy street, the large canopy bears tall art deco lettering that reads "Cavendish House".

Cavendish? That's my last name.

My pulse quickens.

I've got to figure out more about this Rob guy.

On a bench under an almost-bare tree, I pull out my phone and search for Rob Billing, then correct it to Robert Billing.

There are lots of results, and several images too, a few with me in them, glamorous society photos. There's one of us at a Broadway premiere, me in an emerald green dress, Rob in a tux, beaming as he gazes at me. But the photos can wait. I need to understand who Rob is, and why he lives in a building bearing my name.

Robert Andrew Billing is a New York real estate developer and architect. Born June 4, 1979, he is the only child of Seattle real estate developer Andrew Billing and Kim Wade of the Lummi First Nation. Andrew Billing and Kim Wade met when Billing was co-developing a resort with the Lummi Nation on Lummi lands in Washington State.

That makes sense, given the photos of his parents on my phone. Rob looks like he is at least partly of Indigenous heritage.

In May 30, 2011, Robert Billing took over as president and CEO of B+B Developments, a Seattle and New York architecture and development company founded by his father as Billing Developments in 1975. Robert Billing began working there after graduating UC Berkeley School of Architecture in 2005. Robert Billing's most notable development since taking over B+B Developments is a 2015-completed residential building on Union Square named Cavendish House, which Billing designed and which has been featured on reality TV show Luxury Listing NYC.

Of course. I've come across B+B Developments in my job on the radio show. But I didn't know who the boss was. And, apparently, I'm married to him.

PERSONAL LIFE
On October 10, 2015, on the Hawaiian island of Maui, Robert Billing married Josephine Alice Cavendish, a UK-born communications professional and former associate editor at Crain's New York Business. Cavendish is communications manager at Manhattan real estate brokerage Halstein & Faust. Robert Billing's most recent residential development, Cavendish House, was named for his wife as a wedding gift, and the couple lives in the building.

I sit for a long time, staring at the building entrance and the words "Cavendish House" in their graceful lettering. A building named for me, as a gift from my multi-millionaire husband. Incredible.

But this is also a world where I am married to a man I don't know, and David is dead. I mustn't be seduced by its lavishness and its elegant architecture.

I shake it off and go to order a latte at the kiosk. The old guy beams at me in recognition. "Ms. Cavendish herself, a pleasure. How are you?"

"Fine, thank you." I smile back and lift my strapped arm to display my injury. "Apart from the sprained wrist. How are you?"

"Peachy, thanks, ma'am. Here you go, regular latte. Four and a quarter, please." I pull out a chic leather wallet from the Coach purse. Thankfully the back section holds cash, and I hand over a five. "Keep the change."

"Thank you, ma'am. Send our best to your husband. Tell him Luca and Greta say hi."

"I will." I take a sip of the coffee and walk away with an awkward wave of my strapped arm. The coffee is delicious, made with creamy milk. So that's why Other Me doesn't get coffee from here — no 1%. Can't be drinking full-fat lattes with a figure like this. I wonder if I'll wreck Other Josie's body for her in the time I occupy it. I giggle at the thought and sip my coffee.

My merriment doesn't last long. I buy a newspaper and return to my bench, wondering what else is different from my reality. I read the paper from cover to cover, checking for variations in the news. Nope, it doesn't seem like there's been some kind of butterfly effect in which my different life has somehow caused a mass humanitarian disaster. Everything in the news seems in order — or the same disorder as my own world.

The cellphone rings and I pull it out of the purse, Laura's name popping up.

"Hey, Laura."

"Where are you?" My sister sounds a little anxious. "*Is she okay?*" I hear Rob say in the background.

"I'm in the park, reading the paper and acting like a normal person," I say, more breezily than I feel. "How's it going?"

"Good. We're getting hungry for lunch. Want to meet us at Carluccio's? It's near the square."

"Sure. See you there in five?"

"Sounds good."

Passing a homeless guy on the path, I find a handful of quarters in my purse, which I drop in his upturned ball cap. "Would you like this paper? I'm done with it."

"Thank you, love," he replies with a warm smile. His accent is Irish. He's quite good-looking, around forty, fair-haired, chiseled jaw, with one blue eye and one green. I wonder what path he took that caused him to end up there. And what other versions of him may exist in other realities, perhaps in better circumstances. I imagine him in a suit, on Wall Street, and smile back at him before walking away.

"And how about your number, too?" he calls after me. I glance back with a laugh but keep walking.

Mum and Laura are already in the café, ordering three ham and Swiss on rye.

Mum gives me an assessing look. "You seem cheerier, darling."

"I was hit on by a hot panhandler." I hand my trench to the server.

"Josie! Really!" Mum mock-scolds.

"Well, he made me smile. How was your morning?"

"Fine," replies Mum. "Discussing next steps for the next few days. Laura and I have to fly home on Tuesday."

"Oh. Of course." Any cheerfulness dissolves. They're leaving me here?

"Sorry, Bosie," says Laura, "I've got to get back. It's tough on Adam taking care of Theo alone. And I've used up my Christmas holiday leave to be here."

"And I've got my art students," adds Mum. "The studio isn't going to run itself."

"Of course. You must go home. I'm fine, and this . . . confusion might take a while to sort out." I don't want them to go, but I can feel their anxiety. I put on a brave face. "Anyway, Rob will look after me." Although I'm not sure how I feel about *that*.

"Exactly. Even if it takes time to remember him, he'll take good care of you, you needn't worry." My mother examines my face.

I smile. "It's all good."

My sandwich arrives and I pick at it, barely able to join their conversation about little Theo. I will probably never be able to talk to Mum and Laura about my real life again. They won't accept it — it's not their truth. I'll have to keep pretending this is genuine amnesia. Who would believe anything else?

After lunch, I pay the check. "I guess I can afford it," I tell them.

"You need a distraction," Laura muses. "How about MoMA? We have a couple of days left and I want to do some New York things."

"Sounds great. I don't want to go back to the apartment yet."

"You two go," Mum says. "I'll go back and read. Rob's catching up on work, but I can give him space."

I kiss her on the cheek. "Thanks, Mum."

An afternoon strolling around MoMA is, as Laura predicted, just what I needed. Here, among all this art and artifice, is some semblance of real life. This is something she and I would do if she were on a regular visit to New York. For a moment, I let myself imagine I'm back in my own reality, where we'll get the subway home to Brooklyn and she'll sleep on the futon in my tiny second bedroom.

That's not what happens, of course. After a cup of tea at the crowded café, we get back on the subway to Union Square. The train is packed, and I struggle to hang onto the rail with my left hand while attempting to protect my injured arm.

Laura looks irritated as someone bashes me. "You realize you can afford cabs and cars everywhere, don't you? We don't have to rough it anymore."

"I don't care how rich Rob is," I reply. "It's not my money to waste, it's his."

"Actually, you can afford cabs all by your lonesome," Laura points out. "Your job is very well paid. If that helps."

Yes, it does. A bit. If I'm stuck here, at least I can work and get my own place. I can recreate my normal life. But there would still be no David. No Peter. Unless, perhaps, I rejoin choir. Now, there's a thought.

I smile at my sister so she doesn't guess what I'm thinking. "Thanks, but I suppose if I want to live in that penthouse, I'll have to keep relying on Rob."

"Yes," she replies with a wry grin. "You *poor* thing."

We enter the apartment to delicious cooking smells.

"Roast chicken for my girls," Mum calls from the kitchen as we remove our coats. It's a comforting aroma, and it's heartwarming to see her cooking in this glamorous kitchen. Rob is nowhere in sight.

"Is there wine?" I ask, finding a bottle of Sauvignon Blanc, my favorite, in the refrigerator. I hold it up.

"Ooh, please," Mum says.

"And me!" Laura calls from the bedroom.

"Where's Rob?"

"In the den. See if he wants a drink, darling." Mum frowns when I hesitate, so I acquiesce.

I take the corridor to the right of the kitchen. Several more pieces of artwork adorn the walls, two of which I recognize as belonging to me. So some things have crossed over to this new reality. How does that work?

Maybe it's just stuff from before I supposedly met Rob. All the paintings here that are mine, the vase for my thirtieth, my bike helmet, are all from my Murray Hill days. I suppose that's what I would've brought with me into this marriage, if I'd met him back then.

At the door to the den, I can hear strains of a jazz piano piece being played. I knock. "Rob?"

The music abruptly stops. "Come in."

I open the door and find a generous but cozy den entirely painted in the same dramatic blue as the art wall in my bedroom. Next to the double-sided fireplace, which adjoins the living room, is an open pullout sofa. My sister's suitcase is lying open on top, clothes draped everywhere, as usual. Rob is sitting at a baby grand piano near the window. He looks up at me and smiles tiredly. "Josie. How was your day?"

"Not bad, thanks. I feel better. After last night . . ." I stop. I don't want to think about David. About him not being here.

He nods solemnly. "I'm glad." He stands, looking uncertain. "Dinner smells amazing. I'd forgotten your Mum is quite the cook."

"I wondered if you'd like some wine. We've got the Sauvignon Blanc open."

"Thanks, yes, but I'll have red. There's some Shiraz left. I'll come out in a moment."

"I'll get a glass out for you." I hesitate, glancing around the den once more.

"Do you like this room?" Rob sounds curious, as if the answer is important.

"It's lovely. It's the first time I've seen this one." I pause, blushing as I realize what I've said, how odd it must sound. "I went into the master suite when you were out, but I missed this one. It's a bonus room, almost hidden."

"I designed it that way. But you picked the color." He half-smiles. "I said you were crazy choosing dark blue for a smaller room, but you were right. It looks so beautiful with the piano."

"I heard you playing." I should go, but something makes me linger. "Mum said that's how we met."

"Yeah, in the W Hotel lobby. I learned the jazz classics as a kid. That's what my dad is into. Mum never had stuff like piano lessons growing up, so she wanted me to have it. I was lucky."

"Nice." I nod, not sure what to say next. "Well . . . See you in a bit."

I leave quickly, somewhat flustered. Any man who can play jazz piano like that is extremely attractive, at least to me. That's possibly even sexier than Peter's guitar skills. It's not surprising Other Me fell for Rob so hard.

But this is *her* husband. Not mine.

Over dinner, though, it's hard not to be distracted by Rob's presence as he skillfully carves the roast chicken. My imagination wanders to what it must've been like for Other Me, lounging in the den, singing along while Rob played Gershwin. I take frequent sips of the wine, trying to concentrate on the meal and conversation, but my eyes keep sliding to Rob's plate, his hands, his generous mouth.

Okay, so this guy is hot. There's no denying it.

I realize I may be tipsy, and I'm ashamed at myself for thinking about someone else's husband in that way, when Peter and I are just starting out. That's what I've wanted for so long. Isn't it?

My head throbs and I excuse myself after dinner, retiring to my room with a Kate Atkinson novel, a cup of mint tea, and my painkillers. Dosing myself, the drugs eventually kick in, and I sleep.

I dream of a huge grand piano inside MoMA. I keep trying to play, except I hit the wrong keys every time. There's nothing but discord.

CHAPTER 4

Early December

"You'll be okay, won't you, darling?" Mum asks for the third time as she puts on her coat.

"Fine, Mum. I'll call you tomorrow when you're home in Cornwall."

"Lovely." But she looks worried. "Got everything, Laura?" My sister is famous for losing things.

"Yes, Mum." Laura turns to me. She looks like she's going to cry. "We love you, Bosie. Everything will work out. Promise."

"Of course," I say firmly. "Love you. Give Theo a snuggle from me. And Adam. Well, a chaste hug to Adam." I smile, a lump forming. "Off you go."

"Let me get that, Iris." Rob grabs both their bags, ushering them out of the apartment.

I watch from the doorway, giving one last wave as they disappear into the elevator. I return to the living room and slump down on the couch.

Christ, it's been wonderful to have them with me, but I'm also relieved not to be hosting my family while I'm in a parallel universe where I have no idea what's going on.

Now there's only this Rob guy to deal with. Hmm.

When he returns to the apartment, I pick up my book, hoping to dodge a "now what?" conversation that we inevitably have to have at some point. Just not now, I hope.

Rob walks into the kitchen. "More tea? Or have you overdosed?"

"Please. Never too much tea. English Breakfast, please."

"At 5.30 in the afternoon? You crazy Brit." He covers his awkwardness after the over-familiar tease by filling the kettle. "There is no food. Your family has eaten everything, including those weird crackers that you guys love so much. We could go out for dinner? Start from scratch." He shrugs. "I can tell you about my work. It's real estate, so you'll find it interesting . . ." He trails off into silence.

A dinner date.

"Okay," I reply finally. "I'll resist the temptation to bring my notebook and interview you."

"I wouldn't mind." He looks at me, his face earnest. "I want you to get to know me, Jose, to start jogging memories." He runs a hand through his thick, silky hair. "I'll call for our usual table at the W?"

We have a regular table at the W. Very fancy. "Sure."

After showering, I blow-dry my hair, which takes way longer than I'm used to, as there's more of it. I fix my makeup in a soft, smoky style and pick out a mid-length blue dress with a fine-pleated skirt that's totally unfamiliar, but definitely something I would have chosen.

"You look great," says Rob when I finally emerge. He's trying to sound casual. He's looking pretty great himself, in a slate-blue shirt over dark jeans. My stomach flips. "Hope you're hungry."

"Ravenous," I tell him.

We pull on our coats and exit the building into the dark night. The trees in the park square are strung up with glittering fairy lights for the holiday season, and a cluster of warmly dressed tourists are sipping from steaming cups at Luca's kiosk.

At the W hotel, a few buildings away, we are greeted by the maître d' of the restaurant. "Mr. and Mrs. Billing, good evening. We have your table."

"Thank you, Ben." Rob helps me out of my coat, hands it over to the maître-d.

As Ben leads us through the warmly lit, high ceiling restaurant, Rob murmurs, "Do you recog . . . have you eaten here before?"

I appreciate his effort, and smile at I take my seat. "No, I've never been inside the hotel. I was supposed to come to a conference here a few years back, on my birthday, in fact, but I sprained my ankle and never made it."

He raises his eyebrows, looking surprised. "You mean . . . that's the day we met, three years ago, at the Inman conference."

I stare at him. "Right. That day."

The awkward silence that follows is broken by the arrival of the server. Rob doesn't even bother looking at the drinks menu. "Bottle of the Pinot Gris, please, Cameron."

I place the linen napkin on my lap. "I guess you and I eat here often."

He grins. "Every couple of weeks, when there's no food at home. Like tonight."

"And your development firm worked on the hotel?"

He nods, looking a little more relaxed as he leans forward. "Yes. It was still Dad's company then, but we were subcontracted for part of it by another developer. I moved here from Seattle to manage our side of things. Then I took over all the New York projects. And now that Dad is retired, we only do New York developments — like our building." He pauses. "You've done some research on me, then? You don't remember."

"No," I say, aware that he sounded almost hopeful. "Of course, I had to research you. I'm living with you, so I should figure out who you are. Your parents sound interesting."

"Mum and Dad are awesome. Wildly different from each other, but still going strong after forty-five years. They've been asking after you. They're very fond of you."

"They sound cool." I'm not sure what else to say.

Thankfully, Cameron returns with our wine. I watch as he expertly uncorks the wine, pouring a little into Rob's glass. Rob sips at it, then, after a moment, nods. Cameron fills both our glasses. "Any decisions on dinner?"

"Do I have a favorite?" I ask Rob.

"I'd say the seafood linguine, although you've been getting the ahi salad recently."

I nod. I've always liked seafood. "The linguine, please."

"Two, and let's split a beet salad," adds Rob. "Thanks, Cameron."

"Man," I say after Cameron leaves. "You know everybody, don't you?"

"Well . . . around Union Square, maybe, and at a few hotels and restaurants. Development and real estate people, really. Generally, I try to keep to myself."

"That photo of us on the red carpet doesn't seem that way."

"You saw that? It was more your thing than mine." He smiles. "I was just happy to watch you having fun in a foxy dress."

"It looked fun. I don't get to go to stuff like that."

His smile falters. "Since you've been at Halstein & Faust, you've been to some very glamorous events. Lots of real estate parties. You've even appeared on *Luxury Listing*, when the cameras follow Hans into the office to film his meetings. The producers interviewed you — you've been on screen a few times."

"Wow, that's so cool!" I shake my head. "I can't even get Hans to come on my radio show."

Rob hesitates, clearly unsure how to proceed when we're talking about two very different versions of my life.

I break the silence again. "So, tell me about Cavendish House."

Over the linguine, awkwardly eaten with my left hand, Rob tells the story of the building, which was originally dubbed Union House, "—until I decided to rename it, as a wedding gift to you. But even before I met you, I knew I'd want to move in. I designed the penthouse and four sub-penthouses with extra ceiling height, and we kept 1802 aside for us."

"Why not the top penthouse?"

"That's where the real money is. Although it's still for sale. But we think Hans may have found a buyer."

"So Halstein & Faust are your brokers? That makes sense."

"Yeah, it's all a tight circle. Even in New York."

"I guess I've seen that, from the outside, through my radio show. It's interesting to see the inner workings."

Rob is silent again as Cameron clears the table. "Anything else, sir, ma'am?"

"Not for me," I say. "That was delicious." It really was.

Rob pays the check. I notice he tips generously. Always a good sign. He watches Cameron leave, then leans back in his chair, presses his lips together. "This is hard, Josie. You talking about a different life."

I nod. I don't want to hurt this man, but he's basically a stranger to me. "Yeah. But I don't know how else to do this. Do you want me to pretend this is regular amnesia? It isn't. I mean, you're a great guy, and I've had a nice evening, but I have to be myself. I'm happy to get to know you, but you have to get to know me, too. The real me. If that means we have super-weird conversations where you say, 'This is your favorite restaurant' and I'm like, 'That's cool, I've never eaten here before' — can you handle that?"

Rob looks down at the table. "Guess I'll have to." He half-smiles. "Promise me one thing? Don't stick to your version of events out of stubbornness. Because I have a different truth. So if you start to remember any of our shared history, will you tell me?"

"Deal," I nod, then stand as the maitre d' approaches. He helps me with my coat as Rob shrugs into his. "Thank you." I turn to Rob. "But I don't want you to hold out hope."

We walk out into the crisp night air, our breath misting.

"You'll see the consultant?" he asks, breaking our silence, as we stroll back to Cavendish House. It's late, and the streets are starting to empty.

"I'm going this week."

"It might help, right?" He's trying not to sound too hopeful. "I meant to tell you, I spoke to Mike. They're good with you taking another week off work."

"That's good. My wrist won't be strapped by then, so I guess I can start. It's weird — they'll have all these expectations, but for me it's starting a job I've never done before."

"You'll be fine." We're back at the apartment building. Rob steps back to let me enter first as Ed holds open the door. "Good night, Ed."

We ride up in the elevator and enter the apartment in silence. I'm exhausted and as confused as ever. Trying to keep the mood light, I say, "Well, I'm developing a deep relationship with Kate Atkinson, so I'm taking her to bed with me. Along with a cinnamon tea to spice things up."

Rob smiles. "You and Kate have fun. I'll be watching game highlights in our — my room. I'll be at work when you get up, assuming you're still a lazy ass who sleeps till 9.30."

So some things don't change. "Yes," I say, filling the kettle from the island sink. "I am. Where is your office?"

"On Lexington, near the Chrysler. A source of art deco inspiration." He gestures at the ceiling, the moldings.

"Indeed. Well, good night. Thanks for dinner."

"You're welcome, Josie. Sleep well."

I watch him walk away, trying to make sense of how this evening made me feel.

Perplexed, definitely.

Comforted? Perhaps a little.

And, I have to admit, attracted.

CHAPTER 5

Early December

Dec 8, 2017

This is the diary of Josie Cavendish, British expat in New York, living in some kind of parallel universe/alternate timeline of her own life.

I'm starting this journal to document the extraordinary events that seem to be happening to me. I say "seem" because I'm aware this will sound crazy to anybody other than myself. And perhaps I am crazy — in which case, this journal could be useful to the nice people in white coats when they come to cart me off.

But there are only two people this is intended to be read by, and they're both me. Me, and the woman whose life this is, who is also me. The Other Me.

I realized something last night. The reason I want to start documenting is because, if She exists as a separate person from me, and if we've switched lives, it's also feasible we might switch back one day. If so, she'll need to know what went down while I was living her life. Or maybe I've somehow shifted into an alternate version of my life, but there's only one me. Or I could just be nuts.

As I write this, it's 7 a.m. on Dec 8, 2017, and I'm in the guest bedroom of the apartment owned by Rob Billing and Josie Cavendish, on Union Square in Manhattan, New York. I guess the only way to start is from the beginning.

It happened on November 30, 2017, my 36th birthday. I was riding my bike to meet my friends for dinner when . . .

I spend the next hour propped up in bed, documenting the extraordinary events of the past few days. I get almost up to date when, twisting to find a back-pain-free position, I close the journal. It's a beautiful notebook, with a lavish green-and-copper cover. I probably shouldn't be defacing its pristine pages with my scrawl. It isn't really mine to write in. It's hers. Uncomfortable with both that thought and the too-hard mattress, I decide to get up, like a normal person.

It's 8.15 when I finally enter the living room in my robe. Rob is there, dressed in a well-cut suit, drinking coffee at the kitchen island. He starts when he sees me.

"What's this? Josie up before 9 a.m. when she doesn't have to work? We really have slipped into a parallel universe."

He's trying to make me laugh, but the joke grates.

"Too soon?" he asks, seeing my expression.

"A bit," I say with a half-smile. He really is very nice. "I'm having a hard time with my mattress. It's a bit firmer than I'm used to."

"Has your back pain returned? I figured it might, in that bed. It's only been better since we got our fancy mattress. I'd switch them, except yours is only a king, not a super-king."

"Don't worry. I've got painkillers. Plus it's only a problem if I'm lying awake in bed for ages, so I'll have to start getting up at a reasonable hour, I guess. I have an appointment with that consultant Dr. Weinstein today, although not until after lunch."

Rob nods, moving to the espresso machine. "Sit down, I'll make you coffee."

I perch at a bar stool as he makes me a latte with the skim milk. "Have you eaten breakfast yet?" I ask him. "I bought eggs, thought I'd scramble some. Even if it is a weekday."

He checks the kitchen clock, hesitates. "Thanks, but . . ." He stops again. "Yeah. Eggs would be great."

"Good. I'll do the eggs, you do the toast."

"I've only eaten toast with my eggs since I met you." He's smiling as he puts thick slices of bread in the toaster while I reach into the fridge for the carton. "It's you who hasn't been eating much bread. You cut out most of your carbs."

"Right." That explains a lot. I crack eggs into a large bowl and whisk them with a fork. "I guess I must've lost a fair bit of weight since we met."

"You wanted to, just a little, for the wedding. But then, after Hawaii, after David, you lost a lot more. Since then, I guess you figured you may as well stay slimmer. But I miss the delicious enjoyment of food you used to have. Still, it seems you've gotten that back since your accident."

"I'm not sure I was meant to be this slim." I watch the butter sizzle in the hot pan and stir the eggs. "I want to eat toast, goddammit."

"Then you shall eat toast," Rob laughs. "And here, *Madame*, is your toast."

As he leaves for work, we've had such an amicable breakfast, it's almost weird he doesn't kiss me on the forehead. There's a moment I think he's going to, as he pauses, but then remembers. He turns away.

"Back around six. Good luck with your appointment. Call if you need me."

"Thanks. Good luck with the penthouse buyer."

The huge apartment seems very empty with Rob gone. I'm glad of the appointment that will keep me busy. After showering and dressing in the same burgundy blazer and gray pants I came back from the hospital in a week ago, I decide to leave several hours early and walk most of the fifty-six-block journey to the doctor's office. I head out into the cold, sunny day. "Okay, boots, let's see if you were made for walkin'."

My boots and I make it almost thirty blocks to Grand Central Station, which I think is quite impressive, before my feet are hot and aching. I realize Rob's office is nearby, and my stomach repeats its weird flutter, which I ignore. It's still way too early for the appointment, so I step inside Grand Central and spend time enjoying the cavernous space, imagining couples waltzing to some unheard music as the sunshine streams through the vast windows. A scene from *The Fisher King*. I buy a soda and pastrami sandwich from a vendor and sit people-watching, then read *The New York Times* for a while.

This feels good. This feels normal.

With twenty minutes until my appointment time, having read the entire paper, I take the subway a few stops to 68th Street. The consultant's office is on the ground floor of an imposing Fifth Avenue building overlooking Central Park.

I stop outside, suddenly panicking. What am I going to say to this doctor? How can I tell him the truth? But what's the alternative? Lie, and tell him I don't remember anything from the past three years? Why in the world didn't I come up with a plan before now?

It's 12.58, and my appointment's at 1, so there's no time to worry about it now.

"Yes?" The woman at reception is flicking through a binder. She doesn't even look up.

"Josie Cavendish for Dr. Weinstein," I reply, with a warmer smile than she deserves.

"Take a seat at the end of the corridor."

"Thank you so much." I give her another brilliant, but rather pointless, smile as she still has her head down.

The corridor opens up into a seating area with a view of a lush patio. I have just managed to take off my trench when a door with a gold name plate reading "Dr. Abraham Weinstein" opens. A short man with curly hair and glasses steps out.

"Ms. Cavendish?"

"That's me." He gestures me inside, then follows me in.

"Welcome." Dr. Weinstein crosses the room to his desk, picks up a file, opening it. He lowers himself into a leather desk chair. "Please, sit."

I sit on the couch, wondering how many of his patients lie down. Or is that a myth?

"So, Ms. Cavendish—"

"Josie, please."

"Josie. I understand you had a cycling accident and you've been having some trouble accessing some memories. That you have some," he hesitates, "*replacement* memories. Is that accurate?" He peers at me over his glasses.

I smile. "That's about it."

"Fine. I'm a neuropsychiatrist, I help patients with psychological problems associated with damage to the brain or nervous system. The Bellevue referred you to me since I have also worked with amnesiac patients."

"Sounds good."

"Why don't you tell me in your own words what you feel has happened over the past week?"

He's going to think I'm crazy.

I describe what I remember about the bike accident, and the first few moments in the hospital, how I didn't recognize Rob.

"It was weird, though," I add, thinking on my feet, trying to come up with a story that seems plausible. "Instead of simply not remembering my husband, or where I lived, or worked, for the past three years, it was like I had been someone else during that time. Someone who wasn't married, who lived in Brooklyn, and worked at a radio station. But . . . that's all fading now. I mean, I still don't remember Rob, our home, or my job at the real estate brokerage. But the memory of my other life is fading. It seems more like a dream now."

That's not even a lie — not really. My old life is already starting to feel distant.

"I see." Dr. Weinstein taps his pen against the desk. "Perhaps your brain, attempting to fill in lost memories caused by your amnesia, has latched onto some other ideas, maybe experienced by you in a dream or fantasy, or created by your subconscious. And it's made those memories seem more real than your actual reality. Especially as the last version of yourself you can remember was unmarried. That would make more sense to you than the reality of being married. And your brother was alive three years ago, so it would be understandable that you want to believe he is alive somewhere. Does that make sense?"

"Yes, it does."

It really does.

Fuck.

Is that what is happening? Is my old life a trick of the mind, filling in the gaps caused by genuine, plain-old amnesia? Is this world my real life?

Dr. Weinstein asks me more questions and I answer, but my voice sounds like it's far away, and I'm on autopilot. After another half-hour, he is done.

"There was no visible trauma to the brain on your MRI," he concludes, "so we can only hope your memories will return. They don't always, but for most people they do. We'll pick this up again in a month and see how you're doing. Please make an appointment with Marie on your way out."

"Thank you." We both stand, and my legs are like jelly. He holds open the door, and I walk unsteadily out of the office, past reception, ignoring the instructions to book a follow-up.

I push my way through the heavy door onto Fifth Avenue. Through charcoal clouds, dramatic sunbeams are now illuminating the park. I cross Fifth and enter the park at 69th Street, crunching over the last of the fallen leaves, my mind racing. Is none of my old life real?

There's a crowd ahead — the ice rink. The ideal spot to people-watch and ponder. I buy myself a hot chocolate from a vendor and sit on the bleachers, double-wrapping my scarf around my neck for warmth.

The scene in front of me is a classic movie image. Skaters of all shapes and sizes, wearing a wide array of colorful knits, glide or falter across the ice. Behind them is the southern edge of Central Park, the almost-bare trees still showing flashes of red and gold. Beyond them, the towers of Manhattan rise up majestically. At least New York and its beauty are consistent.

I sip the syrupy hot chocolate and take some calming breaths.

Okay, let's think about this. Is it possible the doctor is right, my old life a construct, filling the void left by amnesia?

I consider this for a long time. On the surface, logic suggests he is right. It makes more sense than my belief that I have switched places with another version of myself from an alternate reality. Obviously.

But, no. It can't be true. My old life is too detailed. If I had only a vague picture, then perhaps. But I can remember the minutiae of the last three years in my old life, and nothing of my current one. My home in Brooklyn: moving in, hauling furniture up all those stairs, hanging the forest painting — that now admittedly hangs in Rob's apartment — Mum visiting and her complaints about the futon in the second bedroom. The dinners I've hosted around the tiny table. My radio job. My chipped desk always covered in cracker crumbs. The feel of the headphones over my ears. Even the radio voice I use. My friends and mentors at the station. And my brother. David.

If he's really been dead more than two years, how do I remember a conversation with him three weeks ago about Trump's presidency? And what about this past September, when I flew to France to join him and other friends on a surfing vacation in Biarritz (the guys surfed, our friend Mel and I played with her baby)? And last Christmas, when I went back to the UK and my family had Christmas Day at David's flat in London. There are so many, many memories that can't be explained away.

Did I really imagine them all?

The doctor has to be wrong. Understandably, considering the information he's been given, but wrong. He just has to be.

On the other hand, I'm not sure that is such a good thing, given that *my* truth is that I am stuck in an alternate timeline with a husband I don't know and a brother who is dead. In many ways, it would be much easier to accept this new world. And yet believing my old life exists and David is alive, somewhere, even if beyond reach, is immeasurably comforting.

I watch the skaters whirling about while I think about my two worlds. When I realize I am getting too cold, I check my watch. It's almost 4 p.m. and the sky is darkening. How did two hours fly past?

Back in my new neighborhood, which is becoming familiar, I stop to pick up some fresh tagliatelle, smoked salmon, dill, and some crème fraiche at the local store.

Rob gets home as I'm chopping the herbs. "The famous smoked salmon pasta," he comments as he shrugs off his overcoat. "Are you trying to impress me?"

I blush, realizing I might have told him at some point that this is a favored date-night meal. "It's easy." I shrug. "Make a salad, would you?"

"Sure," he says, but his eyes are smiling and he's not making a move toward the fridge. "How was the doctor?"

"Interesting. I'll tell you about it. Did you guys pin down the penthouse deal?"

"We did!" Rob declares. He pulls out a bottle of champagne from behind him. "Seventeen-point-seven-five, including the furniture. Everybody's happy. I thought we could celebrate. This will be delicious with dinner, too."

"Congratulations." I examine the bottle. "Wow — the good stuff."

"Nothing but the best." Rob puts it in the fridge to chill. "Okay, salad."

Later, at the dining table, Rob waits until the pasta and salad are plated and then pops the champagne, pouring into tall-stemmed flutes. "What should we toast to?"

"To the sale," I reply. "To 17.75 million. Nice work."

We clink glasses. "To our success," Rob adds. "And to getting to know each other. Whether for the first time, or all over again." He smiles, then knocks back a generous glug.

I take a sip of the cold, crisp bubbles. "That too."

Rob swirls the pasta expertly on his fork, "So . . . tell me about this consultant."

"Dr. Weinstein. Well, he was smart. We had an interesting chat. I told him . . . a partial truth, about believing I had been living a different life for the past three years. I played it down, saying I was unsure now, although I still couldn't remember anything from since I met you. Didn't want to seem too crazy, in case he had me taken away by men in white coats. He had an interesting theory." I spear some lettuce onto my fork and look up. "Kinda threw me."

Rob arches an eyebrow. "Oh?"

"He thinks my brain, having lost short-term memories, is reacting against that void by filling it with false memories. Stuff that could have been from dreams, my subconscious, my life before you — about David being alive, me being unmarried, working another job, and so on. And they seem real, because my actual memories of that period are gone."

Rob picks up his glass, absently swirling the champagne around. "What do you think?"

"It's a sensible suggestion, I guess. Given the information available."

Rob's eyes are on my face as I take another mouthful of the creamy pasta. "But? I feel like there's a but."

I swallow. "But. I thought about it — for a long time, I sat in the park for hours — and I can't believe he's right. I can't have imagined every single memory for the past three years. I lived them. As real as you've lived the past three years. I remember being in my Brooklyn place, Skyping with David a few weeks ago, talking about current politics. That couldn't have happened three years ago. I remember a holiday in France with our buddies this past September, including a baby who wasn't even born three years ago. I have so many memories of the past few years, and it was a *different* life. It can't all be imagined."

Rob frowns. "I guess not. I'd find it pretty weird if everyone told me I'd never met you, I had a different wife, I lived in a different part of town, and I didn't have my job. I've been trying to imagine what that must feel like."

I lean toward him, putting my hand on the table near to his. Not quite touching. "I appreciate that." And I mean it. "All this must seem crazy. And so hard for you. Me not remembering you. You've been so kind."

Rob inclines his head and half-smiles. "So, I guess the big question is, what do you think happened? Really? I won't judge, I swear." He tops up our glasses and waits.

I push away my plate and grip the edge of the table. "I know this sounds nuts, but . . . I think the impossible happened. I've been somehow jolted out of my reality, my timeline. My life split, three years ago, when I did or didn't meet you. And that was because of a near-miss on my bike that day — because in my world, I sprained my ankle, and missed that conference, never met you there. Then, at the moment of my recent bike crash, at the exact same spot, I was shifted onto this alternative path. The road not taken.

"Think about it," I add, warming to my subject. "The Josie in your reality was also riding to meet you at a gallery, right? And our paths would have *crossed*. Maybe because they crossed at exactly the same time, or because we both crashed at exactly the same time *and* exactly the same place, this shift happened. Of course—" I break off, aware of how nonsensical it all sounds. "There's no logical explanation. Unless a tear in the fabric of the space-time continuum is, you know, a real thing." I laugh, trying to brighten the mood.

Rob smiles uncomfortably but says nothing. He takes another sip of champagne and stares past me, toward the sparkling lights of Manhattan.

I hesitate, then add the kicker.

"There's one other thing I'm wondering. Whether there's only me, and I shifted from one path to another, and that's it. Or whether there are two Josies, and two realities. And in the crash, we *switched*. So your wife, your real wife, is stuck in my life. Without you. Probably trying to work out how to get back to you."

Rob's eyes snaps back to me, his expression dark. "No. No way. *You're* my wife."

He picks up the dinner plates, stacking them with a clatter, and takes them up the steps to the kitchen.

I follow him with the salad bowl. "I get that it's not what you want to hear, Rob, but we have to at least consider the possibility that if I'm here, from another life, she might be there. But . . . who the hell knows? Maybe there's just me, and I'm on an alternate path, and that's all. Maybe I've plugged in fake memories, like the doctor said, and there is no other reality. Maybe I'm losing my goddamn mind."

I grip the cold salad bowl, the scent of the vinaigrette sharp. Sobs rise in my throat. I swallow hard. "I don't understand what the hell is happening."

Rob takes the bowl from me, placing it on the counter, then unexpectedly pulls me close. He wraps his big arms around me, and I sink into his chest, his bearded chin against my forehead.

"You're not crazy," he murmurs against my hair. "I promise. I'm going to take care of you. It will work out."

I say nothing, letting my cheek rest on his collarbone, feeling myself calm. Nobody has held me like this in a long time. In this world or any other. It feels warm and safe, and for a moment I believe him. Everything will be fine.

We stand in silence for a while, clinging to each other. Then he strokes my hair and pulls back to look down at me.

"What do you want to be the truth?" he asks. "To be right, about your belief in another life? Wouldn't it be easier to be wrong? To be amnesiac, and be my wife, even if you don't remember me?"

"Sure, easier. One world, no crazy parallel realities, the laws of the universe as we know them fully intact. Boring old amnesia. But I have to believe I'm right."

"Why?" Rob asks, in a small voice.

"Because in this world, David is dead." There, I've said it out loud. "In the end, it doesn't matter where I live or whom I'm with. Here, David is dead. I have to believe there is a world where he is surfing in Australia right now. And that world is my home."

Rob pulls away. "That's what this is about? David? That's why you've barely cried for him since we told you?" He turns to me, his face drawn. "*You still think he's alive.*"

"He is to me. Somewhere."

Rob shakes his head. I put my hand on his arm. "Rob, I'm sorry. But I won't lie to you, or lie by omission."

"So . . . what? You hang out here a while until you go . . . home? Back to your old life? Are you planning on leaving?" His voice breaks.

"I've no idea." I really don't. I can feel the pull of him, and of this life, conflicting with my need to find a way back to my old reality. "I'm trying to make the best of everything. I'm trying to live this life. I'll do this new job. I've even emailed my old choir director to rejoin the group in January. I don't know if I'll ever be able to go home, and I'm utterly confused about it all. Because, the truth is, I like it here. I like being here with you. It's a dream home. And you seem lovely. But David's my brother, you know? And we're really close. I can't abandon him."

"I'm sorry." Rob steps back, rubbing his face. "I can't stand this. You're my wife and I love you. I need you to remember me, our whole life together. I'm trying to be strong for you, and I'll be as patient as I can. But it's so messed up. How is anyone supposed to handle this?" He looks so miserable.

"You're being amazing, I swear," I sniff. Everything's blurring. I dab at my eyes with a hand towel. "There's no guidebook for how to handle parallel-universe switch-ups." Even saying that sounds insane. "You haven't had me committed to a mental institution, so I figure you're doing great. And I'm sorry for crying. It's so unattractive."

Rob picks up the plates. "You could never be unattractive to me."

He turns away.

CHAPTER 6

Mid-December

On a lazy Sunday in the living room, as I'm journaling about Dr. Weinstein, Rob looks up from his iPad. "Hey, I meant to mention a couple of things. Stuff we need to plan."

"Yeah?"

"There's this thing we have here — it's called Christmas. You're familiar with it?" He waggles his eyebrows.

I laugh. "Some ancient festival, I believe?"

"Exactly. We were supposed to go to Seattle to spend it with my folks, since you and I were here without them last year, and we went to England the year before. Mum and Dad figure it's their turn with us. I wasn't sure you were up to a trip to Seattle, so they suggested they come here instead."

Rob's joviality has turned to uncertainty. He rushes on. "They'd stay about eight days, arrive Christmas Eve, leave after New Year's . . . You get along with them so well, and they can't wait to see you. What do you think?"

"I must know them pretty well, huh? It must be weird for them, too. You've told them I don't remember anything since the time we met?"

"I said you have amnesia going back three years, not . . . anything else." He grins. "Dad said it's nice they get a second chance at a first impression with you."

I smile back. "That's sweet. Of course, they should come. You're right, I'm not ready for Seattle, but it'll be nice to spend Christmas with good people." I glance about the apartment. And I'm getting used to this place. This life.

"It'll be fun." He turns back to his tablet.

I pick up my journal, then remember. "You said there were a couple of things?"

"Right. The other thing is a party to celebrate the penthouse sale. Hans wants us to host it, as we're in the same building. They're filming the new season of *Luxury Listing*, which has been following the sale, so they want to bring the camera crew in, shoot the party, all that jazz. Of course, I told Hans I'd run it past you."

"Wow. That sounds like a lot."

I'm not sure I'm ready to be a glamorous party hostess on TV yet. If ever.

"Yeah. We've had parties like that before — not with a TV crew, but similar events. It'd all be party-planned and catered, you'd only have to show up in the living room in a great dress. Or even go stay with Suzie for the night, if you can't handle it — I could do it solo." The reluctance is evident in his voice.

It doesn't seem fair to leave him to host it alone. The sale is a big deal. "How soon are we talking?"

"February, I guess? Something like that."

Two months. It's hard to imagine still being here then, but it's also hard to imagine I'll have worked out how to get home.

"I'm sure it'll be fine." I sound more certain than I feel. Rob's been so kind, and it is his home. "Tell Hans yes, we can host."

"Yes to everything! I knew I liked you." He gets up, stretching. "Soup for lunch?"

I laugh. "Sure. Did Mike tell you he's stopping by this afternoon to talk to me about coming back to work?"

"He did." Rob walks up into the kitchen. "I think it's also a social call. He wants to watch hockey on our big screen. They're bringing beers — Hans is coming too," he explains at my quizzical look. "Mike's your boss, but it's cool. You'll like them. They're close friends of ours."

Rob's right. When Mike and Hans turn up a few hours later, I warm to them immediately. Mike is a stocky, attractive guy with a trim goatee beard. He's about Rob's age and was in his year at Cal. His partner, Hans, is a familiar face, of course. Apart from wanting to get him on my radio show, I've watched him for years on *Luxury Listing NYC*. The tall, blond man makes me a little starstruck, but the feeling soon dissipates with his friendliness. Mike and Hans make a great couple and clearly adore each other.

"Josie, darling, you're looking gorgeous," Hans says in his still-thick German accent. He grabs my shoulders with both hands, bending to kiss me on each cheek, his affection for me obvious. "We've been missing you. And I know you haven't been missing us, because you don't even remember who the hell we are. But you're going to love us."

As Hans and Rob settle down to watch the pre-game on the projector screen in the living room, Mike and I slip into the den for a chat.

"So, this is weird, but you *do* work for me." Mike laughs. "We're hoping you'll come back soon. We miss you in the office. Professionally and personally. I'm just wondering where your head is at." His honesty is refreshing.

"That's very kind," I tell him. "It is weird, because I don't remember the job and I haven't had a comms role before. I don't want you to have high expectations and be disappointed. I'll have to learn everything from scratch. So if you want to hire someone else, someone with experience, or whoever has been filling in, I completely understand."

Mike's response is immediate and flatteringly emphatic. "Thanks, but no. We hired you based on your experience working in real estate journalism at Crain's, and you still have that, right? And when we took you on, you adapted so quickly, you're a natural. Even the person who has been filling in, Angela, she's fine, but she isn't as good as you were even in your first week. It's you we want."

"Wow. I appreciate the validation." And I do. It's good to know I'm good at my job. Even if I can't remember how to do it. "Okay then. When do you want me to start?"

"We only have two weeks until the office closes for Christmas, so it's an ideal time to ease into it — do some retraining, strategy meetings for 2018, and Angela can hand back projects. Then you'll be able to hit the ground running in the New Year. Sound manageable?"

"Perfect. That makes it a bit less pressured. So . . . I'll start tomorrow?"

Mike considers this. "Let's make it Wednesday. And you guys are coming to our Christmas party, right? We've booked the private room at Lafayette again. It's Thursday. Everyone's coming, partners too. Hans and I will be there, all the staff, plus Rob's team. Didn't he tell you?" I obviously look blank.

"Not yet. There's been a lot to take in. But it sounds fun. I'll have been at the office a couple of days, so I'll have learned some names by then."

"And Rob said you guys are up for hosting the *Luxury Listing* party?"

"Yeah, in February — we'll have to see how fast it can be planned. Not much will get done till after New Year's. Actually," I pause, "now that I think about it, perhaps it should be around Valentine's. We could even have it themed. Right? Set up a hashtag, #LoveLuxuryListing, or something—"

Mike throws his head back with a booming laugh. "Ha! You're worried about this job? You've come up with an amazing party theme with a social hashtag in two seconds. You, my dear English rose, are going to have zero *problemo*."

I'm excited for the first time. This job sounds kind of great. Mike seems like a fun boss, as well as a friend. Plus I know I have a talent for this kind of stuff.

Mike gets up and opens the door. "Right, I'm having a beer before our husbands drink them all. Coming?"

Rob is in the living room. He grins at my expression. "All good?" He pats the seat next to him, a warm invitation.

"Yeah, actually." I sit down, tucking my feet under me and accepting the beer Mike passes over my shoulder. "I restart next Wednesday. And I'll get to meet people at our office party Thursday."

Rob nods, but he's watching me carefully. "You okay with all that?"

"Sure. I've heard Lafayette is fabulous."

Finally, he smiles. "You helped Angela organize the office party there last year."

"Right. Still getting used to having been places I don't remember."

"More fun things to do for the first time." He inches closer to me, glancing at the giant screen. "So, do you want the lowdown on the game?"

* * *

Mike steps into my small interior office at Halstein & Faust, where I'm reading through the winter PR campaigns I've apparently put together. My first day yesterday was a whirlwind of information and introductions, but today I'm beginning to figure out my responsibilities.

He pulls up a chair. "Going well? Anything too weird?"

"It's a lot, but nothing's weird. I can see my thought processes. I can execute on these. I'll figure it out as I go."

"No doubt," Mike agrees. "We worked on all these together, so I'm always here to ask. The other task is the *Luxury Listing* party at your place. You'll have to work with the producers, as they'll be filming it. You can do it in office hours, as it's part of your job, working with party planners. Is that a good first project until we wrap for Christmas?"

"Perfect."

Rob texts me in the afternoon.

Hey, hope your second day is going well? I'll be done by 4.30 so figured I'd come to your office first, if you're all leaving at 5.

Yes, going well, thanks for asking. Angela said we're leaving around 4.50 as we're booked at Lafayette at 5, so if you're delayed, meet us there. We're in the private cellar. See you later.

As I'm finishing my makeup in the restroom, Hans's assistant, Angela, bursts in. She's sporting a tight green dress with a plunging neckline, her hair bouffant. "Rob just showed up. He's having a drink with Mike."

"Thanks." I apply lip gloss and spritz the mini bottle of perfume I found in an evening purse. It's a good scent for me. "How do I look?" I'm in a silver chiffon cocktail dress that I found in the dressing room, and I've gone all-out with smoky makeup, my long, blonde hair piled up at the back.

"Great. As usual. How 'bout me?" She puffs her hair and pouts into the mirror.

"Sensational." She does. She's really pretty. "Okay, we're ready."

Rob is in Mike's office, sitting back on the leather chair by the bookcase and laughing, swirling whiskey around in a large glass. The door is open, so I step inside, feeling unanticipated nerves. Rob turns and gives his easy smile, his eyes meeting mine full-on.

"Wow. My stunning wife."

"You don't scrub up too badly, either." I find myself blushing at my teenage-level flirtation, but he's nothing short of dashing in what's obviously a designer dark gray suit and a white shirt that's open at the throat.

"C'mon, you two. Drink up, Rob." Mike hustles us out of his office.

We weave through throngs of holiday tourists and revelers along the couple of blocks to the restaurant, Rob noticeably turning the heads of several women along the way. He doesn't see it though, focused as he is on supporting me in my heels. We arrive at Lafayette and descend into a spacious wine cellar. Two lavish tables are laid beautifully, seating at least fifty, with a separate bar and lounge area. "This is a big space," I comment to Rob. "I think there's only twenty coming from our office."

"The B+B folk are coming too. Combined party, remember? It made sense, since we do so much work together. There are twenty of you, nearly forty of us. I think it was your idea, originally."

"Right. No wonder Angela is so giddy. I can't imagine she'd be this excited about the H&F agents."

Rob laughs. "My team will be here soon to make it worth her while. Drink?" He puts his hand on my back and guides me toward the bar as more people pile into the room.

Most of the H&F agents are pretty full of themselves, but conversation with Rob, Mike, and Hans proves as fun and sparkling as it was at our apartment. Hans has shown up in a tropical-print shirt, declaring, "Screw Christmas."

At dinner I sit next to Rob, with Angela opposite and Josh, the office's young receptionist, on my other side. Angela doesn't seem interested in engaging, talking intently to a slick-haired guy beside her but occasionally casting strange, narrow-eyed glances my way. Ignoring her, I devour the delicious steak-frites and enjoy chatting with Josh, who is outspoken and hilarious.

Hans stands up, dinging his fork against his glass, and the room falls silent.

"As you all know, I'm the shy and retiring type. I hate the limelight—" cue snorts of derision and loud heckles "—so I'll keep this short. Thank you so much to my team at Halstein & Faust, and to our friends at B+B. Great job on a wonderful year of success. Even though the last unit of Cavendish House is now sold, as of last week, we have the new Tribeca building to work on, so long may this relationship continue.

"Speaking of relationships, on a personal note — Josie, welcome back to our family — we're so glad to have you with us, my dear. Thanks to everyone, and happy holidays to you all. *Cheers*! *Prost*!"

"Prost! Cheers," come the calls from around the table. Then, "Rob! Speech!"

Rob raises his hands in protest. "No, no, I don't . . ." He relents as the chants become louder.

"Fine, to shut you all up. I don't have a speech prepared — it was always the deal that Hans, the very *un*-shy and retiring one, would do this. But I suppose my folks at B+B deserve their own message, so . . . thanks, guys.

"It's been a great year for us at B+B, very much helped out by our friends at H&F. I'd like to thank everyone for that. And of course I would like to echo Hans's words about Josie, my lovely wife, and the inspiration for Cavendish House." Rob's voice softens. "As you've all heard, Josie is suffering from amnesia, so this has been a challenging time in many ways. But I'm thankful she's still here with me, and I know you guys at H&F will take care of her. So thank you for that, too."

He raises his glass, his eyes on mine. Everyone raises their own glass in response. I blush at the attention, but Rob's adoration feels wonderful. Confusingly so.

"To our continued health, happiness and success, this holiday season and in 2018. Merry Christmas."

As the others echo the toast, Rob leans down and kisses the top of my head. I put my hand on top of his, where it rests on my shoulder, the champagne forgotten.

"Everybody up." Hans is waving his hands in the air. "Let's move these tables because, by God, there shall be dancing!"

Much champagne later, the evening is getting fuzzier, and I find myself on a slippery stool at the bar with Josh, who is complaining about his absent boyfriend.

"Screw him. I gotta pee," he declares, abandoning me. Our colleagues are dancing to pumping music, but I can't see Rob. I'm about to go find him when a guy in a pinstripe suit and slicked-back hair — Angela's dinner companion — squeezes in next to me.

"Josie, right? We met last year . . . you won't remember. Kyle," he says in my ear. "Drink?"

"Thanks," I gesture at my full glass. "I'm good."

"I'm business development at B+B. Veep. Awesome company. Eighteen months now, love it. But I've been buddies with Angela on your team for years. We go way back."

"That's great."

"Josie, I'm, like, super-curious. You've got full-blown amnesia, right? Angie was telling me. Can't remember a thing?" He's slurring his words, his gaze half-focused.

"Well, nothing since around three years ago. My long-term memory is fine. But I've only been at H&F two-and-a-half years, so nothing about my job. I restarted yesterday from scratch."

"That's wild. What about Rob? How long have you guys been together?"

"About three years. Married for two." I look past Kyle, scanning the room. Where did Rob and Mike get to?

"You can't remember your relationship at all? You woke up not recognizing your husband? That's what Angie said."

"Right." I sip my wine. This guy is making me uncomfortable.

"I figure, it must feel like you're single, right? Like, you don't know Rob or remember marrying him?" He leans in closer, the whiskey heavy on his breath, and, to my shock, slips his arm round my waist. "If you don't want to be married to a guy you don't even remember . . . You've got options, is all I'm saying."

He lurches, tugging my body toward his. I slide off the slippery stool, wine spilling on Kyle's expensive suit.

Furious, I stand upright and look him square in his unfocused eyes. "Don't you worry about me. Being married to a man I don't know is a hell of a lot less painful than listening to your greasy bullshit." I take a defiant swig of wine, hesitate for a moment, and then throw the rest in his face. "Asshole."

As I turn, I spot Rob, Angela and Mike standing at a distance, watching the exchange. Angela has her hand up to Rob's ear, telling him something. Rob's brow is furrowed as he tracks my approach. I smooth down my dress and weave past sweaty, dancing colleagues toward them.

"I'm all out of drink, apparently," I tell Mike, feeling exhilarated. "But it's time I was cut off anyway." The song "Fairytale of New York" begins, one of my favorites. I turn to Rob. "Dance?"

"Hell, yes," he says with a short laugh. He turns to Angela. "Excuse me." His voice has an uncharacteristic frosty tone, and her jaw slackens.

Rob pulls me to the center of the room. As our colleagues cavort around us, he twirls me around the dance floor, an easy mover, pulling me in close in the quieter spots, pushing me away as the music livens up. It almost feels like we've danced together before, many times. Some kind of muscle memory, perhaps. Either way, there's no denying that in this moment, I feel something close to joy.

Much later, back at the apartment, we're still laughing about the sleazeball who got a faceful of Sauvignon Blanc.

"He'll probably send me his dry-cleaning bill, he was that kind of asshole," I say.

"Man, if anyone deserved it." Rob chuckles. "I'm sorry about him. I knew he was a douche — just didn't realize how much. If he has any pride, I'll have his resignation on Monday."

"Don't fire him. Not on my account."

"I'll see how he handles it." I note Rob makes no promises.

"You know he's a friend of Angela's? I got the impression she encouraged him to approach me, which is weird."

Rob nods. "She was strange with me, too. When Kyle was hitting on you. She made sure I saw it. Like she was trying to get you into trouble. But she's always been jealous of you, ever since you got the comms job. She applied for it at the time. And she's been covering it while you've been away."

"I did wonder about that." I remember the way she looked at me earlier in the evening.

"I don't want to waste another moment thinking about Ange or Kyle. Want another drink?"

I hesitate. It's so tempting. But I'm aware I smell of white wine and sweat, and am already a little too tipsy. Plus, there's work tomorrow. Most of all, I don't want to lose control around Rob. It's been such a great evening. I could almost imagine this life were mine.

"Thanks. But I'd better go to bed. I do have to work tomorrow."

"Of course. Well, good night, Bruiser."

I grin. "Night. And thanks, I had a great time. Sleazeballs notwithstanding."

"Me too. Sleep well."

Rob leans forward to kiss my cheek, his lips grazing my skin. It tingles.

CHAPTER 7

Christmas and New Year

Rob's parents show up Christmas Eve, all smiles and warm hugs. Andrew is a tall, gray-haired man with rimless glasses over piercing blue eyes. He has a definite Seattle architect vibe. Kind of an older Steve Jobs, with a quick wit and very little filter.

"Rob, my boy!" Andrew presents a half-case of wine, pretending to stagger under its weight. "Help your old man out, would you?"

Rob's mom, Kim, is the one who interests me most, though. A short Indigenous woman in her early seventies, her long hair is mainly jet-black but streaked with silver. Her face is pretty and inviting. She speaks in low tones that force me to listen and, unlike her husband's, her words are carefully chosen. Kim reacts to all of her husband's unfiltered comments with a small, wry smile, waiting to ensure he's done goofing around before she quietly takes charge. I envy her serenity and patience.

"They're a sweet couple," I tell Rob while they unpack in the green room.

"They've never fought much, that I remember. I'm sure Dad irritates Mom, but she's so Zen, she lets it wash over her."

Seems like her son takes after her — Rob's been pretty calm about all my craziness.

"That's good. Different, but complementary. Your mother met your Dad when he was working with the Lummi Nation on a resort development, right?"

"Yeah. It took a while for them to marry, though. My grandmother relied on Mum a lot, so she remained on the reservation even after marrying Dad in her early thirties." Rob smiles into the distance, a look of nostalgia passing across his face. "We still have my paternal grandparents' old house in La Conner, north of Seattle. That's where she would stay with my Dad a few days a week. But she kept living with my grandmother until she got pregnant with me, and Mum and Dad decided to move to Seattle as Dad's business was taking off."

It's fascinating to watch Rob with his folks and understand where his looks come from. His height and easy grace are his father's, but his light brown skin coloring, thick black hair, deep brown eyes and wide, open facial features are all his mother. He's a perfect mix. And it's hard to stop staring.

"So, Josie," Andrew says, as we enjoy our Christmas Eve dinner. "I heard some douchebag hit on our girl at the office party?" His eyes are glinting with laughter. Rob must have told him.

"Yeah." I glance over at Rob, whose smiling face is lit beautifully in the candlelight. "A total sleaze. Said if I couldn't remember being married, he wanted me to know I 'had options' if I felt single."

"Unbelievable." Andrew shakes his head. "Even if that were in any way valid, which of course it isn't, who hits on his boss's wife? What a dick—".

"What did you say, Josie?" Kim asks, shooting Andrew an admonishing look.

"Well, I seem to remember it involved me calling him greasy and throwing the rest of my wine in his face. Then going over to Rob for a slow dance. We didn't see him after that, funnily enough."

Rob eyes crinkle in amusement. "He came into my office a few days later, tail between his legs. Said something like, 'I believe I owe you an apology, I had too much to drink at the party and I may have said something inappropriate to your wife. I will of course offer my resignation if you think it's necessary.' Something lame."

"What did you do?" Kim's expression is gentle as she looks at Rob.

"I'd've fired him," Andrew declares. "That kind of lapse in judgment tells me he's not right for the company. What a fu—" He breaks off as Kim gives him another look, flopping back in his chair with an audible huff.

Rob shrugs. "We had a formal meeting with HR, who gave him a warning, but then we let it go. Josie didn't want him fired on her account. He's got a lot to prove, though."

"I think a lapse in judgment can be a wake-up call," I add. "Maybe he'll think twice about getting wasted at work events."

"Your girl has a good head on her shoulders, Robbie." Kim smiles at me.

The accolade is wonderful to hear, although it also makes me uncomfortable. They wouldn't like me if they knew. I'm not Rob's real wife. I'm an impostor.

Christmas Day dawns with a mild hangover, cured by coffee and Rob's production of a full English breakfast — "a treat for my English wife." Then the gift-giving begins. Fortunately, any Christmas gifts from me had been ordered or bought before my accident. Other Me had helpfully written a gift list on her phone, and various packages arrived over the past few weeks. All I had to do was wrap them. It felt particularly duplicitous, wrapping gifts chosen by someone else. But what else could I do?

Kim is the first to open the small, soft parcel from me. A gorgeous silk scarf in blue and gray tones, bought from an expensive boutique. She seems to love it. I could've picked that out for her myself.

Andrew's gift from me is a hardback copy of Douglas Coupland's *City of Glass*, about Vancouver, signed by the author. He's impressed and curious about how I got the autograph, but I have no clue and Rob is also unable to answer.

Rob's parents' gift to me, presented in a huge box, is a silvery-brown faux-fur throw with matching pillow from an exclusive home store. It must've cost hundreds, I think with a pang of guilt. "It's a gift for Rob too, so we didn't hold back," Kim comments, reading my expression.

"I love it. Thank you."

"My turn to open something." Rob grabs the large cube I wrapped for him in silver paper. I'm not sure how it will be received, considering the circumstances. I'd have never given this to him myself, but of course it's from Other Josie, really.

He pulls open the bow and tears off the paper, finding a box with a lid. He lifts it to find another box inside, and then three incrementally smaller boxes, with the last a six-inch cube. Inside, among silver tissue paper, Rob finds the gift — a red envelope containing a voucher for a two-night stay and dinner for two at the Blue Harbor Inn on Orcas Island in Washington State.

He looks up at me from his position cross-legged on the floor, his eyes moistening. "Wow. Thank you so much, baby. That's going to be amazing." He turns to his mother. "Look, a weekend on Orcas Island. Isn't that awesome? We've always wanted to stay at Blue Harbor Inn, the food is pretty famous, but we've never gotten around to it. We could stay a night in La Conner, too."

"That's wonderful." Kim turns to me. "You'll love it. Andrew and I have stayed and eaten at the inn a number of times. It's fabulous. You must visit us in Seattle while you're in the area."

"When will you come?" asks Andrew.

"I don't know. Maybe sometime in the spring?" Rob's face is lit up. He's so happy.

"Sure, around then would be ideal." I wonder if I'll still be here. But I'm excited by the prospect of the Blue Harbor Inn, as I've heard of it myself. "Actually, I learned about the inn well before I met Rob," I tell Kim. "I remember reading about it in *The New York Times* many years ago — top restaurants worth getting on a plane for, or something. It sounded so wonderful. I've always imagined the Pacific Northwest as a wild, romantic place."

"Thank you, my darling." Rob kneels down. He wraps his arms around me and pulls me in, kissing my temple, pressing his mouth against my skin for a moment, his beard tickling my cheek. I blush, a teenager again.

"You're welcome." But when he pulls away, I give him a sheepish half-smile, as if to say, we both know that gift wasn't really from me.

"Now for you." He picks up a flat red box, trimmed with a huge white bow, and places it on my lap.

"Very festive."

Pulling apart the bow, the lid falls off. And inside, folded in black tissue paper, I glimpse rich, deep red silk. A dress? Yes. I pick up two ribbon-width straps and pull the dress up high, letting the box fall. It's long, slinky and divine. Thank God I've now got the body for it — I'd have never been able to get away with this a month ago. The straps divide at the back, both continuing down to the deep V and crossing each other. The front neckline is a simple V, edged with the ribbon of the straps. Simple, yet extravagant. Gorgeous.

I can't help but laugh. "This is incredible." I lean toward Rob, sitting on the floor against the arm of the couch, and kiss the side of his head.

"I hope it fits." He's watching me indulgently.

"It should. I'll try it in a bit. Really, thank you so much."

"Hey, it's as much a gift for me as for you, right?"

"You'll be lovely in it." Kim smiles.

"You could wear it for Hans and Mike's New Year's Eve party," adds Rob.

"I might save it for the Valentine's *Luxury Listing* party. It'd be so perfect for that. I've already got my eye on another dress for New Year's Eve."

* * *

When New Year's Eve comes, I set aside the red dress, even though it does indeed fit my new body perfectly, and pick out a knee-length cocktail dress with a black lace overlay and long chiffon sleeves instead. I pair it with an extra-long silver necklace and a pair of strappy sandals. I've blown out my thick hair to up the glamor. Now, I'm ready to hit an exclusive Manhattan New Year's Eve party.

Rob and his parents are waiting for me in the living room. Rob is very handsome in yet another of his fine gray suits with a slate-blue shirt beneath. "You look amazing." He pulls me close to kiss my forehead. It's probably not something he would have done if his parents hadn't been here. He clearly needs them to see we're a happy couple, even if I do have amnesia and am sleeping in the guest room.

The party's at Hans and Mike's place in Chelsea. I'm not sure what to expect — a super high-end condo with fine finishings, maybe. Hans opens the door to usher us inside, and I gasp. It's a super cool, quintessential New York loft, with a vast footprint, soaring ceilings, and exposed brick, pipes and ductwork. There are rows of massive windows and distressed, painted plasterwork. A few glass-brick room dividers and clusters of furniture create room-type spaces. A pair of leather sofas here, a contemporary dining table and chrome chairs there, a big desk in the corner. There's a DJ on decks at the far end of the room.

Hans catches me examining the huge windows. "You don't remember being here, my dear?" I shake my head. "Last time, you were surprised we didn't have an elaborate apartment with opulent trimmings and marble everywhere. Like yours, only with more gold."

I laugh. "You've got me."

"Well, it would have been," Hans whispers conspiratorially, "but Mike was the driving force in these design choices. Between you and me, he's just not as gay as I am." He nudges me with a wink, and I laugh again.

"Such interesting couples we have in our lives," I observe later to Rob as we pile our plates with food from the buffet. "So complementary. Your parents, Hans and Mike. Suzie and Donald, of course. I must go over to Brooklyn and see the twins."

I have a moment's panic. Do the twins even exist here? If they do, should I not remember them? They're only two years old.

Rob interrupts my thoughts. "What did you tell Suzie, about how you're feeling?"

"Same thing I've been telling everyone — amnesia mixed with confusion, not believing I'm married to you, believing David's alive."

"Sure. And yeah, you should visit the twins. They're adorable."

I relax at the news. "I will."

A couple of hours later, the loft is packed with scantily clad partygoers, pop music pumping. I steal a moment alone, helping myself to a gin and tonic in Hans and Mike's divided-off kitchen. Andrew appears.

"There's our girl." He leans up against the concrete counter. "How is the evening going? I've been meeting some . . ." he peers around in a comic fashion, "pretty fascinating types. They all seem to love Kim. She's having a ball."

I grin. "I'm good. Taking a quiet moment, before midnight hits."

"Ah, New Year. Time to take stock. Lemme ask you something." Andrew hesitates. "Kim would kill me for asking but, with you still sleeping in the art room . . . Obviously you feel like you only met Rob recently, so it's gotta be weird. But how's it going? Since your memories haven't returned, is the relationship developing anyways? From where I'm standing, it seems like it is, but that you're holding back . . . It's none of my business, of course."

I sip my drink, unsure of what to say. "It is weird for me. Rob is a wonderful man; he's been taking care of me. Not pushing at all. I know when we met, everyone says we fell hard for each other, very quickly. But it's not the same this time. There's so much more at stake. We're already married and living together, so there's much more to lose by rushing things. I have to be sure. Not only of loving him, but also of wanting to spend the rest of my life with him, as his wife. Because that's what it would mean."

I've never put this into words before or even admitted it to myself. But it feels good to say it. I turn back to Andrew.

"It's not that I'm *not* falling for him. I'm still me, so of course I'm bound to. But I have to be sure of never wanting to go back."

"Of course." Andrew pulls me into a hug. It's comforting. "You'll get there."

I squeeze him back. "Don't tell him, okay? This is between us."

"You got it, kiddo. Come on. It's nearly midnight."

In the living area, the party is in full swing with Hans now sporting a flapper dress, singing "Young Hearts Run Free," complete with a dance routine.

"That guy can sing. I should recruit him for the choir," I half-shout in Rob's ear when I find him.

"Yeah, he'd bring quite the flavor to your shows," Rob agrees. "Where've you been?"

"A paternal talk with your dad in the kitchen," I reply, with an air of mystery.

"Ah, the Papa pep talk." He smiles. "I can't hear a thing. Come here."

We weave through dancing guests to the far end of the loft, away from the DJ. It's a little quieter here, and a few people are lounging about on the sofas. Out of the tall window, I can just make out Chelsea's patchwork of rooftops in the dark night. I turn to Rob.

"I need you to know—"

"Raise your glasses, the balls are dropping!" Hans's voice bellows through the speaker system, interrupting the moment. "We are go in . . . TEN, NINE, EIGHT, SEVEN, SIX, FIVE, FOUR, THREE, TWO, ONE . . . Happy New Year!!"

"Happy New Year!"

Dozens of silver 2018 balloons are released from a net across the high ceiling. Everyone's laughing, cheering, hugging, kissing, as the music starts up again.

I turn back to Rob and shrug, raising my glass to him with a shy smile. "Happy New Year."

Slowly, he takes my glass and sets it down on the window ledge. He takes my face in both of his hands and puts his mouth against mine. But gently — he's waiting for me to kiss him back. I ache to do so, to push through that soft beard and press hard against his lips. But an image forces its way into my mind, pushing everything else out.

Other Me at midnight on New Year's Eve, out at a bar, or maybe drinking Prosecco on Suzie and Donald's. She's thinking about me, in this moment, being with her husband. Wondering where we are, and whether I'm kissing him, right now. And this woman is me. I can't betray her. I can't betray myself.

So instead of kissing Rob, I pull back, although every fiber in my being screams against it. I look at him helplessly.

He pushes his lips together, looking as crushed as I feel.

"Happy New Year."

He walks away.

CHAPTER 8

Mid-January

Disproportionately nervous, I step into the choir practice room and shrug off my coat. It's sweltering, the creaking radiators overcompensating for the icy January night outside. Lisa is helping a couple of the tenors unload stacked chairs.

"Josie!" She drops the chair she's holding with a clatter and rushes over to give me a hug. "How are you? We haven't seen you in forever! So happy you've come back."

"Thanks," I reply, a bit thrown. I saw her last at rehearsal at the end of November. But for her, I haven't been a choir member for more than two years. It's going to be so weird, pretending I don't remember people, or the music. "With my . . . amnesia, it doesn't feel as long for me."

"That makes sense. If you've lost three years, then the last time you remember, you were in the choir. So it must feel like you still are." She laughs, pushing back her hair. "That's crazy. Too bad you only know old repertoire."

"I'll catch up. I learned the newer songs during the holidays, after I decided to rejoin. I'll be fine."

A group of men enter the room and my heart pounds. The reason for my nervousness, all six foot two of him, is walking toward the coat rack, laughing with Ryan. Peter takes off his dark coat, removes his woolen beanie hat and runs his fingers through his sandy hair, glancing toward me. He pushes his glasses up the bridge of his nose and gives a polite half-smile before turning back to Ryan. Of course, he doesn't recognize me. But it still hurts.

Lisa follows my gaze. "That's Peter. Cute, right? He's been in the group a couple of years now, joined just after you left. I introduced you and Rob to him and his girlfriend, Michelle, when you came to last year's show, but you won't remember."

"No." This is so weird.

"He's fun — you'll like him. Always cracking jokes and getting into trouble with Kathryn."

The director herself walks into the room and stands at the front, clapping for attention. "Happy New Year, everyone," Kathryn greets. "Welcome back." She claps her hands. "Right, catch-up is over, let's get settled. There's a lot to do and a few announcements before we start. First, we have a returning member, so let's welcome back Josie Cavendish, who left us, what is it, two-and-a-half years ago?"

I nod as the gathering group offers generous applause, with a couple of whoops from Lisa and Ryan.

"For those of you not in the loop," Kathryn continues briskly, "Josie has suffered amnesia and has lost the past three years of her life. Even if you have met Josie before, she might not remember you. Don't be offended. Reintroduce yourselves in the break."

The director glances at her notes. "Next up, we still need a soprano for the 'Can't Sleep Love' duet in this year's summer show, along with our charming Peter here. It's a tricky part, but I'm sure one of you could take it on." She looks right at me. "Josie? I realize you're newly back with us, but this would work well with your voice, if you're willing to try? It would require some extra rehearsals."

My eyes widen in surprise. She's talking about the same duet I've spent weeks rehearsing with Peter, in my real life,

84

before my accident. I know the song inside out. I've sung it with Peter many times. It's a much easier task than she thinks.

All eyes are on me. "I could give it a go."

Aside from already knowing the song, all I can think is that it's time with Peter, to resolve the issue of whether there's anything between us in this world. I turn to him, my eyebrows raised in a question — okay by you? He gives me a quizzical half-smile, and I realize my look might seem overfamiliar. I turn away, embarrassed.

"Atta girl. Speaking of Peter, one final announcement. Very happy news. Peter and Michelle are expecting a baby! Isn't that wonderful? Congratulations to you both, Peter."

What?

The other members turn to congratulate him, asking him how many weeks along they are, whether it's a boy or girl, and whether they'll continue living in their Greenpoint apartment.

I open my water bottle, attempting nonchalance. But my mind is racing.

A baby? How can they be having a baby?

Six weeks ago, this guy was about to become my boyfriend. He didn't even have a good relationship with Michelle. They were breaking up!

But that was when I was in his life. Maybe I was the reason for the deterioration of his relationship. In a world without me around, maybe Peter and Michelle overcame their challenges and got stronger.

I can barely concentrate on the music, and just go through the motions. At the break, friends I've known for a couple of years introduce themselves, assuming I don't remember them, even though I do, and I stammer my way through awkward conversations. By the time we pour into the nearby bar for drinks afterward, I'm hopelessly confused. And I still haven't spoken to Peter.

"This amnesia is hitting you hard, huh?" Lisa's studying me curiously. "You seem discombobulated."

"That's the perfect word for it," I agree. "I'm all over the place. It's crazy what a head injury can do."

"I hope you're not riding that bike home, especially with the roads this icy."

"No. Electra got mangled. Rob bought me a new red bike last week, a surprise extra gift, but it's been too dangerous to ride."

"You should hop in with Peter, he always drives. He and Michelle live in Greenpoint, and I think he's been taking the Midtown tunnel, so Union Square isn't far out of the way." Before I can say anything, she calls out, "Hey, Peter!"

He picks up his beer and saunters over. "Hey," continues Lisa, "remember meeting Josie and her husband at our show last year?"

Peter sits down on a stool opposite us. "Sure." He gives me a smile, "I remember you both. You won't remember me, of course. Peter Klavins, bass extraordinaire."

"Nice to meet you." I'm having trouble looking at him. I feel such a fraud. "To meet you again, that is."

"And you. Thanks for saying you'll try the duet with me. I've been wanting to do it, but Kathryn hasn't found the right soprano to blend with my voice. You're my only hope, Obi Wan." He's so easy with me. "I'll email you the sheet music and part recording, and we can take some extra time before or after rehearsals. What's your email address?"

As I'm writing it down, Lisa jumps in. "Hey, you go back to Greenpoint via the tunnel, right? Could you swing by Union Square and drop Josie home? It's only a few blocks along 15th. She's not riding her bike since her crash, and we need to take care of her."

Peter seems caught off guard but quickly recovers. "Of course. Sure. But I need to leave soon. I have to get back to Michelle. She's been having morning, noon and night sickness. That work for you?"

"Fine." My nervousness is returning. I take a swig of my wine but leave the rest. Peter finishes his beer.

Lisa nods at us, obviously relieved that someone is taking responsibility for me. "You get your ride, Josie, the wine's on me. Get me back next week."

"Thanks," I tell her, pulling on my coat. "You can hold me to it."

Outside, I recognize Peter's restored Chevy instantly, but at the last moment remember to act like I don't know which vehicle is his. Inside the car, it smells the same. My memories of our extra rehearsals and flirtatious rides to Brooklyn come flooding back.

I've had such a crush on him, for such a long time. But do I really feel the same now? Now that Rob's in my life?

As he pulls off, I inhale deeply. "Congratulations. A baby. That's amazing."

"Thanks. We're very happy. Michelle and I have had our ups and downs, but we decided a few months back we would make a go of it. And now we're pregnant. Seems meant to be."

I can hear the warmth in his voice, and an unexpected feeling comes over me. I'm actually happy for him. I care enough about this man to want the best for him, even if that means he's having a baby with another woman.

With little traffic on the roads, he is soon pulling up to Cavendish House.

"He named this place for you? That's so . . . baller."

"Isn't it? A wedding gift to me, one of many, apparently . . . I don't remember meeting him, or our marriage. It's all in the time I've lost."

Peter smiles. "Then there's good news. You get to fall in love all over again. And that's the best feeling in the world. He must be crazy about you, if he's naming buildings. He's a cool guy, right?"

"He's wonderful." And I mean that. Rob is great. "Well, thanks for the ride, Peter. I hope Michelle feels better."

"You're welcome, Josie. See you next week." I give him a little wave as he drives off.

Riding up to the eighteenth floor, I am strangely at peace. I let myself into the apartment and drop my keys on the foyer table. I can hear Rob moving about.

"Hey," I say, as I walk into the kitchen. He smiles at me and, for a moment, it's almost like he's going to kiss me on the cheek. But he doesn't.

"Hey yourself," he replies easily instead. "You realize this is the first evening we've spent apart since your accident? I missed you."

CHAPTER 9

Valentine's Day

I zip up the red dress and turn sideways in front of the mirror in the art room. The stick-on bra I bought is working with the plunging back, but my underwear is giving me a visible line. It's no use. I'm going to have to go commando this time.

The caterers need supervising, and the band guys want to block my bedroom door. I pick up a pair of Louboutin's with a red undersole and open the door with care.

"You done in there, ma'am?" asks the guitarist.

"Knock yourselves out," I tell him with a smile, stepping over a cluster of black cables. I scan the living area. It's been taking shape over the past couple of days, but now that the finishing touches have been put to the Valentine-themed decorations, it looks spectacular.

Instead of the usual lofty space, an installation of thousands of fine gunmetal chains in undulating lengths, hanging from a grid of wires across the ceiling, has transformed it into a much darker, more intimate room. I spot-check the hundreds of small, fat hearts hanging from the lowest of the chains — chocolates for the guests to pick off — all with #LoveLuxuryListing on the red foil. The dining table is covered with lavish food in pink, red and white. I straighten the plates bearing four whole baked salmons and glance over the ring of huge prawns with a pink dressing, a large chicken-cranberry dish, white bread rolls, tomato and bocconcini salad, the tiered tower of pink and white sushi, and trays of white- or dark-chocolate-dipped strawberries. Several silver buckets on the sideboard hold pink champagne on ice.

"Everything is wonderful, Erika," I tell the catering manager. "Thank you."

Rob emerges in a navy suit with a pale gray shirt and a dark red tie, loosely tied with his top button undone. He lopes down the steps and stops when he sees me. He shakes his head and laughs.

"What?" I say, self-conscious, smoothing down my dress. "I know it's long, I haven't put my heels on yet."

"No, it's ridiculous how perfect you look," he says, the easy smile on his face. "That dress is insane. I'm not going to be able to stop staring at you."

"Oh," I say, flustered. "I do feel like a million bucks, I've got to admit." I move toward him, shoes in my hand. He seems very tall when I'm in my bare feet. I reach up and adjust his tie. "We coordinate tonight. You look very handsome."

"Thanks, shortie." That smile again. He surveys the room, nodding approval. "This is quite something. When does the TV crew arrive?"

"Not for two hours. The guests will be here when they come. I've given them a one-hour window as they'll be in the way. They'll get some party footage, couple of moments filming some of their agents, and Hans's big speech at nine. Then I want them gone for the rest of the night, so we can relax."

Rob smiles at my excitement. "Can I do anything? Put something on ice?"

"No, we're good. Let me lean against you. I can't have guests arriving when I haven't got shoes on."

An hour later, most people have arrived. The band is playing in the corner and the guests are laughing, chatting and devouring the buffet. As well as almost everyone from work and Rob's office, I've invited the choir, most of whom have shown up, keen to see inside Cavendish House. Peter has sent his regrets, with Michelle still unwell. Frankly, it's a relief. He and I have had some extra rehearsals to practice our duet, and it's been fine, but I could use not having him and Rob in the same room.

Suzie arrives, glamorous in a sky-blue jumpsuit, red lips and sky-high heels. "Wow," she exclaims, turning me around by the shoulders. "The famous dress. It lives up to the headlines."

"Thanks. You look fabulous. Come sit with me. I can't stand all night in these heels and the TV crew will be here soon."

The *Luxury Listing* producer — a hot, short-haired Portuguese woman — turns out to be a dream to work with. Suzie admires her lasciviously, despite her own happy, heterosexual marriage. There's a moment of staged rivalry between two TV agents, facing off over the kitchen island. "Eric, that listing was mine and you know it!" "All's fair in love and real estate, hotshot." Hans intervenes dramatically, but it's all for show. After Hans's grandiose thank-you speech about the penthouse sale and toast to the successful season, the TV crew and rival agents make a dignified exit.

I blow out a breath as Rob comes up to me, a fresh glass of pink champagne in each hand. "Better?" he asks, handing one over.

"I can relax now," I reply. "Anything bad happens, at least it won't be broadcast to millions."

Mike and Hans, both dashing in their different ways, join us. "Some of the guests want to tour the penthouse upstairs," says Mike, "while it's still unoccupied. What do you think?"

Rob swallows some champagne. "I guess — a small group. No drinks up there. The buyer is getting all the furniture, so we don't want any damage. You have the keys."

As Mike moves off, I tell Rob, "I'd love to go up, I've been dying to see it."

Hans turns to me in surprise. "You've never been in the penthouse?"

"Not that I remember," I say, looking at Rob for an answer. "Not since my accident."

Rob raises an eyebrow, strangely sheepish. "I've shown it to you before. But yeah, not for a while." He glances down with a wry smile.

"Well, I'd love to see it now," I reply.

"Those of you who want a penthouse tour, put your glasses down and follow me," calls Mike from the foyer. He leads well-dressed guests to the elevator, with me and Rob following.

"What was that about?" I ask Rob, as we wait in the corridor. "About being in the penthouse before?"

Very deliberately, Rob lets his eyes wander around my lips and down to my décolletage. He slips his arm around my waist, puts his hand on my bare back and leans in close. His beard tickles my cheek. "We've been up there many times, often very late, usually with all the lights out. We've . . ." he hesitates, leaning in even closer so his voice resonates deep inside me, "*fucked* in every room, on every surface, in every imaginable position, on every stick of that staging furniture." He lets his hand trail down and runs his thumb across my butt, making sure I know that he knows I'm wearing no panties.

It's possibly the single hottest moment of my life.

The elevator dings and we squeeze in, Rob's arm still around me. On the 20th floor, he strides ahead and takes charge.

I'm so blown away by what Rob said, and did, that I can barely take in the penthouse's 360-degree Manhattan views and lavish finishings. I want to sit, but I'm worried about what kind of moisture mark sitting would make on the back of my dress. I look around, and instead of marble and Italian tile, all I see are surfaces on which we've apparently had lots of hot sex.

Hans catches up with me and takes my arm. "Someone's getting lucky tonight," he says with a wink. "I feel like I witnessed something I shouldn't have."

"You saw that?" I blurt, embarrassed. "That should've been private. Sorry."

"Don't be. I love a nice big thumb on the ass. Or, better yet . . ." He giggles.

I punch him on the arm. "Hans!"

"Sorry not sorry. He's so damn hot, your husband. Please tell me you've resumed marital relations. Because if you don't, I'll bone that hunk of man meat myself. Mike will totally understand."

I laugh, shaking my head. "Oh my god. First, hands off. And, second, no we haven't. I haven't been ready. I feel like I've only met him recently. I've got to get it right."

"Sure, girl, but remember that amnesia movie, *The Vow*? We're all screaming, Rachel McAdams, if you wake up and Channing Tatum is your husband, you *do not argue*."

"Okay! I hear you."

I make my way back down to the party, seeking another drink. Josh comes over to chat with me as the guests start to thin out. As the band moves into their final number, a ballad, I feel a tap on my shoulder.

"You've been hostess all evening, and we haven't even danced," says Rob as I turn around. Josh takes my glass and nudges me toward him. "Off you go," he says with a meaningful nod.

Rob leads me into the center of the room, where a few die-hard couples are dancing, Mike and Hans among them. Suzie is on the couch, deep in slightly drunken conversation with Lisa. Rob slips an arm around my waist and pulls me into him, his left hand holding mine to his chest. I give myself over to the moment, resting my head on his shoulder, listening to his breath and the singer's voice. "*Lover man, oh where can you be?*"

I'll find you, Rob. If I do have to leave you, if I am ever able to get back to my world and to David, I will come and find you.

I jerk my head up. Of course. Why didn't I realize before?

If Other Me is in my old life, she'll have gone to find Rob, immediately. Maybe they're together there. Maybe she's happy. Maybe she doesn't want to come back to this life.

"What?" asks Rob quietly, lifting my chin with his finger.

"Nothing," I tell him. "I'm fine." I lean my head back against his shoulder and pull him a little closer. He responds by leaning his cheek on the top of my head and twisting a piece of my hair around his finger.

The song ends and the moment is gone as the guests applaud, and the singer acknowledges the band.

"Thanks, Josie, Rob, it's been wonderful," slurs Suzie. "You guys are great. So grrreat together. Gotta scoot, my car is here. Thanks for an amaaazing party."

"Thanks, honey. Safe journey."

After the place has emptied out, I'm still energized. I grab my coat and step onto the cold terrace for some air. The space is lit with hundreds of string lights, more chocolate hearts hanging from them.

I'm gazing out across the city when the terrace door opens behind me. "We have a leftover candy problem," Rob says.

I turn and smile. "We'll have to take them into work. If we get through all those, we'll be too fat to ever leave this apartment."

"Doesn't sound terrible," he says, joining me at the barrier. "We could live off takeout and watch movies, like we did in Snowmaggedon." He's referring to the huge snowstorm at the end of January that had us holed up for several days.

"That was fun," I admit, smiling at the recollection. "Successful party, don't you think?"

"A triumph. You were a goddess. What's the time?"

"After midnight," I reply.

"What a wonderful Valentine's Day," he says, turning to face me. "You made the most perfect Valentine tonight."

He reaches out and strokes the side of my face with the back of his fingers. Slowly, deliberately, he moves his hand round the back of my head, entwining his fingers in my hair. I tilt my head as shivers run over my body. "Thank you," I whisper.

This time, when Rob touches his lips to mine, my lips search for his mouth, my tongue for his tongue, as his hand holds my hair and I cling to him. He pushes me against the pillar, kissing me searchingly, desperately, lovingly, moving to kiss my eyes, leaning to kiss my hairline, my neck. There's nothing to do but give in.

But then the image is back, refusing to set me free. Her. Other Me, imagining me, with him, on Valentine's Day. Hating me for being with her husband, where she should be. Or perhaps tearfully giving me her blessing, because I *am* her. Or both. Or neither. Who the hell knows?

"Baby, why are you crying?" Rob says, pulling away. I hadn't realized I was, and shake my head, unable to speak. He wipes tears from my face with his thumbs. "Oh, Josie. I get that you're still confused, but you can't be confused about us, can you? Doesn't it feel so right? Why won't you let go?"

He searches my face for answers. But I can't look at him. If I look at him, I'll kiss him again. And if I kiss him again, I'll go to bed with him. And if I go to bed with him, I'll be his wife, completely. And I'll give up everything for him. My old life, my brother — and, most of all, my own sense of self.

"I'm so sorry," I say, and pull myself free. I let myself into my bedroom at the end of the terrace, lock the door and close the blinds.

But there is no escape from this world and its impossible decisions.

CHAPTER 10

Easter

"You ready?" Rob picks up my case.

I glance around the floral-wallpapered room with its brass Victorian bed, antique wardrobe and old-fashioned dressing table. "This has been lovely. I'd love to come back for longer."

In the sloped ceiling, a dormer window offers a view of the historic Washington State town of La Conner and the river by which it stands. The heritage house we've been staying in is perched on a bluff above the town, currently packed with tourists here for the Easter weekend break. There's also the draw of the tulip festival. I close the window, hesitating for a moment to take in the sounds of the street.

"It's like summer out there." I turn back, smile at Rob. "This room is charming. Thank you for letting me stay in here, when it's always been your room."

On Thursday, we flew to Seattle to stay with Andrew and Kim at their huge, detached house in the Queen Anne neighborhood, and then Rob and I drove on to La Conner for the night to his family's weekend house here. We toured the lovely tulip farms. But now it's time to go to the Blue

Harbor Inn for the weekend, my Christmas gift to my husband. I can't wait.

We drive to the ferry dock at Anacortes, where we drive right onto the ferry. The blustery ride to Orcas Island weaves between several other pretty islands. Landing at Orcas, we drive around the stunning West Sound inlet, past the small town of Deer Harbor and out to the inn on the island's western coast. Once checked in, we have to drive a little farther to our off-site accommodations, about a half-mile along the waterfront.

"I upgraded us," Rob explains. "The rooms at the inn look great, but I figured we could use more space. We've got a one-bed-plus-loft cabin on the beach."

"Good thinking, Batman," I reply, with mixed feelings over expectations of the sleeping arrangements.

The large, rustic-chic cabin is glorious with its cathedral ceiling and huge ocean view windows. A perfect, peaceful retreat. We explore the comfortable living-dining area and kitchen, and I climb a spiral iron staircase to find a mezzanine loft bedroom with sloped ceilings. Below it, at the back of the cabin, is a bathroom and the primary bedroom.

Rob's watching me as I descend the tightly curved stairs. "You can have the big bedroom." He takes my small case into the room. "It's your turn. Plus neither of us wants you negotiating that loft staircase to visit the bathroom four times in the night. And we both know with a fancy dinner like tonight's, and the inevitable quantities of wine, that's going to happen."

"Fair point. What time's our reservation?"

"In an hour." He leaves me to unpack. "It's a set menu and everyone eats at 6.30. So meet you in the living room at ten past."

I take a shower and pick out a slate-blue Helmut Lang blouse and indigo jeans, deciding my gray-blue wedges work with the outfit. Whether they'll work for a stony walk along the beachfront is another matter, but it's either these or the sneakers that are way too dirty from yesterday's visit to the tulip fields.

Rob looks up idly when I finally emerge into the living room. "Nice."

He's very handsome in a black linen shirt and blue jeans, his thick black hair slightly damp from the shower. "All set?" I nod.

We walk the easy, paved road to the inn and settle into an ocean-view table in the busy restaurant for a dinner of hyper-locally sourced food, fished off the island's coast or grown on the inn's grounds. As Rob pours the wine, appetizers of pickled oysters and salt cod donuts arrive, which we devour quickly.

"To great food, great wine, great company." He raises his glass, looking directly into my eyes. "And thanks for this weekend."

"I didn't do much, but you're welcome. I'm glad we're here." I take a generous sip of the very mellow wine and gaze out at the sun lowering over the ocean. This place is so calming. Not like New York. Here, we're both so relaxed.

We enjoy the view of the ferries and far-off islands for a while, Rob pointing out what each island is called. He explains that we visited Orcas Island and the nearby Lummi reservation two years previously, and that I met his maternal grandmother, before she died last year. From his expression, she obviously meant a lot to him.

We eat from beautifully dressed plates of decadent sea urchin with shaved truffle, and we savor the rich delicacy. It's followed by an entrée of fresh halibut and sea asparagus.

"I was very fond of Nana. She was an awesome woman. So sparky, and funny."

I smile. "She sounds wonderful. Did I get on well with her?"

"Of course. But . . ."

"But what?"

Rob chases a piece of halibut around his plate with his fork. "It was only about six months after we were married, after David's death. Things had been tough for us. You'd kinda thrown yourself into work and social events, going to parties with Mike and Hans, that kind of thing. I think it was a way for you to get out of your head, to stop thinking about David all the time."

He spears the fish but doesn't move to eat it. "You once said to me, in one of our rare fights, that if we hadn't gotten married, or at least gotten married in Hawaii, there would've been no helicopter crash. That David would still be alive. You were carrying around a huge amount of guilt.

"We still really loved each other, but it was hard. I often wondered if you blamed me. Nana picked up that something was not quite right. She asked me if I was happy with you."

I nod. "That makes sense. But that was two years ago. So, after that — before my accident — how were things between you? Sorry, *us*. You get what I mean."

"Things got better. You weren't so sad. But it was never quite the same as before the wedding, when we were so happy. We'd lost our previous . . . joyfulness."

Rob reaches across the table and puts his hand on mine. "But since your accident, at least since you've been coming to terms with it, it's been better for me. Like a reset button has been pushed. You don't have any of the guilt associated with our wedding and David's death. Hell, as far as you're concerned, we're not even married and David is still alive. Which is a bucketload of bizarre in itself, we both know that.

"But what it's effectively done is give me back the original you, the woman I fell in love with. No guilt, no working ten hours a day then coming back half-wasted after some premiere and not wanting to talk. I mean, you also have your issues, to put it mildly, but you're still so . . . *you*. When we're having dinner, it's so much more like I'd always envisioned having dinner with my wife. I don't know if you know what I mean."

He pulls his hand away from mine as the server comes to clear our plates. We're silent, instead turning to witness the sun setting over the islands, the last light casting a warm glow on the wisps of cloud above.

The server promises us dessert and departs. I look at Rob and shake my head.

"Wow. I had no idea. You seemed — I mean, *we* seemed like a perfect couple. Marred by tragedy, but still loving and happy."

"And we were — we are," he interjects. "There was nothing really damaged. Only challenged."

"I get it. What happened in Hawaii . . . it's brutal. It would take its toll on any relationship. I'm glad to have restored things to a happier place, even if it is because I have no memory of those events."

"Me too." Rob smiles, leaning forward, pouring the last inch of wine into my glass. "It is weird that, even though my wife doesn't remember me and is sleeping in the guest room, I've been happier these past few months than before. It's crazy."

I smile back at him, unable to stop myself feeling joy at bringing this wonderful man some happiness. Both our spirits seem lifted as we finish the wine and eat the delicious local berry sorbet with mint the server brings, before leaving the restaurant.

"Walk back along the beach?" Rob suggests. The sun has gone, but the sky is still a deep orange, the islands silhouetted in the distance.

I peer down at my shoes. "We'll see how I fare in these wedges. Firm sand I can probably handle, major rocks not so much. I may need assistance."

He laughs and helps me step down onto the beach. We walk in silence for a while, him sturdily, me a little unsteadily. "Is that the wine or the shoes?" His face is obscured in the twilight, but I can hear the smile in his voice.

"Both. Here, help me out on this bit." A cluster of rocks blocks our path.

He steps up gracefully onto a flat rock and holds out his hand. I take it and he pulls me up beside him, guiding me across the outcrop and down the other side, making me feel secure.

"I'm better holding on to you." I hold on to his hand, even when we're on firmer ground. He says nothing, only adjusting his grip when I wobble, waiting when I slow at the rockier sections.

It's almost dark by the time we get back to the cabin. Rob lets go of my hand to unlock the door. It leaves me feeling bereft, wanting more. I kick off my wedges and flop down on the couch as Rob goes into the kitchen.

"I could handle another glass of wine. You?" he calls.

"Sure." I'm not at all sure I should drink more, but I want to prolong the evening. It's been so wonderful.

Rob returns with an open bottle and two stemless glasses. He puts them down, turns on some Ray LaMontagne on the iPhone dock, and sits next to me. He pours the wine and raises his glass. "Another toast," he announces. "To amazing food and a beautiful evening. Thank you for sharing it with me."

We chink glasses, suddenly shy. The air is thick with tension.

"So," Rob elongates the word. "I was saying I've been happier recently. And I guess I was wondering how you're feeling. I know things are messed up, but lately you seem better. Even happy. To start with, you were understandably freaked out, but no . . ." He swirls the wine in his glass, watching me.

I nod, wondering how much to say. A huge part of me wants to tell him he makes me feel safe and happy, and lean forward into his arms. To kiss him again, like I did on Valentine's Day. But those floodgates, once opened, cannot be closed. And is that right?

"I guess I have been happier. It was all too weird at first. Living with you, our home, the new job, everything. But this is my new normal. And it's a wonderful life. We have so much. An incredible place to live. And I've met fantastic people, I have a fun job . . . Yeah." I shrug, more nonchalant than I feel."

Rob's gentle smile wavers. He presses his lips together. "That's good."

And you, I want to say. Now I have you, and you love me, and you're the most incredible, kind, beautiful man I have ever met. I'm so lucky to have you. I don't deserve you.

Why can't I say it? I want to, and it's what he wants to hear.

"It seems to be going really well for you at H&F," he continues, and I'm relieved for the break in tension. We spend another hour chatting about my work and B+B's new Tribeca project. But something is missing — a gaping hole of unfinished business.

After finishing my wine, I go to the bathroom and realize the room is tilting. "I'm cutting myself off," I tell Rob when I return, leaning on the wall for support. "I've been matching you drink for drink, and you've got a hundred pounds on me."

"Probably for the best." Rob's tone is carefree. "You're enough of a lush as it is. I might stay up a while. It's only 10. Hope you're comfortable in there."

"Thanks, I'm fine. See you in the morning."

"Good night, Josie." He pours himself another glass of wine, then turns and raises it to me. "Sleep tight."

In the bedroom, I change into the silk pajamas and crawl between the sheets. I expect the wine and food to knock me out, but sleep doesn't come. The light from the living room creeps in under the door, and I find myself listening for tiny sounds. Quiet strains of music, Rob occasionally putting down his glass, sometimes changing position. I listen intently, as if his mundane movements will provide me with clues to . . . something.

To what? What am I listening for? To hear heavy, lovesick sighs? Or . . . a quiet knock at my door?

After almost an hour, I give up, turning on my side to sleep. But I'm not comfortable, as it's a firmer bed than I prefer. I'm considering taking one of my sleep-inducing painkillers when a switch clicks, the living room light vanishes, and Rob thuds up the spiral staircase to the loft.

I'm overwhelmed with acute disappointment, as though an opportunity has been lost. To do what? But I know the answer.

To be with him. Tonight. Completely. I blew it.

I continue to lie still, eyes wide open in the dark, listening to Rob's footsteps on the ceiling above, more alert than I've ever been in my life.

He's still awake. I haven't blown it yet. I could still go upstairs.

Refusing to think about it further, I climb out of bed and open my door. Every hair on my body is on end as I walk into the living room, which is lit by the glow of the loft light. I pad to the foot of the staircase, my stomach in knots, not daring to breathe.

Am I doing this? Don't think, don't think.

I take a silent first step up the curved staircase, then realize it would be creepier to be quiet. I blow out a stream of breath, ignore the screaming in my head, and walk as confidently as I can muster up the stairs. "Hey," I say as I climb up, my head appearing above the loft floor. "You still up?"

Rob is sitting on the bed in a white T-shirt and black boxer briefs, bathed in the light of the bedside lamp. He stares at me, clearly shocked. "Err . . . hey. Everything good?" He unfreezes, picking up his phone, pretending to set an alarm.

I'm suddenly ashamed, verging on humiliated.

What am I doing? What if he doesn't want me?

"I'm fine," I reply. "It's the bed. It's firm for me, I can't get comfy. I wondered if it's a softer mattress up here. Sorry."

"Oh. Sure. You'll like this one, it's squishy. You wanna try?"

"Thanks." I sit on the other side of the bed. The mattress gives beneath me, inviting me to lie down. I sigh. "This is much more like it."

Rob turns to me. "You should have it, then. I'll go downstairs."

"Oh, no. I mean, you don't have to. I don't want to throw you out. There's plenty of room."

"Okay. If you're sure." He hesitates, then gets under the covers, not looking at me. I do the same and lie down. We're both rigid, awkward. Then Rob reaches to the nightstand and switches off the light.

I lie there for a moment, my sight adjusting to the darkness, my heart racing. I move my pillows, stalling for time, then turn toward Rob. He is facing upwards, his profile illuminated by the bright glow of the moon from the skylight in the sloped ceiling. The line of his forehead is flat, his nose strong, his profile fuzzing as it reaches his beard, with a deep crevice where it parts for his mouth. Every few moments, his long eyelashes blink.

He is waiting, in the dark, beside me. Waiting for me to say, or do, something.

And in that moment, I am no longer afraid. Still, I let him wait a beat longer.

"I didn't come up just because of the bed."

He turns his head to me but says nothing, still waiting. I wish I could see his expression, but his features are now in total darkness.

"I came up here to be with you. Completely. As your wife."

That's it. That's all the invitation Rob needs. He rolls toward me and, in one fluid motion, slips one arm beneath my waist, the other across me, under the sheet, pulling me firmly into his body. He pauses for a moment, before kissing me more deeply than I've ever known. And then kissing me more. And more. And more, pulling off his T-shirt and unbuttoning my pajamas with fervor.

What happens next is beyond any physical, emotional, or sexual encounter I've ever experienced before — a spiraling, dizzying, all-consuming blur of desire, urgency, passion and joy.

Here, in this little loft, I lose all sense of time and place, of where I am, of *who* I am, of where one of us ends and the other begins. The bed, the headboard, the chair, the dresser, the floor, pushing against the sloped ceiling, leaning over the railing and even clinging onto the hard, spiral staircase . . . There is no surface in this self-created paradise that doesn't bear witness to this joining of bodies and souls. And no inch of my body he doesn't explore and devour, nor me his, from the nape of the neck to the navel to the inside of the thigh.

The tiny universe we create between us is neither his world, nor mine, but a third place, a transcendent place, where only he and I exist in space and time.

* * *

I awake, still half inside a dream of the two of us alone on a distant planet made up entirely of pale blue ocean and gray shingle beaches. We were walking, no destination in mind, the journey along the beach an end in itself. Rob would stop to help me over a rocky outcrop and lift me into him, kissing me each time, before continuing on.

For a moment, I'm not sure where I am. What's a dream and what's reality. There's a bright light dazzling me, preventing me from fully opening my eyes. The bed is unfamiliar yet soft, and my head is aching. There is a beeping in the distance. For a moment, I am struck with terror.

Am I back in the hospital? Or waking up again, for real this time?

Tilting my head away from the light, I see the loft, the bed I'm lying on, the sheets and pillows in disarray, my pajamas and lace panties on the floor, the chair in an improbable position. Evidence of last night.

Thank God.

It was real.

I'm lying in a pool of sunshine beaming down through the skylight. There's a sheen of perspiration on my bare skin. No sign of Rob, though.

Rob. I recall snatches of moments from last night, some making me smile, blush, or shake my head in disbelief. And his absence makes me ache. Where'd he go?

A trio of beeps again — this time I recognize it as a microwave announcing its task is done. Moments later, heavy, slow footsteps clang on the staircase. A lowered head of tousled black hair appears, then a wide, brown chest bearing a smattering of dark hair, then finally a large tray full of breakfast delights being carried very carefully. Rob, in nothing but a pair of white briefs, steps up into the room. He looks up at me, his expression triumphant.

"Those stairs are so tight, I didn't think I'd make it without the whole tray going overboard." He sets it on the bed.

"Wow. You didn't have to do all this." Although I'm glad he has.

"Well, I was hungry. And I didn't, really. The inn doesn't normally serve breakfast to the cabins, but I have ways of making things happen." He winks comically. "The lattes got a little cool, so I nuked them, but otherwise it's all fresh."

He leans in for a kiss, his movements natural. "Morning, beautiful." He smirks at me. "You're . . . disheveled, to be honest. And a bit sweaty. But still gorgeous." He kisses me again.

I laugh, and then cover my mouth with my hand. "Thanks. And probably suffering from dragon breath, too."

"I didn't like to say anything, but . . . Have a reheated latte. That will help."

He waggles his eyebrows and gestures to the tray with a flourish. "*Madame*, for you we 'ave herbed pancakes with poached eggs, because it *is* Easter Sunday, cured salmon, cheese scones and homemade yogurt. And plum nectar, I think they said."

"Fantastic. I'm starving. Also, slightly hungover." I grab a plate and a fork and dig into a pancake with some salmon and a poached egg on top, the yolk oozing.

"Yeah, well, I had to get you drunk enough to finally get you into bed, didn't I?" he jokes. "But not so drunk you'd pass out. Had to make you think it was your idea. All part of my cunning masterplan." He rubs his hands together then takes a large bite of a cheese scone.

"Your evil genius worked. Well played, sir. I am but putty in your hands."

"Yeah, you are." He takes another bite and chews. "Okay then, today. We could stay in bed all day." He looks at me suggestively. "But then again, it's beautiful, clear, sunny. We should probably make the most of being here and go outside. It's 10.45 already."

"What?" I mumble through the delicious pancake. "I thought it was earlier."

"I guess we were up pretty late. I don't think we got to sleep until maybe three. Four? It's kind of a blur."

I grin. "Yeah, I was having some fairly pornographic flashbacks. Last night was incredible. The most incredible ever."

"Oh, yeah? Best ever?" He lifts an eyebrow.

"Well, don't get all cocky on me now. It's probably muscle memory, right? I mean, for me it was the first time we've slept together, but not for you, far from it. And not even for my body. It was probably all programmed how to please each other. Nothing to do with any skill on your part, of course." I poke him in the ribs as he takes a forkful of my pancake.

"Is that right?" He grins back at me. "We'll have to try again and see, won't we?"

Two hours later, we're still in bed, the square of sunlight in a different spot, now highlighting the sheen on Rob's bare chest. Lying against his shoulder, I trace my fingers across his smooth skin, stroking the patch of hair on his chest.

"I feel so lucky to have met you. It could so easily have never happened."

"Me too." Rob kisses my head and keeps his mouth there, murmuring into my frizzed-up hair. "I've always felt so lucky that we met, but even more today. The luckiest guy alive." He squeezes me.

I squeeze him back, then lean back to look up at his face, my head resting in the crook of his elbow. His eyes are damp.

"Hey," I say, reaching up to touch his face.

"Sorry. It's just I — I've been waiting for this. I'm happy." He wipes his face against his free arm, and looks back at me. "I love you so much, Josie. And I wasn't sure you were going to come back to me."

He's so sweet. "I know. But I'm here now. I'm not going anywhere. I'm . . . so in love with you. Totally, completely, in love with you. I guess it was always going to happen. I'm still me, and you're you, so—"

But his kiss stops me, and we fall into each other yet again, both of us saying, "I love you, I love you," more times than I can count. Now we've started, it seems almost impossible to stop.

It's late afternoon by the time we make it out of bed, and that's only to take a shower and brush our teeth.

"I reek," I admit, putting on a white bathrobe.

He nods. "Yep, you do. But so do I. You're getting a five-minute head start in the shower, then I'm coming in."

We never make it outside that day, despite the sunshine. We order dinner in and eat in our bathrobes in the living room. Then we make lazy love on the couch, sliding onto the floor, eventually lying on our backs on the carpet, spent, and deliriously happy. But the floor is too hard to relax on, so we drag ourselves up the iron stairs again to the mussed-up bed in the loft, which becomes our private paradise for a second night.

I don't want to leave this place. Or him. Ever.

I'm sorry, David.

I don't think I'm coming back for you.

PART TWO: HER

CHAPTER 11

November 30

Man, that hurts.

The pain radiated from wrist to neck, from knee to buttock.

Owww.

The ground was impossibly hard, gritty, ice cold. It was dark. There were street sounds, car horns, people.

"You okay, ma'am?"

A large hand came into view, offered kindly. But it was all too confusing.

"What happened?"

Josie's voice sounded distant in her own head.

"You came off your bicycle, ma'am. Can you get up?"

The hand was still there. This time, Josie took it.

He pulled her up so that she was sitting. She took a moment to get her breath back, do a body check. Nothing broken. At least, she didn't think so. She rose painfully to her feet.

"I'm fine," she managed, taking off her brown and green bicycle helmet with caution. "Just bruised, I think. Thank you for stopping."

Other people had stopped, were watching, their breath fogging the night air; a few had already started to move away.

The man's brow was furrowed under his threadbare beanie as he watched her. He looked up at the remaining bystanders. "She's good."

Josie straightened. She could already feel her body stiffening.

"I'm okay," she assured him again, more confident than she felt. "I'll go get a cup of tea. I'll be fine. Tea solves everything." She smiled shakily.

The man gestured to where Electra lay, front wheel bent, handlebars at an improbable angle. "Your bike is mangled."

Josie looked over. "Oh no! I love that bike. Guess I'll lock her up for now."

"Coulda been you got squished," the stranger observed, as he helped Josie lock her damaged bike to a stand. "Lemme get you to a café. Where you headed?"

He handed over her purse, which had fallen out of Electra's basket, and walked Josie to a café on the corner.

"I'm meeting my husband at a gallery in Midtown. I'll text him that I'll be late." Josie stopped at the door. "Thanks for helping me." She hesitated. "Do . . . may I buy you a coffee, or something else?"

The man smiled. "I'm good, ma'am. Don't need anything. You take care."

"I will," she assured him. "Thanks again."

At the counter, Josie ordered a London Fog from the barista.

Hold on. Why did she have her old black purse? That thing was ancient.

Josie thought back. She distinctly remembered picking up the burgundy Coach purse this morning. To go with her outfit. For the PR meeting earlier, and for the gallery.

"Ma'am? Four and a quarter."

"R–right, of c-course," she stuttered, reaching into the black purse and pulling out a fabric wallet, again one she hadn't used in ages, not since Rob gave her a leather one. What was going on? Maybe she'd hit her head? At least the wallet contained cash. She paid up, silently starting to freak out, and moved through the other customers to sit at an empty stool at the counter across the front window. She stared out at her bike on the stand across the street before focusing on the distorted reflection of the woman staring back at her in the double-glazed window.

This was really weird. She had no idea why she had her old bag. She closed her eyes; she'd figure it out. She must've picked up the wrong purse from the closet.

Josie took slow sips of the tea and some long, calming breaths. She felt shaken to the core, and her wrist was throbbing.

God, Rob! He was still waiting at the gallery. And they were supposed to be getting dinner after, for her birthday.

She looked at her watch, then swore. Its face was smashed, the hands stuck at 6.17. Josie dug in the bag for her iPhone and pulled out an old model in a green case.

Where had that come from?

She examined the screen-lock display. "Josephine Alice Cavendish; blood type O+; no medical allergies; no medications." Josie always had that on her phone display, in case of an emergency.

She tapped in her passcode, and it unlocked. The time was 6.33 p.m. — she was supposed to be at the gallery at 6.30. She took another deep breath. She had no idea what was going on, but speaking to Rob was the priority. They'd figure it out together.

Josie scrolled through the contacts, down to the R's. Ryan, a guy in the choir she used to be in. Ruben, a former colleague at Crain's.

She scrolled down, then back up again.

Where's Rob? Where the hell is Rob's number? Think, think.

She didn't know Rob's number by heart — who remembered numbers, these days? Perhaps it was entered in a different way.

Josie flicked through the names, looking at them in random chunks. Most she recognized, but many were unfamiliar. Who was Abby Crawford? Brent Thomas? Caitlin Abbot?

Increasingly uneasy, she checked her texts, relieved when she found a new, unread one from Suzie. Thank goodness. Something normal.

You nearly here, birthday girl? We've got the table, but it's packed and I'm getting evil stares from servers who won't take our orders until you get here. Get your 36-year-old ass over here!

But she wasn't meeting Suzie tonight. She was late for Rob. Josie called Suzie's number.

Don't cry, don't cry.

Suzie answered, the restaurant's chatter and music loud in the background.

"HEY, YOU CLOSE?" her friend shouted. "I'M WITH YOUR CHOIR BUDDIES, BUT WE CAN'T HANG ON TO THIS TABLE WITHOUT YOU."

"No, honey . . . I was in an accident. I crashed my bike." Josie rubbed her forehead, noting her grimy hand, the sore, red scratches. "I'm sorry, am I supposed to meet you? I guess I double-booked. I'm late to meet Rob too, but I crashed . . . I'm in a café."

"OH, CRAP. ARE YOU HURT? LISTEN, I CAN'T HEAR YOU . . . LET ME COME GET YOU. I'LL TAKE YOU HOME, OKAY? TELL ME WHERE YOU ARE."

Josie looked around her. "I'm at the Bel Air café on Third and 25th, by Baruch College. I must call Rob, but I don't have his number—"

"BEL AIR? THIRD AND 25TH? GOT IT." Suzie was making Josie's head ache. "SIT TIGHT, I'M COMING."

"Sure, but can you text me Rob's nu—"

But she'd gone.

Rob would call eventually, when Josie didn't show up. He was probably schmoozing and hadn't even realized she was late.

Josie examined the other texts. Nothing from Rob — no sign of him anywhere. But then, texts from him would be on her real phone, in her usual purse. Not this old phone.

She tried not to think about the phone and the purse, and focused instead on her tea, the familiar Earl Grey flavor soothing her. She practiced the mindfulness exercises Suzie had been teaching her, since David.

Pick up the cup. Feel its warmth. Take a long, careful sip. Feel the texture of the frothy milk. Taste the sweetness, the spices. Move them around your mouth. Swallow slowly. Enjoy the sensation as the warm liquid flows down your throat.

By the time Suzie burst through the café door, Josie was almost in a trance.

"Josie! Are you okay?" Suzie turned Josie's stool around and touched her jaw. It was tender. "That's a nasty graze, I'll bet you're bruised all over. You poor thing, on your birthday too. We need to get you home. Got everything?" She picked up the bike helmet from the counter.

"Yes, only it's not the right purse — and this phone—" Josie rose, but the floor seemed to be shifting beneath her.

"Honey, do we need to go to the ER? My cab's waiting. Home or hospital?"

"Home. I need to call Rob." She grabbed Suzie's arm and took an unsteady step.

"We can see what you need to do later, right? Come on."

Suzie wrapped Josie's scarf around her neck and led her out into the cold evening, where a cab was waiting. Suzie leaned in the window to give the driver the address while hustling Josie into the back seat. Josie could feel every ache, every bruise. The taxi's heater was on full blast and, as the driver pulled away, Josie tugged the scarf from her neck.

She looked at the silver and black material in her hands. This was definitely not her scarf.

She couldn't even think about that right now.

"I've lost Rob's number. I have to call him, Suze — he's waiting for me."

Suzy frowned. "You double-booked? For a date? On your birthday? You weren't even coming to the restaurant? That's not cool."

"I have no idea, I'm sorry . . . I don't remember arranging a night with you. I have to call Rob, because he'll be worried. You've got his number, right?"

"Why would I have your date's number?"

"A date? I'm talking about Rob. *Rob*. Don't you have his number?" What was going on?

"Honey, I haven't even heard of this Rob. Now, I'm taking you home. We'll work it out."

Dumbfounded, dizzy and nauseated, Josie stared out of the window.

Deep breaths, deep breaths.

Then she realized they were driving across the Williamsburg Bridge.

"Hold up . . . why are we crossing the bridge? I meant my home, Suzie, not yours — we should be there by now. Where's this guy taking us?" The panic heightened.

"Calm down — we're going to your place in Brooklyn, Josie . . ." Suzie turned to Josie, peering into her face. "You live in Williamsburg. You remember, right?"

"No, Suze! I live in Manhattan, you know that. Have ever since I moved to New York."

"Shit. This is worse than I thought. You've lost some time, Josie, you must've hit your head. Dammit, I should have taken you to the hospital."

Suzie knocked on the clear plastic divider. The driver flicked open the hatch.

"Change of plan. We need to get my friend to the hospital. Woodhull, that's close, right?"

"Yes, ma'am, maybe ten blocks. You got an emergency?"

"I think we're okay." Suzie looked at Josie. "But I need to get her checked out."

Within minutes, the cab pulled up to Woodhull Medical Center's ER entrance. Suzie hustled Josie into a busy waiting room and helped her to a plastic chair, the only one available, next to an obese woman who glared as Josie squeezed in next to her. She watched as Suzie spoke to the staff at the desk. She was so hot. Josie shrugged out of her coat, earning another glare from her neighbor. But Josie was focused on the raincoat: that wasn't hers either. Or the oversized gray sweater underneath.

There was something very, very wrong here.

That was Josie's last thought before she slumped into the woman next to her, darkness taking over.

* * *

Josie awoke in a hospital bed, surrounded by green curtains. Next to her, beyond the fabric, a man was groaning.

Right. The bike crash. Birthday . . . Something bad about Rob.

She tried to push herself upright, but her left hand hurt when she put pressure on it.

A doctor with hair graying at the temples pulled the curtain open, stepped in, and closed it with a swoosh. He gave Josie a wide grin, white against his dark skin, and picked up a chart.

"You need to be more careful on your bike, Ms. Cavendish, I think." His voiced was heavily accented. South African, or maybe Zimbabwean, she thought. "You fainted in reception, but you're okay, a little bruised on your wrist and hip, but no head injury." He smiled again. "Your friend is finishing up your paperwork, and she'll take you home. No need for you to take up a bed here. Some strong painkillers will do fine."

"Thanks, doctor."

"You're most welcome, Ms. Cavendish. Now take better care, you hear." The doctor flashed a final grin, then swooshed out again.

Josie sat up, gingerly swinging her legs off the bed. She was upright, at least. And still dressed. The man next door groaned again, his piteous noises apparently unheeded.

Josie's mind flashed to Rob. He'd be frantic with worry by now.

"Can I come in? I can't knock, with these curtains—" Suzie's drawl was unmistakable.

"Sure. Come in."

Suzie pushed the curtain aside, looked at Josie critically. "Good, you're up. Let's go. I filled out your paperwork from the insurance details in your purse, so we're set. A car is picking us up." She held out her arm. "On your feet, sister."

"Thanks. What an idiot. Sorry I ruined your night."

"*Our* night. And it's fine. What are friends for?"

She grabbed Josie's coat, the one that wasn't hers, and the old purse. Josie's head was still spinning, more from confusion than trauma, as they walked out to where their car-share ride was pulling up.

Suzie confirmed her identity to the driver as they climbed inside. As the car pulled off, Josie asked again, "Have you called Rob yet? He'll be frantic."

Suzie gave her a strange look. "I don't have a number for a Rob — is he someone you're seeing? You haven't mentioned him before tonight. We had dinner plans, with some of your choir. Were you meeting him later?"

"Suzie, what are you talking about? Rob! The guy I married? You were at my wedding, Donald too, and everyone. Even David. Before . . . you know. The helicopter crash."

"Married? Helicopter crash? What?" Suzie was staring at her as if Josie was crazy.

Josie shook her head in disbelief. "The crash that killed my brother, and Charlie. Right after my wedding. Two years ago. You were there. You were . . ." She ran out of words.

"Sweetie, I think you had some pretty vivid dreams when you were knocked out. You've never been married, and I can promise you David and Charlie are alive and well. You're just confused, honey. Everything's fine . . . I'll get David to call you, how's that? You'll feel better. I'm taking you home with me. I'll send Don to yours to fetch some things."

"Sure . . . Thanks."

But all Josie had registered was that David was alive. How was that possible?

Josie pressed her lips together. The way Rob did when he was trying not to say something.

They pulled up to Suzie and Donald's Brooklyn brownstone — at least that was the same. Donald was already at the door, the lights in the hallway behind him bright. Suzie helped Josie up the stoop and on the top step, kissed Donald.

"The twins were feeling a wee bit better after dinner, they're zonked out now," he said, stroking Suzie's short hair. "Hey Josie. You gave us all a scare." He pecked Josie on the cheek.

"Sorry, Don."

"Don't fret. Come on in." He stepped aside, holding the door open.

Suzie ushered Josie straight upstairs. "Try not to wake the twins." Her voice was a stage whisper. "The bed's made up in the guest room. Back soon. I'm bringing you some codeine and water, okay?"

Suzie left Josie in the pale blue guest room with pretty, floral bedding and calm prints of sandy beaches and ocean. Josie slumped down on the bed, her confusion eased by the downy softness of the bed, the low lighting. She fished around in the black purse for the unfamiliar phone, unlocked the screen, and went back to the list of contacts. She scrolled back to the Rs, checking she hadn't missed Rob's number last time. *No.* Was it in the Bs, under Billing? *No.* It was clear the names were ordered by first name.

She scrolled further, then stopped when she saw it.

David Cavendish.

David's number. Right there.

Josie had deleted his number from her own iPhone about 18 months ago. About six or seven months after he died. Him and Charlie. But then, this was an older phone, so it made sense it would still be there.

She scrolled up and saw Charlie's name, too.

Josie inhaled and returned to David's entry. She clicked on the contact details. The same number he'd had for years, with all the eights in. Should she call? The bedside clock displayed 11.17 p.m. That meant 4.17 a.m. in London.

A text, perhaps. To see.

She clicked on the text message bubble and typed.

Hi. Are you there?

She hit send.

A soft knock made Josie jump. Suzie nudged the door open with her foot, her hands full with a small tray, not waiting for a reply.

"I made you tea."

"Thanks. On the nightstand, please."

"T-shirts in that drawer if you want something to sleep in, and a new toothbrush in the bathroom cabinet." She handed Josie a glass of water and a couple of pills, glanced at the phone in Josie's hand, as if catching her in some illicit act, then looked back at her with wide eyes. "You all good?"

"I'm okay. Sorry."

"It's fine. We take care of each other, don't we?" She gave a small smile and retreated with a quiet "Night."

Josie changed into a faded T-shirt and climbed into bed, her left hand throbbing. She propped herself up against pillows and picked up the phone again. She clicked on David's name and started to read backwards.

[Nov 30: 11.19 p.m.]
Hi. Are you there?

[Nov 30: 9.52 a.m.] Happy b'day, sis! "Have a nice day!" as they say. Hope you got my pressie in the post, sorry if it's late. Have a good one, call me before my flight to Sydney tonight, mwah XD

[Nov 18]
Screw you! It's hard to buy for her when I'm here. She loves vouchers, anyway. Who doesn't? Jx

[Nov 17]

Hey, cheapskate. Did you seriously give Mum an Amazon gift voucher for her birthday? You're such a loser. You know what you're getting for your birthday now, don't you? :D

> [Nov 6]
> Hey arsehole, or asshole as they say over here. What are you getting Mum for her birthday? Can I come in with you on something? Running out of time to send gift. Get her something lovely and pretend it was my idea. Jx

He had been texting. As recently as this morning.
He *was* alive.

Josie's heart raced, and her fingers trembled as she scrolled more and more rapidly through the texts, a sob thickening in her throat.

The banter between Josie and her brother went on and on, backwards. The texts were only every few weeks, except for a flurry of messages around August and up to mid-September, when it seemed she and David, plus some friends, had met up for a vacation in Biarritz.

Wiping away the tears that had begun to fall, Josie abandoned the texts for Instagram. Sure enough, after scrolling backwards in her account, past some autumnal shots of Williamsburg she'd never taken, she found dozens of photos of herself, David, his two best friends, and their partners, plus one couple's baby, all geo-tagged "Biarritz, France," and dated September this year. Pictures of them lying on a beach next to steep cliffs, at French cafés drinking wine, walking along the streets of an old town, David and the guys carrying surfboards in short wetsuits and damp hair. Tanned, disheveled, happy.

Only Josie had never gone on that trip. She'd gone to Mexico this past summer with Rob, ate something too spicy, and had diarrhea for two days. *That*, she remembered — not going to Biarritz with her dead brother.

Ting-ta-ding.

A text. But it couldn't be David, surely?

> **Peter**
> Hey, are you okay? Suzie ran off, saying you'd had an accident on the way to restaurant. We stayed and waited a while, hoping you'd show up. I'm worried about you — please call or text me! P

Who in the world is Peter?

Josie flipped through her mental contact list. She only knew two Peters in New York. One was an older guy she had worked with at Crain's; the other a tall guy in the choir she used to be a member of. He'd joined after Josie left, but she and Rob had met him briefly at the group's last concert. It had to be the latter, since Suzie said a bunch of choir friends were waiting to celebrate her birthday. But why would he be so concerned? They barely knew each other.

She scrolled further back.

> [Nov 30: 12.15 p.m.]
> Yeah me too :) See you at the restaurant. Jx

[Nov 30: 11.54 a.m.]
Happy birthday, beautiful. Can't wait to see you tonight. :P

> [Nov 29: 9.48 p.m.]
> Stay behind a while tonight? I need to talk to you about something. P

The texts read like she and Peter were friends. Maybe more than friends? But that made no sense.

Josie replied to the new message, mostly to placate whoever this guy was, so he wouldn't keep texting.

> Thanks, I'm not badly hurt, just a crash
> on my bike and I'm a bit shaken up. Being
> cared for by my bestie, so don't worry.
> Thanks for asking after me, sorry about
> not making it to my own birthday dinner!
> I'll catch up with everyone again soon. J

Josie put the phone down and gazed at the sandy beach on the wall in front of her. It could be Biarritz. She took a long, slow gulp of the now-tepid chamomile tea, her head swimming. Was it her dead brother come back to life? Her missing husband? The mysterious Peter? The trauma of the crash itself? Or perhaps the codeine was finally kicking in.

Probably all the above.

Her eyes were so heavy. She glanced at the clock: 1.06 a.m. Maybe David would text back soon.

Closing her eyes, she drifted off into an ocean of unremembered dreams.

CHAPTER 12

December 1

"Morning, Josie."

Suzie's soft drawl roused Josie from a deep sleep.

Josie opened her eyes. Two soulful brown eyes stared back, and Suzie's trademark red lips broke into a gentle smile.

Josie pulled herself up. "Oh. I didn't hear you come in. Sorry."

"It's fine, thought I'd better let you rest. I'm at home again with the twins today. Euan still has a runny nose. How are you feeling?" Suzie placed a cool hand against Josie's head.

"Bit soon to say. Not much pain, just confused. Shaken." Josie sat against the headboard, plumping the pillows behind her, wincing as her bruises made themselves known. Had last night really happened? She tried to look cheerful, but a knot of panic weighed in her stomach.

"I'll bet." Suzie moved over to the windows, opening the curtains, and looking back at Josie, eyeing her critically. "Well, you stay as long as you like. Don can drive over to your place and pick up a few things, if you don't feel like going home tonight. It'll only take him a few minutes."

Josie realized she didn't know where "her place" was but couldn't say as much to Suzie. Her own home was in a Union Square sub-penthouse with her husband, at least twenty minutes away. But that was clearly not where Suzie meant.

"Uh, right. Thanks."

"Cup of tea and more painkillers for you. Fresh towels in the bathroom if you want to shower. No hurry. Come down whenever. Or stay in bed all day." Suzie gave Josie's shoulder a squeeze before leaving.

Josie's eyes filled with tears of combined gratitude, confusion and downright terror as she recalled the events of the previous night.

What the hell was going on?

Her phone on the nightstand was flashing its little notification light.

David.

She grabbed it, hands trembling.

Please let there be a text from him.

There was a text.

It was from him.

> Hey, kiddo. Yep, I'm in Sydney, remember? Heading to the pub to watch footie. What's up? Had a text from Suze, something about a bike accident? Let me know you're okay XD

Josie let out a strangled noise, somewhere between joy and anguish. Then her face crumpled, tears rolling down her face.

So many days and nights, she had begged the universe for a do-over, a chance to turn back the clock and have her brother back. To never have gone to stupid Hawaii in the first place for the wedding. To be able to hang out in a pub with him again, drink too much and laugh themselves silly. And for David to fulfill his potential as a fine man, and hopefully even become a husband and a father one day.

And there he was, texting like nothing happened. Clearly, for him, nothing had.

Wiping her tears away with her fingers, she shakily typed a reply.

It's all okay, I'm fine. I had bit of a bike crash on way to b'day drinks, then nasty dream you died! Needed to reconnect. Love you, big bro. When seeing you next? Jx

She stared at the screen, hoping for a quick reply. It came after a minute.

Ahhh, ya big idiot. Luv you too, softie. You're still coming home for Xmas, right? And no Amazon gift vouchers this time! As you'll be there in person, we want real presents. Amazing ones. :D x

So, she was supposed to be seeing him at Christmas. That was still weeks away.

She tapped her Gmail app and found the "Travel" folder she'd set up years ago. There it was, a British Airways flight, flying out 20 December, returning December 28. The dates were changeable.

She had to see David as soon as possible.

And right now, the UK was the only thing that made any sense. Because *this* New York was apparently not the same New York as yesterday.

Suddenly all Josie craved was being at her childhood home in Cornwall, surrounded by family, including the brother she'd thought was dead. She wouldn't believe it until she set eyes on him.

She typed another text.

Actually thinking of coming early, spending more time with you. When do you get back to London? Not to worry about me.

I'm physically fine, just a bit shaken up. I'm staying at S&D's now. Any gift requests? Jx

His reply was instant.

Glad you're okay, and sure, I'd love to have you stay longer. Back on 8th, short trip this time. You can stay with me for party times in Londinium before going to Mum's for Xmas, if you like. Lemme know. XD

Josie would love nothing more in the world than to stay in London with her brother. She looked back at the flight email, then scrolled through the inbox. What about her husband?

There was nothing from Rob. Neither texts nor email. It was like he didn't exist. She banished the thought of Suzie's reaction when Josie had mentioned Rob. She carried on scrolling. Also nothing from Mike and Hans, who always used her personal number for social stuff.

There were lots of emails from Suzie, but not about anything she recognized, aside from things about the twins or Donald. And their recent social plans were more frequent than Josie remembered. And more Brooklyn-based.

There were also lots of recent messages from friends at the choir, and some from the director about rehearsals and forthcoming gigs. But she'd given that up years ago. Yet, according to this, she was still an active member of Sound Eclectic, and due to sing carols at a children's hospice next week. That must be why this Peter guy was so familiar with her.

She kept reading the email history, hoping she'd start recognizing some messages. Or something that might tell her why her life was so different to what she recalled.

Josie returned to the travel folder, hoping for a shortcut to the answer. The most recent trips were at the top. "Biarritz Sept 2017" was the first, which corresponded with those vacation photos. Then "London December 2016" — so, she had gone home for Christmas last year, too. Then

"Vermont April 2016," which revealed she had gone on a girl's spa weekend, a treat from Suzie, apparently. Josie did remember Suzie offering her that trip, but she'd had plans with Rob, so Suzie had taken another friend.

Below that folder was "Italy June 2015," which, looking at Instagram, looked like a fantastic holiday with Mum in Venice — again, Josie had no memory of it. That would have been about seven months after she met Rob. Josie recalled telling him how much she wanted to go to Venice, and he'd promised they'd go one day.

Below the Italy folder was "Barcelona September 2014" with David, Laura, her husband Adam, and their then-five-month-old son Theo. Now, *that* trip, Josie remembered. She did go on that holiday.

She thanked herself for being disorganized enough *not* to clear out her main inbox. It was full of history. Josie went back to the period when she met Rob — her thirty-third birthday, November 2014 — and it was clear that all the emails before that date related to her previous life. The one she remembered. Anything after her thirty-third birthday, she couldn't. Why?

Yet there were some discrepancies.

Her termination notice and severance pay from Crain's in March 2015 was still there, even though that was after met Rob. However, instead of the Halstein & Faust job offer and contract emails, she came across a group of messages from Talk New York radio station, inviting her first to an interview, then making her a job offer as real estate radio show host and online reporter. She recognized the name of the manager, Abby Crawford, from the green phone's contacts. That must be her boss.

Except that wasn't her job. She worked in communications at Halstein & Faust, and her manager was Mike Jones.

But Rob got her the interview with Mike. So, if she had never met Rob . . .

Josie recalled the day they met so clearly. It was her birthday, three years ago, 30 November 2014 — the day she'd gone to a real estate conference at the W Hotel. She hadn't met him until that evening, but the whole day was still crystal clear in her mind. She remembered that sunny morning, crisp and cold, as she rode Electra from her tiny Murray Hill place down to Union Square. She had been singing a tune as she cruised down Second and turned onto 25th, actually right through the intersection where she'd had her accident yesterday. Then, she'd narrowly missed a group of Baruch College students who had stepped off the sidewalk.

Wait . . . that was weird. Could that intersection be a coincidence? That moment of almost crashing?

What if something *had* happened there, which had prevented her from getting to the conference? If she'd crashed at that moment, if she'd gone home or to hospital, she would have never made it to the conference. She wouldn't have met Rob. She wouldn't have gotten an interview with Mike at H&F, so she would have had to get a different job — the radio station. She remained single, so she went to Venice with Mum. She didn't marry Rob, so she didn't quit the choir.

No wedding in Hawaii. David really was still alive. Charlie too.

Josie was in a life where she hadn't married Rob.

How was this even possible? It wasn't, of course. Was Josie just going nuts? Been watching too many episodes of *Fringe*?

She stared at the beach print on the wall ahead of her but saw only images of her life as she knew it. Her incredible, kind, handsome husband. Their beautiful home, in a tower he had named after her, on Union Square.

If by some impossible truth she had really been flung into a life where she'd never met Rob, that would mean she also didn't live with Rob on Union Square.

So where *did* she live?

Suzie had said it would take Donald a few minutes to pick up some clothes. It must be in Brooklyn.

Back in Gmail, she spotted a folder "Williamsburg flat buying 2015."

Thank you, alternate Josie.

Inside was a link to a listing of a modest but pretty, two-bedroom walk-up in Williamsburg, and then a purchase contract, dated June 2015, along with a series of emails between Josie and a realtor. She'd bought this home more than two years ago.

There was no way she could have afforded it on what the employment contract said she was being paid for the radio job, but Josie had clearly received her grandmother's inheritance in both versions of reality. From the emails, she had invested a 50% down payment.

Josie flicked through the listing photos, to see if anything about it was familiar. Nothing.

Her home was not her own.

Her job was not her job.

Her husband was not her husband.

Her dead brother was alive.

A rush of bile rose in her throat, and the tea came with it. She managed to lean over, panicking as she grabbed the bedside bin and threw up into it. She continued retching until there was nothing to bring up, tears running down her cheeks.

Josie fell back against the pillows, exhausted. Then she sat up, gripped by another appalling thought. If Rob wasn't t her husband in this bizarre reality, did he even exist?

She grabbed the phone again, her hands clammy and slick with sweat as she Googled the name Robert Billing.

A Wikipedia entry came up, and she exhaled. It seemed to be the entry she remembered. Stuff about his parents and B+B Developments. Then she got to "Personal Life."

> *As of April 2017, Robert Billing is dating Surin Chan, a luxury real estate agent whom he met when she pitched him her agency's services. Chan is the daughter of Manhattan real estate tycoon Bernard Chan and society heiress Annabelle Chan, formerly Davis, daughter of the late oil magnate Tyson Davis.*

Stunned, Josie clicked through to photos, her pulse quickening as she saw Rob and a gorgeous, very petite woman on a red carpet, the words "Luxury Listing NYC" printed on the backdrop behind them, Rob and this same woman with Hans and Mike at a party, Rob with this woman at . . .

She turned her head and retched again into the bin, but there was nothing left. Sucking in deep breaths and exhaling slowly, she tried to calm herself, to suppress the panic, to create some order out of the chaos.

Breathe . . .

Think.

Okay.

Rob wasn't her husband.

He was dating some Manhattan heiress.

Her home was some small apartment in Brooklyn she didn't recognize.

She worked at a radio station for a mediocre salary.

So, good stuff?

Breathe . . .

Think.

David was alive. That was better than anything. Charlie too.

She was physically fine, and she did at least have a home.

She had a job. Admittedly doing something she'd never done before.

And Suzie was still her best friend. That was comforting.

But what next? What should she do?

The only thing that made sense was her initial instinct — to go back to the UK. Take time off to figure out what had happened. How she had gotten here. And how she could fix it. If she wanted to fix it. Here, David was alive. He was her priority.

So, if she accepted, really accepted that she was in some kind of alternate life — a *Sliding Doors* reality — if she really accepted that, then what would she do? She had so many knowledge gaps, including how to do her job — she'd never done any radio work. She'd have to claim amnesia and fake not remembering anything at all from the past three years. Of course, that would mean doctors, tests, but what was the option? None, as far as she could see. Who would believe anything else?

Josie went back to the travel folder and clicked through to the London flight booking. She was able to change the flights to a red-eye arriving December 9, returning January 2. That would give her a week from now to recover physically, go to this Brooklyn apartment, and pack for the UK, go to the doctor to be tested for amnesia, and arrange time off work until January.

Josie felt a small sense of relief. At least she had a plan. Feeling slightly more relaxed, she got slowly out of bed, her muscles aching, bruises throbbing. She headed into the bathroom for the first time since arriving at Suzie's. She was so dehydrated from vomiting she couldn't pee, so she went to the bathroom cabinet for the spare toothbrush, glancing in the mirrored door as she opened it.

What?

She closed it again with a slam and frowned at the woman frowning back at her. She looked *so* different.

Aside from the scrape on her jaw, she was very pale, although not that surprising, given everything that had happened in the last twenty-four hours. She was a lot chubbier around the cheeks and chin, more like she'd looked a few years back, and her hair was more its original dark blonde rather than the golden blonde she'd been highlighting it. It was shorter, too, at her shoulders, with no extensions. In fact, her lash extensions were gone too, and her brows unkempt. She looked like the pre-Rob Josie.

She examined her hands. They were also chubbier than usual, and where were her acrylic nails?

She pulled off her T-shirt in one swift, painful movement, looking in the mirror again, then down at herself.

Wow.

She turned herself in front of the mirror, ignoring the bruises on her wrist and hip, examining the mound of belly fat and the cellulite on her butt and thighs. She was easily thirty pounds heavier than she remembered.

She thought about the weight she'd been when she met Rob — somewhere in between, maybe, around ten or fifteen pounds lighter than this. She had lost that weight gradually, a few pounds on purpose before the wedding, but more after David's death.

So, in this life, without the wedding, without David's death, without Rob, and the glamorous life he offered, she had been putting *on* weight over the past three years instead. *Terrific.*

She stepped into the shower, her plumper body feeling weird as she washed. And her pubic hair! It didn't look like it'd seen the inside of a salon in months. Drying herself seemed to take longer than usual: there was more to dry.

As Josie returned to the bedroom, the reality of her situation — or of this reality — began to sink in. She sat on the edge of the bed, burying her head in her hands.

On the nightstand, the green mobile was flashing. She had a moment's hope. David? Rob? She glanced at the screen, the disappointment crushing.

> **Peter**
>
> So relieved you're not hurt. I still really want to see you and talk. I have news that I hope you'll like. Call me when you're feeling better and we can meet up. Thinking of you, P

Gosh, this guy was persistent. Well, he'd just have to wait.

Josie put the phone on silent, then quickly dressed in the black jeans and gray sweater and headed downstairs. Some kids' TV program was blaring away in the living room.

"Hey," she said weakly, walking into the spacious kitchen, where Suzie was at the large wooden table with a laptop.

Her friend beamed, running her red-nailed fingers through her dark pixie-cut hair. "You're alive. I wanted to

132

check on you again, but I didn't want to disturb. How are you feeling? Want some lunch?"

"Not yet, thanks. My stomach is pretty dodgy. I'm otherwise okay, I think. Physically. Only . . ."

She sat down at the table, unable to finish her sentence.

"Only what?" Suzie's brow creased.

"I . . . don't remember stuff. Where I live. My job. I'm really confused."

Suzie's frown deepened. "Wait, Jose! You don't remember *anything*?"

"Well, I know who I am, I know you, this house, and Donald . . . I remember my family, and moving to New York, living in Murray Hill, and working at Crain's. But after that—"

"After that, what?"

It was no use — she would have to tell Suzie the truth. About her real life, her real memories.

Josie drew in a deep breath and recounted an abridged version of her life: meeting and marrying Rob, her brokerage job, their wedding, and the helicopter crash that killed her brother and cousin.

"Our grief has been hard on our marriage, but Rob and I have been making it work," she continued. "And you and Rob are friends, you get on really well — Don too. So . . . that's what I remember from the past three years. But I don't think that's what you remember."

Suzie had been shaking her head the entire time. "Are you serious?"

"Yeah, Suze. I'm totally serious. I get that for you, events were different, I live somewhere in Brooklyn, I've never married — or even dated — a guy named Rob, and David is alive. Which, to me, is a freakin' miracle, because *I* was at his memorial in London, wailing like a baby. But now, I'm in a world where he's alive and we texted each other this morning. It's totally impossible . . . literally incredible." Josie grabbed some kitchen paper from the counter and blew her nose.

"What about the twins?" Suzie nodded her head toward the living-room door, through which two-year-old Euan and Isla were giggling.

"Rob and I came over and gave them giant plushies, just after they were born, and we told you about our engagement. You were trying to decide whether to bring the whole family to Hawaii or leave Donald alone with the babies. In the end, you all came. Your six-month-old babies were at our wedding, and you and Don missed half the ceremony because Euan was crying nonstop."

"Shit. Josie, this is unbelievable. I mean ACTUALLY NOT BELIEVABLE. I've never been to Hawaii. You've never been married. You got your radio show a couple of months after the Crain's layoff. You love it. Then you bought your place in Williamsburg. And you've been single for years, although I know you've been crushing on that guy in your choir, Peter." Suze was talking so quickly it was hard to keep up. "You've no memory of your Williamsburg place at all? What about Peter?"

"No." Josie turned down the corners of her mouth. "That's . . . not what happened to me."

"Fuck!" Suzie ran her hands through her hair, grabbing a tuft. "This is really *bad*. We have to get you checked out. There's something really screwy going on. You might be concussed, have some kind of brain injury. I'll call Don to come home for the kids, and take you to the hospital, yeah?"

Josie shook her head. "I'm sure it's not so urgent I have to go right now. The thing is, it's not like these are weird, screwy memories. These are my actual memories. The hospital won't be able to help with that."

"But last night the doctors didn't know you had these memories, Jose! And they *are* screwy." Suzie put her hand on Josie's, squeezing so hard Josie winced. "What if you've got some . . . some swelling of the brain or something? Some head trauma that could be getting worse? We need to be sure."

"Suze, I just want to get back to London and see David. It's all I can think about. I lost my brother two years ago, in the most brutal way, and now he's alive again? I have to go to him. I've already changed my flight to the UK. I'm going next week."

Suzie frowned. "Okay, flying doesn't sound like an awesome idea when we have no clue what's going on in your brain. I guess I can't make you go to the hospital, but I'm keeping you here with me for a while. You can rest and I'll keep an eye on you. Then, if you really can't remember your place when I take you home, you're booking an appointment for a scan to get checked out before you leave. Deal?"

Josie nodded, truly exhausted. "Deal." She slumped her head into her arms on the table.

"Right, back upstairs to bed with you. And if you slip into a coma, *I'll* kill you."

CHAPTER 13

Early December

"Give me the keys." They were standing outside the Williamsburg building Josie only recognized from the listing images in her email.

Josie found a set of unfamiliar keys in the black purse and handed them over to Suzie. She opened the green door, which had a dozen buzzer buttons next to it, including one that read "Cavendish 3C."

"Recognize anything?" asked Suzie as they walked up the stairs and along the third-floor corridor to apartment 3C. She unlocked the door, and they stepped into a small foyer. Suzie flicked on a switch. Past a short corridor, Josie could see a tiny kitchen on the left with an open, sunny living area beyond. Two doors to her right were closed, as was a door to the left.

If Josie had had doubts before, she didn't now. She'd never been her before, but it was clear she lived here. Her beloved paintings were hanging on the wall, her old, green, velvet sofa in the living room, her enamel jug on the counter. The place was small, but pretty. Charming.

Suzie was watching her carefully. "You don't recognize it at all." It was a statement, not a question.

Josie shook her head.

"Nothing," she admitted. "Except what I saw in the Listing photos. But it looks very different with my stuff in. I do remember the art, the furniture, the sofa—"

"You remember buying this couch with me for your Murray Hill place?" Suzie walked into the living area and laid a hand on the back of the sofa. Josie nodded, examining the rest of the room. Most of the items were familiar, but there was a big mirror above the fireplace she didn't recognize. She gestured at it. "I haven't seen that before, though."

"You bought it for that exact spot." Suze tilted her head, pursing her lips. "I guess we're getting a clearer idea of how much time you've lost. It's more than two years, less than . . . four? That'll help the doctors. You've got to go back for tests, honey, this is crazy."

Josie crossed the room, collapsing onto the familiar couch, swinging her legs up and tucking her feet underneath her.

"I haven't 'lost' the time, Suze. And I've already figured out exactly the point my life diverged. It was when I met Rob. Or, I guess, *didn't* meet him. Which seems to be the case in this version of reality."

The thought of her husband, or lack of, prompted fresh tears. She buried her head in her arms and let them come. Without a word, Suzie moved into the kitchen and made Josie yet another cup of strong, sweet tea.

"Right." Suzie put the mug down on top of Josie's storage ottoman. "I'm going to the store, since you've got nothing but milk and tomatoes in the fridge. You'll have to buzz me back up in ten minutes."

Josie looked up at her. "I don't even know how the buzzer works."

Suzie paused, then started to laugh. "Well, aren't you a hot mess? Okay, I'm taking your keys — you sit tight. We'll figure out the buzzer later. Chill."

Josie sipped the tea, the warm liquid and Suzie's laugh calming her. It was strange, but this place was comforting, with all her things from her life before Rob around her. She could imagine herself choosing it, living here. If she hadn't married into a life of luxury, of course.

She got up and explored, feeling like an intruder. A door off the living room led to a tiny bedroom, only big enough for her blue guest futon and a small Ikea wardrobe. She hadn't seen them in years. The other door, nearer the main entrance, opened to a larger bedroom containing her old bed, the antique armoire she had shipped from the UK to Murray Hill years ago, and her set of oak drawers. All pieces of furniture that she had given away when she moved in with Rob. The green forest painting she had bought for the Murray Hill studio was in pride of place above the bed. This, she still had — it was now in the green room in the Manhattan apartment. She ventured back out across the hall, where she found a small interior bathroom with a lot of the toiletries she used to use.

Josie went back into the bedroom and flopped down on the bed, wrapping herself in the duvet. It was familiar, warm. Maybe things would be okay here, especially if this was a world in which David was alive.

Ting-da-ding.

Hoping it would be David, Josie pulled the phone out of her pocket. It was that damned Peter guy again.

> Hey, are you feeling better? I've been worried, you didn't reply. When can we talk? P

Perhaps if she made it clear she wasn't interested, he'd leave her alone. If she told Peter she had amnesia, that could cause more questions. Better to blow him off.

> > I'm a lot better, thanks. I'm in Brooklyn, but only for a few days. I'm heading back to the UK for holidays. I need to be with family right now. I'll catch up with everyone after that. Take care and have a great holiday season, J

Hopefully that would make it clear she wasn't into him, no matter what their situation before. After all, as far as Josie was concerned, she was a happily married woman.

And Rob?

She couldn't think about Rob right now.

* * *

"Mum, I'm okay. I'm flying home tomorrow. I'll be in London by Saturday lunch . . .

"Yes, it's scary, but I went for an MRI and they didn't find any brain injury or swelling, they said it all seems fine. The doctors said it was amnesia, which can be caused by the shock of an accident, or other trauma, and my memories could come back. There's no real treatment, anyway, so . . .

"Exactly. Plus, I can remember important things, I haven't forgotten you, or who I am . . .

"No, the radio station is giving me a month off. Someone's filling in. Anyway, we can catch up when I see you . . .

"Yeah, I'll be staying at David's for ten days, he'll drive us down on the 19th . . .

"I can't wait either. I'll call you when I'm at David's . . .

"Love you too, Mum. Bye."

Josie hated lying to her mother, but Suzie's incredulity had taught her she needed to be careful with whom she told the truth to. It simply was not their truth. Better to let everyone else believe it was amnesia.

Josie scrolled back through recent texts with her brother, which told him about her supposed condition, that she was flying to London early and would be at his place by Saturday. She read and reread their conversation, grinning like an idiot, and shaking her head in disbelief at this miraculous second chance with him.

But for now, Josie had a list of things to do before she left. She had already emailed Abby Crawford at the radio station and arranged time off until the New Year. Next, she emailed the choir director to tell her about the accident, her "amnesia", and that she was bowing out of Christmas gigs. Josie also asked Kathryn to let her choir friends know what was going on. She figured Lisa would tell Peter, so he would realize she didn't remember him.

It wasn't long before the director replied, telling Josie to rest and heal, and if she was coming back in January, she could spend the holidays relearning repertoire. "Music can be very therapeutic — it might even jog some memories!"

Not a bad theory, except Josie didn't have any memories to jog. It made her wonder, though. *Would* she be rejoining the choir and working at the radio station, in January? Surely something would flip her back to real life? Wouldn't it?

With that in mind, there was one other task before leaving for the UK. The other side of the equation. For the huge thing regained — her brother — it seemed there was something equally huge lost. *Rob*.

It wasn't like Josie could call him and tell him she was his wife, and that she loved and missed him so much. He'd think she was a crazy stranger. But she just had to go to the building where they lived together. To see if it existed. Rob had named it after her.

She would have to get the subway from her place in Williamsburg, as she couldn't take Electra. Her poor, mangled bike was still chained up at Third and 25th, unless someone had taken it. She'd better deal with her today as well. She checked her phone for the nearest subway, about a twelve-minute walk. Probably why she usually used the bike. She walked to Bedford Avenue subway station, boarded the L, and stepped off at her familiar station, Union Square. Walking up the steps, she emerged into the bright, chilly December sunshine on Union Square East.

She saw it immediately.

The building — *their* building — was still there. Only, ever so slightly different. The architectural detail at the top, where it narrowed at the sub-penthouses and then the penthouse, was a little boxier. Slightly less elegant, less art deco. More modern, perhaps.

But the biggest change was on the canopy of the porte-cochère.

Instead of "Cavendish House" in tall, elegant lettering, the name read "Union House" in a crisp, wide font.

It was true, then.

She and Rob had never met.

Josie pushed her lips together to quell her emotions — a habit she picked up from Rob himself, who was always so stoic in the face of tragedy and grief. Turning away from the street and into the square, she headed for the coffee kiosk. Luca was behind the counter. Would he know her?

"Regular latte, please," Josie smiled, wondering if Luca's wife, Greta, was nearby. Luca smiled back without recognition.

"Coming up, ma'am. That's four and a quarter." He smiled at Josie again as he gave her 75 cents change. Still nothing. His lack of recognition pushed a pit of emptiness into Josie's gut.

Taking her coffee to her favorite bench, she sat in the sunshine, watching a cheerful panhandler bantering with passersby.

At least Josie had a home, and a family. What had happened in that guy's life to put him there?

After a while, despite the sunshine, she started to chill. Josie tossed the cup in the bin near the panhandler sitting on the side of the path. He lifted his face to her, with one blue eye and one green, crinkling at the corners. He was surprisingly good-looking.

"Here you go." Josie tossed the 75 cents change into the baseball cap in front of him. He flashed her a grin before she turned to walk away.

"And how about your number too?" he called after her, in an Irish accent. She turned her head back to him with a laugh but kept walking.

She was about to return to the subway, her mood ever-so-slightly lifted, when she glanced back over the street to the now-named Union House.

Josie stopped in the middle of the sidewalk.

Rob. Coming out of the main entrance. Handsome as ever, dressed in a sharp suit, white shirt open at the throat, contrasting with his dark beard. Josie held her breath. Her husband, her Rob, the love of her life. Right there. Surely he'd recognize her, if he saw her?

Rob paused at the door to chat to Ed, the concierge, then looked back into the lobby, seeming to wait. Josie's heart sank when she realized it was Surin, the woman he was dating, according to Google. Rob slipped his arm around her, still chatting to Ed. She was barely half his size, even in the killer platform heels she wore. She was stunning, raven-haired, in a cobalt-blue power suit.

Rob's peacock-green Lincoln pulled into the porte-cochère. Ed opened the passenger door for Surin as Rob came around the front to take the keys from the valet, Ed's son, Will.

As Will moved out of the way, Rob paused before getting into the driver's door. Then he looked up, suddenly, across the street, straight at Josie.

Despite the wide, busy road between them, they locked eyes for a moment. The rest of the world froze. He stared, and Josie stared back.

Did he recognize her?

Instinctively, she half-raised her hand in greeting, unable to stop the urge to make herself known to him. Rob tilted his head, furrowed his brow in confusion — then abruptly turned and got in the car.

He drove off into the New York traffic, leaving Josie standing on the sidewalk, her hand still raised foolishly before her.

CHAPTER 14

Mid-December

Josie felt really, really terrified.

But in the best possible way.

The moment she had been thinking about since she arrived, more than a week ago, in this crazy version of reality, was here.

Standing outside the townhouse, she checked the number beside the door a third time against the Waterloo address on her phone. The last thing she needed was to work herself up to this momentous reunion, only to have the door answered by some old biddy in a housecoat.

It was correct.

She exhaled very slowly, then pressed the buzzer.

A moment's silence.

"That you, Bosie? Hold up, I'm coming down."

Her brother's voice, unmistakable.

Footsteps thundered down the stairs of the two-story terraced house, and the door was flung open.

David beamed at her. Her brother, really him — disheveled, pushing his hand through thick, sun-bleached hair, shirt half-undone, wearing surfing shorts despite the cold, drizzly December weather.

Josie stared at him like an idiot, clutching the handle of her wheelie case as if it were the only thing holding her up.

"Sis! Wonderful to see ya." He flung his arms around her, his hand against the back of her head as he gave her a firm kiss on the temple.

Josie let go of the suitcase and slid her arms around him, fearing he might disappear if she did it too fast. But his wiry body stayed solid. Josie firmed her grip, buried her head in his shoulder, and broke into a flood of tears so violent, her knees buckled.

"Bose, Bose, what's up? Oh, come now! Stop that. Let's get you inside. Here, let me get that." He kept one arm round her, grabbing her case with his other hand, towing her through the open door into a carpeted hallway. He pushed the door closed with his bare foot.

He led Josie up the stairs but let her go to carry the suitcase. Her legs wouldn't cooperate. Still sobbing, she collapsed on the fourth step.

Abandoning the case, David sat down next to her. It was a squeeze. Josie stared at him. She couldn't believe he was here, beside her. He gave Josie a warm hug and waited for her to stop crying.

"I'm sorry . . . I'm a mess," she managed with a snotty sniff.

"You really are, aren't you?" David's smile was kind. "Poor Bosie. I didn't realize your accident had traumatized you so much."

She nodded, gulping the tears down. "I've . . . lost . . . so much time. So much time with you."

You have no idea.

"I know, it's crazy. You really can't remember anything from the last few years? Staying here last Christmas? Biarritz? You going to Venice with Mum?"

She shook her head with another sniff, finally beginning to pull herself together. "No. I've seen photos, but as far as

I'm concerned, I wasn't there for any of it. I don't even know my own flat or job. Even some of the people in my life."

"Man, that's effed up. What a nightmare. Come on, you can make it to the top of these steps." He stood up. "We'll get you sorted."

He grabbed Josie by her armpits, hauling her up the rest of the stairs, then quickly going back to retrieve her luggage. He reached past her, pushing open the door to his flat. To the right was a large living room with a bay window, but he turned left into a small bedroom overlooking a row of tiny backyards.

"You can have my room, since I'm such a gent." He winked. "I sleep on the settee half the time anyway. I made the bed and everything."

The bed was indeed made, with mismatched linens, and a foil-wrapped chocolate placed on top of a folded towel. Overwhelmed with joy, Josie laughed at her brother's trademark gesture.

She turned and hugged him again, this time cheerfully.

"I'll give you a five-star Trivago review. Sorry I'm such a wimp. I've been through a lot, and it's just so good to see you, brother."

David rubbed his knuckles on her head, albeit gently, flashed his megawatt grin, the one that got him in and out of trouble.

"You sort yourself out, I'll put the kettle on. Earl Grey?"

"Brilliant. Cheers."

They were themselves again, and it was like the past few years had never happened. In either universe.

He cooked dinner as Josie sat at the tiny kitchen table drinking tea, watching him, listening to him filling her in on everything he thought she should know about the past three years. Family gossip, plus what he and Josie had done together during that time — the surfing vacation in Biarritz, Christmas in London last year, and his visits to New York, including one a couple of years ago with his now ex-girlfriend Hayley (a trip Josie remembered, but differently — she and

Rob had taken them to Eleven Madison for David's birthday, about six months before Hawaii).

He also spoke about how much he hated his stock-broking job in the City, his recent surfing trip to Australia's Gold Coast, and how amazing it was, plus an update on some major political and world events. Those, Josie already mostly knew, of course. They, at least, were the same in both realities.

"Did anyone tell you yet?" He put down two plates of glistening fettuccine and pulled up a chair to the table. "If you've lost three years . . . You'll never *believe* who's President—"

"Yeah, I know about Trump."

"Right. I guess Suzie filled you in on a lot of stuff."

"Plus I have watched the news in the past week. Still, I'm sure there's a lot I don't know."

Josie took a bite of pasta as David grabbed two beers from the retro-style fridge behind him. He cracked open a bottle, handing her one.

"So," she said, "have you seen much of Charlie?"

He took a swig. "Some. We go for beers Friday nights after work sometimes. Such a tosser, that guy, but he's a laugh. Making a shitload of money at Paribas, and he's still seeing that Zoe, the big-pharma heiress who looks like a bank clerk."

"I'd like to see him while I'm in town. Next Friday, maybe? It's been ages."

"No can do. He's with Zoe's family in the Caribbean until late December. Staying there for Christmas, no doubt to avoid Auntie Jan's sawdust-dry turkey. Wanker." David gave an exaggerated wink and shoved a huge forkful of pasta in his mouth.

They took their time over dinner, David full of information and Josie basking in his company, his laugh, his very existence. Opening more beers, they sat on the leather sofa in his living room and watched *Zero Dark Thirty*. As the credits closed, Josie gave her brother a hug and thanked him for a wonderful evening.

"What, pasta and telly? You're easy to please. You can stay again."

Laughing, she went to bed. As she turned out the light, she thought to herself this was the happiest she'd ever been.

Happier even than her wedding day.

CHAPTER 15

Christmas and New Year

"Darlings! I'm so glad you're both here safe."

Her mother was lit up by the porch lamps either side of the wreath-festooned double front door of Josie's childhood home. As elegant as ever in her flowing Indian-patterned dress, her mum had hardly let Josie get out of the car before hugging her, then holding Josie back to scrutinize her, as if to assess her amnesia. Josie clamped down the guilt that was pushing its way to the surface, reminding herself memory loss was a much easier story for her family to swallow than the truth.

"How are you feeling? No headaches? Dizziness?"

"I'm fine, Mum. Honestly. I've lost some memories, that's all. The brain is a weird thing. But lots of amnesiacs go about their lives perfectly fine."

Josie wondered, not for the first time, whether any of those other amnesiacs were also from an alternate timeline, who weren't admitting to it either.

"Hi, Mum, thanks, yes, I'm fine, don't mind me," David grumbled, as he pulled the cases from the trunk.

"Well, there's nothing wrong with you, dear boy." She absently kissed his cheek. "Laura and Theo are in the playroom, and Adam's napping. Poor man's exhausted, they drove eight hours to get down here."

Josie's mother ushered them across the gravel drive and into the warm, light-filled home. It was a gracious white-stucco house that, in daylight, offered sweeping views of the rugged North Cornwall coast from the gardens at the back. It was still Josie's favorite place in the world.

Dumping cases and bags of gifts on the elaborately tiled floor of the foyer, David and Josie headed straight down to the basement playroom.

"Bosie!" Laura jumped up when she saw her sister, giving her a big hug, as little Theo dragged a wooden train awkwardly across thick carpet toward them. "How are you? How are you feeling?" Like their mother, Laura studied Josie closely.

"I'm fine," Josie told her, getting watery around the eyes. She distracted herself by crouching down to her nephew's level.

"I bet you don't recognize him, if you've lost nearly three years," Laura mused, sitting down on the carpet beside them. "The size of him now! Such a shame you've lost memories of him being a baby. When was the last time you remember him?"

Crap. Josie hadn't thought this through.

As far as she was concerned, she'd only seen Theo four months ago at Laura's house in Sussex, when she and Rob had overnighted in the UK on their way to a real estate expo in Geneva. Theo looked hardly any different.

Laura saw Josie's confusion, interpreting it as the amnesia. "Our trip to Barcelona?" she prompted. "Three-and-a-bit years ago? He was only a few months old then."

"That must be it," Josie told her, staring at Theo, who'd stopped to say hello but was now playing trains happily with David. Josie filed the image away.

"I only remember meeting him twice, right after he was born, of course, when I stayed with you — and then, yeah, Barcelona. It's all . . . muddled after that."

The lies were making her feel queasy.

Josie turned to her sister, adding, "Theo's so big. He talks now. And he remembers me."

"Yeah, of course he does, silly. Well, he saw you on your way to your Biarritz with David. That was only in September. You stayed with us overnight as you had an early flight from Gatwick. Before that, we saw you the Christmas before, in David's flat. Did David tell you about that?"

Josie nodded, swallowing, not wanting to prolong the conversation, as it would only result in more lies or half-truths. Her throat was dry.

She got up, stiff from her crouching position, her body not completely healed from the accident. "I could murder a cup of tea. See you upstairs?"

"In a minute. I have to wake Adam. He's taking a nap. It'll be dinner soon."

Josie climbed the steps back to the main floor, grabbed her suitcase from the hallway, and started up the staircase, the bannister overloaded with a faux-pine Christmas garland.

She called down to her mother in the kitchen. "Am I in the blue room, Mum?" Josie had inherited her penchant for themed rooms from her mother.

"Of course, darling. Be down at quarter past, won't you, to help me finish dinner?"

"Absolutely."

Josie took her case to the blue room. It was a different room from the bedroom she'd grown up in. That was in the converted attic and was now her mother's office. The blue room, always considered the fanciest guest room, was wallpapered in an elaborate pattern of peacocks, trees, and pagodas in greens and blues, and furnished in a rich blue color scheme, from the bedspread, pillows and curtains, to the plush chair by the huge window. The blue sometimes seemed to extend out of the window to the sky and slice of sea visible from this side of the house, but at that moment it was dark outside. Josie smiled. On the dressing table by the window, Josie's mother had put a mini-Christmas tree with tiny white lights, which were reflected back in the mirror.

She flopped back onto the bed, closing her eyes. Perhaps it was going to be okay after all. Through the open door, she could hear David and their mother laughing in the kitchen. She listened intently as Laura brought little Theo up the stairs, past her bedroom door, and up the last flight to the larger attic bedroom that had once been their playroom.

"Let's go and wake Daddy," Laura whispered. "Shall we jump on his bed? That'll be funny, won't it?"

Despite everything, Josie felt wonderful. As long as nobody asked her any questions, she'd be fine. More than fine. David laughed again. This was heaven.

Finally, she heaved herself off the huge bed to unpack and hang up the array of holiday outfits she'd brought with her, including a blue dress she'd bought at the airport to wear on New Year's Eve, when she and David would be back in London. She was due to fly home to New York a couple of days later. She didn't even want to think about that.

Josie changed into a green sweater, brushed her hair and headed back downstairs. She found her family in the kitchen, Theo eating yogurt at the central island, his little bare feet dangling off the edge.

Her mother was at the stove. "There you are. We have to decorate the tree after dinner. I was waiting for you all to get here. I couldn't stand it up by myself. The one they delivered this year is enormous."

"Do you need me to bring the decorations down?" Josie asked.

"I've done it, and Adam's got the tree in the stand — he's putting up all the lights now. Help him, would you? Dinner's under control."

Josie went into the living-dining room, taking a moment to admire the high ceiling with its restored crown moldings. The room stretched from the tall bay window at the front through to French doors at the back of the house, which led out to a stone terrace. It was more elegantly furnished than when she was a child, her mother having spent much of her father's life insurance on renovations.

A huge tree was in place in the front bay window, and Laura's husband, Adam, was on a stepladder, pushing a hand through his curly hair as he fixed the lights. Underneath him were two large boxes, with "XMAS TREE DEX" scrawled in Josie's teenage handwriting. The words brought a lump to her throat.

"Hey, Ad."

Adam turned his head and nodded at her. "Perfect timing. I need someone to turn the lights on, tell me if they're even."

Josie crossed the room, picked up the control and switched on the lights.

"Ta-da!" It did look Christmassy. She stepped back to assess the distribution of sparkliness. "There's a cluster near the top on the left — no . . . Yes! Better."

"Okay, turn them off." Adam jumped down onto the floor. He came over and hugged her. "All right? We can do the official ceremony when the baubles are on."

Dinner was a lively affair, with David taking most of the attention, as usual, regaling them with tales of "totally rad" waves off Australia's Gold Coast and buddies who worked at some investment bank in Sydney. Laura, having put Theo to bed, talked about her son's new friends at playgroup, including rumors from the staff that he'd given little Emily a kiss in the Lego room.

After dinner, Josie and her brother volunteered to wash the dishes while Laura and Adam unpacked the decorations from the boxes.

"How you feeling, sis?"

David stood waiting with a tea towel while Josie rinsed a casserole dish in the farmhouse sink. She looked out of the window. Usually there would be a view of the lawned garden and the coastline beyond, but what was now reflected back was a picture she'd much rather see — her and David, side by side, doing dishes in their family home. She stared for a moment, almost fearful that if she turned, her brother would evaporate.

She took a deep breath and handed the cast-iron dish to him. "Everything's a muddle. I'm so confused." Josie turned to face him. "But being here, with you, with everybody, it's wonderful. It's making me feel so much better. New York is weird for me now. I don't know my job, or my home. Being here is the only thing that makes any sense."

David finished drying and threw his arms around his sister. "You'll be fine. You love your flat, you'll get used to it again — and you love your radio job too. You're brilliant at it. Plus, there's your choir, which you enjoy too, right?" He pulled back to look at her. "New York has always been your dream, and you're making it. And if you can make it there . . . Well, you remember how that goes. Don't give up on it."

Josie nodded as David stepped away. "You're right. I'm still processing, I guess."

"Ach! You said that with an American accent! *Processing?* You Yank . . ." David twirled his wet tea towel into a whip. "You better run . . ."

Josie shrieked, flinging soapy dish water at him, and laughing as he chased her into the living area, whipping his tea towel at her legs.

"I'll thrash every last one of you," he threatened the rest of the family, who were sitting by the fire, sorting out tree trimmings.

"David. Put that down and come help," their mother scolded from the sofa, with a pretense of sternness but a twinkle of joy at her eldest's exuberance.

The tree took a full two hours to decorate, which took them through the whole of the King's College Cambridge's *Nine Lessons and Carols* classical album, plus some of a cheesy Christmas pop compilation. When they were done, David turned off the overhead lights, and Josie switched the tree lights on again.

"Ta-da!" she repeated, with far more enthusiasm than the first time.

"*Aahhh*," chorused her family with varying levels of sincerity. But it was spectacular.

They stood in awed silence for a moment. Then her brother exclaimed, "Presents!" and grabbed the bags full of gifts from the hallway, emptying them out under the tree with little respect for any fragile contents, arranging them in clusters according to who the gifts were from.

"In groups by gift-receiver, surely?" Josie offered. "Then you can see what you're getting and be excited."

David shook his head. "Nope. I want to give out all my presents personally. Plus, if it was grouped by receiver, Theo's pile would be 782% larger than anyone else's."

"Fair point." Josie grinned, then yawned. "Okay, I'm off to Bedfordshire. Night-night, everyone."

"Night, Bosie." David and Laura each gave her a hug.

"Good night, darling." Her mother lifted her face, as Josie bent to kiss her forehead.

Later, Josie lay in bed with the light on for a long time, listening to the sounds of the house settling down, too full of joy from the perfection of the evening to sleep.

All the people she loved the most, safe, in one house, her beautiful childhood home, all at the same time, at Christmas. Well, apart from the fact of Dad being gone, of course.

Oh, and Rob.

Shit.

Mustn't forget Rob.

* * *

"For the sake of Auld Lang Syne!"

The tiny pub erupted in cheers as a dozen of David's closest friends, mostly male bankers and stockbrokers, some accompanied by glamorous partners and wives, toasted the New Year. David grinned, held up a finger in the air to demand a moment's attention, steadied himself theatrically, and chugged down a pint of lager in a matter of seconds. He held up his empty glass to more raucous cheers, wiping his mouth with the back of his hand and shaking out his surf-blond, shaggy hair.

Josie shook her head at him in mock disapproval, laughing. He bared his teeth at her in their trademark fake smile and loped over, slinging his arm around her shoulder.

Enjoying having the floor, he announced to the group, somewhat drunkenly, "Lads, I have news. Those of you who are here pretending to celebrate NY Eve, but are actually here to hit on my NY-*dwelling* sister, in the hopes her amnesia will make her forget what sleazeballs you all are — well, you're shit out of luck because she hasn't lost her senses or taste. So, give it up."

This speech solicited a couple of groans, and one of the guys grabbed his coat and made as if to leave while Josie squirmed. David laughed, pinching his sister on the cheeks. He always managed to make her uncomfortable while focusing enough on her to show she mattered more to him than any of his friends.

"Thanks a bunch." She punched him quite hard on the arm. "I do so love having you discuss me like I'm some trophy."

"Ha! You are most welcome, dear sis. No, seriously, you'll be thanking me when Graeme *isn't* running his hands all over you later. Considering you came out in a slut-dress, I had to do something to protect you. I mean, cover yourself up. Have you no respect?"

Josie smoothed down her blue dress, which was admittedly a bit cleavage-exposing, but nothing outrageous. "What's wrong with it?"

David bared his teeth and ruffled her hair, messing it up. "I'm joshing. And it's thanks a lot, not thanks a bunch. Now go be nice to the Real Housewives of Islington — I'm off for a pint."

"It's my round. What are you having?"

"Thank you, but if I let people buy me drinks all night, I'll never get to chat up that hot redhead at the bar. Wish me luck." He made for the bar, slightly unsteady.

"Good luck!" Josie called after him.

She watched him push somewhat obnoxiously past a couple of people ahead of him at the bar, maneuvering himself next to a pretty girl with flame-red hair who was waiting for a drink. He said something to her, and she turned to him, an eyebrow arched. Then her face broke into a smile. He was a charming bastard, Josie thought with an inward laugh, and kept watching.

They were in a packed, ancient pub on Fleet Street in the heart of London. But as far as Josie was concerned, there could be nobody here but her and David. To be able to celebrate New Year's Eve with him, when he had died more than two years ago . . . it was beyond miraculous.

Her brother's miraculous resurrection had distracted her over the past weeks. It was almost enough for her to stop thinking about where Rob might be, or who with, this New Year's Eve. Almost. But increasingly, as her return to New York approached, she'd been thinking about her husband again.

In this world, she figured Rob was spending the holidays with the glamorous Surin. Horrible as it was, that thought at least made some kind of sense. After all, here, Rob didn't even know her.

But what about in the world she'd left behind?

Had Josie simply disappeared from that Rob's life?

Or had she *switched places* with another version of herself — the Josie who really lived in Brooklyn and whose brother was alive?

Was that Other Josie with her husband, right now?

Had she kissed him at midnight?

Josie swallowed. There was a familiar knot in her stomach, but her dark reveries were interrupted by someone putting their hands over her eyes. "Guess who?" said a gruff, male voice she instantly recognized.

"Charlie!"

She grabbed the hands and turned. Her ginger-haired cousin stood before her, in an expensive suit, his ruddy face flushed from the neck up, very much alive and well. She flung her arms around him, hugging him tightly, which caught him a little off guard, as they had never been particularly close.

"Man, it's so good to see you!"

"Good to see you too, cuz! Wow, that's a warm welcome." He grinned at her, uncertainly. "Hey, so this is Zoe, my girlfriend."

A petite girl with light brown hair stood behind him, seeming overwhelmed as she tried to avoid David's increasingly inebriated friends and their sloshing pints. She smiled at Josie. "Hi, Josie. You might not remember me."

"Hi. I'm sorry, I don't . . ."

Charlie came to Josie's rescue, telling Zoe, "Yeah, remember, baby, the timing of when you and I met, it's all in the period Josie has lost. Right, Jose?"

Josie nodded, still trying to process seeing her previously dead cousin standing alive in front of her. This was the first time she'd seen him since Maui, the day after her wedding. Just two days before he and David died.

Josie turned to Zoe. "It's nothing personal. Lots of friends, my job, my apartment, I can't remember any of them."

Zoe smiled forgivingly.

"I'm off to the bar," Charlie announced. "Bottle of Sauvignon Blanc suit you ladies? Oh, man, check out David chatting up that girl. He's *in* there."

David was now in deep conversation with the redhead. He glanced up, noticed them looking at him, and flashed them a winning smile.

Josie and Zoe made small talk for a few minutes, but Josie's lack of memory and Zoe's shyness made for a stilted conversation. Charlie's arrival with wine in an ice bucket and a handful of glasses broke the awkward moment. He poured generous servings and raised his glass.

"Happy 2018! And to David, and his remarkable ability to pull gorgeous women wherever he goes." They all laughed and clinked glasses.

By 1.45 a.m., Josie and Zoe had become better friends, aided by the bottle of wine. Zoe and Charlie hugged Josie as they said their goodbyes. "How are you getting back to Waterloo?" her cousin asked. "You might be staying at David's place alone tonight."

Josie glanced over at her brother and the redhead. "No problem. I'll wait for an opportune moment and ask him what he's planning. You guys go. Nice to meet you, Zoe. Well, to see you again."

She checked her phone after they left, a digital comfort blanket when alone in a busy pub. To her surprise, it was flashing with a text she hadn't heard come in.

Peter
Hey, how's the UK? I hope you're having a good time with your family. Happy New Year! It's only 8 p.m. in NYC but I figure you've already had midnight. Lisa told me about amnesia from your accident. That totally explains why you didn't want to talk, and I get it would have been hard to explain you don't remember me. But I hope you'll have read our previous texts, so you can see we're good friends. I'm hoping you'll come back to choir when we start back on the 17th. We can get to know each other again. Until then, happy 2018! :P

Josie smiled in spite of herself. This guy did seem very sweet.

She glanced cross at David. At the bar, he was helping the pretty girl with her coat. Josie typed back:

> Yeah, great time thanks, Happy New Year too. I'm out with my brother and his buddies, but we're wrapping up now. I think I may have been ditched for a cute redhead, but we'll see! Flying back Jan 2, and yes, I think I'll come back to choir, so look forward to re-meeting you then. J

She hit send as David and the redhead came over to the high-top table. He leaned in toward Josie. "I'm walking Anna to her cab. You okay in here for two minutes?" She gave him a nod and smiled at Anna. They disappeared outside.

Josie flicked through her Instagram, posting a picture of the New Year's toast earlier, and heard her text ping again.

Happy to hear it. Safe travels. :P

"What are you smiling at?" David asked as he came back inside, bringing the cold with him.

"Texting a choir friend. So, you liked the redhead, huh?"

"Yeah. Sorry to abandon you to my braying banker friends, but she was too lovely." He waved a cocktail napkin in Josie's face. "Like, totally got her number," he added in a bad American drawl.

Josie laughed. "Well done, you. And thanks for your overwhelming concern, but I had a nice time with Charlie and his shy little heiress."

"Zoe's sweet, right? Much too good for Charlie. Well, perhaps now I can join her and Charlie in the world of happy coupledom. I'm telling you, Bosie — that Anna is something special. I'm not kidding, she could be The One. Except she's only here for another six months, then going back to Sydney, so . . ."

"Well, that's your favorite city, right? It's perfect. You should marry her and have redheaded babies that look like Charlie."

He grimaced, then nodded. "I think I might. Come on, let's go home, drink whiskey and binge-watch *Stranger Things* until dawn. No work tomorrow."

"And then I have to fly back the next day."

David frowned at Josie with a pretense of seriousness. "Yep, and go back to real life. Whatever that is."

CHAPTER 16

Early to mid-January

"Which button turns the mike off again? This one?" Josie asked Abby, the ultra-cool producer at the radio station.

"That's it. You'll pick it up." Abby's voice was warm with encouragement. "It's only a run-through, which we can either use as a canned edition or a training exercise. Give it a try, keep an eye on the timer, so you come out around fourteen minutes for the first break. Then Marcella will come in and chat about taxes. You've got your phone interview scheduled after the second break. I'll patch him through. Good to go."

Abby went into the production booth, giving a double thumbs-up after the door closed. The digital timer on the wall began to count up, and Josie inhaled deeply and put a chirpy smile on her face.

"Good morning, New York, and welcome to Open House here on Talk New York — your daily dose of real estate, development and housing issues. And what a show we've got for you today.

"I've got Talk New York's news director Marcella Grande in the studio for the latest on the pied-a-terre tax, and we'll be talking with developer Manny Bellman about the trend of adding housing on rooftops. But first, the hot issue of short-term rentals — are they contributing to our rental shortage? We want to know what you think. This is Open House after all. We're not taking live calls today, but you can email openhouse@talknewyork.com, text the studio at 555387 or leave a voicemail on the feedback line, the number is 212 . . ."

The time flew past, full of lively discussion, making for an interesting hour of talk radio. Josie felt she had a knack for it, although she thought the topic was probably one any interested person could speak at length about. She stumbled over some words but managed to stick to the timings and get all her cues in, as well as a teaser to an upcoming show.

"Man, that was awesome! See? Told you you'd be fine." Abby gave Josie a hug. "We can use that as a pre-taped edition, if you're off. The content will hold for a month or so. But you could have done it live, and you'd have been great. You good?"

Josie nodded, slightly stunned as realization dawned that she was an actual radio show host. "I'm fine." And she was. "As long as you get me a couple of talkative guests each day, I don't think it'll be a problem. That developer guy was ideal."

"It's what I'm here for. You find the stories you want to tackle, or I see something interesting, and I book the guests. Then you write a story for the website in the afternoon. Show in the morning, news story in the afternoon, and boom, you're done. Easy, right?" Abby's bright blue eyes sparkled under her black bangs.

"I think so." Josie smiled at the young woman's enthusiasm. "Yes. I can do it."

"Course you can. Want to get a drink? I think we're done for the day."

It was tempting. "Thanks, but I'm still kind of jet-lagged, and learning a new job at the same time is wiping me out. Maybe tomorrow night, as it's a Friday?"

"Sure. Rest up." Abby was already looking at the clipboard in front of her. "See you tomorrow and we'll find a bunch more guests for when we go live next week."

Josie grabbed her puffy winter coat and left the radio station on Second Avenue, hurrying through the cold to the nearest subway on 33rd. It was only 4.30 in the afternoon, so rush hour was not yet in full swing. The streets were quiet by New York standards and a little shabbier than the neighborhood she had become accustomed to while working at H&F's Spring Street offices.

She experimented with a different route home than she'd taken after her first day yesterday — taking the 6 farther south than Google recommended, then changing to the M, getting out at Marcy Avenue in Williamsburg instead of going to Bedford. It was a longer journey and a longer walk to her place, but if she took the L to Bedford, that would mean transferring at Union Square. And yesterday, she had found it pretty difficult not to exit at Union Square, cross the street to the building that still felt like her true home, and beg Ed to let her talk to Rob. Not wanting to come across as a crazy stalker, Josie figured it was better to avoid that neighborhood entirely.

It was dark when she emerged from Marcy Avenue, and she bundled up against the chilly evening, wrapping a thick scarf around her neck and donning gloves, to walk the fifteen minutes to her building.

Back in the apartment, she turned on the little gas fireplace in her living room, quickly made a cup of tea and fired up her laptop. The digital journal she had started in London was already proving the best outlet for her thoughts, helping her to maintain her calm.

In the beginning, I was so distracted and overjoyed at having David back in my life, it seemed like I was taking a break from my real life with Rob. All I wanted to do was be in Cornwall with my resurrected brother, and that's what I did. I had what was, in many ways, the best Christmas of my life. Not only with David, but spending quality time with Mum, Laura, and little Theo was also to be treasured.

But I've really been missing Rob badly since Christmas Day. That evening, in front of the fire, when we all opened our presents, as David passed around the gift-giving Santa hat, watching Laura being so loving with Adam, I missed Rob so much I almost cried right there in the living room. Later that night in the blue room, I let myself weep for him.

And let myself feel angry, too — jealous he was with another woman, the gorgeous Surin, probably celebrating Christmas with her, possibly also with Andrew and Kim. My parents-in-law. Mine!

The real kicker, though, is that I don't think it's only Surin I'm jealous of — although I am, without doubt, jealous of Surin. Another thought has been developing in my mind, growing in strength.

Josie hesitated, unsure of whether to put down in words the fear that had been gnawing away at her insides. As if writing it down would make it true. She screwed up her face and forced her fingers to move across the keys.

The idea of there being another me. A totally separate version of myself, living my life, as I'm living hers.

I didn't even think of it the first few weeks. I guess being jolted into this version of reality, my amazing reunion with David and the craziness of the whole situation, took up all the space in my head. But on Christmas Day when we were opening gifts, I started thinking about what happened to my old life. Then more on New Year's Eve, watching couples kissing around me in that pub in London.

Is there another me — a version of myself with whom I swapped lives? And what happened to those gifts I ordered, a trip away in Washington State for me and Rob, a designer scarf for Kim, and signed book for Andrew? Did Other Josie give them to them? Did she take credit from them? I feel like I'm going mad, trying to separate out my old life from this one.

I know my life with Rob was real — I lived it. And it is clear that this new version of my life is also real — but a different version of me has lived it. Since I have been somehow derailed into this Other Me's life, it stands to reason She also exists.

If that is true, I know what it means.

It means the Other Me is with Rob. Probably living in our apartment. Of course, she knows Rob is not her husband. <u>She</u> never married him. She is really single and lives in Brooklyn and is a radio show host and has a brother who is alive. Presumably that's a life she wants to return to. After all, she wouldn't even recognize Rob, let alone love him. Other Me might even have been in love with someone else in her Brooklyn life, before the accident. Maybe this Peter guy, who definitely seems interested. Maybe Other Me wants to get back to this life.

Or maybe she doesn't. She is still <u>me</u>, after all. And I fell in love with Rob almost instantly. The night we met, my 33rd birthday, I thought he was some jobbing pianist, playing the bars and hotel lobbies to make ends meet. Whereas Other Me, if she exists, has landed, Dorothy-like, straight into a lavish world of penthouses and parties, with a gorgeous, rich, instant husband who utterly adores her. That has to be almost impossible to resist.

Josie reached for a blanket and wrapped it around her knees, shivering despite the warmth of the gas fire, and kept typing.

Or does he adore her?

Maybe he's figured out she isn't his real wife. Or maybe she's even confessed it to him, made him believe her and understand

164

his true wife is . . . somewhere else. Somewhere lost to him, but thinking about him and missing him. I know myself well enough, and I'd be honest in that situation. I wouldn't lie to a nice man who didn't know any better. And I wouldn't betray myself. Would I?

Are they together? What are they doing? Did they kiss on New Year's Eve? Are they sleeping together?

It makes me sick to think about it. I can almost stomach the idea of Rob with Surin — after all, this world's version of Rob doesn't know I even exist, so there is no betrayal. But the idea of my own Rob, my own husband, sleeping with an impostor, who looks and sounds and thinks like me, is repulsive.

How could he? How could She?

And then there's David. Just as in this world, David's alive; in my world, he isn't. How will she be able to bear that?

Josie couldn't stand it. It was past seven, and she'd been sitting for almost two hours, obsessing. She grilled chicken and veggies for dinner and ate in front of a recorded episode of *Outlander*. Things could be worse. She hadn't gotten stuck in a different time entirely, hundreds of years ago. She was still in the same century, the same kind of world. Her favorite TV shows to distract her.

She'd make it work. She had to.

For now.

* * *

Josie bit her lip and picked up the handset of her cubicle's phone. She missed having a private office to make calls in, but at least nobody was paying her attention. Abby usually made bookings, but this was one she wanted to do herself.

She dialed the number from the results of the online search on her computer screen.

"B+B Developments, how may I direct your call?" a chirpy female voice asked her.

"Hi, yeah, this is Josie Cavendish of Talk New York. Could I speak to, to Robert Billing's office, please?"

She winced. Could she really do this?

"One moment."

An agonizing few seconds passed a voice she recognized came on the line.

"Robert Billing's office, how may I help you?"

It was Dolores, Rob's faithful assistant since years before Josie came along.

"Oh hi, D — hi there. My name is Josie Cavendish and I'm the host of the Open House radio show on Talk New York. I was wondering . . . that is, I'd like to invite Mr. Billing into the station to be a live guest on the show one morning, if he's interested? I understand the Cav — the Union House building has sold its last unit and the company is starting a Tribeca project. I'm sure the listeners would be very interested in . . ." she trailed off.

"Sure, I'll pass that invitation on to him. He'll want to run it by our PR manager, so she'll be in touch. Can I get a number or email?"

"Right, sure. It's usually my producer, Abby Crawford, who does the guest bookings, so let me give you her details, and if your PR manager could email her and copy me, that would be perfect."

Josie reeled off the contact details then hung up, her heart racing. She'd done it. Really done it.

She bit her lip. Was she being stupid? But it was the only legitimate way she could think of to meet Rob and talk to him, to figure out if anything could happen between them. But he had a girlfriend, a stunning one, and he didn't know Josie at all. Why would he be interested in her after one radio interview?

Then she remembered the look they'd exchanged as he sat at that piano in the W Hotel lobby. He'd fallen in love with her before, almost instantaneously. He could do it again. It was surely worth a shot?

Josie looked at her phone — it was after five. Everyone in the station was wrapping up, apart from the evening producers and a couple of others. She had to be on the Lower East Side for rehearsal by six. The sidewalks were horribly icy, so she wanted to give herself time, and it had been too dangerous to commute on the new pale-gray bike she'd bought herself last week.

She bundled up and made her way unsteadily to the subway at 32nd, taking the train five stops south. The rehearsal space was walkable from there, but she wasn't taking any chances on the streets, so she transferred to get to the nearest station. As she passed a busker on the platform singing "It's Cold Outside", she wondered what had become of the holiday party she and Angela had arranged for Halstein & Faust and B+B, just two blocks away at Lafayette Restaurant.

They had probably gone ahead with it. Angela was likely H&F's comms manager in this world, since Josie was not. She should call Angela and invite Hans to come on her show, too. That'd be a blast.

Josie laughed out loud as she pushed onto the packed F train, startling a woman squeezing on next to her. She smiled at the woman, sheepish, then giggled again.

She could really mess with people's heads — Rob, Hans, Mike, Josh, everyone. She knew so much about them, and they didn't know her at all. But the thought saddened Josie as quickly as it had amused her. The people she loved didn't know her.

She exited the subway at Essex Street and treaded carefully down the slippery sidewalk to the church that rented the choir their rehearsal space. Inside, it was far too hot, and she stripped off her puffy coat and long cardigan, finding a clip to lift her hair and cool the back of her neck.

With members running late because of the roads, only a few others had arrived. She vaguely recognized the tall guy who had been texting her, Peter, setting up chairs under the watchful eye of the director. He paused, a chair in each hand, and caught Josie's eye. He walked toward her, a little too close, putting a chair down next to her.

"You missed a bit." Peter reached up, taking a stray, damp strand of Josie's hair in his fingers, adding it to the ponytail she'd just made. His hand grazed her neck as he did so.

Their eyes met. Josie stepped back from him, surprised, suddenly aware of her bare arms and dewy décolletage.

"Thanks," she muttered.

"You're welcome." He gave a small smile, then broke eye contact, and continued to arrange chairs.

It was an overly familiar gesture from someone whom, as far as Josie was concerned, she had only met once. It had been during intermission at the choir's concert last summer, which she and Rob attended. She remembered Lisa introducing them to Peter and a beautiful Black woman called Michelle, who seemed to be his partner. He'd said he was a videogame designer and part-time musician, but that was all she knew of him. Aside from what was in their recent texts, of course.

Josie concentrated on singing, which she found invigorating and calming at the same time, forgetting about the exchange. But at the break she was distracted by Peter as he chatted with the basses on the other side of the room. He was looking right at her — almost as though he were talking about her. Josie turned away. Sure, he was attractive, in a geek-chic kind of way, with that tall, lanky stance, the sandy complexion and those black-framed glasses. But Josie was married. Sort of.

She stepped toward Lisa to find her friend looking between Josie and Peter and back again.

"Hey," Lisa breathed, close to Josie's ear. "Peter can't stop staring at you. Like, not even hiding it!" She leaned around Josie to examine him again.

"Stop it." Josie felt like a teenager. "You'll encourage him."

"And why not?" Lisa raised her eyebrows. "When was the last time you got some, huh? He's so cute! And he's not with Michelle anymore. Oh, you won't remember her. Or even him, I guess. But take my word for it, he's single now, and you guys have got close. I'll get you sitting next to him at the bar later and—"

"No! I'm not interested, okay? You flirt with him, if you think he's cute."

"Well, maybe I will! But I'm not the one he likes, am I?" she muttered, as the director started up again. "He just moved to Williamsburg, too." The director turned to glare at them, and Josie felt like a teenager misbehaving for the second time.

"When you're done gossiping." Kathryn's disapproval was obvious. "I have solo and ensemble parts to work out for the summer show. In the fall, we had been rehearsing Peter and Josie for the duet 'Can't Sleep Love' — Josie, first, welcome back. I know you've lost your memories of the past few seasons, but the song was working very well with your voices together. Are you up for relearning your part and doing some extra rehearsals?"

"W–we were? Sorry, I didn't . . . didn't realize," Josie stuttered. Lisa nudged her and gave her an encouraging wink.

Josie sighed. "Well, I don't want to let anyone down . . ." Out of the corner of her eye, she caught Peter grinning at her from across the room.

"Atta girl," Kathryn approved. "We can start rehearsing it in a few weeks. Hopefully it will all come flooding back. Next up, who's throwing in their hat for the 'All That Jazz' solo?"

By 9.30, the choir was pouring into The Late Late bar and Josie made a point of sitting far from Peter, who was still throwing glances her way. She avoided his looks, introducing herself to some of the women while Lisa sat at the other end of the table with the guys.

After a large glass of wine, Josie considered the journey across the Williamsburg Bridge to home. An easy walk in the summer, but not in this weather. As a subway ride it was only one stop on the M, but then involved sliding along the sidewalks for fifteen minutes, walking home from Marcy.

Not an appealing prospect. As she put on her thick coat, Josie fired up a ride–share app on her phone.

"Hey, Jose," called Lisa from the other end of the table. "You leaving? I found a ride for you." Next to her, Peter stood up and put on a heavy, dark coat that looked great with his fair skin and black glasses.

He raised his eyebrows at Josie. "Need a ride over the bridge?"

"Oh, no. I don't want you to go out of your way. I can get a car, it's no problem."

"Don't worry about it. I recently moved right by the Nitehawk Theatre, so it's easy for me to drop you. I know where you live, I've given you a ride many times. Ready?"

Having been given little choice, Josie nodded. She let Peter lead her out of the pub, throwing a glare back at Lisa, who was grinning widely.

It was even colder outside now, and Josie admitted to herself that she was glad of the ride, even if it was awkward. She didn't want to encourage this guy, so she was a little frosty as she got into Peter's car, a restored old Chevrolet.

Peter was chatty, telling Josie about the duet they had been rehearsing before her accident, and about the apartment he had moved into before the holidays, seemingly oblivious to the curtness of Josie's responses.

They were at her place in a mercifully short amount of time. As she thanked him and reached to open the door, Peter put a hand on Josie's arm, stalling her.

"I get that you're struggling with amnesia, but . . . you and I were close friends before your memory loss. And I think it was about to turn into something more, when I broke up with my girlfriend and moved out. I'm betting you've seen our texts from before your accident, so you can probably see there was something developing between us." He paused.

"But even if you never remember, that's okay. We can start from scratch. We live so close, we can keep it simple, start by hanging out outside rehearsals." He gave her a warm smile. "Are you busy Friday? There's a jazz band playing at a little neighborhood joint — you'd like them."

Josie played with this tassel on her purse. This was awkward. "Thanks, but I'd better not."

"Ah, it'd be fun. You still like live music, don't you?"

"Yeah, of course, but . . ." She hesitated. "I realize you think you know me, but I don't know you. I'm sorry. I'm not being rude, I'm just not in a place to date anyone. And it kinda sounds like a date. So, I appreciate the invitation, but I can't. Thanks, though. And for the ride."

"No problem," Peter murmured as Josie got out of the car.

When he didn't drive away, Josie realized he was waiting to make sure she got inside. Her fingers fumbled over the keys in the frigid air, and as the heavy door opened, she finally heard his car move off.

She didn't look back.

CHAPTER 17

Valentine's Day

Josie peered out through the glass of the studio at the station's reception area, where Rob was kicking back on a vintage leather couch, reading a copy of *The Times*. She had nearly lost the thread of her live telephone interview with the city planner when she'd seen him walk in ten minutes previously, and she was barely keeping it together. She glanced at the production booth, where Abby was giving her a "what the hell?" expression.

"Thirty seconds to news," she said in Josie's headset, glaring at her.

"So . . . thanks for talking with us today, Daniel, and I guess, please keep us updated on the rezoning process. Okay then. You're listening to the Open House show on Talk New York, and I'm Josie Cavendish, we've got a slice of news for you right now. Coming up after the break, one of our city's leading developers on his plans for luxury residential projects around the city, including the buzz on the new lofts soon to be built in Tribeca. We'll be right back."

Abby burst into the studio. "What is *with* you? You didn't even ask about the protests, which I thought was the whole point."

"Sorry. I'm distracted. I'll pull it together, I promise."

One of the interns was getting Rob's attention, and he gathered up his coat and made for the studio.

Oh God. This was really happening.

Abby frowned. "Okay, so next up is Robert Billing, the developer you wanted to talk to. Why this guy?"

"Oh, cool lofts, high-end, nice to have some glamorous stuff . . ." Josie trailed off as the intern let Rob inside.

Abby shook Rob's hand as she departed the glass studio, pointing him in Josie's direction. He strode toward her, fearlessly, unknowingly, with a big smile.

"Rob Billing." He held out his hand with all the dignified ease of a major CEO.

It took Josie a moment to take it. It was so incredible to be up close again, even if all she got was a handshake. She'd almost forgotten how magnetic the sheer physical presence of this tall, broad man could be. His silky black hair was cropped a little closer than usual, and his beard was even neater than when she'd last seen him. But his dark brown eyes had as much soul and depth as ever under those enviable lashes.

She grabbed his hand formally, like they'd never met. "Josie Cavendish." She took a deep breath, smiled. "Please, sit here. These will be your headphones. We still have a couple of minutes for the commercials."

He settled into the chair and picked up the headphones. "So, we're sticking with the talking points we arranged, right?"

"Absolutely, I gave D — your team my key questions, mostly about your upcoming projects, but also some of the objections raised in the Tribeca public consultation, as well as how your luxury homes fit into the overall housing need. I hope you're still good with all that."

"Sure, fine." He smiled broadly.

Her guts were doing somersaults.

"*One minute*," Abby's voice warned over the intercom.

Josie put on her headphones, smoothing her hair back. She tried to calm her breathing. Rob was saying something to her, and she lifted up one earpiece. "Sorry? We have less than a minute until we're live."

"Right, I was saying . . . Do I know you? I feel like we've met before, right?"

Her heart leaped, but she feigned surprise. "No, I don't think so. Maybe at some real estate conference—"

"*Thirty seconds.*"

She added, "You should put the headphones on, and you can adjust the volume there."

He seemed to be thinking about her response and finally put on his headphones.

"*And we're back in five, four, three, two, one . . .*"

"Welcome back to Open House on Talk New York and good morning. You're listening to Josie Cavendish, and I'm here today with my next guest, Rob — Robert Billing of B+B Developments, a luxury developer with exciting but sometimes controversial residential projects here in Manhattan. Robert, welcome, and thank you for coming into the studio today."

"My pleasure, Josie, and it's Rob, please."

"Thank you, Rob. I want to talk about your company, B+B Developments, and the projects you've got upcoming, but of course, we want to know what you folks out there think, or whether you have any questions — this is Open House, after all. Give us a call, the number is 212 . . ."

Twenty minutes later, the show concluded with a rendition of "Home" by Philip Philips. Rob took off his headphones and pushed back his chair with a laugh.

"That was fun! I thought you'd take it a bit easier on me, I have to admit. How'd I do?"

It *had* been fun. Once into the interview, on a topic she knew well, and with a man she knew intimately and exactly how much to challenge, the conversation had flowed. Abby gave the double thumbs-up through the glass.

"You were great," Josie told him. "I also have to write a story on your Tribeca lofts for our website, and I was waiting for this conversation to get some quotes from you. You've given me tons of material."

"That's good. I mean, I'm glad you've got your quotes, but there's a lot more to the Tribeca story than I told you on air. There wasn't the time." He checked his watch. "Are you free now? I don't have to be anywhere for a while. You want more on the public consultation aspect?"

Josie's heart did its schoolgirl flip again. Sure, she wanted more on the story, but more than anything, she wanted time with Rob. So he could fall in love with her.

"Thank you — that would be great. Should we go for coffee? I don't have a private office, and it's a bit crazy in the newsroom."

"Sure." He picked up his coat and a brown leather satchel Josie didn't recognize and gestured to the door. "Lead the way."

Abby raised her eyebrows as Josie and Rob left together. "Rob and I are going for coffee. He's got more on the Tribeca development to share. Back later."

"Take your time," she called after them.

Josie walked him to her favorite coffee place, and he took a seat at a table as she stood at the counter. "My treat. Grande latte?" she asked him, then winced at her familiarity as he looked at her curiously.

"Thanks, yes. How'd you know?" The coffee menu had dozens of options, so it was a fair question. She needed to be more careful.

"Oh, you seem like a latte kind of guy." She turned away, embarrassed, and placed the order for two large lattes.

You seem like a latte kind of guy? What did that even mean?

Sitting down with the coffees, and remembering to ask him if he wanted sugar, Josie stirred Splenda into her cup, focusing on the task longer than necessary. The table was tiny, their knees touching, and the space was intimate. A live, on-air interview was very public, but this . . .

"So," Josie began, "what else can you tell me?"

He spoke with her for more than an hour, offering details about protestors objecting to the gentrification of a warehouse they said should have become social housing, including death threats he received. He shared things about his past career Josie already knew about, and some things even she didn't know, which was a surprise. He gave her a great story and waited patiently as she made notes and checked quotes back with him, looking at her the entire time.

"You're sure we've never met?" he asked again. "I really feel like I've seen you before."

His unabashed gaze made Josie's whole body shiver. "Not that I remember, but like I say, we've probably been at the same events."

Rob smiled, absently. He didn't look convinced. "Well, it's been fun talking with you, Josie. I'm sorry it was about me most of the time. I'm sure you've got even more interesting tales to tell. How you came to be in New York, after growing up in England."

He glanced at the clock above the counter and Josie followed his gaze. 11.45. Josie panicked that he would leave, and that would be it. No more reason to call or see him, unless they bumped into each other at work events. Mere industry acquaintances.

She attempted a winning smile. "Sure I do. Hey, why don't you stay for lunch? The food is pretty tasty. I can regale you with tales from the Motherland."

Rob smiled back, and surprised Josie by putting a hand on her arm. "I'd love to. But I have to meet my girlfriend, and she *hates* it when I'm late. We're helping organize a big Valentine party tonight with the *Luxury Listing* folks, so it's a big day. As fun as lunch with you would be, I have to take a raincheck."

Josie flushed, humiliated that she had asked the man she loved, her own husband, out for lunch, and he'd said no. To set up a Valentine party with his girlfriend. She wanted to cry.

They rose, and he held up her coat. The simple, familiar gesture, one Josie was so accustomed to him doing for her, nearly made her break down. She wanted to turn in his arms, take his face in her hands, kiss him, and beg him to recognize her as his wife.

Instead she shrugged on the coat, thanked him, and left with as much dignity as she could muster. Back at the station, she headed straight for the accessible washroom, where she let the sobs come.

CHAPTER 18

Mid-March

Josie woke in a cold sweat in the dead of night, the street-lights outside her little apartment casting an unnatural glow.

Moments before, she had been on the terrace of her and Rob's home, the sun setting in violent colors over the city. At the far end of the terrace, a couple embraced, indistinguishable in the fading light. They were kissing by the railing, their lovely figures creating a silhouette against the red sky. As she got closer, she saw the couple was Rob and Surin. They turned to her and smiled, smug in their happiness. They kissed again, and Surin's face blended into Rob's, her face morphing, shifting form to become Josie's. But the Other Josie. Kissing Rob. They turned to Josie again and laughed. Laughed and laughed at her. She fled inside, tripping, falling, smashing her face, crimson blood seeping onto the white tile.

She turned on the lamp beside the bed, trying to calm herself. Only a dream. It was 3.12 a.m. She took a sip of water and reached for the sleep remedy she now kept on hand.

She had been distraught for weeks, ever since interviewing Rob. As if that meeting had been her one hope to win him over and make him hers again. The day after Valentine's

Day, she'd read on Page 6 about the party to celebrate the final episode of *Luxury Listing*, hosted at Hans and Mike's place. There was a photo of Surin in a tight, fuchsia-pink dress, a rose in her dark hair, clinging to Rob.

But in truth, it wasn't Surin that Josie was picturing being with Rob. After their coffee chat, and the realization he didn't know her, and really did have a girlfriend, Josie acknowledged that this guy wasn't her Rob. Her own Rob, her husband, already loved her — and this man didn't.

No, since Valentine's Day, what was overwhelming her was the sense of the Other Josie being with her husband in the life she'd left behind.

What were they doing? Were they also having a party, in which She was the hostess? Were they a couple now, even though Other Josie knew Rob wasn't really her husband?

Sleep was no relief: the nightmares had begun that same night. Always the two of them, kissing, laughing at her. Other Josie, knowing she'd stolen Josie's husband, but doing it anyway. And Rob, knowing the woman in his arms wasn't his true wife, still choosing her.

The sleep meds kicked in and she got a few more hours of rest before rising for work, tired and irritable, her back sore. She'd forgotten how not having a super-expensive mattress hurt her back. Josie resolved to save for an upgrade, but she was still paying off her month-long Christmas trip to the UK, as well as Jean Grey, her other major indulgence, the bike she'd bought to replace Electra.

Under the tiny but hot shower, Josie's thoughts turned to the theory she'd been pondering since her stay at Suzie's after the accident. The idea that the intersection at Third and 25th, where she'd nearly hit those college students on the way to the conference at which she'd first met Rob, was some kind of parallel timeline soft spot, a tear in the fabric of the universe, created by that near-miss accident three years ago. A moment in which her life had split, where in another reality, she had hit those students and never made it to the conference, and therefore missed meeting Rob.

One life path had forked into two possibilities in that instant. So when both Josies crashed on the same day at the exact same spot, on her birthday, it was enough to merge the universes for a second, and each Josie had ended up in the wrong life. Of course, the idea was preposterous . . .

But if it were true, it also meant that same intersection was the key to Josie getting back to her own life. If returning to her reality was what she wanted, of course. Yes, she could maybe get back to her Rob — but she would lose David again.

At the radio station, she tried to let the routine of work distract from the memory of her nightmares, which still clung to her like a bad smell. But even lunch with Abby did little to improve her mood. It was only when her phone dinged around 4 p.m. that she felt a tiny hit of endorphin.

David

Hey kiddo, hope you're good. Wanted to let you know Anna and I have booked our flights! We're arriving JFK April 12, give us a chance to get over jet lag before the big celebration. Can't believe I'm getting old!! 40 is the new 30, I guess. :O Mum and Laura etc. have already booked flights and I've sorted their hotel. Glad you'll be putting me and Anna up, it's pricey enough paying for their accomms. ':O Gonna be fun, NYC here we come! :D

Josie smiled. Anna, the redhead David had met on New Year's Eve, seemed to be quite the fixture in his life these days. Perhaps they were getting serious — a first for David. It was certainly a big step for Anna to be part of this family visit next month.

She typed back:

Look out, Brooklyn, the Cavendish clan is descending en masse! Looking forward

to it, old man. Got your pressie already,
don't expect anything fancy just cos it's
your 40th — I'm broke right now. Your
presents will have to be our presence! Ha,
maybe not completely. Jx

The prospect of having her whole family stay in Brooklyn
for David's 40th was just the uplift Josie needed. David had
insisted on them all being together for the big day and had
even offered to pay for the others' hotel in Williamsburg.
Laura and Adam, who hadn't been to New York since before
Theo, and were always keen on a good deal, had jumped at
the chance. Of course, that meant their mother was easily
persuaded.

Josie's spirit was a little brighter riding down to the
Lower East Side for rehearsal. At least it wasn't dark and
cold, as it had been for months. The evening was warmer
than usual, and it was nice to be arriving at the church in
daylight. Josie fastened Jean Grey to the railings and went
inside. Singing would make her feel better.

She was a little early. The basses were running through
their comedic take on "All About That Bass" when she arrived.
She sat in a corner, watching them, enjoying it. Peter, by far
the tallest, was in the middle, and revved up his performance
when he saw her. He grinned during the line, "And I can
make you swoon, like I'm supposed to do," and pointed at
her. The other basses nudged each other and waggled their
eyebrows. Sure, it was all part of the skit that they'd do that
to some other woman in the audience in the real performance.
But it made her laugh. Peter was good at making her laugh.

Throughout the rehearsal, he was in fine form, making frequent wisecracks. At one point, when he was being
reprimanded for talking, he gave Josie a conspiratorial wink
when the director's back was turned. Josie laughed out loud,
and the director whipped around to glare at her too. Josie
made a face at Peter for getting her into trouble, and they
both grinned.

With Josie still catching up on their duet, the two of them stayed behind afterward, along with the director, to rehearse "Can't Sleep Love" for the summer show. Emboldened by their earlier camaraderie, Peter took Josie's hands in both of his and sang words of love and passion right to her face, making her blush and stumble over her lyrics.

By the time they were done, it was after ten, and though tired, Josie was more cheerful than she had been in weeks. She slipped outside while Peter was helping the director close up and went to unlock Jean Grey from the railings.

Oh, crap.

The wheels had been stolen.

Josie was so accustomed to locking Electra anywhere, always safe because of her security locks, she'd forgotten to be careful with the new bike until she had the same locks added.

"*Fuck!*" Josie cursed out loud.

"Now, now, young lady. You realize this is a place of worship?" Peter's voice came from behind her.

"Sorry. My wheels have been nicked."

"Oh shit. They have, as you say, been 'nicked'. That's too bad." He looked around. "How will you get home? I'd offer you a ride, but my car's in the shop, so I'm walking."

"I could walk too. It's not too far, and it's not cold. I'll have to leave Jean Grey here until I can take her to a shop. There's one nearby, I think."

"And one by your place, right? On Bedford? That'd be easier."

"Yeah, but I can't get her there," Josie pointed out. "No wheels. I don't think I can get her inside a cab."

"She's pretty light, I can carry her to yours, if you want."

"Really? Yes, thank you." Josie didn't bother to mask her relief.

She unlocked the bike. Peter took the frame, hooking it over his shoulder, carrying it as if it weighed nothing. They started walking.

"So . . . Jean Grey? Your bike is a she and has a name?"

"Yes. They're always Marvel superheroes. In London, there was Lady Sif, who now belongs to my sister and is sorely neglected, and then when I got to New York, there was Electra, who died in my accident a few months ago. And now Jean Grey."

"Right. How's it going, with your amnesia?"

"It's . . . tough. There are lots of people I don't remember. I didn't even know my job, or my apartment. I lost memories from around fall 2014. All the people I've worked with, or met since then, I don't recognize. Even though I've told people I have amnesia, they still feel hurt I don't remember them. Like they should have left some indelible mark."

"You mean, like me." He smiled, hitching the bike farther onto his shoulder.

Josie grimaced. "Sorry, I didn't mean—"

"I know. No offense taken."

"Are you sure you're okay with that bike?" she asked. "We've got the whole bridge to cross."

"I'm great," he insisted. "Couldn't leave Jean Grey alone and naked on the Lower East Side, could we?"

On the walk home, Peter proved a warm companion, asking thoughtful questions about the effects of Josie's supposed amnesia but also teasing her about her memory. In rehearsals, Peter had emerged as the charismatic class clown — but in their duet rehearsals and one-on-one, he was considerate and kind, even nurturing, while still often a bit silly. Josie was beginning to realize she liked him, as a person, very much.

At the apex of the bridge, they stopped for a moment, looking north over the city lights. "I need to switch arms. Walk on the other side of me."

They continued down the other side of the bridge, walking more slowly, enjoying each other's company. Peter was talking about the funk band he played guitar with on weekends, when he suddenly changed topic.

"Hey, remember that first rehearsal. I gave you a ride home and asked if you wanted to see a gig with me, and you said you weren't in the right place to date?"

"Yes . . ."

Where was this going?

"Was that because you were feeling messed up by your amnesia? I guess it wasn't long after your accident."

Josie wanted to confide in him — but she couldn't tell him the truth, of course.

"It wasn't only that," she admitted, after a moment. "The accident was a big part of it, psychologically. But I also wasn't feeling emotionally ready to date anyone. I was . . . involved with someone. I'm still not over that."

"Oh. You mean, you were involved with someone at the time of your last memory?"

Yet one more thing she hadn't thought through.

"Uh, yes. From before. But to me, it feels like a few months ago. We loved each other, and then I wake up from an accident and he's no longer in my life. I don't know what happened. And my friends haven't been able to help."

"Man, that would suck. But I guess if he wasn't still in your life and your friends don't know about him, he wasn't a serious boyfriend, right? Wait . . . Was it an affair?"

Josie sighed, wondering what hole she was digging for herself. But it was the best half-truth she could give him. "He was married. But I loved him, and last I knew, he loved me too. Before my amnesia."

Peter nodded, his face lit by the off-ramp streetlights. "That would suck," he said again.

At Josie's building's side entrance, Peter deposited the bike in the storage unit, then waited as Josie locked the door.

"Thanks for carrying my bike, it was kind of you. Drinks on me next week."

Peter smiled in the dim light. "I'll hold you to that, English." He turned away but stopped. "You know, that guy? I understand it still feels fresh for you, but he's long gone out of your life now. If he's not kicking down your door to be with you, and only you, then he's a fool. You deserve way better."

Peter hesitated, placed his hand on top of Josie's head and kissed her forehead.

"See you next week."

* * *

"Well, enough about the twins. What's the deal with this Peter dude, then? You keep mentioning him and you're obviously having fun rehearsing this duet." Suzie slurped her third post-work martini at the high-top table.

"God, you're as bad as Lisa. Peter's a lot of fun and super smart — I like chatting with him. He lives nearby, so he drives me home sometimes, and once he walked with me, but I'm usually on my bike. We're friends. Not even that, really, since we don't hang out outside choir. Friendly choir buddies."

Suzie arched a well-plucked eyebrow. "Well, I remember him from your show last year and he is super-fine, so you should get this guy out of the friend zone and into the sack. He clearly likes you. What's the issue? When was the last time you got laid, girl?"

Josie sighed into the dregs of her mason-jar cocktail. Suzie had suggested they go out near her SoHo office instead of the usual haunts in Brooklyn, but Josie found herself exhausted by those kinds of places in a way she never used to when she was with Rob — and had money. She had become accustomed to unlimited room on her credit card for overpriced food and drinks, and getting a seemingly free car home. A home that had never seemed more than a few blocks away.

"You know what the issue is, Suze. I get that it's hard for you to hear, as it's not your version of events, but for me, I'm *married*. I keep telling you that."

Suzie nodded slowly. "I do believe you. At least, I believe you believe it, and that's enough for me. But sweetie, you told me about Rob coming your radio show, and him not knowing you. And that he has some hot girlfriend. So, in this life at least, you're single. Therefore totally allowed to date whoever you want."

Josie pressed her lips together. She didn't feel single. "I suppose so. I like Peter, but I'm not sure it feels right. Let's get the check, this place is crappy," she grumbled, "and I need to go to bed early."

Back home, Josie fired up her laptop to write her journal for the day. She scrolled back through the file to reread an entry from a couple of weeks back, which documented a moment that had been on her mind ever since. A chance encounter with Rob, on the street.

She'd been on Lexington Avenue, not far from the Chrysler Building, coming out of a restaurant where she had been having lunch with a work contact. They had shaken hands goodbye, when she had turned and nearly bumped into Rob on the corner. They were close to his office, but Josie had barely even thought about Rob that day, or the fact he worked nearby.

Rob stopped short. He looked like he was stepping out for some lunch, and seemed as surprised to see Josie as she was.

"Josie. Hey. It's good to run into you."

Josie didn't know whether to expect a handshake, but she was surprised when he took her shoulders and leaned in for a chaste kiss on the cheek. Standard practice, perhaps, with female acquaintances.

She forced herself to sound calm. "Hey, Rob. How are you doing?"

"Fine. I kept meaning to tell you, I read your online piece after our interview. It was great. Very balanced."

"Oh — thanks. I appreciated the story. We don't get a lot of exclusives, being a radio station."

"Glad to help. Were you in there for lunch?"

"Yeah, I've gotta get back to the station. You going in?"

He nodded, gesturing over his shoulder. "Yeah, Surin and I are grabbing a bite before heading off to the Hamptons."

It was then Josie realized that one of the two women chatting behind Rob was Surin, chic in a cream skirt suit and huge black sunglasses, inappropriate on a cloudy March day. Surin had said goodbye to the other woman and walked up to them, removing the shades and linking a proprietary arm through Rob's. She examined Josie, waiting for an introduction.

"Honey, this is Josie Cavendish, the radio host who interviewed me a few weeks ago — you remember? Josie, this is my girlfriend, Surin Chan. She's a realtor, so you guys should connect. I'm sure Surin has a bunch of stories for you."

Surin had shown no sign of remembering being told about Josie. She offered a hand. "So nice to meet you."

"Great to meet you," Josie told her, even though that was far from the truth. "I know who your father is, of course. Let me give you my card . . ." She handed over her business card, which Surin eyed without reading, tightening her lips. Surin turned to Rob.

"Honey, we've got to eat if we're going to beat the traffic." She tugged his arm a little, and Josie saw him wince. But then he smiled at his girlfriend, then back at Josie.

"Good to see you, Josie. We'll connect when I've got more projects to talk about."

"I'll look forward to it. Nice to bump into you."

Surin put her sunglasses back on. "Awesome to meet you," she murmured, without a trace of feeling, as she led Rob away.

Even though Josie had been due back at work, she had walked into Grand Central to think about the encounter. She'd felt somehow detached.

Was it possible she was starting to get over Rob?

Josie wondered the same thing now. The nightmares, so acute in January and February, had calmed down. She was obsessing over him and Surin, even the possibility of him with another Josie, much less than before. Maybe she was beginning to move on.

As Josie pondered, her laptop pinged. She checked her emails, hoping for some distraction.

Distraction obliged, in the form of an email from Peter.

Hey. I've got two tickets for Lauryn Hill, booked months ago, and I need a date. Say you'll come with me! It's next Saturday night. My Easter gift to you. You did say you had no Easter plans . . . :P

Screw it.

She typed a reply, quickly, so she wouldn't change her mind.

Sure. It's a date. J

PART THREE: ME

CHAPTER 19

Early April

Apr 5, 2018
I realize now I've been in love with Rob for a couple of months. I just wasn't willing to admit it until this past, blissful weekend on Orcas Island. I can see how falling in love would have been virtually instantaneous between us, under normal circumstances — as it apparently was between him and the Other Me, when they met. I suppose it was only because of the shock of being catapulted into his world, and having to adjust to a new reality, that slowed my feelings down. That, and the crush I had on Peter at the time of the accident, and the hope he had raised in me about getting together. But with Peter still with Michelle and having a baby — at least in this world — and Rob being so wonderful . . . if I'm honest, I was pretty much in love with Rob by the end of January. Only two months into this new life.

I'm shocked at how easily I've adapted to this "new normal". I've taken over someone else's life, marriage, home, job and friends. In doing so, I've left most of my life behind — aside from a few consistent friends and family members, who are thankfully in both lives. But my Brooklyn home, my radio show, Peter and — most of all — my brother: I've abandoned them all for this new reality. And, aside from missing David desperately, I'm okay with it.

Of course, it doesn't hurt that my new instant husband is smokin' hot and fabulously wealthy. And, I think, the most amazing, gentle, kind man I've ever met.

But deep down, there's still an underlying sense of unease. That this is not my life. That I'm an impostor.

* * *

"So," I tell Suzie, sipping my cocktail, "it's been incredible. We haven't been able to keep our hands off each other for more than a few minutes, since we flew back from Seattle on Monday. We both took four extra days of leave, so we've spent almost the entire week in bed. He's wonderful."

I'm grinning like a teenager, but I don't care.

Suzie gazes at me, rapt. "Wow, Josie. That's so wonderful. So happy for you and for Rob." She takes a glug of her prosecco. "But I'm going to need more details. I mean, exactly *how* great is he?" She raises one eyebrow. "Now you're living as husband and wife, and all?"

I can feel myself blushing. "The best ever. I joke with him that it's all muscle memory, my body remembering how to be with him. But our physical relationship is the best I've ever known. And our emotional relationship. Well, I struck gold." I push the guilt away.

Suzie gives a slow nod. "Yep. Always figured Rob had to be a beast in the sack. Those big hands, big feet — dead giveaway."

"Suzie!" I laugh. "Okay. Yes. Happy?"

"Very. So, you guys are going to live happily ever after, right? Doesn't matter if your memories return?"

"I guess," I reply, ignoring a niggling feeling that this could all end as quickly as it began. "I'll just live day to day.

Get up, go to fun job, go back to incredible home, eat lovely dinner, watch a good movie, have amazing sex with my adoring husband. Then do it again the next day. Doesn't suck."

"That's it?" She sounds as if there should be something more. "I mean, I get it. When Don and I got married, we were deliriously happy for the first year or two, but it gets mundane. It's not all a fairytale. It's only since the twins came along that we found . . . a reason."

I laugh again. "Are you asking if we'll have kids? Play dates with the twins?"

"Yeah, I guess so. You'd make great parents. And a mini Rob or Josie running around, it'd be so cute. Sure, it'd be fun for me and Don. But it's you I'm thinking about."

"Well, you're too kind, but no, we haven't discussed it." I pause. "Yes, Rob and I are in love and very happy. But you've got to remember, for me, it feels like we've only known each other four months, and became a couple last week. It doesn't even feel like we're really married, as I have no memory of our wedding. It's all very new to me, still."

"I didn't think about it like that," Suzie admits. "Must be weird to be married but not remember your wedding. Could be a good thing though, considering what happened in Hawaii." She pushes her lips out, looks thoughtful. "You need a fresh start."

"That's what we have," I tell her. "Rob says it's like we've pressed reset. That it's better now than ever."

And therein lies the guilt.

CHAPTER 20

Mid- to late April

I pick up my iced tea, my feet up on the terrace couch, my trusty journal and pen on my lap. Rob will be home any moment, bearing groceries, hopefully following through on this morning's promise of shrimp risotto. I gaze out through the glass barrier onto the New York skyline, dazzled by the warm April sun.

Breathing deeply, trying to practice the mindfulness Suzie has been telling me about, I take a slow sip of the tea. Concentrate on its sweet flavor, its coolness. I look over the rooftops and think about the magical past two weeks I've had with Rob who, since we got together, has been a revelation in terms of how loving a man can be.

It's been the best two weeks of my life — and there's that guilt again.

It comes to me when I'm lounging around this apartment, a place that now feels like home, and yet isn't really mine.

And today has been tough.

David would have been forty today. Correction: David *is* forty, and I'm not with him. I miss him so much. His cheeky humor, his lack of logic, his ability to turn every event into a party. I wonder what he's doing for his birthday, in our world. It's nearly 11 p.m. in London, and he'll probably be at some pub with his friends, the center of attention, partying up a storm. Maybe with Her, too. Other Me.

A step behind me, and Rob's hand is on my shoulder. "Hey, baby." He leans down to kiss the top of my head. "How was your day?"

I tilt my head back, smile up at him. "Fine—" But I can't hide the dampness around my eyes.

"What's up?" He sits down beside me, lifting my feet onto his lap. "Why are you upset?"

"I'm fine. Only . . . It's David's 40th today. I'm sad, that's all. I'll be fine."

"Baby, I'm so sorry. Of course." He presses his lips together, clearly upset he forgot. "I guess his last birthday was when he came to stay here with that girlfriend of his. Three years ago now." He takes my hand in his.

He's trying to be kind, but I'm irritated.

"It's not that it *would* have been today," I reply. "He *is* 40, today. And I celebrated his birthday with him last year, in London, and the year before, and yes, three years ago, when he and his girlfriend visited me — in Brooklyn, not here." I'm getting more agitated. "I've never missed his birthday, not even after I moved to New York. But this year, for the first time, I am. Missing it." I pull my hand away and pick up my iced tea, taking a gulp.

Rob presses his lips together again, then pats my bare legs, and lifts them from his lap, getting up.

"I'm sorry. I understand it's a tough day. I'm going to start dinner." He goes inside, pausing to stroke my hair for a second on the way.

I feel awful. He was trying to be nice. None of this is his fault. But I can't follow him yet.

I pick up my iPhone and pore over photos of David, as I've done so many times before. The last ones of him, tanned and happy in Hawaii, are preceded by images of his final trip to visit me and Rob in April 2015. They include a photo from David's birthday meal at Eleven Madison, with the smiling faces of Rob, David and his girlfriend at the time, a platinum blonde. What was her name? Ashley? Hayley? I don't even remember. But that visit, three years ago, I *do* remember — although in my reality, they stayed in Brooklyn with me, around six weeks after I had moved into my place. The three of us went to a Greek place for his birthday dinner and got tipsy on cheap house red. The server brought out a mini cake with a sparkler, and the staff sang "Happy Birthday," while David conducted the staff, basking in the attention, taking a grandiose bow at the end.

I smile tearfully at the real memories while flicking through photos on my phone of a more glamorous version of events. The sun lowers over the city skyline, but I linger outside. The evenings are starting to get warm again.

When I finally venture inside, Rob is dishing up a wonderful-smelling shrimp risotto into shallow dishes, grating a little parmesan over the top. I walk up behind him and put my arms around his waist. He pauses as I lean my head between his shoulder blades and pull him back toward me.

"Sorry," I mutter. "You were being lovely. I'm having a hard time, that's all."

Rob puts down the cheese grater and turns in my arms, taking my face between his hands. He gives me a gentle kiss. "I'm sorry too. It's sometimes easy to forget how you feel about . . . being here."

"I love being here with you, you know that, right?"

His lips curve through his beard. "I do. Come on." He turns to pick up our plates. "I'm starving."

"Me too. I fancy a drink, too. Want a glass of something?"

"I picked up champagne, it's in the fridge. It'll be great with the risotto."

"Very fancy." I take it out of the refrigerator door, grabbing some crystal flutes along the way. "We can toast David's birthday."

We sit at the dining table, and Rob pops the cork. He hands me a glass and lifts his to mine. "Happy birthday, David, wherever you may be," he toasts.

"Happy birthday, David," I echo, and take a sip. I wonder if he's celebrating with Her.

"So," I pick up my fork and pile fragrant rice onto it. "What's this about, then?"

"What?" Rob looks confused.

"Oh, come on — nice dinner, champagne . . . And I know it's not to make me feel better about David, because you forgot. So, why the special treatment on a random Thursday?"

Rob grins ruefully. "I can't get anything past you, can I?"

I shake my head.

"Well, I figured we could talk. About us."

"Ruh-roh." I put my fork down, suddenly nervous.

"No," he puts his hand on mine, "it's a good thing. But before we get into that—"

"What?"

"Well, I know you want to be here. I know you love me. I'm not worried about that. But you still seem to feel there's another life somewhere, with David alive. Your life in Brooklyn. I'm not sure you can 100% commit to me, if you're feeling like that. Like, how *present* are you in what we have here?"

"I'm present. I swear, baby, I am. It's not like I'm torn. I don't have a choice, but if I did, I'd choose you." I lean forward. "I choose this life, with you. I love you so much." I'm on the verge of tears again, though these are happier emotions. But, oh, David. I'm sorry.

Rob smiles, his relief obvious. "I needed to hear that, baby. Sometimes I'm not sure if you're here because you're . . . stuck here. I need you to feel this is your real life, the one you were meant to have. This has to be it. You and me, this world, together. Whatever you believe your path was before your accident, this is your path now. The right one, you know?"

"I do. I do," I assure him, leaning farther in for a kiss. I stroke the side of his face, smoothing his beard. "I'm here, and I want to be. This is my life. *You* are my life."

"Well, then. That's what the dinner is about."

He pulls one hand away and reaches into his pocket. As I lean back, he puts a small black box on the corner of the table between us.

"Open it."

I do as he says. Inside is an antique oval sapphire engagement ring, outlined with tiny diamonds.

Rob slides off his chair and drops to one knee.

Wait . . . What?

"Will you marry me?"

"Uh . . ." I laugh, shocked. "This is beautiful, but . . . we're already married."

"*I* know that, but do *you*? I mean, really? You don't remember our wedding. As far as you're concerned, you've never said 'I do' to me — you've never committed to me. I don't think you'll feel like we're married until you've done that. I have to admit, Suzie put the idea into my head, but I realized it's the greatest idea ever. So — again — will you marry me? Slash, remarry me?"

I'm stunned. "A wedding?"

"Yep. A wedding. Okay, I'm getting up, these floors are tough on my old joints." He sits back on his chair, still holding my hand. "Make an honest man of me?"

I laugh. "I can't believe this. I didn't even think of this! I mean, we're married, so it didn't occur—"

"Put me out of my misery, for God's sake." I realize that beneath the bravado, he's uncertain. "Is that a yes? Because if it's a no, then . . . damn, we'll have to get divorced, or something."

I look into his soulful eyes. "Yes. Of course, it's a yes! Of course, I'll marry you. I love you."

Rob laughs too, his face lighting up, all the strain gone. "Thank Christ. You had me worried." He takes the ring out of the box and examines my left hand. "Hmm, you already have an engagement ring from me, not to mention a wedding ring. How do we do this?"

"Here." I take off the engagement and wedding set, and put them onto my right ring finger. I offer my naked left hand to Rob, and he slips the antique ring into place. We look at each other for a second, break into laugh, then kiss again. And again. And again.

"Riiiight — that's what the champagne was for . . ."

* * *

"I wanna see! Lemme see!" Suzie yells from outside my changing stall. She's a little giddy on the free mimosas.

I zip up the dress and examine myself. This is the thirteenth or fourteenth I've tried, but it's the one. It's fabulous.

I walk out into the lounge, where Suzie is lolling on a chaise. I step onto a raised circular platform in front of a trio of full-length mirrors.

"Oh, hell yeah, baby," says Suzie, eyeing me up and down. "Wow. I'd do you myself, in that."

"Who are you kidding? You'd do me anyway," I tease, causing her to snort out the mimosa she is sipping.

"So . . . this is it, right? This has to be the one?"

Suzie wipes her nose. "Yeah. No question. Rob is going to die."

"Well, let's hope not, after what happened last time. But thanks."

"How are we ladies doing in here?" Kate, the store assistant, re-enters the lounge, bearing a selection of glittering tiaras and gossamer-thin veils. "Oh, goodness me." She examines me, approvingly. "Yes, quite lovely."

"It's perfect. This is the kind of vintage style I wanted, but I wasn't sure if I could find it."

I look in the mirror again, turning to view angles. It's a killer dress. Old Hollywood glamor, 1940s in style. A slender, ivory silk number with long buttoned sleeves, slightly squared shoulders, and the neckline a deep V at the front and back. Beneath each V is a flat diamond-shaped panel, out of which the fabric explodes in all directions, in an art deco starburst design. The back of the gown is longer than the floor-length front, with a slight puddle train.

198

"Lana Turner, eat your heart out," adds Suzie.

"Not too . . . bombshell? I don't want to look like a slut on my wedding day."

Suzie shakes her head vigorously. "No. I'd tell if you if it was, but it's not. It flows enough that it's not too figure-hugging. There's lots of fabric. It's super-hot, though."

"Okay, then. This is it."

"Hair up or down?" asks Kate.

"Well, not all up. Not too formal. I mean, Lana Turner always looked best with her hair down, right? This is that kind of dress. And no veil."

"How about a clasp on one side, like this?" Kate delves into a box and pulls out a pearl-studded hair comb, about five inches wide with a curved design. She expertly sweeps up one side of my hair and pins it back. It's stunning. "Then, imagine your hair in smooth waves on the other side . . . Very vintage."

"Perfect. Thank you." I step off the platform, Kate supporting me as I wobble in the skyscraper heels. "These shoes won't work, I can't walk, but we'll find some later. You've been amazing, Kate, thank you."

Once I'm back in regular clothes and have settled the vast bill, I treat Suzie to lunch on the patio of the nearby Standard Grill restaurant. It's just warm enough to sit outside, and a row of trees in full blossom seems to be celebrating my upcoming wedding with me.

"Thank you for helping me today." I take a sip of my wine.

Suzie digs into her salmon. "You're welcome. I love the hair clasp. Definitely right to go the hair down route."

I nod. "I kind of have to. I don't want the nape of my neck showing."

"How come?"

"Well, I've probably told you this before, but I've always kind of wanted a tattoo. I've been quite jealous of the birds on your shoulder," I add. "So I designed one that represents me and Rob, and our lives. I'm getting it done as a sort of

199

wedding gift to him. On the back of my neck, below my hairline."

"Awesome!" Suzie claps her hands together in excitement. "Do you have the design finished? You gotta get it right. It's a big commitment."

"Well, not as big as marrying someone, but I'm sure. I've been thinking about a tattoo for years, and now I have one in mind that means something and a reason to do it. Here," I flick through my phone, until I find it. "I got our marketing designer to draw it out properly."

I show Suzie the design of a stylized tree, branches twisting and curling. "You can make out an R and a J. See?"

She tilts her head. "It's so pretty . . . Oh, that's the R, and then the J there, right? I approve. It's kind of classic, like a book lettering illumination. And I get it. You don't want to be one of those brides with a very visible tattoo. That's not really you." She studies it again. "It's gorgeous, but why the tree?"

I put the phone away. "It's about me and Rob, but the tree represents life in general. Every split of a tree branch is a new branch, and then each of those becomes more and more branches, ending up with thousands of twigs, right?" I lean towards her. "To me, all those splits are like your choices in life, or things that happen to you, and the life path they take you down, which is only one of countless possible paths. You start off as a baby, one individual at the base of the trunk, but then life takes over, and you twist and turn, and there are a million different ways it could turn out. I guess it's about Rob and me finding each other on this path, which is amazing when there are so many others that could have been taken. We might have never met."

Suzie raises an eyebrow. "Well, fuck. And I just thought it looked cool."

CHAPTER 21

Late May

I swipe through the photos on my tablet, Rob leaning into me in the back of the limo for a better view of the pictures. The comforting pressure of his shoulder against mine increases as the car hugs a corner.

I zoom in on one. "I can't believe the photographer sent these already. She must've been up all night."

"Well, that's the VIP treatment, I guess," Rob observes. "Check out this one."

It's a close-up of me and my husband, newly married (slash, *re*married) the day before, gazing at each other as we shared our vows inside the Brooklyn Botanical Gardens Palm House. Our profiles are in crisp focus, the leaves of the huge palms and the brightly attired guests fading into the background, as they had for us in that moment.

I scroll through, getting to the reception photos — my sister, with husband and child, grinning widely, seconds before Theo threw a tantrum and Adam took him back to their hotel. Lots of me with Laura and Mum, who is very elegant and quintessentially English in her mother-of-the-bride outfit and fascinator. Laura is pretty in a pale green dress, and then me, in my Lana Turner wedding gown and wavy glamor-hair. The swing band getting everyone on the palm-fringed dance floor, Suzie in a 50s-style polka-dot dress jiving with Don, plus images of my choir friends singing during the band's break. Me and Rob from behind, his brown hand pushing my hair off my pale neck, his thumb caressing my new tree tattoo, which he can't seem to leave alone. The two of us outside, getting into a limo, confetti thrown with abandon by our cheering guests, the Palm House illuminated in the background.

It's perfect. Well, almost perfect. The only person missing from the beautiful images is David.

"These are gorgeous. It looks like the best wedding of all time." I kiss Rob on the shoulder.

"It was the best wedding of all time." He touches his lips to mine. "And now we're about to have the best honeymoon of all time."

"I don't doubt it. But at some point you need to tell me where we're going."

"True. I'm leaving it until the last moment, got it?"

"Got it. I packed layers for mixed cool and warm weather, as instructed, so it's not the tropics. Having had my luggage whipped away, it's now out of my hands."

Rob laughs. "Don't worry. I'm certain this is somewhere you'd want to go."

"Why, have we ever discussed this place?"

"Well, yes and no. Not since your accident. So no, for you. But I'm sure."

"Okaay . . . I trust you." And I do.

He grins. "No, you don't. But you will."

The car pulls to a stop, and Rob helps me out. There's a huge, sprawling, low-rise building ahead of us, with large rotating doors, and travelers with wheeled cases moving in and out of them.

"Well," I observe, "we're at JFK. No big surprises yet."

Rob places a hand at my waist, guiding me forward. "This way."

I have only an overnight bag with me, as my luggage was taken away before the wedding, so I'm carefree as we approach a small security checkpoint servicing VIP passengers. With me still no wiser as to our destination, Rob leads me onto the tarmac, toward a small jet with an open door and steps leading up to it.

My jaw drops. "Are you kidding me?" I slap Rob on the arm. "You chartered a freakin' private jet?"

He smiles sheepishly. "Yeah. But if we were ever going to do this, it's going to be our honeymoon, right? Plus we have a long flight and I know how cranky you get, even in first class."

That's true. I shrug. "Fair enough." A smartly dressed flight attendant holds a hand out to me as I climb the steep steps. The extravagant interior is fitted out with plush leather seats and a wide banquette with a dark-wood table.

I turn to Rob with an incredulous laugh. "Wow. This is amazing. How long a flight are we talking?"

"Around eight hours. We'll get there at one in the morning, our time. But not local time, obviously."

"And local time will be . . . ?"

Rob smirks. "You think I'm dumb? That would tell you which time zone we're traveling to, so nuh-uh."

"Ah, man! You're killing me." I kiss him, and plop down onto a large leather seat. "I'm good."

In the air, I'm able to figure out we're traveling east over the Atlantic, which must mean Europe. It also means it will be morning when we arrive. After about four hours, without telling Rob my calculations, I recline the chair for a couple of hours' sleep.

The pilot's voice over the intercom wakes me. "Please fasten your seatbelts, we are making our descent and will be landing in twenty minutes. Temperature on the ground is currently 61 degrees, partial sun and cloud, and the local time is 7 a.m." I still have no clue where we are.

Swallowing hard against the pressure of the descent, I try to make out the ground through wispy clouds. They part, and the landscape below is revealed — glittering water, but also a city that seems to be floating, and a single causeway carrying tiny cars and a miniature train from the coastal mainland. I recognize it immediately, having taken that very same train into that city some years ago. It's unmistakable, and I'm thrilled with Rob's choice.

Venice.

I turn to Rob to find him looking at me with anticipation. Perhaps I shouldn't spoil the surprise, and let him tell me.

"Where are we?" I ask. "It's beautiful. Obviously we're in Europe."

"Can't you guess?" he leans into me, looking over my shoulder at the view below.

I feign contemplation. "A city that seems like it's over the ocean, off a main coastline . . . Lots of water . . . Venice, maybe?"

"You got it! Right first time." His enthusiasm is unbridled. "You pleased?"

My lips curve upwards. "So pleased. It's so romantic. Thank you, baby. It's perfect."

"You always said you wanted to go. That's not even the whole surprise — I've got another even more special surprise for you. Later, though."

After disembarking and breezing through another small checkpoint, we pick up our luggage, and get a cab from the mainland airport across the causeway. We are dropped off in the morning sunshine at a plaza. I look around at the Grand Canal, taking in the sights, the unmistakable smells, the babble of nearby tourists, the shouting of the street vendors, the vaporetto and the majestic, ancient buildings surrounding us.

"Not too shabby, huh?" Rob murmurs.

"It's amazing. I love it." It doesn't matter that I've been here before. It's just as incredible as the last time, and much more romantic to be here with Rob. "Is our hotel nearby?"

"No, but this is as far as the cab goes. It's all water taxis and ferries from here. The occasional gondola." Rob winks.

"Oh, we have to take a gondola, I didn't get a chance last ti—" I stop myself mid-sentence.

Rob turns to me. "What?"

I wince. I wasn't sure when, or if, I was going to tell Rob I've been to Venice before. "It's no big deal, but — I wasn't sure how to explain."

Rob's expression is grim. "You've been here before."

I nod, miserably. I can't lie to him.

"With Mum, for a few days, three years ago. To celebrate getting my radio show, I booked myself a tour of the northern lakes and then met Mum in Venice." I tilt my head to him, demanding eye contact. "But baby, I'm so happy to be here with you. I mean, Mum and I had a nice time, but I always dreamed of being here with a partner. It's so romantic. Plus our hotel was horrible, and I'm sure you've found somewhere amazing."

Rob's brow gradually furrows, and he turns away.

I grab his arm, pressing on. "I'm sorry, baby. But this means I get my dream of being here with you. I'm so happy to be here."

I throw my arms around his neck, rising up on tiptoes to kiss his cheek, forcing him to acknowledge me. "Thank you. Thank you." I kiss him again and again. "I love you."

He turns back to me, shrugging it off. "It's fine. Not your fault. No big deal. I guess I wanted to discover it together, that's all. But it's fine."

"And we will discover it together," I insist. "I hardly saw any of the city last time, really, just a couple of major tourist points, then a day out on the islands. There are so many parts of the city I want to explore, and wander round, hang out — we've got ten days, right? It'll be like brand new for me, too."

Rob presses his lips together. "Of course. No problem, Josie, it'll be great. I'm being a baby." He grabs our cases. "Right, let's see about that water taxi."

Rob's mood improves as our boat glides along the Grand Canal, the largest of the canals that snake through the city. We come to a halt at a dock in front of the Gritti Palace

Hotel, an incredible fifteenth-century building that drops right down into the water. I don't need to feign any wonder and excitement as we step onto the dock, hand our luggage over to the porters, and step into the high-ceilinged lobby, filled with art and antiques. Rob's smile is back as he takes in my unfettered joy.

"We could totally do Italian palazzo in our place, if you ever felt like a change of décor," he jokes, pointing out an ostentatious Renaissance painting above a carved antique settee.

"I don't think so, baby." I am relieved at his light tone. "We could pull off full-on black-and-gold art deco with mirrored cabinets, but I think we'd better leave this style to the Italians."

Upstairs, our vast suite, with its ceiling-height windows overlooking the canal, is just as grand as the rest of the building — and the dark green-marble bathroom is utterly indulgent.

I giggle after the porter leaves. "I wouldn't want this décor all the time." I pull the heavy blue damask curtains wide open, revealing the view of the Grand Canal and the gorgeous buildings dripping down into it. "But it's fantastic for a honeymoon suite. Although . . . isn't that bed too posh to have dirty sex on? I'm sure Italian ladies of yore would have had separate bedrooms from their husbands."

"Yeah, but their husbands would have come into their rooms at night and taken what they wanted." Rob comes up behind me, pressing me against the window. I spread my hands on the glass and look out at the canals, the ancient buildings, and the tourists scurrying below, as he pushes my hair away from my neck, tracing my tattoo with his fingers, kissing it gently, then roughly with his bearded mouth.

I can feel how much he wants me as he pushes his whole body harder against me, licking his fingers, and sliding his hand inside my bra to my nipple. I want him, too. I've never wanted anything as much as him, as much as this.

I turn and let him strip me naked in front of the window, not caring whether anyone can see us from outside.

I grab the curtains at each side as he drops to his knees, removes my panties, puts my right leg over his shoulder and explores me with his fingers and tongue, persisting until he hears the first cry of ecstasy from my lips and feels my body buckle. Only then does he stand up, carrying me to the grand bed and doing things to me that would make an Italian lady of yore swoon.

Later, lying in the plush bed, exhausted and sweaty after a long session of lovemaking and very little sleep, I start drifting off.

"Do we have to do anything today?" I mumble into Rob's shoulder. "What time is it?"

"It's around noon. We should sleep a few hours, baby. I've got a surprise for tonight, and we'll need energy."

We wake and shower in the late afternoon, and I'm about to ask Rob what I should wear for the evening's surprise event when there's a knock on our door. Two porters enter, carrying two enormous flat boxes, plus a large cube-shaped one, and place them on the messed-up bed.

"What's this?" I ask Rob, as he tips the departing porters. He has a knowing smile on his face.

"It's your other surprise. Well, the surprise is what we're doing tonight, but this is what I ordered for us to wear. I called ahead and the concierge helped me out. Open them."

I lift the lid off one flat box and find, to my astonishment, an eighteenth-century style male courtier's coat and breeches.

"Ah, that's mine," Rob laughs. "Open the other."

Puzzled, I grab an even larger box.

Wrapped inside, in tissue paper, is an ivory period ball-gown with intricate blue-and-gold embroidery down the front, and a blue brocade trim. I pick it up, carefully place it on the bed, smoothing down the skirts. I am speechless. Silently, Rob places two tickets on the comforter, next to it.

Masquerata Primavera, Venezia.

"*Masquerata* . . . masquerade?" I screech. "As in, the Venice masquerade carnival? We're going?!"

He grins. "Told you it was a good surprise. This is how much I love you — I'm prepared to get dressed up like an idiot for you." He kisses me. "It's not the big Venice Carnival, that's in February, but there's a spring masked ball tonight. It's full eighteenth-century costume dress — hence the hired outfits. Yes, I'm the best husband ever. Go on, there's more stuff, and we have to leave at six."

This is totally unbelievable. I throw my arms around his neck. "Oh my Lord. Thank you, baby. You've made me so happy." I release him, turning back to the boxes, wriggling in a happy dance. "This is better than Christmas."

Rob nods, rummaging in his box. "Check out the square box. I asked for a bunch of accessories to go with these outfits. Masks and hats."

I look. "All kinds of goodies in here."

Two full-length, velvet-lined hooded cloaks to go over our outfits — his brown, mine blue. A courtier's hat, a white ringleted wig and several Venetian masks of all shapes and sizes, including one with a hooked nose, three full-face masks and a white lace one. At the bottom is a small bag of jewelry. No eighteenth-century-style shoes, but I packed my ivory wedding shoes, which should work fine.

"This stuff is amazing." I sit at the dresser and lift the white wig over my hair, which I tuck up underneath. *Cinderella at the ball.* I pick up a full-face ceramic mask painted with gold and blue decorations, and gold lips on the closed mouth. I put it against my face, slip the elastic under my wig and the transformation is complete. I'm unrecognizable, the image of an eighteenth-century princess at a masquerade ball. Which, of course, is the point. It's tough to see or talk, however, so I try on the white lace half-face mask. This one I can change into when I need to eat and drink, I think, packing it into my gold clutch — which is inauthentic but at least coordinates.

"Wow!" Rob's eyes widen. "That wig is magnificent. Okay, I'm dressing in the bathroom so you can see the full effect."

I laugh as he takes his box and the courtier's hat, disappearing with a wink into the bathroom.

I remove the wig, strip down, and replace my underwear with my wedding bra and matching panties. I add nude stockings, then step into the dress. I heave the bodice together at the front, fastening it with dozens of tiny hooks. It's tight but fits pretty well, and looks incredible with its huge skirts, which I swish around.

Now for the accessories. In the box I find a pair of long, off-white gloves, and out of the jewelry bag I select an elaborate necklace of pale blue leaves in an antique-gold setting that picks up the colors of the dress.

The bathroom door opens, and an eighteenth-century gentleman in a cream-and-beige courtier's outfit emerges. He is wearing a three-cornered hat and a half-face ceramic mask with a long, hooked nose.

I've never seen a man look more spectacular. And he's my husband.

"Oh. My. God. Just incredible."

I grab Rob by the shoulders and bob under the mask's nose to kiss the bearded, full lips underneath. "Totally authentic, but like a sexy, mysterious courtier. The one all the court ladies fantasize about, but nobody can figure out where he's from."

He laughs and removes his mask. "Thanks. Wow. That dress is something."

I put the necklace against my throat, holding the fastening for Rob to take. "I'm not done yet. I still have to do my makeup."

Rob moves my hair aside to fasten the necklace. "Doesn't a mask negate the need for makeup?"

I smirk in fake pity. "How little you understand, sir. Yes, I have a mask, two in fact, but only one of them covers my whole face, and there might be times I'm not wearing either."

He grimaces, glances at his watch.

"I won't take long. Give me twenty minutes?"

"I'll have a drink downstairs." He looks for somewhere to put his key card, phone, and wallet. "This damn outfit has no pockets."

"Well, not many cellphones back then. I have a bag, I'll take them."

He hands them over. and kisses my cheek. "See you soon. Don't be late."

I freshen my makeup, clip up my hair and add the white wig, which has a blue feather and brooch attached. I fix it in place with bobby pins and give my head a shake — the wig isn't going anywhere. I pull on the gloves and add my own gold bracelet on top. Smiling at myself in the mirror, I put my compact, lipstick, the ball tickets, two hotel key cards, both our phones and Rob's wallet in the gold clutch, along with my smaller lace mask.

One last thing.

I place the beautiful ceramic mask against my face and pull the elastic under the base of my wig. Now the image is complete.

Staring at myself is pretty freaky. The room behind me is so ornate, the oil painting above the bed adding authenticity, I can easily imagine myself in another life, as an eighteenth-century princess, my suitor waiting to take me to the ball.

But I'm already in another life, living as a twenty-first-century princess, or as privileged as one.

Snap out of it. This is your honeymoon.

Walking carefully, my field of vision compromised, I grab my clutch and carefully descend to the lobby. I can just make out Rob finishing a glass of whiskey on the couch beneath the huge painting. Several other hotel guests stop and stare, and a few take photos as I try to glide as elegantly as possible across the floor toward him.

He stands up, his expression momentarily inscrutable. "You're incredible. Unrecognizable. We have to get a picture at the ball."

I try to laugh as I take his arm, but the mask restricts my mouth. "I can't see a freakin' thing," I mumble, "and I can't talk much. Plus, I'm going to want a drink and some food. So, this mask is not going to last long."

Rob leads me out of the hotel's Grand Canal exit, where a gondola decorated with ribbons is waiting at the dock.

"Oh, baby. Did you do this, too? It's wonderful."

"Well, we couldn't arrive in modern transport, not in these outfits."

Rob climbs in and lifts me by the waist off the dock before I can even object, putting me down onto a seat in the gondola. "Couldn't have you going overboard, could we?"

It's impossible to give Rob a steely glare from inside the mask, so I poke his side. "Not sure lifting is allowed, but we're in character, so you get a pass — this time."

"Got it, Your Highness."

The unseen gondolier expertly steers us down the water, and I catch glimpses of spectacular canal-front hotels, palaces, and churches. Other watercrafts carry a mix of costumed and regularly clothed people. It's like a strange and beautiful dream.

"I'm getting snapshots," I tell Rob. "It's already like a memory."

He peers at me. "Take the mask off if you're missing out."

I shake my head. "I've got to show up in full dress. I'll switch soon."

The gondola veers toward an ancient peach-colored building, the Ca'Sagredo Hotel. As we pull up at the dock, immediately porters rush to help us disembark, a crowd in full costume lining up ahead. Revelers are dressed in every conceivable color and shape — some outfits and masks are quite outrageous. Jester hats in vivid hues with bells on the pointed tips, vast dresses in saturated jewel tones, wigs of every variety, and masks varying from the simple to giant, oversized, papier-mâché heads. All of them laughing, calling out greetings, jostling to get inside the venue.

Arm in arm, my husband and I are swept along with the guests and enter the grand lobby with its huge ceilings and curved staircase. Handing our tickets over to a man dressed like Rob, we are hustled into an incredible ballroom with elaborate wall paneling and oversized crystal chandeliers.

"So elegant," a man comments behind us in a strong Italian accent. He's in costume but with an inauthentic digital camera around his neck. "Your picture, I take it?"

"You want to?" asks Rob. I nod and he turns me around so our backs are against the paneled wall. The photographer positions us in a few poses while he snaps away and then hands over his card. "You email me, you buy pictures if you like, jpegs, *si*?"

"Sure. Thanks." Rob hands me the card, which I put in my clutch.

As a server walks past with a tray of champagne, Rob grabs two glasses for us.

"Okay. Dramatic entrance made, official photos taken — time to switch masks."

I remove the mask and replace it with the half-face lace number, Rob helping me tie the ribbon at the back, and tuck it under the wig.

"Man, that's better." I smile at him. "I can see you now, too. Those eye holes were a bit teeny."

"That mask was amazing, but I like you better in this one. You look like my wife. There's only so long you can wear a mask like that." He hands me a glass and I take a sip.

"You have no idea."

Rob scans the crowd, who are drinking and chatting, but not dancing yet. "So do we have to, like, waltz, or something?"

"I'm sure we can manage some approximation." I sound more confident than I feel. But this event is beyond my dreams. "We'd better find some food first — this bubbly is going straight to my head."

The evening from then on blurs into a delight of music and color. We eventually find the buffet, with various delights on offer, but I don't eat much between conversations with the other partygoers — mostly tourists from all over the world. We meet a charming older French couple whom we talk to for a long time, and they ensure our glasses remain topped up.

For a while, after coming back from the bathroom, I lose Rob altogether. All the men start to look the same, so many of them in three-cornered hats and hook-nose masks. Having made a few circuits of the ballroom with no success, I take off my own lace mask for a clearer view. I am immediately admonished by a dark-skinned man with a trimmed goatee beard, in a deep green costume and black mask that drips down one side of his face.

"Tsk, tsk." But he is smiling. "We must wear our masks at all times." He has a Middle Eastern accent.

"You're right." I tie the mask back on. "I lost my husband, and lots of men are dressed like him."

"Well, now I'm hoping I look like your husband — perhaps I'll be lucky enough for you to mistake me for him." The man seems to wink his one visible eye. "Isn't that what masks are for? We get to be someone else — and even be with someone else, even for one night?"

I laugh at his audacity and gaze out at the crowd, scanning for Rob. "I guess that's the idea. But . . ."

"But what, my dear?"

I turn back to this stranger. "I guess I always feel like I'm someone else."

The man seems surprised by my candor. "Well, my dear. That's true for many of us. Aren't we all . . . faking it? What's the American expression — 'fake it till you make it'?"

I smile. "Right. That seems to be my motto in life these days."

The man gestures to the floor, where couples are beginning to dance, some in a real waltz, others swaying to the lilting music.

"Will you dance with me, madam?"

It seems rude to refuse, and there's something appealing about dancing with a total stranger at a ball in Venice. I take his proffered hand and step farther into the room with him, squeezing between couples, still scanning the room for Rob.

He could be any one of a dozen men talking to other people. Was his hat cream or beige?

The man puts his hand on my waist and leads me in a formal waltz, keeping it respectful. My muscle memory from a short stint of ballroom dancing as a teenager kicks in, and the man is soon spinning me around the floor, weaving between the slower-moving dancers. The ballroom becomes a whirl and I give into it — the moment, the room, this understanding, charming stranger.

I'm euphoric as music finishes and the whirling ceases, and the man before me bows and kisses my gloved hand. Another man, in a cream hat and embroidered coat, with a hooked nose, comes up behind my dance partner and taps him on the shoulder.

"Mind if I cut in and dance with my wife?"

The stranger turns to Rob. "Ah, the lost husband! Well returned, my friend. I was about to fall in love with your beautiful wife, and that would have been trouble for us all."

Rob laughs. "Well, only trouble for you, I think. My wife and I are on our honeymoon, and I think it's safe for her to dance with anyone she likes, without falling in love."

"Indeed, my friend." The stranger turns to me and raises my hand up to his lips again. "A delight, madam. I am very happy to have met you.

"And you, sir, it was my pleasure." He turns to Rob. "I advise you to keep this precious creature close to you. You may not know her as well as you think." With that cryptic comment, the stranger disappears into the crowd.

Rob raises an eyebrow, taking me by the waist and pulling me close. "Making friends, I see."

"Yeah, I lost you for a minute. He was nice. An outrageous flirt, but quite kind. Where were you?"

We sway to the music, smoothly but rather inexpertly in comparison with my previous dance.

"I was accosted by a fifty-something Texan woman who asked me where I was from and then was fascinated with my heritage. The Scottish part of course." He winks.

"Ha!" I exclaim. "You were being chatted up too! I knew it. Told you the ladies would see you as a mysterious courtier."

"Well, I guess she did. Not as mysterious as your new friend. What did he mean about not knowing you as well as I think?"

"I've no idea," I lie, laying my cheek on his shoulder. "Something to do with not being ourselves."

Rob takes a breath as if to reply but remains silent, instead moving me around the room. I relax into the beauty of the moment, soaking it in, filing the memory away.

We last until just after midnight, when the blurring becomes a bit much — no doubt a combination of alcohol, excitement, and jetlag.

Rob, his arm about my waist, guides me towards the entrance. "Time to head back, don't you think?"

He helps me with my cloak at the coat check, and I switch back to the full-face ceramic mask as photographers are lining the lobby. Posing for them momentarily, we look toward the exit of the hotel, where there's a long line for water taxis snaking down the dock.

"That's going to take forever," Rob observes. "How are your feet? Could you walk ten minutes, cut through the streets to the canal a bit farther up, and get a boat there?"

"Feet are fine," I mutter through the mask. "Let's walk."

We leave by the side door of the hotel, and emerge into the cooling night onto a small, cobbled street. I pull my cloak around me as Rob takes his phone out of my clutch to check a map. He's an incongruous sight in that costume with an iPhone in his hand. "In a few streets we'll be near the Rialto, we'll pick up a water taxi there."

We stroll arm in arm, picking our way across the uneven surface. Ahead, a few other carnival-goers are prancing and wheeling about, disturbing the quiet of the night with the occasional hoot and holler.

"It's like a scene from a movie," I mumble. It's hard to talk, but I'm reluctant to take off my mask, as Rob is still wearing his, so I don't want to spoil the effect. "Have you seen *The Wings of the Dove*? The one with Helena Bonham Carter and Linus Roache?"

"Sure. We . . . watched it together. Not long after we met. That was when you said you wanted to go to Venice."

"Ah." We cross a small bridge, and the group in front veers off, leaving us alone in the street. "Tonight made me think of that movie. The Venice carnival scene? Linus and Helena in masks and costumes, and they hide from the other woman, the one he's also in love with, and have sex in a dark corner."

"You mean like this alley here?" Rob pulls me down a tiny, pitch-black side lane. He stops at a battered old doorway and slips his arms under my cloak, around my waist, tugging me close. He takes off his hat and his mask, tousling his black hair, and kisses me on the collarbone, moving me into the doorway, pushing me up against the frame.

"Are we Linus and Helena?" His voice is low, as he bends down, moving his mouth to my décolletage, running his lips over the top of my restricted, pushed-up breasts.

"Yes," I breathe through my mask, arching my back into him, thinking of the other woman in the movie, how she was searching for them while they had sex.

Rob removes his gloves with his teeth and unfastens the top hooks on my bodice, reaching one bare hand inside my dress, finding my nipple. After a moment, he crouches down and lifts the front of the full skirts of my dress, right up to my waist. He pushes aside the silk panties I'm wearing, putting his hand between my legs, his fingers meeting wetness. Then he unbuttons his fly, wraps my leg around him and fucks me right there in the dark alley, the expressionless mask on my face the whole time.

At the moment both he and I cry out into the night, the ceramic mask can no longer take the pressure from my jaw, and it cracks under the chin. I lean back against the wall, spent.

Rob collapses against me. "Take it off," he mutters. "I can't get to you."

I remove the mask, careful not to break off the cracked section. "I remember how, in the movie, it wasn't enough for Linus and Helena that they loved each other, because he also loved the other woman."

Rob seems to know what I'm thinking. "That's not us."

I fasten my bodice as he does up his fly. "I want to believe that. That's why I married you."

"We'll be fine. We're married, and we love each other."

"You're right. I do love you. I love you more than anything."

Even though you're a bigamist.

The thought leaps into my head, but I'll never say it out loud. Even though I've made him one.

CHAPTER 22

Mid- to late June

June 12, 2018
Impostor syndrome update, number . . . I've lost count.

It's now spilling into the office. Working with Hans and Mike is fun, but I'm having a hard time. It should be a dream to get paid a generous salary for arranging parties and doing social media campaigns, all about luxury real estate. But I'm finding it increasingly sickening. All the money, the sales mentality, the push to get every dollar, even though everybody is already rich. The systematic gentrification of New York neighborhoods where nobody can afford to live unless they're wealthy. The parties, the air kissing, so much champagne. I've found it hard to bite my tongue on a couple of occasions.

Added to that, Angela is increasingly competitive. I know she wanted my job, and she can see I'm no longer 100% engaged. She's worming her way into Hans's and Mike's good books. At meetings, when she suggests social campaigns or other communications strategies, which is not her responsibility,

Hans now entertains them. Which would have bothered me before, but these days, it's hard to care.

It's hard to care when my emotions are all over the place. One moment I'm lying in bed with Rob, skin on skin, blissfully happy. The next, I am consumed with guilt that I just married a man who is not really my husband.

He's yours.

I do realize that. I've admitted it to myself. I believe in my heart that you exist separately from me, that we did switch lives that day. That I'm betraying you by being with your husband. And that from the start, I've been writing this diary for you, not for me. So you'll know what happened here, if we ever switch back.

* * *

A familiar, freckled hand with sandy hair at the wrist reaches over my shoulder and places a large glass of wine on the table.

"Congratulations. I heard it was an amazing wedding."

I turn and give Peter a warm smile. "Thanks. Yeah, it was wonderful. I thought you and Michelle were coming, though? We missed your dulcet baritone on 'Can't Sleep Love.' Katie and Allen did an awesome job, but that song is so yours."

"It's yours too. I guess it wouldn't have been right for you to do a passionate duet with another guy at your wedding. Or for me to sing it with you. Michelle's hormones might not have stood for it."

Opposite me, Lisa laughs too loudly. I give her a sideways look.

"Yeah, might have been a touch inappropriate." I pause, craning my neck back toward Peter. "You want to sit?"

Peter pushes his glasses up his nose. "Need to catch up with the rest of the basses. Got to hear Ryan's story about how he hit on one of your relatives without noticing her wedding ring."

I laugh. "My sister, actually. I heard her side of the story. Well, report back. Thanks for the drink."

"You're welcome. See you later, ladies."

Lisa coos a "See you, Peter" at him, watching him lope away. I shake my head. "Want to mop up the drool with this napkin?"

"He's so darn cute!" Lisa shakes her head. "And he likes you, you greedy bitch. What, it's not enough for you that you have this charming, handsome, rich husband — who you've now married *twice*, for chrissake — you gotta steal the attention of the one hot guy in our group too?"

"Hey, enough." I squirm uncomfortably. "He and Michelle are having a baby, remember? Sure, we have our duet together, but that's all. We're both taken, so it's okay for us to be friends."

"If you say so." Lisa smirks. "What does Rob make of your smoochy duet? He's coming to the show, right?"

"He'll be fine. Rob's not the jealous type. I haven't told him it's a duet, only that I got a feature song and have extra rehearsals. But I'll tell him."

Lisa's eyebrow arches. "You better. You don't want him to at the show, and he's like, 'So this hot guy is the reason for all your extra rehearsals, and you failed to mention him?'"

I grin. "For one thing, it wouldn't even occur to Rob that Peter is hot. And I *will* tell him. We have no secrets. Rob will be happy that I've got a moment in the spotlight. No big deal it's with another guy."

I glance along the table at where the basses are laughing at something Ryan just said, no doubt about my sister. Peter catches my eye, stops laughing and smiles at me quizzically. I give him a half-smile, then look away, changing the subject with Lisa.

When I arrive home, Rob is slumped reading on the couch, even though it's late.

"Hey. You're not in bed yet?"

He sits upright. "Wanted to be awake when you got in. How were drinks?"

I walk over and kiss him on the temple. "Great. I like that bar. Gets tiring, though, going out after rehearsal."

"Yeah, your rehearsals are longer than usual. I guess it's to be expected, this close to show time. Is it all going well?"

"Yeah." I remember my conversation with Lisa. "Actually, all those longer rehearsals are because I'm doing a duet in the show. You know the Pentatonix song 'Can't Sleep Love' that's been my earworm? This is like a slushy, duet version. It's a lovely arrangement. Plus, it means I get a nice spotlight moment without having to do a scary solo."

"That's awesome. I know the song. You've been watching the YouTube video of two guys covering it. That American Idol dude. Never assume I'm not familiar with your internet habits, young lady. Who's the duet with?"

"Peter. You met him at last year's show, but he wasn't at our wedding. Tall, lanky dude. Glasses. Good voice."

"Bet it's not as good as mine." Rob grabs me around the legs, pulling me into him, and breaks into wobbly falsetto, crooning the song's chorus.

I laugh. "No, your voice is far superior, honey. You should join our choir, you'd be brilliant — aside from your abject terror of public performance, of course." I pull myself upright, my hands resting on his shoulders. I kiss him again, then step away. "I'm exhausted. Bed. Sleep."

"No!" Rob calls as I ascend the steps toward our bedroom. He croons after me, "Can't sleep love."

He's right. Despite my exhaustion after a long day, the intense rehearsal and the wine, sleep is reluctant. It's been elusive for a while now, slipping away night by night, ever since I agreed to remarry Rob. And in the week since we've been back from Venice, insomnia has crept its way into my bedroom every night, like an old lover with a bad habit.

The few hours I do sleep don't really help. Because, behind that wall, She's always there. She's been there every night since the carnival ball. Sometimes masked, sometimes in a mirror — at other times, she'll appear in front of me when I'll be walking down the street of an unnamed city or along an abandoned beach. Sometimes she speaks, implores me — other times she shakes her head in disbelief.

So I've started to avoid sleep, sitting up in the dark instead, staring out at the Empire State Building, watching Rob. His chest rising and falling. That goddamn duet tune in my head, constantly.

* * *

"Bravo, baby! Or should it be *brava*?" Rob throws his arms open in the theatre lobby and I walk into them. He rocks me back and forth.

I kiss him and smile. "Thanks, baby. And thanks for the drink." There's whiskey for him and a glass of wine for me waiting on the bar. "I didn't realize how nervous I was, but the duet was a big deal for me. Plus the audience was huge. We sold out."

"I could see, honey." He strokes my hair as I sip at the wine. "You were fantastic. Here, take this stool, I'll stand."

I accept, my feet throbbing after two hours in my heels. Lisa, in a tight black dress and a vibrant yellow scarf, flops on the bar next to me.

She smiles sunnily at Rob. "Wasn't your wife amazing?"

"Absolutely. You all were."

"Aww, you're a peach! So, spill. Which song was your favorite?"

"Well, I'm a Bond fan, so I loved 'Skyfall'. 'Under Pressure' was awesome too. But 'Can't Sleep Love' was probably the best."

"Very diplomatic," Lisa winks. "Speaking of . . . Peter! Over here. Buy me a drink, would you? My purse is in the green room."

Peter saunters over, already changed back into a checked shirt and jeans. "Sure. White wine? I'll buy a bottle."

"May the Lord bless you." Lisa, a vehement atheist, laughs.

I turn to Peter. "Hey, you remember Rob?"

The two men shake hands across me. "Hey. Peter Klavins. Yeah, we met briefly this time last year."

"Rob Billing. I remember meeting you and your partner. Congratulations, I heard about the baby. Is your partner here?"

"No, Michelle isn't feeling like sitting in a theatre seat for two hours right now, especially while I'm performing a duet with another woman. We're due in three weeks."

"That's exciting. So . . . Klavins? Unusual name."

"Latvian. I'm first-generation American, my parents immigrated after they married."

"Right. Great job on the duet, by the way. You guys sounded awesome."

"Thanks. Lots of practice. Some tough harmonies, but I think we pulled it off, right, Jose?"

I take a gulp of wine, feeling Peter's casual abbreviation of my name create a slight tension.

"Yeah." I focus on my wine. "It went as well as it could've. Go team."

Rob looks at me, sensing my discomfort. He turns back to Peter. "Josie says you're a videogame designer. Anything I might have heard of?"

"Maybe *Heist*? That's our biggest."

"Wow — I've played *Heist* a bunch. Nice. It's huge."

"And you're a real estate developer?"

"Yep." Rob takes a sip of whiskey. "Did some work on the W Hotel, and then designed and built the tower we live in, Cavendish House, named after this lovely woman, of course. We're working on a loft development in Tribeca right now, plus a bunch of boutique buildings. Business is good."

"Cool."

I keep sipping my wine, feeling like the two men, though cordial, are in some kind of pissing contest. Lisa is watching with unrestrained curiosity. Thankfully Ryan and a couple of others show up, so any awkwardness — perceived or real — dissipates.

After a glass of wine, I'm wiped. Peter picks up the bottle to pour me another, but I put my hand on his arm. "Thanks, but I'm going to ask Rob to take me home. I'm flaking."

"Of course. We've all worked hard. You rest up."

Lisa adds, "No sweat, girl. I'll drink your share. Peter will help me, right, Peter?"

I laugh as I slip off the stool onto my aching feet. "Someone's gotta do it. I'll see you at the choir picnic in July. Peter, I hope you and Michelle will bring the baby."

Rob holds out his elbow and leads me through the busy bar as I say my goodbyes. Outside, in the balmy June night, the Lower East Side is buzzing with people out for the evening. Rob hails a taxi as it turns the corner from 2nd Avenue.

"So, you liked the duet best, then?" I ask him, inside the dark of the cab.

He pauses. "I thought it was the best performance. You guys were very convincing. Your voices sounded fantastic together. But I can't say it was my favorite."

"Oh. Well, I guess I couldn't compete with a Bond theme, could I?" I say, surprised by his tone.

"I don't like the message of that song. I've been listening to you practice, and the lyrics bug me. It's all about this crazy passion, like that's the best kind of love, so superior to every-day, committed love — like growing old together is boring. It bothers me. Watching movies, going for walks, growing old, that's real. That's what I want."

"I guess you're right."

"Plus, I have to admit it's kind of tough watching you perform this passionate song with another guy. You were both so into it. I know I have nothing to worry about, that it's me you love, and you're just acting, but it doesn't seem like you. It's another version of you. A version who's with someone else. It threw me, with everything we've been going through."

The driver's eyes flick to his rearview mirror. He's eaves-dropping, but I don't care. I'm sure he's heard a lot worse.

"Okay." There's a knot in my stomach. "I can see that. I'm sorry it made you uncomfortable. It really is acting. I mean, Peter is a friend, and he's with someone and having a baby.

"There's nothing to worry about with him. Or any man. You realize that, right? You're my world. Any passion I exuded, it's because I'm singing it about you. You're that crazy, passionate love, for me. The one that keeps me up at night — that's you. Literally. This love we have, it's the kind of love they write these songs about."

Rob looks out at the city rushing by.

"Don't you see, Josie? That's the problem. Right there. I don't want you to be awake all night and exhausted in the day. You think I don't know how little you've been sleeping? And you don't seem happy at work. You have this . . . chronic dissatisfaction. Even though you have everything, even though I'm doing everything to make you happy. I know you love me, I even know you're crazy about me, but I don't want crazy. I want happy. I'd settle for content. Why does it all have to be so . . . dramatic?"

The driver's interest is now intense. He's barely keeping his eyes on the road.

"You know why," I reply, in a quieter tone. "I understand you want real life. But for me, this isn't my real life. What do you want from me? I surrendered to this life, because I fell in love with you. I gave up hope of ever seeing my brother again, for you. But yes, it's driving me crazy, because this life . . . it doesn't feel like me.

"I found you, and you're the best man I ever met, but who am I, in all this? I'm haunted by the feeling I've betrayed my own self — for love, for luxury, for this life. My life now is one giant guilty pleasure. My glamorous but superficial job. Our incredible home. My beautiful clothes, the restaurants, parties, TV shows, luxury real estate, private jets, champagne. So much fucking champagne. So much pleasure, and so much guilt." I shake my head. "I feel like I'm gorging on you, on this life, like a . . . bulimic or something. I close my eyes at night, and I see everything other people don't have, that I shouldn't have. I can't stand the guilt."

Rob says nothing, but he's biting the inside of his mouth. I lay my hand over his on the seat between us, but his hand lies unresponsive. As the cab pulls into the porte-cochère of Cavendish House, Rob pays up quickly and gets out. He's already at the entrance when Ed opens my door.

"Evening, sir, ma'am. How was the concert?" He glances at Rob as he holds open the large glass entrance door for me, following me inside.

"Good, thanks, Ed." I force a smile, wobbling in my heels across the marble. "Thank you."

"Thanks, Ed," Rob mutters, striding into the open elevator.

Inside, we stand side by side, silent. I can't think of a thing to say that would resolve this fight. On our floor, Rob marches ahead to open the door. I follow, kicking my shoes off my pained feet.

He's already in the dressing room, pulling his shirt off. The night is warm and a sheen of sweat glistens on his light brown skin. I stand at the doorway, watching him.

"Rob. I'm sorry."

He looks up across at me, undoing the belt on his jeans with one hand, pulling off his socks with the other hand.

"*Gorging*? Like a bulimic? That's what I am to you? Something guilty to consume, and then . . . what? Throw up when you're done?"

He's furious.

"Baby, I'm sorry. I didn't mean it like that. Of course not. I don't know what I'm saying. I'm so tired . . . I'm so sorry." I step around the plush ottoman, now strewn with his shirt and jeans, and reach out. "I love you. Come here."

His dark eyes are glittering with a fire I haven't seen before. He glares at me. "Fuck, Josie! You're sabotaging this, you realize that?"

He pushes past me into the bathroom, slamming the door.

CHAPTER 23

Late August

It's so freakin' *hot*.

I'm lying under a wide umbrella, on a striped lounger at the foot of the boardwalk leading back to Hans and Mike's Hamptons house. Despite the shade, my skin is sizzling. The stretch of sandy beach is almost empty, and the lapping ocean is inviting. But I can't stand the idea of stepping into the blazing sun to reach it. I'm stuck . . . literally beached. And I finished my iced tea an hour ago.

I read yesterday's entry in the green-and-copper journal on my lap.

> *It was supposed to be cooler in the Hamptons — that was the point of house-sitting for the whole of August. A retreat of ocean breezes, turquoise pool, billowing white curtains and fresh seafood. A relief from 24-hour sirens, inescapable humidity, sweaty sex, and short fuses in New York. But it seems as hot, sweaty and ill-tempered here as it did there.*

> *It's mostly me, of course. Rob seems okay, stoic as usual, content to work from the comfort of Hans's air-conditioned*

ocean-view office, taking long lunch breaks to fix crab salads and iced tea. He wouldn't normally be away from the city for so long, but we need to work on our relationship, to spend time away from things that have been making me feel a little crazed.

A lot crazed.

It's also the anti-anxiety meds, I think. I've been seeing Dr. Weinstein again out of sheer desperation. After the row with Rob back in June after the show, and what I said to him that night, I had to get help.

Not that Dr. Weinstein can do much, but I have to talk to somebody about my nightmares and sense of guilt. I see him once a week now, acting out the amnesia storyline, telling him about how, ever since the accident, I have felt like another person — that I can't shake the sense I'm not supposed to be with Rob. That I'm not supposed to be this version of myself. I also talk about David a lot. How I have no closure over his death, especially since I have no memory of it. How I've never properly grieved his loss or been able to accept it. They're all only half-truths, but discussing them in that way seems better than nothing. I can no longer talk to Rob about it, as it always ends in a fight.

Dr. Weinstein started me on anti-anxiety meds, but I'm not convinced they're working. They're not helping me at the office, where I've made a series of ill-judged decisions and said some things I regret. Nothing that wasn't true, but I should've been more diplomatic. Mike practically hustled me out of the door when I agreed to take him and Hans up on their offer of the beach house for August.

The meds make me drowsy, too. It helps with the insomnia, but it's tough in the daytime and I haven't been getting much work done. By the time the evening rolls around, I'm too tired to do much. There have been a few nice dinners at local restaurants, but I'm quieter than usual. Mostly, we fix dinner at the house, eat it with some light conversation about work or the books we're reading — then settle down to read more or watch a movie. If Rob had been hoping for long moonlit walks along the shore, deep and healing conversations, wine-fueled banter and midnight love-making in the dunes, he must be disappointed.

We both are, I guess.

My reading is interrupted by my phone tinkling its pretty notes. It's a text from Mike.

Better get your party shoes on, girl, Hans and I are leaving in T-minus 30 mins and will be there by 6.30 p.m. — whoot whoot!! Get the beers chillin'. Don't worry about dinner, we're bringing appies, then Hans is taking us all out to Oaklands for Friday night lobster around 8.

Mike and Hans are joining us at the beach house for the weekend. They have planned a huge pool party here tomorrow, which most of the H&F staffers have been invited to. Josh and his boyfriend, Austin, are going to stay in the pool house, Angela and her new guy in the beach house's downstairs bedroom. A group of other H&F agents have rented a nearby property for the weekend.

It's going to be chaos. Hot, exhausting chaos.

I pick my words carefully in reply.

Great! We'll be waiting, beers at the ready. Don't trust your appie selection so I'm going to store. Can I pick up anything you want, for later or breakfast? Lobster sounds fun. I'm wiped out from heat but will hopefully manage an evening out with the boyz. Thought it was supposed to be cooler by the ocean?!?! Jx

I press send, then hate myself for giving myself an out, which I'm sure Mike will take as a slight.

For goodness' sake. A whole month in a Hamptons beach house, friends coming for the weekend, a lobster dinner, fabulous catered pool party tomorrow — what more could I want?

I stare at the ocean, where a couple of guys are body-boarding in the swell. It takes me back to my vacation with David in Biarritz.

My brother, alive. And a clear sense of self. That's what I want.

Trying to shake myself out of it, I rise off the lounger. Stepping into the sun is like hitting a wall of heat, and I make a break for it up the steps. I stop for a moment where the boardwalk joins the house's pool deck, looking up at the window of the home office.

Through the bright reflection of the blue sky, Rob is watching me, talking to somebody on the phone. I wave up at him and he waves back, pointing to indicate he'll be down soon. I push through the folding doors and enter the airy living space.

I flop on the soft white couch with its beachy throws and pillows, and sink into its deliciousness. Why didn't I stay inside all day? I shouldn't be sitting on this upholstery with my sweaty, sunscreeny skin, but I don't care. I kick off my sandy flip-flops and put my dirty feet on the silvery velvet ottoman.

Rob thunders down the wide, wooden staircase. "Hey, baby. How was the beach?"

"Too damn hot. Even under the shade. It's lovely in here, though. Thank goodness for air-conditioning."

"Yeah, the office upstairs is nice. Got plenty of work done. That was Hans. They've pre-sold two more Tribeca units. He said they're leaving, be here around seven."

"Nice. Mike said 6.30, but I suspect that's way optimistic. I should go to the store, get beers and appies, maybe something for breakfast."

Rob sits on the ottoman, taking my feet onto his lap, brushing sand off onto the gray hardwood.

"I'm done with work, so I can go, if you're too hot? You seem wiped out. And sweaty, to be honest." He rubs my feet with the pads of his thumbs. I'm instantly less anxious.

"Not yet. That feels lovely."

He looks up from my feet, under his dark eyelashes, and smiles at me again with his lazy grin. "Oh yeah? Need some of my magic healing hands?" He rubs with more intensity, sending all kinds of sensations over my body.

"Mmmm . . . That's wonderful. Takes me back to that spa in Venice." I let my head loll on the pillows, closing my eyes, surrendering to the moment.

"Now that was a fantastic vacation."

Rob pauses, perhaps worried he is implying this one isn't. Then he presses on with his foot rub. He uses the moisture of the sunscreen to massage his way up my bare legs, kneading my ankles, my calves, the backs of my knees, wheeling himself toward the couch on the mobile ottoman, pulling my legs each side of him. He pushes up the light skirt of my floaty sundress, slowly massaging each thigh in turn, letting his thumbs get close to my bikini line, deliberately turning me on.

I lift my head to look at him. In the light of the cool, pale room, he is so beautiful. He is gazing at me with a half-smile, and pulls me closer, dropping to his knees, wrapping my legs around his hips, pushing my skirt right up to my waist. He glances down at where my pelvis is starting to circle against him and traces a hand across my lower stomach, above my blue polka-dot bikini.

He speaks in a low, quiet voice. "You know what I love about this bikini?" He lifts his eyes to me again but doesn't wait for an answer. "These side strings. No pulling it down over your feet. Just . . . this."

Rob tugs, painfully slowly, at the bows of my bikini, pulling each one open so the sides fall away, looking at me the whole time, feeling me arch my back with desire. I haven't wanted him this much in ages. He takes the front of the bikini and draws it out from under me. It pulls between my legs, the back and side strings tugging through my butt cheeks before emerging, slick, from the front. He holds it up high and drops it on the hardwood floor. I giggle, a teenager in love.

He laughs too, then leans down and is silent. As he buries his mouth and tongue into me and I surf the waves of pleasure again and again, I wonder how I thought I couldn't be with this man forever. This incredible, kind, loving man. The best imaginable husband. I roll down off the sofa, stripping him of his linen shirt and long shorts, taking him in my mouth, devouring every delicious inch of him. I grip his back as we make love on the floor, rolling onto the deep-piled fireside rug for comfort, eventually splitting apart and lying back, naked and spent.

"Man," I say, after a while. "Guess this ocean air is doing me good, after all."

"Apparently." Rob gives a low laugh. "I'm getting hungry. You?"

"Yep." I prop myself on my elbows to check the mantel clock. "It's 4.45. We can shower and go to the store, as long as we're back by 6.30."

"You first, you'll take longer. I'm fixing us emergency cheese and cracker snacks, as I don't think we'll make it through."

"Fair point." I clamber to my feet, giving Rob an eyeful as I lean over to pick up our clothes from the floor. "Better clean up after ourselves, or we'll be in trouble when our daddies get home."

Rob's staring at me from his still-prone position by the hearth. "If that's what cleaning up looks like, I'm all for it."

I throw his shirt and shorts at him. "Up! Fix me cheese!"

"Yes, ma'am."

As I step into the lukewarm shower, I marvel at the change in my mood. So irritable and hot an hour ago, now so cheerful and feeling so much closer to Rob. That's one problem with these meds — mood swings. Although I'm feeling better, I'll swing downwards again. Still, one step at a time.

Rob is positively giddy at the grocery store, throwing all kinds of delicious items from the deli counter into the cart, more cheeses, cold cuts, olives, even buying a dozen oysters at the seafood counter. Fresh bread, eggs, and smoked salmon for breakfast. Two boxes of craft beers.

"I'm getting you drunk tonight," he promises as he slips his arm around my waist and kisses the tattoo on the back of my neck. It's like he's been given permission to be in love again.

I revel in it, enjoying his happiness, but at the same time I'm wary, wondering how long it'll last before I'm sucked back into negativity and guilt. I'm bound to say something to ruin it — it's only a matter of when.

Mike and Hans are pulling up in their sports car as we arrive home around 6.45. "We drove like the wind," Hans announces.

Mike is uncharacteristically flamboyant in his greeting, kissing us both on the mouth, his goatee beard tickling so Rob laughs.

"I do love to kiss a man with a beard." Rob scratches at his own.

I kiss Rob on the cheek. "Me too," I murmur in his ear.

We settle down with beers and oysters in the living room.

"How are you enjoying the house, having it all to yourselves?" asks Hans. "You better have not been doing it in our bedroom."

I blush. "Of course not. We're very happy in the guest suite. Wouldn't dream of sullying your pristine sheets."

The men laugh and Mike brushes sand from his bare feet. "Managed to bring a fair amount of sand in, didn't you?" he says with fake severity. Rob and I smile at each other.

"Yeah, didn't have a chance to clean up properly. Buying beer seemed more urgent than vacuuming."

"Wow, you spread this stuff around," laughs Mike, now inspecting the wide expanse of hardwood floor between the couch and the fireplace.

"What were you doing? Oh, I get it . . . You haven't been doing it in our bed, but pretty much everywhere else?"

"Eww, that's disgusting!" Hans is only half-joking as he jumps up from the couch. "Are we going to find stains? You two . . ."

We're still laughing about the sand and which body parts it might have come from on the drive to the buzzing Oaklands restaurant for its Friday night Lobster Bash dinner. We eat a huge amount of lobster, and I share a bottle of crisp white with Mike, while the others stick with beers. Throughout dinner they are increasingly loud, Hans in a bright floral shirt, winding up his partner, Mike shaking his head in despair and giving me exasperated smiles.

I smile back at Mike, fanning myself with a cocktail menu. I'm overheating again, and the rich food and wine are not helping. I took my evening meds a half-hour ago, and the sluggishness is setting in. I stifle an unexpected yawn and Mike catches me. He raises his eyebrows to ask if I'm okay, and I nod.

"I'm stepping out to the deck to get some air," I tell Rob, rising. "Back in a moment."

"You good, baby?" He places a hand on the back of my thigh.

"Fine. Overheating."

I kiss the top of his head, smile at the others and push my way out to the busy terrace, walking down the steps to the marina. I take in the balmy evening, inhaling the air. But it's still sticky, despite being right on the water. Sweat trickles down the back of my neck, and I wipe my hand across my tattoo.

Footsteps thud behind me, and I am relieved that it is Mike, not Rob, who has followed me outside. I smile at him.

"Too much booze and rich food. I'm on meds that make me kind of sleepy. Sorry if I'm a party-pooper."

"Hell, don't worry about it. I'm not crazy about the heat either. You'd think Hans would be the one to hate it, with his alabaster skin, yet he's fine. But it saps me of energy."

I pull a hairband from the pocket of my denim shorts, and pull may hair into a ponytail. "Exactly. Makes it hard to do anything. What's it like in the city?"

Mike grimaces. "Vile. I heard it's been hot out here, but you were right to leave, it's been disgusting. That's why it's so packed in here tonight, I guess. Did Angie tell you the office air-con broke down? Everyone's working from home."

"Then I'm glad we left. At least the beach house is cool."

"Yeah . . . also kinda steamy, from what it looked like," Mike replies with a wink.

I laugh. "Well, we're on vacation. Sort of. And . . . refreshing our relationship."

"Hey, you don't need excuses, you're a married couple. Doubly," Mike observes. His brow creases. "Everything fine with you two? Do I need to worry?"

"Oh, no. We're okay. I've been having a hard time, and it spilled over into our relationship, I guess. I know you've noticed, at work. About which I'm very sorry. I'm having issues adjusting to these meds. They're for anxiety and insomnia."

He nods slowly, taking this in. "Are they helping?"

"Maybe." I turn to the railing, looking out over the marina's bobbing yachts. "I think they've made some things worse — definitely at work. One of the side-effects can be lack of clear thinking, and that's an issue. But they're helping me sleep, which I was barely managing before. They're also making me sluggish." I shrug. "I may have to try another brand."

"Take all the time you need. Angie has been doing a much better job at covering you than last time. We're thinking about moving her up into more of a permanent comms role and hiring a new assistant. If you need more time, take it." He pauses. "Do you mind if I ask whether the anxiety is about anything specific? Are you getting help?"

"I don't mind. It's been under the surface since my accident. It's all to do with my . . . amnesia. My brother suddenly being dead, everything so different. And yeah, I'm seeing someone about it." I turn back to Mike. "Thanks. I need to find my sense of balance. Reconcile my place in the world." I laugh, drily. "With a life as blessed as this, you'd think it would be easy."

"No, I get it. With your amnesia, it felt like you were ripped from the life you knew, thrust into a new world with a different job, a husband you didn't recognize, a different home, and to top it off the brother you feel like you saw recently has been dead for years. It's enough to freak anyone out."

"Exactly. It did freak me out, completely, to start with — but then, well, I had this instant husband, and he's so amazing. I didn't know him, but I fell in love with him, in love with this whole life — with all you guys. For a while I was distracted from being freaked out, and embraced everything, and we had the wedding, which was wonderful but also another distraction . . ." I shake my head. "But now the honeymoon is over, I'm trying to live as a regular person, but I still don't have that understanding of who I am. It's weird . . ." I trail off, aware this is not a full confession, more like the half-truths I tell Dr. Weinstein. Why bother to only half-confide? Nobody but Rob will ever know the whole truth.

I pull myself together, sucking in a breath of humid air. "We'd better go back. The guys will be wondering where we are."

Mike nods, holding out his arm for me, and leads me back inside, where a local band has started up. I sit next to Rob and put a hand on his arm. He turns to me with a quizzical look.

"I'm fine, I needed air. I had a nice chat with Mike," I say into his ear over the music. "I don't think I can drink anything else tonight. Probably shouldn't, with the party tomorrow."

"You wanna call it a night? We can cab back."

"Yeah, I need to sleep, but you don't have to. If you want to stay with the guys, I can cab alone. I'll only be going to bed. Stay and have fun."

"Really?" Rob seems doubtful, but he has a whole pint of frothy beer in front of him and Hans has ordered dessert, so they're not ready to leave.

"Absolutely," I assure him. "You enjoy. I'll call a cab and wait outside. It's too hot and crazy in here for me right now."

I get up and kiss him on the temple, then call across the table to the others. "Hey, so, I'm out — too wiped. Have fun, I'll see you for breakfast."

Hans puts down his drink and looks like he's about to say something, but Mike lays a hand on his arm. Instead, Hans lifts his fingers to his lips and blows me a kiss. I wave goodbye and head to the front desk.

I'm at the beach house within twenty minutes. Most evenings since I've arrived, I've stood on the deck for a while before going to bed, listening to the ocean, trying to soak it in, thinking about my life and how I can make it work. How I can be happy as *this* person.

But tonight, I go straight upstairs and close the blinds. I insert premium-grade earplugs, anticipating the guys being noisy when they get home. Rob will smell like a brewery when he comes to bed.

Tonight, I don't want to think. I want to sleep. And, hopefully, dream about nothing. After all, tomorrow will be another exhausting charade.

How much longer can I do this?

PART FOUR: HER

CHAPTER 24

Mid-April

Josie padded into her living room in her cozy pajamas and robe, opening the blinds to reveal cherry blossoms blowing off the trees. No stirring yet in the tiny second bedroom — they were still asleep. She fired up her laptop to continue her journal entry from yesterday.

> *Peter's nothing like Rob, and I think that's a good thing. I can start to forget my old life when I'm with Peter. He's so much more gregarious and extroverted, so much more talkative. He's kind of fearless. Rob is gentle, stoic, and always very kind and thoughtful with his comments, whereas Peter has virtually no filter. He's very kind, too, but it takes a while to see it, as he doesn't pull any punches.*

> *When I married Rob, I thought he couldn't be more perfect for me. It was true, and remains true. But this time away from my life and my marriage, and spending time with Peter, has shown me there are many ways people can be right for each other. Just because you can be happy with a quiet, gentle*

man doesn't mean you can't also be happy with an outgoing,
charismatic joker.

In a different life.

Or maybe even both in the same life.

Quiet voices drifted from the spare bedroom, prompting Josie to put her thoughts on hold. Stopping first in the kitchen to switch on the kettle, she knocked on the door. "Are you two up?" she called. "Anybody for tea?"

She heard footsteps and David opened the door. Behind him, Anna was sitting up in bed, wearing a lilac silk camisole that contrasted with her vivid red hair. Josie felt dowdy in her faded robe.

"I could murder a cuppa Rosie, thanks Bosie. Hey, that rhymes." David laughed. "Babe, do you want tea?"

"You Brits and your tea. Got any decaf coffee?" Anna replied with a winning smile. Wow. She was so gorgeous Josie could almost jump into bed with her.

"Sure, somewhere," Josie said. "One tea, one decaf, got it."

"Thanks," Anna said.

"No problem. Happy fortieth, bro. How are you feeling after last night?" Josie added, as David followed her into the kitchen.

"Bit delicate. Feeling . . . you know. Old." He glanced around. "Your new fella joining us again?"

"No, his band has an event today. Plus it's too soon to subject him to the entire family. Last night's double date with you two was quite enough. We've only been out a few times, it's early days."

"Fair enough. I like him, he's all right. For a Yank. At least he can play guitar, which makes up for it."

"That's how I see it," Josie replied, hunting for decaf and her French press. She missed the fancy coffee machine she and Rob had. Those delicious lattes.

"What's up?" asked David.

"Nothing. Hangover." She turned back to him. "I'm very happy you're both here with me, of course." She bared her teeth. "See?"

"Evidently. And you need to brush your teeth. Man, it's nearly ten. What time are the others coming over?"

"Well, Laura and Adam will be enjoying their hotel breakfast, which of course Mum will spurn and then be hangry until lunch. I guess . . . eleven? Official gift ceremony at 11.30, lunch at noon." Josie looked down at her robe. "I'll need to be dressed by then. Mother won't approve."

"And showered. You stink," added her brother. "I heard you fart through the wall last night."

"And yet you, dear brother, didn't mind having noisy sex with Anna, despite said paper-thin walls."

"Shit, you heard us? Sorry. I thought we were being quiet."

Josie laughed. "Right. Here's your tea, Romeo. You can do the coffee; I'm getting in the shower because I stink."

As predicted, Laura, Adam, little Theo and their mother arrived just after eleven. Their mother was carrying no gift for David, only a card.

"No birthday present for you, this is it, I'm afraid," she reminded David as they settled in Josie's small, sunny living room. "You had birthday and Christmas all in one, with that wetsuit."

"Fine, Mum. As previously agreed," he replied, with an eyeroll to Josie. "Hey, we met Josie's new squeeze, Peter, last night. He seems like a nice bloke. You like him, don't you, Bosie?"

"Well, we've only had three dates. But yes, I like him," Josie said, putting a fresh pot of coffee on the ottoman.

"Lovely, darling," her mother replied, although whether this was directed at the coffee or the new romance was unclear.

Laura and Adam were still organizing themselves and Theo, now four years old, in the hallway. They had several enormous bags with them. Children seemed to need so much stuff. No wonder they hadn't shown any signs of wanting another child.

"Hi, Bosie. Sorry about all the junk." Laura hugged Josie.

"No problem, baby girl. How's my little guy?"

"I'm good, thanks," joked Adam, leading Theo into the living room. "Oh, this little guy? He's a monster. Don't be fooled by the puppy-dog expression. He'll tear out your very soul, won't you, kiddo? Say hello to your Auntie Josie."

Theo looked up at her with his huge blue eyes, reached his still-chubby arms up to her and said, "Hello, Auntie Bosie." She picked him up and snuggled with him on the couch as David opened birthday gifts. Theo also presented both David and Josie each with a paper plate covered in tiny seashells, sprinkled with glitter.

"Thanks, buddy," Josie told him. "I love it. I'm going to hang it on my wall."

"The shells might need more glue," apologized Laura. "And the glitter gets everywhere, so don't brush against it."

Lounging on the couch, Adam sighed at his demure child sitting on Josie's lap. "He's a different child from the one at four o'clock this morning, isn't he, honey?"

"Unrecognizable," Laura replied.

"But worth it, though — right?" asked David, uncharacteristically interested in his sister's parenting experience.

"Sure," Laura replied with a shrug. "It's a nightmare half the time, but you love your child so much you wouldn't trade them for anything."

"That's good to hear." David flashed his girlfriend a smile and raised his eyebrows in question. Anna nodded.

Josie looked at each of them in turn. "What's going on?"

"Well, sorry to distract from important fortieth birthday business," replied David, "but there was a reason I made such a fuss of us being in New York together on this auspicious occasion. We're rarely all in one room, and Anna and I have important news. Actually, two lots of news. Well, three, really . . ."

"You're pregnant?" squealed Laura.

David winked, as Anna beamed beside him. "We are," she said. "Ten weeks, so it's early days. Due in early October. This is a bit embarrassing, but we conceived about a week after we met. It wasn't . . . planned."

"But we're so happy about it," David added. "And for us, it was love at first sight. We knew straight away we wanted to be together. Which brings us to our second bit of news." David paused and looked at Anna again. "We're getting married."

Laura squealed again and threw her arms round her brother. "Wow, congratulations."

They all stood to hug David and his new fiancée. "That's wonderful — I'm so happy for you both," Josie told them, tears forming.

Her crazy brother — now going to be a husband and father. And she had thought this would never happen. Now, not only was he alive, but he was becoming the man she always knew he could be. It was more than she could've dreamed.

As they sat again, recovering from the bombshell, David added, "I realize it's soon, we only met in January but . . . this is it, for me. We both knew."

Anna smiled and kissed him, adding, "Yeah, I never imagined I'd go to London for a year and meet the man I'd marry. To think, I almost didn't go to that pub on New Year's Eve."

Adam finally got a word in. "So what was the third bit of news? You said there were three."

"Right," replied David, more nervous. "Here's the thing. Anna wants — we both want — to raise our child, and hopefully more kids, in Australia. It's important to her to be near family after the baby comes, and you know how much I love Sydney. So . . . we're moving to Sydney. Probably in July, before Anna gets too pregnant to fly long-haul."

"Plus my work visa expires then," pointed out Anna. "Since we won't be getting married until after the baby is born, I can't stay in the UK after the end of July."

They all sat for a moment, absorbing the news.

Sydney.

Josie had emigrated to New York herself, but Australia was a lot farther to fly. She'd hardly ever see David. And he'd be so busy with his new baby, as well as his new wife and her family . . .

"Wow," Josie said. "That's great. Really fantastic. We're all excited for you, aren't we?" She turned to the others.

Adam replied, "Yeah, it's brilliant — congrats." Theo was looking around at all their faces, sucking his little thumb, wondering what was going on.

Josie's mother seemed stunned, clearly thinking about her new grandchild being so far away. But Laura piped up, "Absolutely. It makes total sense."

David, eager to convince his family, pressed on. "And those guys I was surfing with last time, you remember — Brad is already hooking me up with an amazing job at one of the big Sydney investment banks. Like, top notch, a big pay bump. We'll be able to get a big house near the city. It'll be a good life for us and our kids. Better than London."

"Of course, darling," said their mother at last. She nodded, visibly adjusting. "It may be far away, but it's only a plane ride, isn't it? That's what we found when Josie moved. We thought it'd be hard, but we've never felt very separated."

"Totally," replied David, earnestly. "Plus we'll come back around once a year, either to London or New York, and we'll all get together like this, and it'll be fine." He didn't sound too certain.

Anna clutched his hand. "I'm not taking him away from you, I promise. Seriously, with the salary at his new job, we can afford to splash out on flights, or fly you guys out to see us."

"We'll work it out," Josie told them both, getting up to hug them again, trying to smile. "Congratulations, on all of it. I'm sure you'll be very happy." She exhaled. "Okay, now. Lunch."

Later, in bed, she couldn't help it . . . the tears came.

They were going to be so far away. She knew David had every intention of visiting, but with the baby and his new life, she'd see him every couple of years, if she was lucky.

She was going to lose him all over again.

Josie lay in bed, sleepless. Her mind traced back to her hardest time with Rob, her husband holding her as she wept over losing her brother after their wedding. She tried to imagine she was in Rob's arms again. To feel like, if she didn't get to have David in her life, at least she had Rob.

But the truth was she no longer had her husband, and soon, she'd barely have a brother.

When Josie had woken up that morning, being in this world had made some kind of sense, with her brother and his girlfriend in the next room, and her family all together in New York for his fortieth birthday. And since starting her fling with Peter, she'd been so much more cheerful. He wasn't Rob, of course, but he was a great guy who cared about her.

Now it looked like she didn't have long with David, even if they were in the same world.

What would she have then, besides Peter?

The man who was — let's face it — her second choice.

CHAPTER 25

Mid-May

Peter turned toward Josie, pulling her pillow closer, slipping his arm under her. Their naked bodies were pressed together, her face in the side of his neck. Of course, this was no way to sleep, but she and Peter seemed to sleep very little anyway. She'd sleep later, after he'd gone.

It was around 7 a.m., and they hadn't gone to bed until past three. After going to a *Star Wars* costume party where Peter's band was playing, the two of them had gone back to Josie's place. They had shared some more wine, Peter geeking out about the new Han Solo movie, mansplaining the details of the fabled Kessel Run.

He had then dismantled her elaborate "Rey" hair buns and taken off her costume, layer by layer, as she removed the long-sleeved T-shirt and cargo pants he had been wearing under his Boba Fett armor. They'd had sex in front of her little fireplace and then dragged themselves to bed.

But she always found it hard to sleep next to him. For some reason, they seemed to generate so much heat that, even in May, with the window open, the room was stifling.

Peter moved away, sliding out his arm from under her, their bodies slick. "You're a thousand degrees." He flung the covers off, turning to the window.

"You are," Josie mumbled into the pillow. She left a gap between their bodies but still felt the need to touch him, so she traced the outline of the guitar-strings tattoo on his upper arm.

Peter seemed entranced. He lay on his back and turned his head to Josie, taking her in, allowing her hand to wander over his chest, down his stomach, still tracing light swirling patterns. Josie pushed the covers away and continued down to his genitals, which responded appropriately. In a blissful state, Peter closed his eyes, a faint smile on his face. He gasped out loud when Josie slid down the bed and took him into her mouth.

After a while he pulled Josie back up the bed, turning her onto her side, facing away from him, lifting her thigh and pushing himself into her. They made love in a cross shape until they both came, loudly, crying out at the same time. They remained in that position, gasping, chuckling at the suddenness and intensity of the sex.

The floorboards above their heads creaked, and they both laughed again. "Guess we woke up old Marcus." Peter wiped the sweat from his brow.

"I'm not surprised." Josie was breathless. "Oh my God. Holy simultaneous orgasm."

"Yeah."

They untangled their limbs and lay still, allowing the morning air to bring their body heat down.

Josie was starting to drift off when Peter leaned over to kiss her forehead. "I'm taking off," he whispered. "I'll leave you to sleep. I've gotta be in Queens by eleven, bearing Mom's ingredients for my sister's birthday meal, or I'm in trouble."

"No problem, I am sated. You are dismissed." Josie gave him a lazy smile. "I'll let you out."

She stood naked in the bedroom doorway, watching Peter in the living room as he found his clothes and collected his costume armor, Boba Fett helmet, and guitar.

"Next time, leave the helmet on. That bounty hunter thing is hot."

"Noted." Peter kissed her. "In return, a Leia thing with the hair? More my generation."

Josie laughed. "I'll try to source a gold bikini."

"Ah yes . . . That would be a perfect birthday treat. You know my birthday is in a couple of weeks, on the 27th?" He stopped, then added, "I was thinking we could go away for a night or two. I've got a family thing that Saturday, but the day after my birthday is Memorial Day, so we could go on the Sunday. It's a long weekend."

A mini-break?

"Great idea," Josie replied, not at all sure it was a great idea. "Sunday 27th. Leave it with me. You may have to drive, but I'll do the rest."

"Perfect." He kissed her again. "See you at rehearsal."

She opened her apartment door, hoping nobody was in the corridor to glimpse her nudity, and let him out. Then she climbed back into bed, much cooler, pulling the discarded covers around her.

A night away — that was a big step. They'd spent quite a few nights together, but going away meant at least twenty-four hours straight in each other's company. They had never even eaten breakfast together, and that somehow seemed more intimate than the act they'd just engaged in. Consuming each other could be dismissed as casual sex, but consuming food was something a real couple would do.

Josie went from satisfaction to a sense of unease. She knew Peter wanted to be a real couple. Problem was she didn't know what she wanted. He was funny and kind, and piercingly intelligent. She loved being in his company and their physical intimacy.

But it still seemed . . . wrong. Off. And it was that, not the overheating, that was preventing Josie from sleeping.

The fact was, as far as she was concerned, she was still married. Rob might not know her in this life, but her real husband was out there, somewhere. And she was being unfaithful to him.

Then again, she was pretty certain he was being unfaithful to her, too.

CHAPTER 26

Late May

"To being here with you, on Memorial Day." Peter raised his flute of prosecco.

Josie clinked glasses with him, trying to enjoy the moment. "Cheers. Happy birthday weekend." They both took a sip and dug into their tiny quinoa and beet salads. The huge glass doors leading to the hotel's terrace were open, and a balmy breeze drifted in.

"It's beautiful tonight." She finished the salad with the fourth bite.

"Yeah, we could wander the grounds after this," he replied, looking out at the warm spring evening.

Josie scanned the room. Virtually all the guests were couples on similar retreats. Two beefy guys feeding each other oysters were still in their spa robes, as were a few others. But she couldn't face eating a fancy dinner in a bathrobe, so she had worn her new green shift dress. It was the first time she'd ever seen Peter in a shirt and tie.

"Although," he continued, "I may be so relaxed after dinner that I want to go upstairs and veg out."

"Yeah, screw the gardens. A spa is the perfect place to do nothing," Josie agreed. "And I got us a late check-out for tomorrow, so we can stay in bed awhile."

But the truth was, as pleasant as this mini-break had been with its treatments and hot tubs, Josie was itching to return to the city. She hated taking time off the radio show, and she didn't want to miss rehearsal with the show coming up in a few weeks. Being holed up with Peter in a big hotel should make her happy. So why didn't it?

Peter raised his eyebrows at her. "You don't seem very relaxed for someone who spent the day being massaged, bathed, caressed and made love to."

Josie inhaled deeply. She studied his face. He really was lovely. "Sorry. I guess I've been having a hard time unwinding. Work is super-busy. Plus this whole couples retreat thing — I've never been comfortable with it. But I am having fun."

Peter nodded slowly. "I'm not sure what your issue is with coupledom, Josie. I can't figure out how you see me — whether as a boyfriend, a casual lover, or a friend with benefits. It's been a couple of months since our first date, but I'm not sure what's happening here."

The entrée, a miniature portion of ling cod on top of six green beans, arrived to break the awkward moment. Josie looked down at it. She'd be starving again in a half hour.

"I don't know," she told him truthfully. "I'm not very good at this. I don't know how to be with anybody new. But I'm trying. You're so lovely, and I do care for you. I definitely don't want this to stop." She took a sip of the prosecco. "You're a lot more than a friend with benefits. More than a casual lover. But it's hard to label it."

"Not for me." Peter put down his fork. He reached out and laid his hand over Josie's. "It's not hard for me. I don't know what's going on with you, but I know how I feel." He paused. "I'm in love with you, Jose. Totally in love with you. I realized this even before I broke up with Michelle. I know it's harder for you, because you don't remember us from before. But for me, it's easy. I want to be your boyfriend, and one day your partner. I want to call you my girlfriend and take you to visit my family, who you haven't met, even though I jumped at the chance of meeting David and Anna. I want our relationship to develop, and someday live together."

He squeezed Josie's hand. "We're so right for each other, but you have to let go of whatever is holding you back. It's you and me now, okay?"

Peter didn't wait for an answer, or seem to expect one, letting go of her hand and digging into his dinner, as though he had said what he intended, and could now relax. Josie pushed her plate away, no longer hungry.

"I'm sorry. I haven't been fair." She hesitated. "It's partly the amnesia. There's this whole period missing, so it feels like there are unresolved feelings I don't have closure on. But it's not your fault, and I'll try not to let it affect us."

Peter finished a mouthful. "It's the last guy, the married guy? You never got closure on that?"

Josie shrugged. "It's tough, because for me, it never ended. There was no break-up, no falling out of love. One moment we're together and the next, I wake up and . . . he's no longer around. It screwed with my head. No matter how much I care for you, I feel conflicted."

"I get it," he replied. "But it's not like, even if you had all your memories, he was a viable option for you. Whatever the circumstances of your breakup, it was the right thing. You probably ended it yourself. You know you deserve a man who loves only you." Peter took her hand again. "That's what I'm offering you, Jose. You and me.

"Let the past go. Hey, if you want to get in touch with this guy to find out what happened, get closure — do it. I trust you. Hell, invite us both for dinner, we'll talk it out, the three of us, like adults."

Josie almost laughed at this. Peter's confidence was so unwavering. He was so convinced he was right for her, and his love would win the day. Then again, he didn't know the whole truth — that the man she was struggling to get over wasn't an affair, but her husband. She felt so sorry for Peter, being so disempowered without all the facts. She leaned over the table to kiss him.

"Not a good idea. But you're right, I need to move on. I'm working on it. And you're helping."

After a delicious but tiny dessert, they went up to their room and raided the mini-bar for candy. They pigged out on overpriced chocolate, watched a slushy romantic comedy, which Peter admitted he enjoyed, and made love in the way they'd gotten used to. He fell asleep almost immediately.

Josie tossed in bed, unsettled. The sugar high diminishing, she drifted in and out of sleep, with the occasional unconscious fondle from Peter preventing her from going under for long.

She must've dozed off, because sometime later she awoke, bolt upright in bed, sweating. A split second earlier, she had been in some beautiful city, with hundreds of people in lavish clothing, and extravagant buildings. Also water, so much water, all around.

Venice.

But in her dream, it hadn't been present-day Venice — it couldn't have been, as everyone was in period outfits, huge ballgowns with ruffles, men in courtiers' clothing. All wearing masks.

Then she had turned to a giant, gold-framed mirror, and she too was wearing a huge dress and a wig, and a full-faced mask. Rob was beside her, smiling, so happy, so in love. She had stepped toward the mirror and lifted off her mask. And that was when she woke.

Josie wiped the sweat from the back of her neck.

Was it her, under there? Or Other Josie? And why was she dreaming of them in Venice?

It was a city she'd never visited, though she knew Other Josie had, with her mother. But she and Rob had only talked about going, after watching *The Wings of the Dove*. The one where Linus Roache has to choose between two women who love him, and he hides with Helena Bonham-Carter from the other woman, and has sex with her, in a dark corner, during the carnival.

Josie stayed upright in bed, nauseated. And it wasn't the candy.

CHAPTER 27

Mid-June

Suzie and Josie strolled in Central Park on a hot Saturday afternoon, twins Euan and Isla running on ahead. Suzie craned her neck to check what they were up to. "So how's it going with Peter? And why haven't you invited us to meet him? You've been together, what, four months? Isla! Stay on the path!"

"Not yet three months," Josie protested. "And you'll meet him after the concert next weekend. We're performing a duet together."

"A few minutes after a show isn't much. He's your boyfriend. We need to meet him properly."

"I *guess* he's my boyfriend . . . he says he loves me and wants to be my boyfriend. But I'm not sure just because he says something is so, makes it so."

"What are you talking about? You've been together for months, he loves you, he's met David and Anna. If that's not being a boyfriend, I don't know what is. If it looks like a duck, and walks like a duck, and freakin' quacks—"

"I get it. It's a goddamn duck. So he's my boyfriend. But I don't feel 100% like I'm his girlfriend. He's so confident he can make me happy, it's like nothing else matters. It's not that I'm saying no, but this is a guy who won't take no for an answer. You realize I turned him down three times when he first started asking me out?"

"You can't blame him for being persistent, especially when you obviously liked him. Isla! Leave those crows alone."

"Sure, but it's not liking him that's the problem. He's super-cute and . . ." Josie checked around for eavesdroppers, "great in the sack. But I'm not in the right frame of mind to fall in love with him. I just can't get there."

"Why not?" Suzie asked.

Josie turned to her. "Oh, I don't know, Suzie. Maybe the fact I have a husband in another life." Her voice was harsher than she intended. "Isn't that enough?"

Suzie kept her eyes on the twins, pursing her red lips. "Okay, Josie. No need to be snippy. I get that you're conflicted because of all your old memories. But surely, at some point, you have to accept this life as your new reality. Right?"

Josie puffed her cheeks. "Do I? It's hard. I still really miss my husband. I know that's weird for you to hear, but it's the truth."

The serious Euan pulled on the pink sleeve of his gregarious sister, who was amusing a group of onlookers by flapping around with some crows.

"But Peter is so loving, and smart and charismatic, I find myself forgetting all about Rob for a while. And then, after Peter's gone, I remember, and I'm wracked with guilt. It's not a healthy way to conduct a relationship, is it?"

"I guess not," Suzie replied. "But maybe you can eventually get over that. Those old memories will fade, and you can be happy with Peter. In the meantime, don't push a great guy away."

Euan and Isla came running back. "Ice cream!" they demanded. They'd reached the lake, and Suzie bought the kids waffle cones while she and Josie each got a small cup of gelato. Suzie plonked the kids on the bench, where they could all watch the ducks.

"Sit nicely and eat your ice cream," she told them. "Hey, check those out, Josie! Looking and walking and quacking like ducks. I wonder what they are."

Josie stuck her tongue out. "I know. I'm just feeling messed up."

"You're going to London for the big send-off, right? It'll be therapeutic to spend time with your family." Suzie took a big mouthful of gelato.

"Yeah, flying next Sunday, day after the show. Their farewell party is the following Saturday, and then David and Anna fly to Sydney after that. Then I'm going to spend the next week with Laura and Theo. I miss that little guy so much."

"I'll bet. When is David and Anna's baby due?"

"October. Did I tell you? They're having a girl. We found out a few weeks ago."

"Oh, how cute! A baby niece for you. Too bad she'll be so far away. When will you meet her?"

"I'll fly to Sydney mid-November for the wedding. It'll be spring there, so it's perfect, and the baby will be a month old. After that . . . who knows how long before I see them again? David says they'll visit either London or New York once a year, but I suspect that's ambitious."

"Yeah, it's tough with little ones. I haven't been home or seen my brother or nephew in two years. And they're only in Ohio."

"Wow. I can't imagine not seeing David or my niece for that long."

"Well, it's so hard, when you all have small kids. But it won't be like that for you and David, I'm sure. It'll just always be you who's the one to visit him in Australia, as you're so much more mobile. Don't expect Anna to schlep her kids across the world to visit you on a regular basis."

Josie finished her ice cream. "You're right. It's always going to be me making the effort, as a childless, single person who can fly anywhere."

Suzie nudged her. "Maybe if you let this thing with Peter really happen, you won't be childless or single. I'll bet Peter wants kids."

Josie took Suzie's empty ice cream cup, slotting it into her own.

"Then I'll really never see David or my niece. No thanks."

CHAPTER 28

Late August

August 24, 2018

Man, it's hot. Any time I share a bed with Peter it feels sti-fling, and I can't tell if it's us as a couple, or just me. Doesn't matter how wide I open the window, or how light the sheets. Sometimes I sleep in the second bedroom for a few hours, to get some distance and coolness. He grumbles about that, though.

We've been bickering a fair amount. He's mad I still haven't told him I love him, even though he's said it lots, and we've been together a while now. And I get mad at his over-con-fidence, and because I'm frustrated I can't let go of my old life. But I care about Peter so much, I also don't want to lose him. So, it's better to put a bit of space between each other. He's been spending fewer nights at mine. Even now, after five months of dating, I've never once stayed at his place.

I'm so tired. I've been having a lot of nightmares — about you, and mirrors, and masks. Sometimes in Venice, and sometimes on a remote, west-facing beach. Always Rob, with you, often both of you laughing at me. I ask you why you're doing this to me, stealing my husband, my life. I beg you to give him back. I plead with you. I wake up exhausted.

And recently, a new fun thing — panic attacks. At home, at work, riding my bike, watching TV, in bed with Peter . . . I've been having them quite badly, every few days. A flood of gut-churning panic rises in my stomach and waves through my body, hitting my head a few seconds later, making me dizzy and almost unable to stand. Even on days without the attacks, my appetite has diminished and my stomach is over-sensitive. My insides have gone squishy.

I realize I'm pretty much clinically depressed at this point. If I went to a doctor and listed my symptoms, that's what they'd say. I'd be referred to therapy and prescribed anti-depressants or anxiety meds. And if I took them, they might make me feel better.

But I don't want to feel better. I don't deserve to feel better. For most depressed people, I wouldn't hesitate to recommend they use whatever was prescribed. But I don't have a valid illness, a chemical imbalance that is messing with my brain. There is an actual reason I'm depressed, and it isn't okay to numb that with medication. Plus it wouldn't help to see a therapist, only to lie about the truth.

I'm in the wrong life. The wrong goddamn universe. And I'm in a relationship with the wrong man. A wonderful man, but the wrong man.

The one thing that has made living in this world worthwhile has been having David back. Miraculously, incredibly alive again. But now, he's in Australia with his new wife and soon their new baby, and I'll barely see him. Or even get to know my new niece as much as I'd like to.

Staring at the bright laptop in the darkness of her bedroom, Josie slowed her breathing, trying to subdue the melancholy that seemed prevalent these days. She glanced over at Peter, who had his back to her, sound asleep.

Thinking of her soon-to-be baby niece, Josie turned to the pictures Anna had emailed. She traced her finger over the latest sonogram of the unborn baby. This little girl who would think of her only as the distant Aunt Josie who lived in New York, who mailed her birthday and Christmas gifts and visited every couple of years.

Josie let a tear fall on her bare chest. Peter sensed something and stirred, rolling over toward her in the darkness. He looked at her face, lit by the cold whiteness of the screen.

"Honey. Whatcha doing?" he muttered.

"Just the pictures Anna sent me. She has a big belly already. Go back to sleep, I won't be long."

"Are you crying?" He sat up in bed and tried to put his sweat-sticky arm around her, but she pulled away.

"It's too hot . . . I'm fine. A bit emotional about David having a baby in Australia. I can't wait to meet her."

"We'll be there in November for the wedding. We'll meet her then."

Josie winced. Peter had assumed he would accompany her to Sydney for the wedding, and she didn't know how to handle it. Part of her wanted him there, and she knew they could make a bigger trip of it. But mostly she wanted quality time with her family and no other distractions.

"What?" He eyed her suspiciously.

"I'm not sure." Three in the morning was probably not the best time to resolve this.

"What?" he repeated, more irritably. They sat in the dark, a slight orange glow coming in from the streetlights outside.

She braced herself. So, it looked like it was going to be now, after all. She closed the laptop and put it on the nightstand.

"I'm not sure you coming to Australia is the best thing." The best thing was to be honest. "I'm unsure, because we'd have a great time, and I know you're keen to see the Gold Coast. But there's another part of me that longs for a close family holiday — with the baby, and the wedding, and all."

Peter sat upright and switched on his bedside light. Josie blinked in the sudden brightness.

"Are you kidding me, Jose? You don't want me to come with you?"

"I'm not sure, that's all. I'm torn about it, and I thought I'd better be straight with you. There are two options, for two very different visits, and I can't figure out which I'd prefer."

"Well, shit, Jose. What about what I prefer? Don't I get a say? Is this trip *The Josie Show*? Most women would 'prefer' to have their boyfriend with them at a family wedding, and for an amazing Australia vacation, you know that?"

"Of course — and I didn't say I don't want you there, only that I'm uncertain."

"Give me a break. That's bullshit."

Josie rose and pulled on her robe, unable to be naked in bed if they were going to fight. Peter stared at her. Josie's knees trembled, so she sat again, this time at the foot of the bed.

"I'm having a hard time. You know that, P. I'm feeling shitty all the time, and I am having a real challenge being in such an intense relationship. I really care about you, a lot — but sometimes it's too much. I understand you're making an effort, and I appreciate it. But two weeks in Australia, with all my family, with the wedding, and the baby . . . That's a lot. Maybe a little more than I can handle."

Peter shook his head. He stared down at his hands, less furious than defeated. For some reason, that was worse.

"You care about me, a lot," he echoed. A redness appeared around his eyes. She'd never seen him cry. "But you don't love me. You still don't love me. You're depressed, Josie, but no matter what I say, you refuse to get help. And I can't make you happy. You won't let me." He grimaced.

"I'm so sorry. I really am." Josie reached out and put her hand on his leg. "You deserve better than what I'm giving you, we both know that." For some reason, she wasn't crying, despite her misery.

Peter looked up, stricken. "What are you saying? That it's over?"

"I'm not saying anything. Only that you deserve better, which is true." Josie also felt panicked at the idea of a breakup. What did she have in this world, without him?

"Damn straight. Question is, are you going to give me better?"

That confidence. He was expecting a yes.

"I've been trying to give you better for months, and I'm doing worse than ever. I can't say yes. I have no promises to offer." She shook her head, exhausted. All she wanted was sleep.

Peter stared at her, stunned. They sat in tense silence for a moment, and then he swung his legs out of bed, tugging on his briefs and jeans. He stood upright, pulling his T-shirt over his head.

"I'm going home. When you decide you want to be in this relationship, you give me a call."

He stopped at the bedroom door. "Otherwise, you likely won't see me for a while. I wasn't sure about rejoining the choir this fall, with the band doing so many gigs, so maybe it's better if I don't."

He didn't move, probably hoping she would try to talk him out of quitting choir. But the truth was it was kind of a relief. If they had to break up, Josie didn't want him at rehearsals.

She gave him a tiny nod. Peter shook his head and walked out. A minute later, Josie heard him slam the main door downstairs. Even above the bridge traffic's drone, she could make out his footsteps as he walked away from her building.

At least now she would be able to get some rest.

PART FIVE: ME

CHAPTER 29

Mid-October

It's all starting to crumble.

The more Rob and I try to hang on and tell each other everything is fine, the quicker it seems to turn to dust.

He texted me earlier today.

> Hey baby. Sorry I didn't see you for breakfast. I remembered what day it is, so I wanted to say I hope you're having an okay day and not feeling too sad. Let's order in tonight and watch a movie — your pick. Love you. R x

That was sweet. I look at my reply.

> Thanks honey. It's always a crappy day without David, but I appreciate you thinking of me and remembering the anniversary of his death while you're so busy at work. I know Hawaii wasn't all bad, it was our first wedding after all, even if I don't remember, so we should

celebrate. Takeout sounds good, maybe Malaysian food? I'll pick a movie that D would have appreciated. See you later tonight Jx

I lean against the barrier of our terrace, unafraid of the eighteen-story drop, staring over the city but seeing only my brother's laughing face.

Where is he? London, or somewhere more exotic? Is she with him — Other Josie? Has she become as entrenched in my old life as I have in hers?

Would she trade with me, if she had the chance? With David back in her life, after losing him, would she trade him to have her husband back? If she's met up with the Rob in her timeline, too, she has them both. Perhaps she's laughing at me, figuring I got the raw end of the deal.

It doesn't feel like that, though. The nightmares keep coming, Other Josie visiting me almost every night, imploring me to give her life back to her. Like she'd do anything to be back with Rob. Even lose David again.

I stand on the terrace a long time, the westerly sun still high and warm on my skin, thinking of all the people below who would do anything to have a life like mine. One of the many aspects of my guilt is the sense of disgust at my own ingratitude, my inability to embrace all I've been given. Who gets thrust into a life of love and luxury and gets depressed?

I try to shake it off, and with one last look at the view, go into the master bedroom through the door at the end of the terrace. Opening the media cabinet, I turn on the huge TV, browsing for movies to watch after dinner. I add six to the playlist as the apartment door closes with a thunk.

"Hey," I hear Rob call.

"Hey," I call back, going out to the kitchen. Rob is unpacking boxes of Malaysian takeout, which I have little appetite for. "This good?"

"Great, thanks. Want a drink? I'm on G&Ts."

"A beer, thanks."

I pop a beer and hand it over while he spoons cod and rice into shallow dishes. He kisses me on the side of my head, absently.

"How are you doing?"

"Okay. Not amazing. I was distracted at work today, thinking about David — and I totally forgot a 3 p.m. meeting with Hans and the *Luxury Listing* producers, I didn't show up, so Hans had a go at me about that. It's more than today, though — my brain sucks on these meds. I'm going to have to stop, or switch again. I'm useless."

We take the plates to the dining table.

"That sucks, baby, I'm sorry. Talk to Dr. Weiner, I guess." That's his name for Dr. Weinstein.

"I will. How was your breakfast meeting? Will you get the hotel job?"

"We got it, already! The meeting was awesome, but we weren't expecting to hear back for a week. Then they called back this afternoon! Such a relief."

"That's amazing, honey." I lift my glass to him. He's brilliant. "They decided that quick, huh? They must've loved you guys. When will it start?"

"After we've completed the Tribeca lofts, early next year. We should slide straight into the new project. Oh, Hans has a buyer for 701 at Tribeca. He tell you?"

I shake my head. "He was too busy asking me where the hell I was at 3 p.m. The answer being sobbing about my dead brother in the washroom."

Rob puts down his fork, hesitates, then looks me in the eye. "Josie, I'm sorry about David, and I understand it's hard today. But can we not make this about you and your issues right now? I'm trying to celebrate a major achievement here."

I nod. He's right. "I'm sorry. This is a good day for you. You deserve your moment." I raise my glass to his again. "Congratulations, my love." I lean across the corner of the table, and go to kiss him on the cheek, but he turns and meets my lips with his. He tastes of fish and beer.

After dinner, the mood is amicable but fragile, and I'm glad to move into the bedroom for the movie. As I dim the lights and turn on the big screen, he settles down in his armchair, giving me the chaise as usual.

"I made a playlist," I tell him, tucking a leg underneath me. "I wasn't sure which you'd seen. Any of these and I'm happy."

I start scrolling through.

"*Australia*? That's the only Baz Luhrmann I haven't seen."

He shakes his head. "That thing's more than three hours long."

"Fair enough. What about a foreign film, one of the Oscar winners? This one is supposed to be incredible: *The Lives of Others* — fancy it?"

"Nah. Josie and I saw it a few years ago and . . ."

The air in the room freezes.

"What did you say?"

In the light of the TV, Rob is staring at the screen, the beer suspended halfway to his lips. He lets out a slow, steady breath, clearly working out how to recover. He puts the beer down and turns to me.

"You know what I mean — the *old* Josie. The old you, before your accident. You get what I mean."

I shake my head. "Rob. You've never spoken about her as a separate person from me. Ever. You know you haven't. You've always believed I'm her, I'm your wife, your original wife, just . . . with different memories. Haven't you?"

He's silent for a moment, pressing his lips together. His tell.

"Josie. What do you want me to say? I got nothing. I have no idea what the fuck to think about any of it. What difference does it make?"

"*What difference?* Are you kidding me?"

The magnitude of this moment is dawning on me. "I'm now discovering you think of me as an entirely different person to the woman you originally married — a woman

269

who, what, disappeared on the day of my accident? And yet you proposed to me, and married me! And, what? You don't think of me as your first wife? I'm your second wife? I'm Josie 2.0?"

He gets up and paces across the room. Even in the low light, the fire in his eyes is back. Only I can make him angry like this.

"Yes. Okay? YES. Is that what you want to hear? Fuuucckkk . . . Why shouldn't I believe it? It's what you believe. Isn't it? You don't think you're the same person — you think the original Josie is somewhere living your life, as you're living hers. Why shouldn't I think so too? You've spent the past year proving to me you're not the same person, that you're a different Josie. Why act surprised now? Really, why?"

He's glaring at me, demanding an answer.

I hesitate, trying to get the words right. "Because even though I always felt I was betraying her by marrying you, I didn't know you felt that way too. But now . . . you can't tell me you don't feel you've betrayed her by being with me. If you think of her as separate from me, then for as long as you've believed that, you've realized you're being unfaithful. And you've never shared that with me. Not once."

"Oh, it's worse than that. Much worse." Rob's even madder now, but I'm beginning to realize he's as angry at himself as he is at me. Probably more so. "I know you're a different woman, and I married you anyways. I'm a *bigamist*."

He starts at the sound of the word escaping his lips. It hangs in the air, making me nauseated, the cod dangerously close to coming back up again. He's only saying what I've thought myself, many times — but hearing it out loud is shocking.

Rob presses on. He's on a roll.

"You know what else? I never even grieved the loss of the first Josie. The loss of my *wife*. Not really. Because I believed, foolishly, stupidly, it would be better with you."

Rob presses the heels of his hands to his face, and it's a moment before I realize he is sobbing. His knees buckle, and he collapses to the floor by the chaise. I lean forward and half-catch him in my arms as he crumples at my feet, his head on my thigh.

He's speaking in gasps now. "And the thing is, we would've gotten through it, she and I . . . our issues, the loss of David, her pain after Hawaii. We were still okay, deep down. But then you switched places with her and I . . . *abandoned* her." It's almost a wail, and he finally loses it completely, the build-up of grief coming out after staying stoic all this time.

I hold him in my arms a long time, letting him get it out, sobbing myself, fat tears dripping off my chin. I hold him and hold him.

When the sobs subside, he looks up at me. "It's not you I'm angry with." A new tear forms, glinting in the low light.

"I know. I know." I stroke his black tousled hair. I want to kiss him. Instead I ask, "How long have you felt this way?"

He shrugs. "Honestly, I pretty much believed you from the outset. I knew you were telling your truth, about your old life, but we had agreed you were still the same person, right? That you'd somehow slipped into a different timeline, but not *switched*. But you were so different in a lot of ways, and I kept dreaming about the old Josie trying to reach me — I never told you about that."

"What? No, you didn't."

"I guess I had the strong sense of you being a separate person from early on. But I suppressed it. I distracted myself by falling in love again with this new, seemingly improved Josie. Then we had our incredible weekend on Orcas Island when we got together — and sure, I pretended to myself it was us getting back together, but it felt like getting together for the first time. It was all so great after that — my proposal, our wedding."

He rubs his eyes, his long lashes clumped with moisture. "Then in Venice, when you said you'd been there before with your Mum . . . That was a gut punch. I knew then, truly knew, I'd remarried a woman who wasn't my wife."

He searches my face, but he's seeing something else. "It was so freaky with the masks, at the ball. Like, you could've been either of my two wives at that moment. And I knew you felt it too. I was messed up about it, but it turned me on so much, too." He winces. "What a cliché I am — turned on by the idea of two identical wives."

I kiss the top of his head. "None of this is your fault."

Rob kneels, gathering himself together, taking my face in his hands. "It's not yours either. You tried to be everything for me. You've been trying so hard to live her life, to be her, that it's so obvious you aren't."

He kisses me, the taste of our streaming tears salty on my tongue. He kisses me harder, leaning me back on the chaise, kissing my neck, burying his face in my cleavage, undoing my shirt buttons.

We silently, tearfully make love under the light of the big-screen TV, the words *The Lives of Others* lit up above our heads.

CHAPTER 30

Mid-November

> *Nov 15, 2018*
>
> *I've been extracting myself from H&F. I feel like I already have one foot out the door, and they don't need me anymore, they need a new assistant to replace Angela, who is pretty much doing my job. Our job. Your job, really. I feel almost as much of a fraud doing your job as I feel being your husband's wife.*
>
> *Ever since I moved back into the art room a few weeks ago, to give us both some space, Rob's become pretty withdrawn. But it helps me, being in here, surrounded by things that make sense to me, by art from my previous life. Or, should I say, our previous life. From when you and I were the same person.*
>
> *I wish I could go back to being that person. Do you wish it too?*
>
> *It's all I think about.*

I put my pen down on the dressing table and scan the artwork on the gallery wall. It always gives me comfort.

But then my gaze rests on a large piece that has been in the room only a few months. Above the bed is giant, near-life-sized photo of us in Venice, at the ball. Rob contacted the photographer without my knowledge and had it framed and delivered. I jumped around with excitement as he pulled away the brown paper and bubble wrap protecting it at the time.

It's fabulous. We're in front of the ballroom's elaborate paneled wall, in full eighteenth-century dress, wig, hat and masks. It's beautiful, but terrifying. We're unrecognizable, me even more than Rob because of the full-face mask. We could be total strangers — impostors. It seems unfathomable the woman is me.

I turn back to my journal. For months now, I've been addressing everything to her. Other Josie. I realized some time ago that chronicling my journey was not only for my own record-keeping, to try to stay sane. I've also acknowledged that I'm figuring my way out of this life, and this is a year's worth of information she'll need, if she comes back.

And I think she's coming back.

So then, the question is . . . how would she do that?

It's one that is easily answered, because she's me. All I have to ask is: what would I do?

And it's a no-brainer. I'd recreate the conditions that got me here in the first place. A bike crash at that intersection, at that same time and date. The first time, we managed to swap with each other by being in an impact at the exact same place and time in our respective universes. So it stands to reason, if it can be called reason, we would switch back the same way.

There's a catch, of course. We'd both have to do it at the same time. I'd have to take the same life-threatening risk, as she would, for it to stand any chance of working.

I think about what Other Josie will be doing in preparation, if that's what she's planning. She'll have probably been in the UK, spending time with David. She'll let him go — knowing that, truly, he's not her brother anymore, he's mine. Hers died in Hawaii, at her wedding. At least this way she was able to have some time with him, and say a real goodbye, before giving him back to me. Before taking back her husband.

I never meant to steal your husband. You know that. The guilt of betraying you has been unbearable.

I know what you want me to do. You tell me in my dreams, insisting I give you back your love, your life.

I know you're coming for him. I know how and when. It's soon. And the answer is yes. I'll do it.

Rob can't bear it either and it's been tearing us apart — first gradually, now rapidly. We have no way of coming back from this. His guilt is even worse than mine now. He feels he should have admitted to himself that he knew I wasn't you, right from the start. That he should have rejected this new version of his wife and searched for a way to get you back. He's in agony over it.

If our plan works, if you get back here, if you're reading this — you have to forgive him. Please, please forgive him and try to move forward. He's suffered enough, and he does love you. And since I turned out not to be a new-and-improved Josie after all, quite the opposite, I think he'd be much happier with you. With you, he can be at peace again. You are his true wife, after all — I'm merely an unwitting impostor.

If you're reading this, I hope you've read all my journal, from the start. I'm sure you will. You'll also understand this couldn't have failed to happen. Of course I fell in love with him — I'm you. And of course he fell in love with me — I'm YOU. Mostly you, anyway. Altered by circumstance, by life choices — but fundamentally you. It was the only way it could have gone.

But if our plan doesn't work, if we're stuck here, in each other's lives — I'm going to try to make it work with him. Because I'll have done everything I could, and I don't think I'll feel the same kind of guilt. Rob may, still. But he'll also realize nothing can be done, and, well . . . you know him. So goddamn stoic. He might learn to live with it.

Don't forget, I love him more than I've ever loved anyone.

Still, if our plan doesn't work . . . well, you won't even be reading this, and I'm just talking to myself, shouting into the wind. I guess I'll stop this journal after that. Then, maybe it'll work out between me and Rob — or maybe it's too late, we're too damaged. Maybe we'll split up anyway. But that's a decision we can only make after D-day.

I look back up at the intimidating Venice picture.

She'll have a terrible shock, if she does return, when she finds out Rob and I got married. Slash, remarried. And that we went to Venice, where she wanted to go with him. And that I tattooed the back of her neck.

It's all in the journal, though, so I have to trust she'll read it and gradually understand.

Until then, I have little to plan. Aside from leaving behind as much information as possible, both in my journal, and my extensive notes at the H&F job, I'm all done. It's not as though I can even pack a suitcase for a journey to another universe. No passport required.

Just nerves of steel and the resolve to do the right thing.

Even if it means losing the greatest love of my life.

CHAPTER 31

Thanksgiving

The apartment door slams, and I look up from the couch. Rob is at the top of the steps, taking off his coat. He's tired and drawn. "Hey."

"Hey. You're back earlier than I thought."

"Yeah, I don't want us to be late for this party. You gonna get ready? I have to change my shirt."

I nod, mustering the energy for the dinner. I've been feeling okay, relatively speaking, and I've been sleeping better, even though I'm off the meds. The dreams are all but gone. They stopped when I made the decision to do what I'm going to do, one week from now.

Someone, my mother probably, once told me depressed patients with a suddenly improved mood are a much higher suicide risk, as people often feel better when they've decided to end their misery and have formulated a plan. I wonder if what I'm feeling is like that. A sort of attempt at suicide — from this life, at least. Considering the risk I'll be taking, possibly actual suicide.

I step into the art bedroom, changing into the cobalt-blue dress I wore the first time I had dinner with Rob, piling up my hair. When I emerge, Rob is at the kitchen island. He smiles as I come up the steps.

"You look great. I like this dress on you." He leans in for a soft kiss, careful not to smudge my lipstick. "You realize you'll have to smile tonight, right?"

I grin at him to show I'm quite capable of smiling. "Actually, I'm in a good mood. You ready?"

"Wow. Put her in a nice frock and she's transformed. It's a miracle cure. Okay, let's go."

I laugh, a little forced, but at least the mood is light as we get a cab to Mike and Hans's loft. A few of our other H&F colleagues have already arrived — Josh and Austin, Angela and her boyfriend, and several of the agents I've come to know well. At the center, Mike and Hans, the perfect hosts, pouring glass after glass of champagne, their caterers serving up a turkey dinner at a long table.

I uncharacteristically stick to virgin mojitos, not wanting to get drunk and maudlin. Better to avoid alcohol tonight. I don't want to start making confessions.

Rob, on the other hand, is clearly drinking away the pain, downing glass after glass of bubbly, then switching to whiskey. He's making an effort to be sociable, but I can tell a lot of it is for show.

When the Thanksgiving toast comes, I kiss my husband. Suddenly wondering if this could be one of the last times, I linger in the kiss, then lean into it, more passionate than is perhaps appropriate for the table. We even attract a couple of whistles from Hans, and one "Get a room!" — which we ignore.

Breaking free, I hold Rob's face in my hands. "Happy Thanksgiving, baby."

He looks at me, sensing something is up. But all he says is, "Happy Thanksgiving, my love."

By midnight I'm done, and Rob is decidedly drunk as we return home. Back at the apartment, he throws his coat and shoes off in the lobby and follows me into the kitchen, where he leans in for another kiss.

"Okay, booze breath." I half-laugh, pushing him gently back. "Bed, I think. Drink some water." I kiss him firmly on the cheek. "Night, honey."

I head into the art room, wondering if I should sleep in the main bedroom tonight. But Rob's drunk. Better to have a quiet night's sleep.

I'm climbing into bed when the door opens. Rob leans against the frame.

"Don't sleep in here, baby," he slurs. "Be with me tonight." He stumbles into the room and nudges me to the other side of the bed, taking off his pants and shirt, getting in. He is drunker than I thought.

"Rob, you're kinda wasted. We'll talk tomorrow."

I try to ease his body off the bed. But he's a big guy and barely notices. He pulls the covers over him and lies down, facing away from me, turning out the bedside light.

"Just lie with me," he mumbles, already falling asleep. He reaches back for my hand and pulls my arm over him.

Holding him feels so good, I quit resisting. With one arm across him, I stroke his thick black hair with my other hand, feeling him drift off. It's comforting to watch him sleep. Even if it is alcohol-induced.

I don't know how many hours later, but it's not yet dawn when I wake to find the bedside light on again. Rob is no longer beside me, and I sit up with a start. He's at the dressing table, the ceramic mask staring at him. Then, with a lurch of my stomach, I see what he is doing.

I sit up, with a sinking feeling. We're in for another Big Talk.

Rob looks up at me, meeting my eyes in the mirror. He shakes his head. He holds up the journal. My journal.

"I couldn't resist. I couldn't not read it."

"I'm not mad. Honestly, if you had a journal, I'd have probably done the same thing." I pause. "How much have you read?"

He swivels around to face me. His eyes are bloodshot, his hair all over the place. He's a mess.

"I started from the back. All the recent stuff, the past few months. When you started writing everything to *her*."

"Right."

The air in the room is thick.

He takes a sharp breath. "Are you leaving me? Is that 'the plan'?"

I bite my lip, thick saliva building at the back of my mouth, then give a tiny nod. "I think she's coming back for you. I need to let her."

"What? How is that even possible? What are you planning, Josie?"

I can't tell him.

"Come on, baby — none of this says what you're planning to do. What *is* it? You going to pack your bags and disappear?"

I press my lips together. "I'm not going to tell you the plan, Rob. I've no clue if there's any chance of it even working. I can tell you it's happening soon, and then we'll know. If it works, she'll be back, and she'll be your wife — your *real* wife — and I'll be gone. If it doesn't work, I'll still be here, and I'll have done everything I could. I'll be absolved, and you will be too. There will be no more guilt. I hope."

Rob throws the journal on the floor and comes to the bed, climbing on it, kneeling over me. "I don't *want* you to go, Josie. I love you . . . so, so much. Don't leave me." His voice breaks, and he buries his head in my shoulder. "Don't leave me, baby, please."

"You love her, too," I remind him, stroking his back. "And she's your real wife. We love each other, but it's not enough. I told you in Venice I hoped it would be enough, but it's not."

He lifts his eyes to the giant photograph above our heads, and his face contorts with despair. He punches the bottom of the frame, splintering it. "Fuck Venice. Fuck all of it. What am I going to do without you, Josie? I love you so much." His body collapses on me. "Don't leave me."

280

I hold him. "If the plan doesn't work, and I'm still here, then I'll never leave you," I murmur in his ear. "I'll know we're meant to be. Trust me."

We both sob ourselves into a restless sleep, the beside light left on the whole time.

CHAPTER 32

November 30

D-day.

Also, my thirty-seventh birthday. Not that it matters.

I wake before the alarm and lie staring at the ceiling, trying not to dwell on what I'm planning for 6.17 that evening.

Get through the day. Don't think about it.

I shower and dress in office clothes. A regular Friday at work. I'm relieved of an excuse not to hang around at home today.

The day after Thanksgiving was truly a Black Friday. Rob was all misery and hangover, dark circles under his eyes, loafing in the bedroom in his sweats all day, watching action movies, saying nothing. Nothing to say, I suppose.

Today it's a bright, late-autumn day, cold and crisp, just like one year ago. Thank goodness. No reason to leave the bike at home today. The plan is a go.

In the kitchen, Rob is in his suit, eating oatmeal at the island. "Happy birthday." He turns to me, "I made you oatmeal."

"Thanks, baby." I manage a smile, kissing him on the temple. I fill a bowl with oatmeal I don't want and sit next to him. I force a few spoonfuls down. When did food stop being good?

Rob picks up a blue envelope and holds it out to me. "I thought you might like this."

I open the envelope to find a birthday card that simply says, "Happy Birthday, Josie. All my love, always — Rob xo"

Out of it drops a smaller envelope, which contains two gift cards for a weekend luxury spa hotel package in Vermont, one bearing my name, the other for Suzie.

Rob gestures to the voucher. "You haven't spent much time with her recently, so I figured you'd like it. I ran it past Donald, too. I can even go to a game with him and the twins, or something."

I'm filled with love for him and give his cheek a lingering kiss. "Thank you, honey. Such a thoughtful gift." My voice thickens.

He has no idea today is the day. He still thinks we have time.

Rob gets up, his jaw set, putting his bowl into the dishwasher. "Well, I have to go. See you tonight. I'll cook you a birthday meal, or something."

I stand, emptying my uneaten oatmeal into the garburator, stalling for time. I'm filled with panic. I may never see him again.

No, no, no. This can't be it.

He sees my anxiety and misinterprets it. "You'll be fine at work, baby. Have a good day." He pulls me close for a moment. I want to kiss him, one last time. But his face so drawn, this is not the moment — this cannot be our last kiss. Better to leave it as that kiss at Thanksgiving — passionate, heartfelt. Not . . . sad, like this.

Rob takes my shoulders, presses his lips to my forehead, then lets go. He pulls his coat from the closet, and lets himself out the front door, giving me one final look. One last sad smile.

I collapse against the kitchen island, sobs taking over, tears ruining my office makeup. I slide down to the floor. But the tears subside, and my need to fulfill the plan gradually takes over.

Pull your shit together, Josie. It's D-day.

I go into the bedroom and fix my makeup. I spot the journal where Rob flung it to the floor. This is for Other Josie, now. I prop it up against the dressing table mirror, next to the mask, which looks at me accusingly.

"Okay, okay," I tell the mask. "I'm doing it."

Downstairs in the parking garage, I unlock Daredevil, the red bike Rob bought me to replace Electra after my crash, and ride out into the cold November air.

Pushing down the fear building inside me, I spend my day at the office completing my recap of the past year at H&F — everything Other Josie missed. If she returns to this job, the amnesia routine won't fly a second time — she'll need to "remember" the last twelve months of campaigns and meetings. Beyond that, she's going to have to wing it. That is, if she wants the job, after all this time away.

If this plan even works, of course.

My only real interaction is lunch with Angela, which is unusual in itself. She dodged me at Mike and Hans's Thanksgiving dinner but then insisted on having lunch today, not that she seems to care it's my birthday. She seems like she has something to tell me and has trouble meeting my eyes.

"Josie, I'm sorry," she blurts, "but I did a comms plan for next year, which I gave to Mike before Thanksgiving." She looks up to see my reaction. "I get that it's your job. But you've kinda been—"

I put a hand on her arm. "Ange. It's fine. I'd have done the same thing. Good for you."

She takes a bite of her sandwich, clearly relieved. But I can barely eat, I'm so nervous about The Plan. I push my plate away. "Confidentially, I'm not sure if it'll work out for me at H&F. This week, I need to decide whether to give it a real shot or consider my options."

Angela examines my face with curiosity. "You do what you gotta do. But seriously, what's up with you? Both you and Rob have been weird. Rob was super-drunk at Thanksgiving."

I take a sip of my water. "I've been having a hard time, a lot of anxiety. To do with my amnesia — not fully grieving my brother, all kinds of shit surfacing. It's been hard on Rob, too."

"You poor thing." But she says it without feeling. "Could be you need a longer break. I'm not saying that because I want your job, I swear!"

"Ha, right." I half-smile, getting up and pulling on my coat. "We both know you want my job. But, like I said, I don't blame you."

As I finish up my handover notes and hit the "save" button, my hands start shaking. I rest my forehead on the desk and take a series of long, steady breaths. At this rate, I'll be such a wreck, I'll never make it to the crash spot.

Calm down, calm down.

I check my phone's clock yet again, which is ticking agonizingly toward the alarm I've set. I have to time it right, so I'll go to the spot early, in case of unforeseen delays. Leaving the office at 5.45 p.m. will be plenty.

Mike and Hans are out, so I won't see them again, and I've already said goodbye to Josh and other colleagues, none of whom noticed the weight of my farewell. As the alarm sounds, I turn out my desk light, and head down to the bike lockup. No backing out now.

I put on my helmet, tightening the strap. It quite possibly saved my life last time. I turn on my lights and ride out onto Spring Street. I take the exact route Other Josie would have taken that night, riding to meet Rob at a gallery opening in Midtown East.

She'll take my route from that evening, and I'll take hers.

I ride until I'm a few yards away from the crash spot at Third and 25th, Baruch College on my left. I look at my watch. 6.09. I'm eight minutes early.

It has to be 6.17.

How do I do this? Ride out into traffic on a red light? What if she also waits for a red light? We could so easily miss each other.

There's no way of knowing. If she's on the other side, she'll be thinking the same thing.

Okay, as soon as the clock says 6.17, I'm closing my eyes and riding out. And she'll have to, too.

I spend the next minutes trying to ignore my rising panic. I keep checking my watch, then my phone, to be sure of the exact time. When it says 6.16, I stare at it, waiting for the moment. It takes forever.

6.17.

This is it.

Do it, do it.

I push off the curb and cycle hard to the intersection, not checking whether the light is red or green. At the moment I cross the line, I pedal harder and close my eyes.

I hear, seemingly in the distance, a car horn, someone shouting, tires screeching. An image leaps into my mind.

Rob in that loft on Orcas Island, his brown skin against white sheets, eyes shining, smiling at me. As clear as if I were back in the room with him.

And then, nothing.

PART SIX: HER

CHAPTER 33

Mid- to late October

"Oh, look at her. Those tiny fingers. She's the cutest thing."

"Yep, she's a keeper." David laughed, cradling his infant daughter.

Josie smiled at the baby on the screen, in the arms of her father, and shook her head in disbelief. Three years ago, her brother had died in Hawaii. Now he was a new father of three days, about to get married. And living in Australia.

"Man, I really wish I was with you guys," Josie said. "It's so emotional seeing you with Daisy. Thank goodness for Skype. At least we can sort of hang out."

The scene behind David's head was of a large, high-ceilinged room. The pink-orange light of sunset poured through tall windows, Anna moving in the background. Minutes previously, Josie had been making faces into the webcam at Daisy as the baby stared at the screen. So gorgeous — and so unaware of who Josie was.

In contrast, the inset image of Josie in the corner of the screen was one of her apartment at night, a weak table lamp lighting up half her face. About how she felt these days.

"Yeah," David looks tired. "But it's not the same. You're coming for the wedding, so that'll be brilliant. There's bags of space here. We have a guest room for you and Pete, a single room for Mum, and the basement suite for Laura, Adam, and Theo."

Josie inhaled. She hadn't told him about Peter but thought her mother would have by now. Clearly her mum was leaving Josie to do her own dirty work.

"Well, you can put me in the small room, because it'll only be me." She avoided looking into the webcam, ashamed. "Peter and I broke up six weeks ago."

Her brother frowned. "What? What happened, Jose? He's crazy about you. You can fix it, right?"

"I can't fix it, David. I don't want to. He was so great, *is* so great, but I never really fell in love with him. He knew that, and gave up. He said I could call him when I decide I want to be in the relationship, but the truth is, I never felt it was . . . right. So I haven't called him."

David looked gutted. She wished she felt the same. "Bosie, that blows. I thought he was perfect for you."

"Well, some things don't feel right. I know you liked him. It sucks for me, too. I do miss him. I realized after we broke up, he had become one of my closest friends. He was so fun to be around and brought so much music and laughter to my life. But I couldn't get there."

"I'm sorry, Bose. We'll cheer you up. When are your flights?"

"I'm arriving on the 7th, so I'll have a few days to get over jet lag before the wedding. Flying back on the 24th. I have to be back at work after that."

"You won't be here for your birthday?" David frowned. "That's a shame. You should've booked more time off."

Josie could have done, he was right. But she couldn't tell him why she had to be back that day.

"Yeah, but it's too long off the radio show. I've got fillers set up while I'm away, but the 26th is the first day back after

Thanksgiving. I have to be on air again." It was partly true, at least.

She heard Anna calling David for dinner.

"Guess you won't be going out too often, huh?" Josie said, changing the subject. "Our New Year's Eve in London seems a million miles away now."

"Yeah," David replied with a laugh, "and don't forget, it's because of New Year's Eve and meeting Anna that I'm here in Sydney and not going out. Possibly never going out again." He glanced lovingly at the baby.

"Oh, you will," Josie assured him. "When Daisy is eighteen, you'll have a social life again. Unless you have more kids, of course."

David laughed. "Thanks for that, you smug cow. I'd better go. Our neighbors brought us a casserole, and it smells incredible. Thanks for Skyping, sis. It was lovely to chat."

"You're welcome, and congratulations again." Josie's anxiety over the impending end of the conversation was kicking in. "I've got to go, anyway, it's nearly 2 a.m. I haven't had my Friday yet. Miss you loads. I can't wait to see you. Give Daisy a big snuggle from her Auntie Bosie."

"Will do. Gotta run. Bye."

The familiar bleep sounded as the call ended, and her screen went dark. All the light and joy of their home, many thousands of miles away, gone in an instant. Josie felt bereft. She hadn't even told her brother she loved him.

At least she'd see him again next month, she told herself. She could tell him she loved him then, in person.

She looked around her apartment. Despite the comfort it brought her, things were not great these days. She had figured that since she and Peter broke up, the anxiety might ease. That she'd have less guilt because she was no longer sleeping with a man who wasn't her husband.

But if anything, her depression had deepened. With Peter in her life, at least she'd had a lover. Someone to hold her and make her feel safe and adored. Someone to distract her from her grief.

Because grief it was, and she'd never fully processed it. The grief of losing her husband, of being thrown into a world where he was with someone else. Instead, she had drowned her sorrows in a pseudo-relationship with a good man who deserved better.

Now that Peter was gone, although she missed him a lot, it was Rob who had come back to the forefront of Josie's mind. She yearned for her husband and their life together, so much so she ached from it at every moment.

Josie downed a sleep aid and added a strong painkiller, her head pounding. She slid into bed and thought about her lost husband. And whether she would ever get him back.

Yes, she had reason to be back in New York. It was an idea that had been growing inside her for several weeks now.

The thought that maybe she *could* go back to her old life. That there was a way to do it. A terrifying and incredibly risky way. But one that left her with a small glimmer of hope.

Sleep finally came, and it was less of a nightmare. She felt she had some control. In her dream, on that sunset beach, she told Other Josie, "I want my husband back. I'm coming for him."

* * *

Lounging on the green velvet couch, Suzie put her feet up carelessly on Josie's shabby ottoman. "So, you feeling any better about the Peter breakup?"

Josie sat down beside Suzie, tucking her feet under her. "I guess. It's been weird at choir without him. I think everyone's a bit mad we got involved and then broke up, since it resulted in Peter quitting. Ryan said to me, 'This is why you don't shit where you eat.'" She screwed up her nose. "A delightful analogy. Anyway, choir aside, I'm feeling . . . better, yeah. It's been two months, and it was the right decision." Josie gave a small laugh. "Thank God I have you. Lord knows I can't afford a therapist. This is my therapy couch, right here, and you're my shrink. I hope you realize this." She shuffled down and lifted her bare feet onto Suzie's lap.

Suzie smiled, somewhat half-heartedly. "If you believe ending it with Peter was the right thing, it must've been. It's too bad, though, I really liked him. From what I saw of him."

"Peter was great. But you know how I'm feeling, Suze. He's not my guy. I'm not going to change how I feel about my old life, about my real husband. I understand you still want me to adjust to the new normal, but it isn't going to happen."

Suzie pursed her lips. "But, Jose, how are you going to live with that? Are you never going to be with anyone new, because you believe you have a husband in another goddam universe?"

Behind Suzie's head, Josie watched the first of fall's auburn leaves drop outside her living room window.

Should she tell her?

"Josie?"

Josie lifted her head to take a fortifying sip of her wine. She'd better tell someone, and Suzie was the only candidate.

"I think I might be able to go back," Josie's voice was small.

A crease appeared on Suzie's forehead. "Go back? Wait . . . you mean to your old life?"

"Yep. I think there might be a way." Josie sat upright. "I told you ages ago that I think I switched lives with another version of myself, the one who belongs to this life. And this Other Josie came from here, but is now living with my husband, right?

"But here's the thing. Maybe Other Josie and Rob aren't together in my old life. Maybe he realizes she isn't his real wife, and they aren't actually a couple, she's just stuck there. Or they are together, but it isn't working out because they know the truth — or at least she does. And think about it, there's David too. She's now in a life where David is dead. So it's possible Other Josie wants her old life back as much as I do."

Suzie pushed her scarlet lips out, looking doubtful. "Okay. But how does that get you back?"

"Well, if that's true, she'll have been thinking about how it could be done, just as I have. And there's only one answer to that question. We've got the same brain, so we'll come to the same conclusion."

"What's that?"

Josie bit her bottom lip, wondering if she should continue. "So, don't freak out, but . . . We have to do what got us here in the first place. But in reverse. We have to crash again — no, listen, Suze — in the same place and at the same time and date as last time. The date that caused our paths to diverge in the first place, my birthday, right?"

She took a deep breath. "If we both did that, at the exact same moment, *maybe* we'd switch back. I've been dreaming about Other Josie constantly, and I feel like she's going to do it. So I have to, as well. It's worth a try at least."

Suzie shook her head vehemently. "No, Jose, it isn't. It's stupid and dangerous. You could get hurt."

"That's the risk I'm willing to take," Josie replied firmly.

Suzie was silent for a moment. "Okay, even if what you're saying is real, and it works, you'd be going back to a world where David is dead again. No more David, ever, and where little Daisy never even existed. Can you do that?"

Josie watched another leaf drift past the window. "I've thought a lot about that. Of course I have. But I have to pick my poison. Ultimately, which is worth more to me? A brother and niece to see every couple of years, or a loving husband to spend my life with? I've made my decision on that, Suzie."

Suzie drained the last of her wine. "Clearly I can't stop you, you crazy-ass woman. But for God's sake, wear a bike helmet."

CHAPTER 34

Thanksgiving

Josie stretched out in the sunshine by the pool. It was her last day in Sydney, and she was still blown away by the place. David and Anna's cream-colored detached home in the Watson's Bay suburb was stunning, with its wide, lush garden overlooking the water, downtown Sydney shimmering in the distance. They must be paying David a fortune at the bank.

"How long have you got?"

Josie shaded her face. Anna, red hair gleaming in the sun, in a light blue sundress and red flip-flops, had six-week-old Daisy at her shoulder and an iPad tucked under one arm. Anna lowered herself onto a lounger, allowing the tablet to drop.

"Still a couple of hours. I'm all packed," Josie replied. "The taxi's booked for three. Is David on his way?"

"Yeah, ten minutes with the groceries, and we'll have a farewell lunch for you. Turkey sandwiches, by way of celebrating Thanksgiving. I can't believe you're going! I'm not sure when we'll see you next."

Josie felt a lump form in her throat as she set her lounger upright and held her arms out for Daisy. Anna handed her over and the baby snuggled happily into her aunt.

Josie closed her eyes. *Never again.*

"I know." Her voice was husky. "I'm going to miss you all so much. Especially seeing this little one grow."

"Well, hey," said Anna, brightly, "I have just the thing to keep us occupied until lunch, I was just showing Iris and Laura. The photographer emailed me the wedding photos. Wanna see?"

"Fantastic," Josie exclaimed, making an effort to cheer up.

Anna pulled her lounger closer and started flipping through images of what was a glorious day, in those very same gardens, two weeks before.

They began with Anna getting ready in the hotel the women had stayed in the night before the wedding, while David had stayed at home. The obligatory hair up-do shot, white strapless dress laid out on the bed. Josie remembered thinking she wouldn't have chosen a strapless dress and an up-do if she had been Anna, with that dolphin tattoo on her shoulder. But Anna didn't care.

The next set showed the wedding car bearing Anna and her parents to the house, a parade of family members greeting the bridal party. David was nowhere in sight, as was befitting, but their mother was dressed in her finery, holding a prettily dressed Daisy, with a bow tied around her head. Guests settling into the chairs lined up in the garden, in front of the flower-covered pergola, the bay glittering silver beyond. There was Josie herself, beaming away in her poppy dress. And then David, at the end of the aisle in a beige summer suit.

Josie welled up at the pictures of Anna being led down the aisle by her father and greeted by David, who was almost in tears. The vows, the rings, the kiss. Their mother handing the baby to them as Daisy had started bawling, the congregation laughing. It was a lot like Josie's own Hawaiian wedding to Rob.

Finally, the garden reception, a dance floor and string lights on the pool terrace, live band at one end. The speeches, including the best man's offering, which had half the guests falling about laughing while older guests were shocked by tales of David's wilder days. Sunset over the bay. Cavorting revelers, loose from free-flowing champagne.

Glorious, glorious day.

Josie wished she could forward these images to herself in her other life, to remind herself of this extraordinary time with her brother and niece. But it was impossible. No, if the switch-back plan worked, her memories would be the only thing she had. Other Josie would see the photos, though, if she returned. At least Josie had witnessed the real thing.

"You're so sweet." Anna reached out to stroke Josie's hair, misinterpreting Josie's emotion. "It was a beautiful day, wasn't it?"

Josie nodded. "Could you send these to me?"

"Of course." She took back her iPad, typing on it, as Josie snuggled Daisy again, breathing in her baby scent. "There, I've emailed you the Dropbox link."

Hearing the front door slam — David and Adam back with the groceries — Anna rose, taking Daisy back from her aunt's arms. "Perfect timing — lunch. You chill here, I'll get you when it's ready. We'll make sarnies and bring them outside. Hopefully your mum will be fine if we put her under the umbrella."

Josie nodded again, glad of the chance to compose herself. But the foreboding sense of imminent goodbyes — possibly forever — made her panic, so she went inside to eke out as much time with David and Daisy as possible. Even the simple act of putting away groceries, and making her brother's favorite sandwich, precious to her.

The turkey and avocado baguettes were delicious, and it was a beautiful setting, with those Josie loved most around her — yet she picked at her lunch. She felt like she was going to lose it at any moment, weeping and flinging her arms around her brother's neck, clutching Daisy to her chest, and swearing to never let her go.

But she didn't. She wanted her last moments with them to be a happy memory.

Maybe the plan wouldn't work. If she ended up staying in this life, it wouldn't be goodbye forever. She might even see them again in a year.

But Josie knew that wasn't enough to make her happy. She had to get her life with Rob back. If David and Anna's marital bliss had shown her anything, it was that.

"You okay?" Laura was watching her sister carefully. "Not like you to snub a tasty sarnie."

Josie attempted a smile. "I'm fine," she lied. "Emotional about leaving, especially Daisy. I don't know when I'll see her again, and she'll change so much. I'll definitely never see this little baby again." That last bit did it, and a tear spilled down her cheek.

She excused herself before Laura could comment and went to the bathroom to blow her nose. She looked at herself in the mirror, trying to pull herself together. She didn't want her last memory with David and Daisy to be of her sniveling.

When she emerged, her family was sitting around the living room with coffee. As Josie finished the last dregs of her tea, car tires crunched on the gravel drive, and a horn beeped.

She inhaled deeply, then rose to her feet. "That's the cab, guys."

"You've got everything?" asked her mother.

"Thanks, Mum, I'm good." Josie hugged her, as well as her sister, Laura, and little Theo, grabbing him as he ran around the kitchen island. Josie wasn't worried about them — they existed in whatever life she chose. She'd see them in a few months either way.

"It's been lovely to have you. Thanks for coming all this way." Anna gave Josie a side-hug, Daisy on her shoulder again.

"I wouldn't have missed it for the world," Josie told her with a warm smile. She reached out to hold Daisy one last time. The infant stretched her fat little hands as Josie took her in her arms.

"Say bye to your Auntie Bosie," Anna told Daisy. The baby looked up at her aunt's red-rimmed eyes and seemed to understand the gravity of the situation. Daisy stuck her thumb in her mouth as Josie kissed the top of her finely haired head.

"Bye, baby girl. I love you," she whispered, giving her a final squeeze before handing her back over.

"Come 'ere, ya big softie." David gave Josie a sudden, big hug as the taxi honked again. Their mother went outside to tell the driver his passenger was coming, but Josie was in a panic. This was really it.

She dropped her carry-on bag on the floor and hugged her brother with all her might, burying her head into his shoulder, trying to disguise her sorrow. He laughed, patting her back. Composing herself after a moment, Josie looked up at him.

"I love you, bro. I love you and your family. I'm going to miss you so much."

David ruffled Josie's hair, gave her another squeeze, and pulled away, picking up her shoulder bag and grabbing her suitcase handle. "Love you too, ya dork. Don't be sad, sis, we'll see you soon, okay? We'll work something out. Come on, let's get you in the cab, before it drives away."

David put Josie's luggage in the trunk and slammed it shut.

"Good to go."

He stepped back onto the porch and put his arm around his wife and child. Josie looked at them all one last time and took a mental photograph. So beautiful, so happy, so perfect.

This, exactly this picture, was what she would take back to her old life.

As the cab pulled away, Josie's whole family stood in the driveway, waving farewell.

At the airport, in the lofty waiting area beyond security, she opened her email to pore over the wedding photos again. She could have gazed at them forever. She had never seen anyone happier than those two on their wedding day. It made her ache for Rob once more.

As much as she was going to miss David and little Daisy, even Anna, it was the knowledge they existed, in any world, that gave her courage. Instead of David dying tragically without ever having been truly in love or becoming a father, Josie had had the privilege of witnessing him experience both those things. It wasn't something she could have ever thought possible.

Knowing that, in some universe, her brother was happy with a wife and child — their happiness set Josie free.

CHAPTER 35

November 30

Josie awoke alone in the dark, well ahead of the alarm.

It was her birthday, and the day of The Plan.

She'd lied to Abby, saying her return flight wasn't until Sunday, so the next live radio show was still a few days away. She had guests lined up for the next few weeks, which meant if this worked, and Other Josie wanted her job back, she'd be set. She had left a comprehensive handover guide for Other Josie to find, and Other Josie should be up-to-date on real estate news, assuming she'd been working at H&F this past year.

Suzie had called her last night, remembering Josie's plan, and worried she was going ahead with it. She'd tried to persuade Josie to forget the crash and meet her for birthday drinks instead. Josie had gently told her there was no way to change her mind, but that if it didn't work, she'd meet Suzie at the Standard at 7 p.m. Neither of them mentioned that Josie might be too hurt to make it.

For that matter, how did she even know Other Josie hadn't been badly injured on the other side the first time? Maybe she was dead, she'd been dead all along, and she wasn't coming.

Josie forced herself to breathe calmly. There was no point dwelling on any of those possibilities.

Today, Josie had one last thing to do before leaving on her bike. She had to finish the journal of events she'd been writing for Other Josie.

Since I left them standing on that porch in Australia, I've realized it is the complete happiness David found there that makes me able to give up seeing him, and Daisy, ever again. Because this time, I got to say goodbye, as opposed to having him ripped away in a horrific accident, which is how I lost him before. If anyone had told me then that I could have another year with him, and see him marry and become a father, I'd have been overwhelmed with joy. And I am — I'm so very grateful for the extra time we've had. I won't get to see Daisy grow up, and one day have a baby brother or sister — but you will. That will have to be enough for me.

I realize the chances are high you're in love with my husband. After all, you're me, and there was nothing that could have stopped me from loving him. But I remain hopeful you told him you're not me, because that's what I would have done. I have to hope he understands this, and believes it, and still loves me. If I make it back to him, I'll do all I can to make it work.

I'm sorry that, if and when you get here, you'll find in this world Rob is with someone else. Perhaps the "me" in this life wasn't meant to be with him. All I can do is wish you love and happiness. And you should keep doing the radio job. It's the best.

I guess we've both learned a lot about ourselves (ourself?!) in the past year. I've learned it is possible to sacrifice a huge amount, even the prospect of seeing family ever again, for a great love. But more than that: being true to who you are is essential for peace of mind. Without that, you're lost.

Perhaps Whitney Houston had it right about what the greatest love is!

Good luck, and please, when you see David again, and meet Daisy, please give them huge hugs and kisses that are secretly from me. Tell them you love them, but also please tell them I love them forever.

Gotta go — it's time. Good luck to us both today. And, assuming this works and you're reading this — thanks for giving me my life back.
J

Josie had been writing so long, it had gotten dark outside. She looked around the small living room. It was bizarre to be planning on leaving a place forever but having absolutely no need to pack a case.

She put on her puffy winter coat, grabbed her purse and helmet, and locked the apartment behind her. She touched the brass 3C on the door before making her way downstairs to retrieve her bike.

It was sunny but bitterly cold as she rode Jean Grey along her street, down Bedford, and onto the Williamsburg Bridge. The frigid air was a useful distraction from what was about to happen, although Josie feared she'd wipe out on hidden ice before she even got to Third and 25th. She rode with care. She had plenty of time, and it was imperative she got there in one piece. Before deliberately riding headlong into traffic.

By the time she made it to the junction of Third and 25th, it was already 6.13. Less than four minutes to go — too close. Fortunately, she had already worked out the direction she needed to head from.

They were recreating the accident of one year ago, but in reverse — which meant Other Josie would be riding north from the H&F office, the direction she herself had been going to meet Rob at the Midtown gallery. That meant she needed to come as if from the Talk New York station, riding south to meet Suzie in SoHo.

Josie waited on the curb, thinking only about the logistics. At exactly 6.17 she would have to turn left, whether she had a green light or not. When her phone told her it was 6.16 and thirty seconds, she pulled across the traffic and waited in the left lane, ignoring the honks from drivers swerving round her when she didn't move on the green light.

It was too soon.

She checked the clock on her phone again. The moment it turned to 6.17, she put it back in her pocket, didn't even look up at the lights, started pedaling and turned left.

Josie saw a flash of bright headlights ahead, heard a shout, and shut her eyes.

An image came into her mind: her brother, with his wife and baby, standing in the sunshine on that Australian porch.

Then, nothing.

CHAPTER 36

December 1

She saw the headlights again. They were so bright. And everything hurt. Everything.

The headlights swished before her. Left, right. Up, down.

Someone was holding her eyelids open. She wanted to close them and sleep away the pain. But, at least, she was lying somewhere soft and warm. People were talking nearby.

Wait . . . what?

She was not where she had been a few seconds ago. Josie snapped open her eyes. A doctor was putting a small flashlight in her pocket.

"Ah, Josie. Welcome back. Second time in one year, and again a cycling accident." Her tone was stern, her smile unfeeling. Josie didn't know her, but the doctor clearly recognized Josie.

Did it work?

Josie made a small, strangled noise. It felt like she hadn't spoken in a week. She looked around and saw she was in a bright, private room. The doctor held a cup of water with a lid and a straw to Josie's mouth.

"You're at Bellevue," the doctor explained, sounding a little kinder. "You've been here since last night. You broke your ankle and several ribs, and you were unconscious for some time. You remember me from last year? Dr. Lin."

Josie croaked again, taking in the fiberglass cast on her lower right leg, which lay above the sheets. And her ribs — she couldn't move a muscle without screaming agony in her torso. Dr. Lin gave her more water, and Josie nodded when the thirst started to dissipate.

"Thank you," she whispered in a hoarse voice.

The doctor moved to the end of the bed, writing something on a chart. Behind her, the door opened. Dr. Lin turned, obscuring Josie's view.

"Come in," she said to whoever had entered. "She's awake."

She stepped aside, and Josie's world fell away.

Rob.

Standing at the foot of the bed, taking up her entire field of vision.

Her husband. Her real husband, whom she hadn't been with in a whole year.

He seemed tired, drawn, older — but he beamed a huge grin of relief and rushed to Josie's bedside. He pulled up a chair and grabbed her hand. Her pain almost disappeared, she was so overjoyed to see him — and for him to be so happy to see her, after all this time.

"Baby." He leaned down to kiss her hand, reaching up to stroke the hair from the side of her face. "I was so worried about you. What did you do? You had me terrified . . . Thank Christ you're okay. I love you so much." He kissed her hand again, burying his face in it.

"I'm okay," she whispered. "I'm back, for good. I'm never leaving you again. I've missed you so badly."

Rob looked up, staring at his wife with an expression she couldn't translate. "Missed me? I thought you were leaving me, baby . . . but I'm so glad you're still here, and you're not more badly hurt."

"What . . . Rob . . . It's me, Rob. It's me. Josie. Your wife. I'm back."

He sat up, his skin draining to a sickly pallor.

"Rob, I've been gone a whole year. I haven't *seen you in a year*. Please, tell me you know this already."

He faltered and creased his brow. "Josie?"

"Yes, baby, it's me. It's me." She didn't understand why Rob had been so overjoyed to see her and was now being so weird.

"You're back? Is that really you?" His voice was weak.

"It's really me," she told him. "Aren't you pleased to see me? Didn't you know I was gone?"

He stared down at his hands, now lifeless over hers. He shook his head ever so slightly, dazed. "I . . . wasn't sure it was *you*. I didn't realize you were back, baby, I'm sorry." He looked like he was going to pass out.

Josie twisted, the pain in her ribs and leg now acute. Her mind raced.

He wasn't happy to see *her*. He was happy when he thought she was Other Josie.

She opened her mouth to speak. "Did you and . . ."

That was when her world went dark again.

* * *

She woke sometime later, people fussing around her. Suzie was beside her bed, Rob standing at the window. The sky was dark; she had been at the hospital the whole day. Her stomach growled.

Suzie immediately started speaking. "What happened, Josie? With the bike? *Again*? The doctor said the ambulance picked you up in the same spot as last time. The exact same accident, how is that even possible? Jose, you have to take better care of yourself."

Josie opened her mouth to say she was sorry, but no words came. She was dehydrated. She tried to pull herself upright to drink some water, but the pain was excruciating.

Suzie grabbed the water, lifted Josie's head and held the straw to her lips.

"Thank you," Josie croaked. "I'm sorry."

"Don't worry, hon. As long as you're okay. Rob's going to take you home in a few days, when you're on crutches. He'll take care of you, and you'll be fine."

Josie looked over at Rob, standing in silence by the window. He gave Suzie a small, weak smile.

A nurse entered with a tray of food. "Hungry?" She nodded. "Someone might want to help you with this. You're pretty banged up." He left it on the bedside tray.

"You want me to?" asked Suzie to both Josie and Rob. Josie nodded. "Thanks."

She offered Josie a forkful of chicken. "I brought you some trashy magazines," Suzie said. "Enjoy the extra time off work, and the painkillers. Rob's told the office you won't be back for a while, haven't you, Rob?"

"Huh? Yeah. I called Mike. Whenever is fine."

Suzie did her best to keep Josie occupied with snippets of celebrity gossip for the next hour, then finally rose to leave. "I have to help Donald get the twins to bed, but you're in good hands. We'll celebrate your recovery, and your belated birthday, another time. I'll visit you this weekend." She walked over to Rob and startled him out of his thoughts with a hug. "Take it easy, big guy."

After she left, Josie was filled with dread. Now they'd have to talk to each other.

Rob went back to staring out at the city, where he'd been for at least an hour. It was almost like Josie wasn't in the room.

"Rob."

He turned to Josie, crossed the room and sat in the wide armchair beside her, arms crossed over his chest. Pressing his lips together, in that gesture that was so familiar, he shook his head. "I . . . don't know what to say."

"Well, maybe we need to discuss the fact you thought I was the Other Josie, the one who's been living with you for the past year, the one you were pleased to see when you thought I was her?"

"Yeah. I guess we need to talk about that."

She nodded, dread tensing her already agonized body.

"So. The Josie who has been here, presumably living with you, as husband and wife, for the past year . . . you were *fully aware* this Other Josie was not me, that we are in fact two different versions of the same person. Am I right about that?"

"I knew."

"And when I came back, you thought I was her, and you were happy to see her until you realized it was not her at all. That it was your boring old original wife. Please, correct me if I'm wrong."

Rob looked up at her. "I knew she was not you — that she was an alternate version of you. But she was still my wife, and she was still *you*, right? And of course I'm happy to see you, baby. It's just a shock, that's all. I had no reason to believe she was going to — to change back. At least, I didn't think she'd actually do it."

Josie tried to shift position and winced. "Well, she did. We did. I came back for you because you're my husband. *My* husband. I guess she left because she knew she didn't belong with you, and that I would come back for you."

The sobs that had been building finally escaped her, and only increased her rib pain. Josie struggled for breath, unable to believe her deepest fears had become reality — despite, perhaps, their inevitability.

She exhaled. "Okay. I didn't really expect you wouldn't have been sleeping together. I figured you would have been — she's still me, like you say. I've been thinking about it, imagining you and her together, for the entire year I was gone. But actually knowing it happened still hurts. So badly."

She paused. "Still, I'm guessing she wasn't happy with you. Otherwise she never would have gone through with the bike crash."

Rob seemed puzzled. "That's how you did it? That was 'The Plan'? Recreating your bike crash?"

308

"You knew about the plan?"

He nodded. "I read her journal. There's a journal, which she wrote for you, in case you ever made it back," he added.

Josie took this in. "I guess there would be. I mean, I wrote one for her, too."

He surprised her by taking her hand in his. "Josie. Clearly, I messed up spectacularly here. But you have to try to understand, there's no rulebook for what to do when your wife who is living with you isn't really your wife, but a different version from a different reality . . . I mean, there's no precedent for this shit. Was I supposed to not live with her? Send her away? She was still technically, legally my wife, and still, basically, you. I made the best out of what I thought was an irrevocable situation."

Josie tilted her head. "Did you? Or did you fall in love all over again? That's my biggest fear, Rob. I mean, let's face it, we'd been having a hard time ever since Hawaii, after David. Then, along comes a new version of me who I'll bet was all chirpy and happy, whose brother didn't die, who held no resentment against our marriage because of it. New and improved Josie. Am I right?"

His silence was all the answer she needed. She pulled her hand out from beneath his.

After a moment's pause, he asked, "David is alive, then? Have you seen him?"

"I saw him alive and well a few days ago, at his house in Sydney, with his new Australian wife and their baby girl. My niece."

Rob shook his head in disbelief. "Wow. That's — David alive, and with a wife and daughter."

"Yes. None of whom I'll ever see again, because I came back. For you."

"Is that where you've been this past year? Australia?"

"For their wedding only, these past couple of weeks. No, I've been living your new Josie's life, as she's apparently been living mine. I've been in her flat in Brooklyn, doing her job at the radio show, and spending as much time with David as possible. Before he moved to Australia."

Rob looked thoughtful. "She'll be so happy to see him and meet her niece," he murmured, almost to himself.

"Honestly, Rob, considering she's been screwing my husband for the past year, I don't really care about Other Josie being happy right now." Josie was aware she sounded petulant, but this wasn't what she'd expected.

What had she expected?

Rob raised his eyebrows. "I get it. I do, Josie. But I have no idea what to do or say here. What would you have done, in my — or her — position? We know what you'd have done in her position, because you *are* her. You'd have done exactly squat different."

Josie sighed. He was right, of course. And there was Peter.

Still, she muttered, unreasonably, "But you should have realized I would come back for you."

He pressed his lips together again. Nothing more to say.

The cheery nurse returned, clearing the dinner tray and giving Josie strong pain medication. He sensed tension in the room and backed out quickly.

Rob used the interruption as an excuse to leave, picking up his coat. "I'd better be going." He looked down at Josie, leaned down to kiss her on her forehead. "I'll be back tomorrow."

Josie lay alone under the harsh lights, sobbing from her pain and heartache, until the meds kicked in. Then, mercifully, she drifted into sleep.

CHAPTER 37

Early December

"I'm fine."

Josie heaved herself out of the car onto the crutches Rob was holding out for her.

"Get the door, please."

He held the building's door open, and she looked up at the "Cavendish House" sign before she entered.

"In the Other Life, this building is called Union House. Because you never met me," she told him as they walked into the elevator, Josie hobbling awkwardly on the crutches.

"Did you go there? To this building?"

"I never went inside. But I saw you there once, when I was checking it out."

"You never spoke to me? I'd have thought you'd have sought me out. The other version of me, I guess. Other Rob."

"I didn't speak to you then. But I did meet you later. Other You."

The elevator dinged their arrival on the eighteenth floor. Josie felt a pit of nervousness about being home. Maybe it wasn't her home anymore.

Inside the apartment, nothing seemed to have changed. Her favorite flowers were on the foyer table, perfectly complementing the ocean painting she had chosen for the wall. Saying nothing, she let Rob remove her coat and slipped out of the single shoe she was wearing. In the open living area, she looked around as if seeing it for the first time. Josie had craved home so much, but now that she was here, she could hardly bear it. She was terrified of coming across something Other Josie had introduced over the past year, evidence of her imposition.

Maneuvering down the steps, she flopped on the couch, letting her crutches fall and putting her cast foot on the glass coffee table. Rob filled the kettle in the kitchen.

"When did you meet Other Me? What was I like?"

"I invited you to the radio show for an interview about the Tribeca project. We went for coffee after. I wanted you to get to know me. Because for you, I was a stranger. I didn't think I could ever come home, so I figured we should meet. I ran into you later, too. We got along well. I guess we would, of course."

He put teabags into mugs. "But nothing happened?"

"No. Other You has a girlfriend. Some hot woman called Surin."

"Surin Chan, the realtor? I'm — I mean, Other Me is dating her?"

"Yeah. You know her, too? Well, I guess you would."

"I've known her through work for a while. She's kind of an ice queen. I thought she was attractive when we met, but we've had some dealings since then, and she's pretty controlling."

"Well, I guess you weren't dating me, so you must've acted on that initial attraction, because in the Other Life you're together. I didn't get it either, she seemed pretty frosty to me."

Josie watched his furrowed expression as he brought the tea to her. She took the cup. "Why do you care? It's not your life."

He sat by the gas fire, turning it on.

"I'm bummed to think there's another version of me, in another reality, who didn't meet you and is in a relationship with someone like that. I can't imagine he's happy. Or that he's experienced the kind of love we have. I feel sad for him." Rob shrugged. "And he's me."

Josie blew on her tea. "Well, I feel sad for us."

They sat in awkward silence. Josie stood it for as long as she could before she excused herself. She'd soon be sleepy anyway, as she'd taken her next round of meds.

"I'm going to drink the rest of this in bed. In the art room. I can't move into our bedroom with you, I'm sorry."

Rob looked at her, eyebrows raised.

"You're not surprised?"

Rob shook his head. "No, it's not that."

"What?"

"Well, that's where Other Josie was sleeping. The last month, anyways. After it started to fall apart. The sheets are clean, but there might be some stuff of hers. Plus her journal is on the dressing table."

Josie felt nauseated.

"Right. Well, I'd better see."

She lifted herself onto the crutches, as Rob picked up her mug. He opened the door to the art room, setting Josie's tea on the nightstand. The canopy over the bed was down, but at least the art wall was the same as she had left it.

Josie examined the items on the dressing table. Rob stood at the door, waiting to assess the extent of the damage. The journal was left out for her to find. A couple of lipsticks and a half-used bottle of perfume she didn't recognize. But the main unexpected anomaly was a ceramic mask, the decorated kind worn to a masquerade ball. It seemed somehow familiar. Josie picked it up, examining its pretty paintwork in blue and gold.

How fitting.

She noticed a crack across the underside of the chin and laid it down. Rob's eyes were boring into her.

Josie picked up the journal. "Guess this is my bedtime reading. Could you pull back the canopy, please?"

"Sure." He tugged back the gauzy white curtains.

That's when she saw it.

Above the headboard was a huge, almost life-sized, framed photograph of a couple in elaborate period dress.

At first, Josie wasn't quite sure what she was seeing. It was a stunning image. Against the paneled wall of some formal state room stood a slim woman in a white ringleted wig, dressed in a gorgeous Renaissance-style gown, wearing the mask on the dressing table. Alongside her, with his arm around her waist, was a tall, broad man in a half-face, hooked-nose mask and a courtier's outfit, complete with a three-cornered hat.

The man was clearly Rob — enough of his beard and mouth were visible to see that. Her nausea returned as she realized who the woman was.

She sat on the side of the bed, staring at it. Rob stood at the door, awaiting her response.

"So," she said finally. "I guess that's you and her, then? At some masquerade ball?"

Josie saw his nod out of the corner of her eye. He cleared his throat and said, "In Venice."

She snapped her head toward him. "You and she went to Venice?"

His face was ashen. He leaned on the dressing table and slumped into the chair, staring away from Josie, at the mask.

"Yep. Yes. I'm sorry."

"That was supposed to be—"

"Our place to go. I remember. I was looking for a fresh start. I thought she was . . . permanent."

"She wasn't."

"I know." He buried his head in his hands. "There's something else I have to tell you."

Josie said nothing, waiting for another blow to hit.

"The trip to Venice. It was our honeymoon. That is, mine and hers."

She stared at the photograph. A honeymoon?

The room started to spin, and she sat on the bed, ignoring the pain in her ribs.

Rob turned to her. "Josie? Did you hear—?"

"A honeymoon? But we were already married."

"Well, yeah. But Other Josie and I weren't. We were, technically — but of course, she had no memory of the wedding. She wasn't there. She never felt like she was really married to me. That's why we got remarried. In May."

Josie shook her head, trying not to hear his words. It made no sense. How could they have gotten married?

Rob added, with more energy, as if it somehow excused everything, "Being with her, it was like living with you, but with amnesia. That's what everyone thought it was, anyways, so it made sense she had to relearn everything — our friends, her job, me — and for us to have a second wedding."

Josie felt woozy. The meds were kicking in, making the whole situation even worse. She sat back against the pillows.

"You married her?" she managed. "You had a wedding?"

Rob came and sat on the edge of the bed, clearly distressed by what this news was doing to his wife. "I'm sorry, Josie. I'm so sorry."

"But you knew she didn't have amnesia. You *knew* she wasn't me. But you married her anyway."

"I was only sure about that later. I mean, she told me she wasn't you, from the start. It wasn't her fault. But the first time I truly believed it, or admitted it to myself, was in Venice, on our honeymoon. And by then—"

"By then you were already in love with her."

"Already, or still, in love — with my wife. She was still *you*, Josie. I had to give it everything."

Josie shook her head, fighting through her fogginess. "You should have realized sooner. You should have listened to her. You should have said no, and waited for me to come back. I was your wife, and I was . . . I was *missing*. Jesus, Rob, did you even try to get me back? You should have . . . fucking torn through the universe yourself to get your real wife back."

He stared at her. "I know, okay? I gave up on you. But I didn't think you were ever coming back. Why would I, when I had a version of you right there? And how could I even have found you? Where were you? What were you doing all that time? Living the single life in Other Brooklyn? If you were so desperate to return to me, why didn't you come back earlier?"

David.

Peter.

A flash of guilt must have passed across Josie's face, as Rob examined her closer. "Josie?"

She took a sip of the tepid tea, and inhaled, her head swimming.

"I didn't want to come back straight away, because of David. He was there, alive, like nothing ever happened. It was a miracle, you know? I spent a few weeks with him in the UK, and when I got back to New York, I needed more time. Then, I guess, Other Josie's life became the new normal. Her place in Brooklyn, the radio job — it all fit. In some ways, more even than life here with you. Because it's what would have happened if I'd only had myself to please, only me making life choices. So, yeah, to start with I was freaked out, but after a while, I kinda liked it. Plus, at that point, I didn't think there was any way I could even get back."

She paused. She was going to tell him about Peter, but he needed context.

"And then, after spending time with David, I figured if I could be with you, Other You anyway, I'd have everything. That's when I invited you on my radio show, and we went for coffee. I knew you were dating someone, but I thought if you spent time with me, you'd realize I was the one for you, and we'd be together. Then life would be perfect. I'd have both you and David . . .

"But it didn't happen. You didn't fall in love with me, you went off to meet Surin, and you seemed happy without me. So, after that, I was in despair. I didn't want to leave a world with David in it, but I was lonely. Then, when a guy in my choir asked me out . . . I guess it was seeing you with another woman that made me rationalize it. Anyway, I started seeing this guy, Peter. Having him around took the edge off. But it never felt right.

"Obviously, I still felt married to you. I still loved only you. After a while, I ended it. David had met Anna, and had a baby, and emigrated to Australia, so I knew I'd hardly ever see him. That's when I knew I had to find a way back. Back to you."

She stopped. She had been staring at the mug in her hands for her entire confession, but she put it down and looked at Rob. His eyes were fire and steel.

"Peter? That video game guy? You've been with him this whole time?" A jealousy she'd never heard before was in his voice.

"Well, not the whole time, but . . . It doesn't matter who. Clearly you know who I'm talking about, but it's not relevant."

Rob twisted his mouth. "Yeah, I met him. At your concert. You . . . well, Other Josie and him, they had this duet together. The chemistry was noticeable. We had a row about it that night."

"Right. That happened in my version too. The duet, I mean. But yes, Peter and I were dating at that time."

He glared at her. "*Dating* him? For fuck's sake, Josie, you were married to me."

"I know, I know. But not in that world. In that world, you were with someone else, and I was really goddamn lonely. You reacted to the situation you'd been put into, with Other Josie, and so did I. Like you said, there's no rulebook for this."

Rob stayed silent.

"I'm sorry, Rob. I really am. I couldn't get back to you, and it took a long time for me to figure it out. But it didn't take long to realize I had to find a way. That all I wanted was to get back to my husband, the man I really love."

Josie slumped down into the pillows again. She was exhausted. "I can't do this anymore, Rob. This is all we've talked about since I got back. I'm wiped out, and in so much pain, and on these meds . . . I have to sleep."

He rose, picking up the journal as he did so. "Sure. You sleep. I'm wiped too."

Josie thought he was leaving, but he paused at the doorway.

"I know that, right now, you think what I've done is terrible, Josie. That I married another woman while you and I were still married. But she was still basically you — the same woman, the only woman I've ever loved. I was trying to make it work. But you . . . you were dating someone completely different from me while still married to me. Think about that, before you decide not to forgive me."

He tossed her the journal and it landed, pages splayed, on the comforter. "And give this journal a thorough read before you start judging."

CHAPTER 38

Mid-April

Josie reread the last pages of her counterpart's journal for what must have been the seventh or eighth time over the past few months.

> *I never meant to steal your husband. You know that. The guilt of betraying you has been unbearable.*
>
> *I know what you want me to do. You tell me in my dreams, insisting I give you back your love, your life.*
>
> *I know you're coming for him. I know how and when. It's soon. And the answer is yes. I'll do it.*

She put the book down on the terrace coffee table.

It broke her a little every time she read the diary of the year Other Josie had spent with Rob. But it healed her a little more each time, too. Seeing how gradually their relationship developed, how hard Other Josie had tried not to betray her, how impossible it was for them not to be together. It made sense. It hurt, but there was no other way it could have gone.

She could forgive Other Josie.

And if she could do that, surely she could forgive her husband?

Then maybe he would forgive her.

She circled her right ankle, a habit she had formed ever since it came out of its cast after the New Year, and looked out over Union Square's cherry blossoms. Today, in another world, it was her brother's forty-first birthday. An occasion he would be celebrating with his wife, baby, and possibly even his sister Josie. His real sister in that life.

Hearing Rob come into the apartment, Josie raised her glass of wine in salute to David, to Daisy, and to any other future nieces and nephews she would never meet. "To you," she saluted, draining her glass, before going inside.

Rob was unpacking groceries in the kitchen. He looked up and smiled.

"It's beautiful out there," Josie said, returning the smile.

"Yeah. I've been stuck in the office and haven't been able to enjoy it. It finally feels like winter is over and spring is here. Did you go out, or were you writing all day?" He walked over to the refrigerator, stowing some items.

"Got an article done this morning for that interior designer you connected me with. He said he'd recommend me to a bunch of home stagers and realtors who need blog content, so I feel like I'm finally getting this freelancing off the ground. Then I just finished re-reading the Book of Revelations. I got so caught up in it, I didn't even go out. I've done zero exercise today."

Rob glanced toward the terrace windows, through which the spring sunlight was streaming.

"How about we pack up some food and take it to the park? Have the first picnic of the year? It might do us good to eat al fresco. Remember what Dr. Palmer said about doing things together for the first time since . . . everything."

Josie nodded. "Great idea. I'll go change. Give me ten minutes."

In Union Square park, under a tree bursting with blossoms, Rob spread a blanket while Josie laid out cold chicken and salad. Rob poured them each a plastic cup of wine from a water bottle.

"I didn't forget what day it is today." He raised his cup to her. "To David. Happy birthday."

"To David," Josie echoed, and took a sip. She laughed. "But you did forget last year, right? Isn't that what you're referring to? Remember, the Book of Revelations reveals all."

Rob looked sheepish. "Yeah. I did. But the Book . . . Man, how many times have you read that thing now? You must know it by heart."

"A bunch. More than you, that's for sure. But then, you were there, so . . ." She shrugged.

"True. I've only read it twice, but I remember everything that happened. Including the reason I forgot David's fortieth birthday that day. Which, since you've just re-read the journal, you probably know too. I dunno, I figure we should talk about it, be open. Share what we're feeling, like Dr. Palmer said."

"You're right," Josie agreed, more than a little nervous. "Okay. You forgot David's birthday because you were distracted, as that was the day of your remarriage proposal. To Other Me. You had the sapphire ring in your pocket, and you made her a fancy dinner."

Rob looked equally unsettled. "I did, yes. So . . . how do you feel about that now?"

"Honestly? It's never going to be great," she admitted. "But better. Much better. Rereading all her thought processes, and how you both acted through it all . . . I guess I get it now. I'll never like it, but I get it."

Rob nodded. "Yeah. That's about where I'm at, in terms of what happened with you while you were away. It still hurts you were with someone else, but I understand. And seeing you gradually work through your pain has helped me work through mine."

He paused, and added, "I know you were initially planning on removing the tattoo Other Josie had done. So when you cancelled your tattoo removal sessions, that was a big deal for me. I didn't want to make a fuss of it, but it felt huge. Like, you were beginning to accept you and she are one. That your love for me, both of your love for me, is the same."

Josie reached to the back of her neck. "Yeah. I'm used to the tattoo now. I'm even beginning to like it. It's beautiful, but more than that, it's joyful. It's a celebration of you and me, our life path, no matter how many twists and turns we've gone through. No matter which 'me' we're talking about. Accepting the tattoo feels like accepting you being with Other Josie, since she's a part of me."

"Exactly, right? It's got to be about acceptance and moving on. And as much as you've had to find a way to forgive me, I've had to forgive you too, Josie."

"I get it, baby. I do." Josie put her hand on his. Was that the first time she had called him "baby" since she'd returned? It was hard to tell, it came out so naturally.

She looked into his deep brown eyes. Behind them, she saw her soulmate, the man she married, the only man she'd ever love.

"You know I still love you, don't you?" Her voice caught at the words. "I still really love you. And even though I betrayed you, I never loved anyone else. It's always been you. It always will be."

"I know, baby. I love you too. So, so much."

Rob brushed some hair away from her face and kept his finger under her chin, waiting for her response. She held the moment, let it stretch out, feeling the weight of it. A life decision. But not a hard one to make.

Josie smiled at him, reached out to stroke his beard, and brought her face to his.

EPILOGUE: US

CHAPTER 39

November 30

I can't quite remember what I was doing, but I'm sprawled across an icy-cold, flint-hard pavement, my face in a freezing puddle, my foot entangled in my bike.

Of course. D-Day. The Plan.

I move slowly, seeing if anything hurts. My face and wrist are both sore, but other than that, all seems as it should be.

"You okay?" a woman asks, although she doesn't offer to help me.

I look up. "I'm good, thanks. Just came off my bike." I remove my foot from the bike frame and clamber up, adjusting my crooked helmet.

"Cool." The woman gives me a wan smile and walks away.

I prop the bike against the nearest wall. Then look at it properly, a weird excitement buzzing through me.

This is not my bike.

The expensive red bike I've been riding around, Daredevil, which Rob bought me after Electra died, is now a gray cruiser I don't recognize.

I check my clothing in the orange glow of the streetlight. Thick black ski gloves. Puffy winter coat. Scruffy boots. This is not what I was wearing a few minutes ago.

The Plan.
It worked.
It freakin' WORKED!

I lock the bike at a nearby stand and walk into a café across the street, almost unable to contain my excitement. Standing in line, I realize my purse is the old, black, tasseled one I loved from years ago. Paying for my London Fog with money from a wallet I don't recognize, I sit at the counter and tip out the contents of the purse, searching for a phone.

It drops down with a thud on the bar, the same model in the same green case I had in my old life, before my world changed. Entering my usual password, I go straight to the text messages. The most recent one is from Suzie. That makes sense, if I'm truly back in a world where I'm not married to Rob. We're probably going out for my birthday. But that's not what I'm looking for, so I flick past without reading it.

I scroll farther down, and there it is.

David.

Glad you got home safe, Bosie, and Happy Birthday! It was amazing having you here Down Under with us. Anna, Daisy and I all miss you already, we'll work something out for next year I promise! Luv ya XD

It's from earlier today.

My brother is alive, and he texted me this morning, apparently from Australia.

I'm home. I'm really home.

I text him back immediately.

Miss you too, D. But I'll see you soon.
I'm sure of it. Love ya billions. J xo

My heart full, I delve into recent emails and find one from the mysterious Anna, whom my brother referenced, with no text in the email, only a link to a Dropbox file. The subject line reads "Wedding Photos!!!"

Clicking on the link with trepidation, I find a folder full of the most stunning wedding photos I've ever seen — aside from mine and Rob's at the Brooklyn Plant House, perhaps. A cream-colored house with a large green lawn and a blue bay beyond. My brother, alive and well, in a suit, getting married to a gorgeous red-headed woman. A baby girl, dressed up with a daisy headband, photographed in his arms and in my mother's. My sister and her family, laughing on the lawn. And me, my old self — regular Josie, with shoulder-length dark blonde hair, and a bit of extra weight — in a poppy dress, looking wistful.

The phone dings. It makes me start.

Suzie: You OK??? It's 6.37 and I know you planned your dumb switch-back crash for 20 mins ago. I'm so worried about you. I've got a table at the Standard, but I'm getting side-eye from hostess. Are you still coming? Are you still even the same Josie?! Are you alive?? Call or text me RIGHT NOW!!

I laugh. It had never occurred to me that Other Josie would tell Suzie the truth about it all, including today's plan. But then, I guess Other Josie had nobody else to talk to about it. Not like me and Rob.

I type a reply, smiling.

OMFG she told you?!! Hahaha, no, I'm not same Josie :'D Our plan worked!!! It actually worked! We crashed, switched back, for real! I'm fine, not hurt. Getting cab, be there by 7. Hold that table! It's me!

Finishing my tea, I grab my items from the counter and head outside. I'm almost giddy. This morning I said goodbye to a great love; now, a huge weight has been lifted off my shoulders.

I'm back in a world where my brother is alive. Not only alive, but apparently married, and a father. I laugh again as I go out into the cold night and hail a taxi.

"Standard Hotel, please," I tell the driver. "It's my birthday. I've got some celebrating to do."

CHAPTER 40

Valentine's Day

I examine myself in the full-length mirror on the back of the door. The green shift dress I discovered in the armoire upon my return is new — to me, at least. It looks lovely, despite the extra weight I'm carrying. Maybe even because of it.

Other Me has excellent taste. Well, she would have.

I go to my tiny bathroom to fix my hair and makeup. It's all working, but that doesn't do much to quell the fluttering in my stomach. I've barely been able to eat today and I've been distracted at the radio station all week, ever since he asked me. Eventually, this morning, I confessed to a curious Abby that a guy I like, the one I went for lunch with in December, invited me to his dinner party tonight. As his date.

That lunch . . . that lunch was something else. And now, a real date.

I had not expected anything, having read the journal Other Josie had left on my laptop. After my birthday drinks with Suzie, at which I astounded her with my tale of the past year, I stayed up all night, reading everything Other Me went through. Her trip to the UK that first Christmas and being reunited with David, so joyfully. Meeting Rob, but finding he was dating another woman, someone called Surin. Then getting involved with Peter — which was inevitable, I guess, since he had split from Michelle and had been all set to get together with me. But then, about how Other Josie broke his heart, because she was still in love with her husband.

It was her news about this world's Rob having a girlfriend that hurt the most. Of course I had thought about coming to find him, if the plan worked and I returned to my old life. It's not like I stopped loving him.

I hoped with all my heart Other Josie had been reunited with Rob, her true husband, and they were making a go of it, even after everything we'd all been through. But I wanted my happy ending too. Living in a world with David in it would be enough, but having Rob as well would be perfect. A new Rob, undamaged by any prior relationship with me.

But Other Josie tried to get to know him, and it didn't work.

What she didn't realize, though, was that on the evening of D-Day itself, Rob emailed an invitation for lunch. I came across it when I returned to work at the station.

I went in and acted like nothing had happened, letting Abby and everyone believe I was the same person, just returning from vacation in Australia. I didn't even tell them about the latest bike crash. Sure, I've made a few mistakes since I've been back and "forgotten" a few key things, including some newer colleagues' names, but otherwise, with the help of Other Josie's handover documents, I've been able to wing it just fine. It's the same job, after all.

Plowing through the backlog of work emails, I came across Rob's invite.

November 30 | 6.17 p.m. | From: B+B Developments

Hi Josie,
Long time no see. I hope you're doing well. I thought I'd tell you we have a bunch of new projects coming

up and I can give you the exclusive on how we landed a pretty sweet deal on a hotel redevelopment, if you're interested. Do you want to catch up over lunch sometime in the next couple of weeks? My treat. (And just FYI, I'm not with Surin Chan anymore, so I promise no early exits or interruptions!) Let me know how you're fixed, if you want to meet. Rob Billing

Holy fuck.

I called him immediately to accept. It was surreal to hear his voice, seemingly happy to talk to me, but also slightly formal — clearly not knowing me very well. Utterly ignorant of the agony I caused him in another life, mere days before.

At lunch, two weeks later, it had been almost impossible to concentrate on what he was saying. I just wanted to stare at him. This new Rob. So shiny and clean. Not the tired, drawn Rob I left behind in the other life. This one had never been hurt by me and had never betrayed his wife with me. This guy had never even been married. And this guy was so enthused to tell me all about his new development projects and share his life story with me, like we barely knew each other. I just gazed at him, rapt, across the table. Then, when he asked me questions about my life, my family, where I was from, he gazed back, his handsome face lit up. Under that dark beard, he just smiled and smiled.

New and improved Rob 2.0.

I wanted to kiss him afterwards, outside the restaurant, but I remembered it was still just a work lunch and he hardly knew me. Instead, I shook his hand — and then held it as he kissed me, gently, on the cheek.

He hailed me a cab. "I'll look forward to the article — and hopefully we can meet up again soon." He waved as I drove off, staring after the cab longer than a regular work acquaintance usually would.

Then in late January, the craziness of Christmas over, he called to invite me to a Valentine's dinner party at his place.

"It's at Union House — the west sub-penthouse on the 18th floor." He sounded somewhat sheepish. "There'll be some great people for you to meet, my friends from Halstein & Faust. You said at lunch you wanted Hans to come on your radio show, so this would be perfect. But," he added, shyly, "that aside, I would like you to come anyways. As my date."

* * *

The app on my phone beeps to say my car has arrived. I apply another layer of lip gloss, smooth the green shift dress down over my hips for the hundredth time, and slip on a pair of black heels and my new winter coat.

In the cab, my mind races. I'm returning to the gorgeous home I shared with Rob for a full year. And I have to act as though I've never been there before. Plus I have to pretend I've never met his friends.

How will I handle it? Will I slip up?

But the scariest thought of all . . . what if it goes well? What if Rob and I start seeing each other again? Can I really have a relationship with a man whose alter-ego's heart I tore into pieces a couple of months ago?

Will I ever be able to let go of what we were, and just be who we are?

The cab pulls up in the porte-cochère of Union House, and I get out, wobbling on my heels, knees trembling. Ed opens the main door. "Good evening, ma'am." He smiles with no familiarity. "A guest of Mr. Billing?" I nod, dry-mouthed. "Eighteenth floor, ma'am."

I ride the elevator, checking my reflection several times. At the double doors of sub-penthouse 1802, I knock, terrified of the life that could be beyond.

But I also wouldn't be anywhere else in the world right now. Knowing Rob is single and unencumbered, nothing could keep me away.

The door opens and he is filling the door frame, wearing a white shirt and a heart-stopping smile.

"Josie." He ushers me in, taking my coat. "I'm so happy you came. Here, let me hang this."

I look around as he hangs my coat in the hidden closet. The picture on the facing wall is a modern red abstract, and the round table is missing from the foyer. It's clear the place has been decorated by him, without my input. But it's still stunning.

"You want to meet everybody?"

I turn to him and pull in a breath. "Absolutely."

Rob leads me into the living area, pausing at the top of the steps. Seated around a modern glass dining table, pouring wine and laughing, are Hans, Mike, Josh and his boyfriend, Austin. They fall quiet as they turn to look up at us. Their lovely, familiar faces smile at me with no trace of recognition. Still, they are full of warmth and welcome.

Rob places his hand on my back, where the green dress meets skin, and gently encourages me forward, down the steps.

"Everyone," he announces. "This is Josie."

THE END

AUTHOR'S NOTE

I've always been fascinated by the concept of the multiverse. As a child, I was prone to asking my teachers precocious questions about parallel universes and alternate timelines. And it's been a treat to see so many cultural outlets embrace this idea in various forms, from books like Kate Atkinson's inspiring *Life after Life*, TV shows such as *Fringe* to movies like *Sliding Doors* — all three of which played a role in the creation of my own version of this story. Although today I'm agnostic in terms of belief in the multiverse, I love to ponder the infinite possible outcomes of our lives through decisions made and actions taken — both significant and miniscule.

Writing one's first novel is just such a decision, as is emigrating to another country — both actions I've taken in recent years in order to become the woman I want to be. The best possible version of myself, by my own standards. I hope my novel will remind readers that there are infinite paths their own lives could go down, and all we need to do is take those steps, large and small, to move toward that best life.

I have many people along my writing journey to thank for helping me become the "published author" version of myself. First are my agent, Victoria Skurnick of Levine Greenberg Rostan in New York, and my publisher, Kate

Lyall Grant of Joffe Books in London. I wouldn't have the immense pleasure of even writing these acknowledgments if it weren't for these wonderful, smart, creative women taking a chance on me and my somewhat quirky tale.

I'm also extremely grateful to the fellow writers, beta-readers, editors, and advisers who have counselled me along the way. These include invaluable help from my talented editor friend Susan Boyce, as well as my beta-readers, Paula Radell, Kathryn Sievert, Monica Storms, Terri Brunsting, Brittany Moss, and Jennifer Marra, all of whom assisted in improving this story immensely. Very importantly, I would also like to thank the various Indigenous advisers (whom I know would prefer to remain nameless) and numerous BIPOC writers who have shared their wisdom on how to sensitively portray an Indigenous character in a book that does not claim to tackle Indigenous culture or challenges. Indeed, I am indebted to the wider online writing community of which I am an active part, as the support and willingness to help has been incredible. We are all on our individual paths to success, leaning on each other along the way.

Finally, I would like to express my deep gratitude for the people in my life, and especially my loved ones, who have supported and even sparked my storytelling. From the guy I once met only briefly near Seattle who ultimately prompted the character of Rob, to two recent boyfriends I've had (not simultaneously!) whose traits and qualities between them made up the Peter character, to my wonderful brother Richard who was the basis for David — I'm thankful for the men who inspired me.

To the incredible women I'm so lucky to count as close friends, and from each of whom different pieces were taken to create the Suzie character — and a special name-check to Shona, Becky, Sarah, and Libby, you all mean the world to me. To my fabulous sister, Alice, whose love and whose two gorgeous sons are the great joys of my life — thank you for being all I need. And to my dear mother, Claira, and her husband, Ian, my eternal gratitude for your unwavering love and support, and for showing us all it's never too late to take a new path toward joy.

Thank you for reading this book.

If you enjoyed it, please leave feedback on Amazon or Goodreads, and if there is anything we missed or you have a question about, then please get in touch. We appreciate you choosing our book.

Founded in 2014 in Shoreditch, London, we at Joffe Books pride ourselves on our history of innovative publishing. We were thrilled to be shortlisted for Independent Publisher of the Year at the British Book Awards.

www.joffebooks.com

We're very grateful to eagle-eyed readers who take the time to contact us. Please send any errors you find to corrections@joffebooks.com. We'll get them fixed ASAP.

Made in United States
North Haven, CT
20 May 2023

36796154R00205